# In From *the* Rain

ALSO BY WILLIAM EFFORD

PICAROON

# In From *the* Rain

## William Efford

iUniverse, Inc.
Bloomington

# IN FROM THE RAIN

*iUniverse books may be ordered through booksellers or by contacting:*

*iUniverse*
*1663 Liberty Drive*
*Bloomington, IN 47403*
*www.iuniverse.com*
*1-800-Authors (1-800-288-4677)*

*Because of the dynamic nature of the Internet, any web addresses or links contained in this book may have changed since publication and may no longer be valid. The views expressed in this work are solely those of the author and do not necessarily reflect the views of the publisher, and the publisher hereby disclaims any responsibility for them.*

*Any people depicted in stock imagery provided by iStockPhoto are models, and such images are being used for illustrative purposes only.*
*Certain stock imagery © iStockPhoto.*

*ISBN: 978-1-4620-4933-2 (sc)*
*ISBN: 978-1-4620-4934-9 (ebk)*

*Printed in the United States of America*

*iUniverse rev. date: 11/10/2011*

This book is dedicated to my
two talented children:
John Scott, and Maureen Hilary;

to my grandchildren
Jessica, Andrew, Sonya, and Nicole;

and to the memory
of my late mother, Olive,
1920-2002.

A special thanks to my ever supportive wife, Vicki, whose editorial wisdom and constructive input were invaluable to me throughout the preparation of the manuscript.

Thanks to Jessica Cripps, of Minneapolis, for the cover design.

And to the following people who have inspired me in various ways: the late Ross Taylor; the late Dr. Grant Huber, Ph.D., former professor of Mechanical Engineering at McMaster University, and his wife, Mary; Dr. Fred Templeman; Bill Fredericks and Rosalie Inglis; and the alpine adventurers with whom I have stood on San Juan summits and touched the clouds.

I expect to pass through this world but once;
any good thing therefore that I can do,
or any kindness that I can show
to any fellow creature,
let me do it now;
let me not defer or neglect it,
for I shall not pass this way again.

Etienne de Grellet du Mabillier

# CHAPTER 1

## *Howard*

THE ACADEMIC YEAR HAD come to an end and so had Howard Munro's tenure. After twenty years he was resigning as head of the English department at St. Martin's College.

He leaned on the stone windowsill in the empty second-storey lecture hall and surveyed the heavily treed campus. The groundskeepers were hard at work with shears, hoes, and spades: pruning the shrubs, weeding the flower beds, and spreading bags of red mulch around the plantings.

On the flagstone path below, a few of his colleagues had gathered for an impromptu meeting. Each juggled armfuls of books and bulging attaché cases as they paused to socialize and trade anecdotes on students. Their laughter spread across the green that was bordered by the ivy-covered stonework of the gothic building. It was the first day of summer break and each of them shared their personal vacation plans.

George Houghton was off to an archaeological dig in the South Dakota badlands; Celia Phillips was heading for Germany to tour castles on the Rhine; and the faculty's ever affectionate lovebirds, Ken Ellsworth and Marsha Sproule, were going camping in New Mexico. He envied their relationship, lusty and spirited, the kind Howard had had with his late wife.

He tapped on the leaded window. His colleagues looked up and waved, except the lovers, who could not take their hands off each other.

"Hey, you two," shouted Howard, "get a room."

Ken Ellsworth laughed, "Don't forget, we're picking you up tomorrow night."

"Oh yes. Where're we going?"

"Venezio's for Italian. Can you be ready for six thirty?"

"Yes. I'm looking forward to it."

He drew back into the lecture hall and checked his watch. There was, he decided, time to have a coffee before he began the dreaded job of cleaning out his office.

His lone footsteps echoed on the terrazzo floor as he walked the corridor to the staff lounge, coffee mug in hand. En route, he stopped for a last look at the row of painted portraits of St. Martin's former deans. All were regally dressed in their commencement gowns; each distinguished face peered out from a gilded frame highlighted by its own spotlight. The last portrait was of the current dean of the college, Richard McKnight.

McKnight was a bear of a man with thinning hair and a strawberry complexion, the upshot of too many bourbon and sodas. His formal likeness belied his gregarious manner. He was unaffected by his high position and no matter how hurried, always stopped to chat with anyone he passed on campus from department heads to the janitor, a trait that made him popular, but chronically late for meetings. Richard McKnight was the most unpretentious and approachable man Howard Munro had ever known, someone people were eager to follow so they could bask in his wit and geniality. Howard admired the man, but because of his own self-effacing manner, was unaware that he too was as well loved at St. Martin's as his mentor. Yet the two men could not have been more opposite.

Whereas the dean was an impeccably groomed and well-dressed man, Howard was the embodiment of casual. His wardrobe consisted of two threadbare sports jackets with bulging, marsupial pockets. Disheveled was Howard's middle name: clothes rumpled and creased, shirt open at the neck, and a tie, often bearing food stains, loosened and yanked to one side. He resembled a worn, but well-loved teddy bear. Female colleagues and students were always trying to mother him.

When he reached the staff lounge, he shoved open the wooden door. The coffee maker carafe held stale dregs and the basket was full of grounds; he decided to make instant. He filled the electric kettle at the double sink, and then wandered as he waited for the water to boil. At a small table he picked up a tissue to clean his smudged bifocals. As he wiped the lenses, he perused his reflection in a mirror.

Staring back at him was a six-foot, fifty-year-old with square face and hazel eyes, a man on whom the passing years had left their mark. His thick head of sandy hair had thinned on top, leaving a prominent island of bare skin like a patch of clear-cut forest. The remaining hair was heavily tinged with streaks of gray, as was his full beard, something that gave him the professorial look he wanted and hid the prominent birthmark on his chin. Although his belt size had increased by a notch or two since his teens, he had kept himself fit enough to stave off obesity.

He looked around. The place was still a mess; the caretaker had not yet made his rounds to sweep the floors and tidy up. The stove top was spotted with pasta sauce, and a single noodle straddled a heating element like a damsel tied to railroad tracks in a silent movie. On the cluttered countertop a half-eaten bag of nachos lay open, surrounded by a debris field of broken bits. He popped a few into his mouth, then carried the bag to the black leather couch and stretched out.

From the coffee table he grabbed a rumpled copy of the *Unicorn*, the campus newspaper, and flipped the pages. His eyes widened when he read *Viewpoint*, the editorial by his protégé, Bernard Lewis, an articulate student with journalistic ambitions who Howard figured was destined for a promising career.

Lewis chronicled Bush's two terms in office, the last of which was now in its waning months. It was, he opined, an administration fronted by an inept figurehead, manipulated by darker forces around him—a federal government characterized by systemic incompetence and duplicity. He touched on a variety of issues and their implications: the opposition to embryonic stem cell research; the vindictive leaking of an undercover CIA officer's identity to the press; the government's unconstitutional intervention in the Terri Schiavo right-to-die case; and the bungled response to Hurricane Katrina. But the major thrust of his editorial focused on the war in Iraq, including an acerbic denunciation of Canadian-born, Father Robert J. Newton, a prominent Roman Catholic cleric, influential member of the theoconservative movement, and unofficial advisor to the president:

> ". . . Newton endorsed Bush's phony invasion as being
> a theologically just war. Then, when the conflict proved to
> be anything but just, when weapons of mass destruction and
> Iraqi government links to Al Qaeda failed to materialize,
> when a post-invasion Iraq descended into anarchy and
> violence, Newton 'hid in the weeds', dodging accountability

3

for his role in contributing to the country's entry into another Vietnam-like quagmire.

Bush's religio-political presidency has set a disturbing precedent in this country that should serve as a sobering wakeup call to voters. Unless the theoconservative agenda is vigorously challenged at polling stations and in the courts, America is in danger of devolving into a theocracy, modeled on a single, state-sponsored faith—the very antithesis of what Thomas Jefferson envisioned—a spiritually myopic and oppressive regime that uses scripture to sanctify its discriminations, that stifles secular dissent and freethinking, and that pursues an anti-science agenda which will impede medical advancement and downgrade the quality of the nation's education systems.

Jefferson must be turning in his grave, given his efforts to enshrine the separation of church and state within our Constitution. Ditto, our nineteenth-century freethinker, Robert Ingersoll—the man who once warned us: 'Give the church a place in the Constitution, let her touch once more the sword of power, and the priceless fruit of all the ages will turn to ashes on the lips of men.'"

The article concluded with a tally of the war's financial contribution to the national debt, and its burden on future generations of taxpayers.

By the time he had read all the letters to the editor, the kettle whistled. He made his coffee, added sugar and whitener, and retraced the corridors to his office.

He leaned back in his swivel chair, rested his heels on the edge of the desk, and tried to ignore the chaos. Shingled layers of yellow post-it notes curled out from the wall. Amid the mounds of papers on his desk, were coffee cans packed with pencils and markers and three photographs in mismatched cardboard stands. As he sipped his coffee, he reflected on his life in the Glass City.

He had been born and raised in the wealthy suburbs of Toledo, Ohio, the only child of Dr. Cameron Munro, a successful orthopedic surgeon, and his mother, Yvonne, a lab technician; both worked at the same medical center. They were loving parents when they had time to be, but young Howard took a back seat to two busy careers.

Dr. Munro worked long hours at the center and at the hospital where he was one of the leading surgeons. In the evenings he brought his job home. After supper, he typically retreated to his study where he kept up with the latest medical procedures and consulted with his colleagues by phone.

Several times each week, Yvonne Munro flung a quick meal on the table, and then dashed out the door to her evening university class. When she was not in class she spent her off-duty time studying.

Although they all lived under the same roof, the busy parents were distant figures in their son's life, a situation worsened by the fact that neither was openly affectionate.

The pictures in the family photo albums, however, showed a contented baby with twinkling eyes and a broad smile. Except for major tumbles he was the kind of kid who bounced back easily and seldom cried. An inquisitive boy, he did more than play with toys; he would turn them in his hands and study the relationship of their moving parts if they had any. He liked puzzles, especially those that required him to match colors or shapes. By the age of four he could unscramble a Rubik's Cube in under two minutes.

From the earliest grades, Howard did well academically. He had a quick mind, an eagerness to learn, and a compliant nature, three things that made him popular with teachers, but marked him for scorn by his peers. In the harsh and unforgiving crucible of the schoolyard, Howard's studious nature soon earned him cruel nicknames.

Despite the family's prominent status in the community, young Howard was not the typical spoiled rich kid. His parents were determined to instill a strong work ethic in their son; they expected him to pull his weight in the Munro household and in return gave him a generous allowance. But his ambitions went beyond helping with domestic chores.

By age ten he was a budding entrepreneur: cutting grass, shoveling snow, running errands, and walking dogs for pet owners in his large subdivision, all solitary jobs, but well suited to his independent nature. Howard was fifteen in 1973, the year he met the Matsuos.

The Japanese couple lived on the next block from the Munros and ran a successful import business. Thirty-five-year-old Takumi spent much of his time in Asia on buying trips while his diminutive, twenty-eight-year-old wife, Hina, anchored the American side of the operation out of their suburban home office. Unable to maintain the property on her own, she posted a help wanted notice at the local grocery store.

Eager for summer work, Howard quickly answered the advertisement, first by phone, then with a follow-up visit to the Matsuo's home, complete with letters of reference in hand. With his solid build and mature demeanor, he seemed older than his years and made a favorable first impression on the young woman. She hired him on the spot.

In short order, he proved himself, and then some, to his employer. He was dependable to a fault, a confident can-do type of kid who paid attention to small details and who worked with speed and efficiency. Although he was originally hired to maintain the swimming pool and cut the lawns, he was soon doing a wide variety of other jobs for Mrs. Matsuo, including re-staining her backyard fence, a job that would bring him into contact with his first girlfriend.

In the full heat of summer, young Howard worked bare-chested, clad only in a bathing suit, sandals, and sunglasses. There was no fat on his adolescent body. He was lean and well muscled, and his tanned skin was set off by a thick head of sun-bleached hair—appealing eye candy. Often, when he looked up from his work, he noticed a girl watching him from the cedar deck of the house next door. The week he started staining the fence, the girl found excuses to come down into her yard and hover nearby.

He did not know her name, but recognized her immediately as a student from his school. On his way to the cafeteria, he regularly passed her locker and recalled that, unlike most girls, she was not someone who hung with a crowd. She had a couple of close girlfriends, but he had never seen her with a boy. When she was not looking, he dropped his paint brush into her yard.

"Do you mind helping a sloppy painter," he remembered calling out to her.

"Good thing it wasn't the paint can," she had replied, grinning as she handed back the brush, "or you'd be in a lot of trouble."

She stayed close to him after that as he worked his way down the fence, board by board, spattering as much stain on himself as on the fence. Conversation came easily as she opened up and talked about her family.

Like Howard, fifteen-year-old, Lisa Crandall was an only child and lived a similar lifestyle. Her parents were also self-absorbed people: Jim Crandall was a highly paid executive of a multi-national construction company, a driven workaholic with a sixty-hour work week; Muriel

Crandall was deeply involved with church work, serving on several diocesan committees and acting as the minister's full-time personal secretary. Lisa spent many of her nights at home alone while her parents pursued their own agendas.

But Howard's attraction to Lisa was not based on their mutual plight of parental neglect. Neither was it based on appearances, despite her slender figure and cute face—rare attributes in a high school where so many girls were frumpy and overweight. They discovered that they shared a few common interests; both were movie buffs, and enjoyed dancing to popular music.

Howard wasted no time asking her for a date. Thrilled at his interest in her, she readily accepted. They went to the movies a lot that summer and saw each other on a daily basis as Howard worked next door on the Matsuo property.

On a balmy August evening, not long before the new school year started, Howard, with the culinary help of his employer, planned a special dinner for the two of them. He floated lit candles on the surface of Mrs. Matsuo's swimming pool, and then dined with Lisa on the patio as Japanese koto music played from outside speakers. After dinner, he opened a small box and slipped a topaz ring on Lisa's finger; they were now officially going steady.

Not long after, he took Lisa with him to a tattoo parlor. So smitten was he with her, so certain that their relationship would be a forever thing, that he braved the needles as the artist inked two entwined hearts on his right arm: one with the letter H inside, the other with an L.

When school started, they were inseparable: eating in the cafeteria, taking the same study periods, and attending all the dances and basketball games. Howard adored her and loved to surprise her with slipping love notes into her locker or between the pages of her textbooks.

Outside of school, they were regulars at the local cinema, taking in all the popular movies of the day, then stopping for a pizza and ice cream.

Lisa's parents admired the personable young man and were thrilled to see their daughter's self-esteem blossom. They even invited the non-religious Howard to attend church services each Sunday and had him over to their house for supper. On special occasions, the Crandall's took their daughter and her attentive boyfriend to celebrate at a fancy restaurant.

Like many kids in their mid-teens, both Lisa and Howard were virgins. For a time, the couple's romantic activities were confined to necking and heavy petting. They talked of going further, but were too frightened of an accidental pregnancy to follow through with the act. But the longer they were together, the more they were tempted.

When his parents were away in the evenings, Howard's bedroom became the ideal love nest; Lisa's parents were too involved with their own lives to keep track of her activities beyond the Crandall home. Still, Lisa took no chances. She told them that although she was studying regularly at the Munro household, Howard's parents were always at home, an effective smokescreen that covered her tracks and opened the door to new freedoms.

As the school year progressed, both of them decided they would take their relationship to the next level. After a trip to Walgreen's Pharmacy, Howard bought a package of condoms, a novelty to the young lovers. Both of them laughed as they blew it up, and then released it like a party balloon to fly erratically around Howard's bedroom. Neither of them thought to use a fresh one; the damaged condom later broke inside Lisa. When she missed her period, the couple panicked; a pregnancy test confirmed their worst fears.

The resulting scandal tore the Crandall and Munro families apart. After cross-examining his daughter, Jim Crandall learned the details of her sexual activities. On pain of physical harm he banished Howard from any further contact with Lisa, and immediately removed her from school. Within weeks the Crandall's had moved out, leaving the real estate broker to sell the house and remove their furnishings.

Howard was devastated at the sudden loss of his girlfriend, feeling as though she had been criminally abducted. He made enquiries about the family's forwarding address, but learned nothing.

A month later, he received a one-page letter from Lisa, mailed from the United Arab Emirates, but with no return address. She explained that her father had taken a foreign job posting with his company to oversee a five-year construction project in Dubai. Then Howard read the final paragraph that cut him to the quick. Lisa's father had made arrangements to take her out of the UAE where abortion was illegal, and have her pregnancy terminated abroad. She told him that the following day she would be leaving to have the abortion.

Clearly then, it was not her idea to terminate the pregnancy. She was being forced to do it under duress. Both he and Lisa had agreed that they wanted to keep the baby regardless of the ensuing problems—and they knew there would be many. But it was too late now. He stared at the postmark on the envelope and felt sick to his stomach. The abortion had already taken place. Their child was dead.

Howard's world collapsed. He felt powerless. Lisa was half-a-world away and there was nothing he could do. The thought that his unborn baby was gone brought him to his knees. Logically, he knew he was not equipped for the responsibilities of fatherhood, yet he cared deeply for Lisa and was prepared to stand by her and the baby until they were old enough to marry. After all, their child had been conceived with love. Did that not count for something? Was a father's humiliation at his daughter's ill-timed pregnancy justification to condemn a fetus to the garbage bin? To discard it like uneaten food scraped from a plate?

He cried for months, suffered from insomnia, and lost weight. Depressed, he quit the basketball team and plodded robotically through the rest of the school year. Gradually, he got on with his life, and devoted himself to completing his entrance requirements for college.

He dated no one during his freshman year at St. Martin's, then, halfway through his sophomore year he met Suzanne Hewitt. Late for a lecture and in a hurry, she had fallen on the flagstone; her attaché case sprung open and the wind had scattered her papers across the common. He rounded them up for her and his chivalry earned him a date. After that, he was in love for the first time since Lisa. Life was good again.

Suzanne was attracted to Howard for his quiet, laidback temperament and found it easy to overlook his untidiness. He loved her sociable, outgoing nature, and they quickly developed a small circle of friends. They shared a love of traveling and the outdoors, of books, and of American history. They graduated summa cum laude and married the following year.

He remembered how excited he was when she got pregnant: feeling the baby move for the first time, buying a music box during her last trimester and playing the enchanting melody for his unborn child. He remembered being in the delivery room to witness the miracle of his little girl making her debut into the world; two years later he did it all again for his second child.

He smiled at their framed photos on his desk: Tina, the more fun-loving and outgoing one, now aged thirty, posing with her husband, Gerry; and Lynn, his youngest daughter, an unsmiling and serious young woman, still single and a champion swimmer, standing on a dais with an Olympic gold medal around her neck.

Neither daughter had shown any intention of having children, something that was a source of great disappointment for Howard. Worse still, both girls were fiercely independent and did not need their father anymore, at least not like when they were younger.

He reached for the photo of Suzanne, taken in Montana and traced his fingers over her face and recalled the happy times: their decades of contented home life as they raised the girls and watched them grow to adulthood, the many Christmases and birthdays, and the languid summer holidays spent traveling across America. He thought about their parallel teaching careers. After college, he had taught English in Toledo's high schools and then babysat the girls in the evenings while Suzanne taught English-as-a-second-language at night school, something she continued to do even after the girls had grown and Howard had joined the faculty at St. Martin's.

When Lynn left home their time was their own. They continued traveling during summer breaks, but then able to do the kind of things they loved and that the kid's had always hated—visiting historical places. The previous year they had retraced some of Lewis and Clark's original route in their motor home. He glanced again at Suzanne's smiling photo, taken at the base of Pompey's Pillar National Monument beside the Yellowstone River east of Billings, Montana. Her hair was windblown after climbing the monolith to view William Clark's famous signature inscribed for posterity in the rock. It was the last picture ever taken of her.

Later, on their way back to Toledo, they had stopped for a few days to camp beside the Mississippi River—Tom Sawyer and Huck Finn's river. The air was still and the heat and humidity were stifling. In the trees and bushes, legions of cicadas droned their deafening chorus, a rasping that drowned out all other sounds. Hand-in-hand they had walked its muddy banks and studied the footprints of the animals and birds that came to drink. They paused to watch the long commercial barges, low in the water with their heavy cargoes, and piloted by watchful men in tall bridges that towered sharply above the decks. They had made wishes for themselves and their adult daughters, then tossed sticks far out from shore, hoping the currents would carry them downstream to the delta and the Gulf of Mexico. In the copper light and long shadows of dusk, when the worst of the day's heat had dissipated, they found a private place beside the great river, spread a blanket, and made love while birds canted their heads and watched them curiously from the branches of the silver maples and the cottonwoods.

On their last morning by the river, the day they were to press for home, Suzanne rose early. She made a coffee in the motor home's galley, and then told Howard she was going to sit by the river. An hour later Howard dressed, and went to join her. In a sheltered grove he spotted her empty coffee mug on the shore, and beside it, her shoes, neatly placed. But Suzanne Munro was nowhere in sight. He called for her and got no answer. He scoured the banks without success. He returned to the motor home in case she had come back barefoot. Nothing. In a panic he ran to the campground office, thinking she might have gone there to turn in their site permit, but the owners had not seen her. He waited for several hours, and then called 911 to report a missing person, but the police would not respond until a full day had passed. Howard did not sleep. It was the longest and most stressful night of his life.

When the police arrived, the commotion drew a small crowd. Investigators cordoned off the scene, and after a thorough examination of the evidence, they ruled out foul play. She had, they concluded, gone wading in the river and must have been caught in the notorious Mississippi currents. But that was impossible, Howard told them; Suzanne was a strong swimmer who knew enough not to fight the current, but to swim with it until she reached shore. The lead officer called for the department's search helicopter to fly the river.

Howard's daughters flew out to be with their distraught father while police teams searched the banks and dragged the river for days, without success. Suzanne's disappearance made the news and alerted the public.

Finally, on the fifth day, a telephone call led to her recovery. A group of kayakers on the river had stopped to camp and discovered a woman's body wedged between the shore and a grounded log.

With his daughters at his side, Howard stood in the ceramic sterility of the county morgue and wept as he identified the bloated and grotesquely decomposed body of his forty-nine-year-old wife. An autopsy revealed that she had suffered a massive heart attack while standing in the river, collapsed, and been swept downstream.

Overcome with grief, Howard had Suzanne cremated, then, accompanied by his daughters, he returned to Toledo to hold a memorial service for her. Hundreds came to pay their respects: friends, family, faculty members and students from both St. Martin's College, as well as the school where Suzanne had taught night classes.

When that horrific summer had ended, forty-nine-year-old Howard went back to St. Martin's. His colleagues and students rallied to his side and for everyone's sake, he tried his best to soldier on. But the loss of his wife had broken his spirit and drained the life force from him. The man who had once taught English with the fervor of a televangelist, the man who had inspired and instilled in hundreds of students the joy of learning, was a shell of his former self. There were too many memories for him at St. Martin's College: memories of strolling the grounds with Suzanne, of attending lectures together, of laughing as they shuffled through fallen leaves on crisp, October days. Every time he walked the path where she had first dropped her attaché case he thought of her pretty face, so full of life, then, an instant later, the image of her death mask in the morgue would intrude and he could not erase it.

A knock on his office door made him look up.

"Come in."

"I saw your lights on," said Calvin Summers, the caretaker, sticking his head in. "Thought you might've forgotten to turn them off."

"You're working late tonight, Cal," said Howard.

"Yes, but I'm heading home now," replied Summers, looking decidedly tired. "I've secured the building except for the exit to the maintenance area. Will you do the honors and close up for me?"

"Sure Cal. I'm sorting the last of my stuff now. I'm afraid you're going to have quite a pile to throw out come garbage day. Do you mind?"

"Course not. Just wish you weren't leaving us."

"Me too. By the way, are you coming to Venezio's tomorrow night?"

"Wouldn't miss it for the world."

"Good. See you there."

The caretaker quietly closed the door. Howard listened to his footsteps retreat down the hall, and the sound of his car as it headed out of the parking lot. He looked at his watch; it was 10:00 p.m.

An hour later he had finished cleaning out his office. He put his personal files and keepsakes in a leather satchel, switched off the lights, and headed for the exit. He armed the security system, locked the building, and walked across the darkened campus toward the maintenance yard. Under the solitary lamp was his motor home, connected to the maintenance building by an electrical cable.

He made himself a late supper and turned back the covers of his queen-sized bed at the rear of the coach. After his usual pre-bedtime read, he turned off his lamp. For a long time, he lay awake, staring at the RVs roof vent above him, unable to shut his mind off as he mulled over the journey he was about to make. What, he wondered, would his new life be like. Had he made the right decision by leaving St. Martin's? Or would he regret having resigned his tenure, something he had not come by easily? After an hour, his eyelids grew heavy and he fell into a dream-haunted sleep.

# CHAPTER 2

## *Greeks in the Park*

THE MORNING SUN SHONE through the venetian blinds and cast stripes on Howard's face. He glanced at his watch with sleep-encrusted eyes; it was almost eleven o'clock. With students gone for the summer, the campus was quiet, save for the singing of birds and the territorial scolding of squirrels. Given the late hour, he decided to forego breakfast.

He showered, then donned his threadbare track suit and jogged across the campus and into the streets of Toledo. The rush hour was long over, but traffic was still hectic. He noticed many motorists talking on cell phones, the reason he was especially vigilant when jogging.

Howard knew the streets of Toledo like his hip pocket. Historically, the city was an amalgam of Port Lawrence, and Vistula, two towns that had sprung up when the area was resettled after the War of 1812. Cherry Street formed a common meeting point for the original municipalities. Howard always knew when he had crossed from one side to the other; the angle of the streets to the northeast of Cherry differed from those to the southwest.

His jogging route, a large loop that started and ended on St. Martin's campus, had not varied for years. It took him through established residential neighborhoods of homes built in another era and shaded with mature trees, and through commercial districts with businesses that had been around since he was a kid. He had run it in all seasons and in all weathers. He knew every crack in every stretch of sidewalk. The faces of the people he passed on the streets were familiar: the homeowners; the shopkeepers and neighborhood "characters" like Isabel, the bag lady; the

14

undercover cops in their unmarked clunkers; the courier drivers; and the city sanitation workers who picked up the trash.

As his feet pounded familiar pavement, other memories flooded in: eating Hungarian hot dogs at Tony Packo's Café on the city's east side; cruising the Maumee River on the *Sandpiper* on silken, summer days; watching fishermen casting for walleye from the banks; and visiting Cedar Point, the roller coaster capital of the world. Best of all, he remembered cheering the Toledo Mud Hens at Fifth Third Field the year they beat the Indianapolis Indians and won the Governor's Cup, and the following year when they did it again and whipped the Rochester Red Wings.

Near mid-day he slowed to catch his breath as he approached his favorite city park. People were seated on benches and around picnic tables that were scattered on the green. A young boy was operating a radio-controlled boat in the large pond. At the main entrance was the familiar catering trailer that arrived each weekday morning to feed the hungry lunchtime crowd. It was a daily event that brought a bit of Europe to the middle of Toledo.

Bouzouki music played from the trailer's outside speakers; a few local Greeks, toothless old men, unselfconsciously linked arms and danced while smiling onlookers clapped. Inside, three members of the Xenakis family operated the mobile kitchen: Spiros and Helene, a stocky couple in their late fifties, cooked the food while their grown son, Nick, took the orders and served the customers. The serving hatch was already open; patrons were lining up to place their orders for souvlaki, gemista, moussaka, kabobs of pork, lamb, and chicken, and Howard's favorite, lamb gyros with onions, tomato, and tzatziki sauce.

Howard had known the Xenakis family for years. Spiros was a short, powerfully built man with a thick neck and calloused, peasant hands. His gray hair was wild and tangled, like the windswept branches of an olive tree and he had the fiery eyes of a Greek warrior. Before coming to America, he had worked in his family's olive groves and vineyards in the Attica region of Greece. His English was broken and limited, unlike his wife, Helene, who spoke none at all. They were passionate people who used their hands when they spoke and were not afraid to embrace or sing. But the star attraction was their son and only child.

Like the legendary Adonis of Greek mythology, Nick Xenakis was a youth of unusual beauty, a lady-killer with a muscular build and dashing good looks. He wore his shirt half-open to the waist, and draped gold chains around his neck that contrasted with his ebony chest hair and swarthy Mediterranean complexion. Office girls for miles around came to the park for lunch and to lust. He flirted shamelessly with them and taught the cheekier ones seductive words in Greek. Like his parents, he remembered the names of every regular customer who patronized the family's catering business, either at the trailer, or at their permanent banquet hall in downtown Toledo. He smiled as Howard approached the trailer.

"What'll it be professor—the usual?"

"No gyros today, Nick," said Howard, shaking his head. "I'm in the mood for something else."

Nick turned to his father, working the grill. "Hey, Papa, the professor wants something different today."

Spiros stooped and peered through the serving window. "Hello, my friend. How about I make for you, keftedes . . . something you not had before?"

"What's that, Spiros?"

"Fried meatballs with oregano and mint. I put with salad: olive, zucchini, feta. Is very good."

"Sounds great," said Howard, and then stepped aside for a female customer.

He caught the eye contact between her and Nick. It was electric. Dressed in a sleek business suit, the voluptuous woman wore high heels with spaghetti straps that drew attention to her pink-painted toenails. She was lean and attractive, in her late forties, and married.

"Hey, lover boy. What've you got for me today?"

"Now or later?"

"Both."

"Good," he said, fire coming into his eyes.

"For now, gemista and a small salad."

"Home?" he whispered quietly.

She shook her head, and made a subtle hand signal on the counter.

"Your order will be ready in a minute," he said, smiling lecherously.

The woman wandered over to the fountain and sat down. She pulled a lipstick out of her purse, applied it, and then ran her tongue along both lips for the titillation of the young Greek.

"OK, Nick," said Howard, grinning curiously. "What was that about?"

"Sshh," he whispered, putting a finger to his lips and leaning forward. "The old man's right behind me. I gotta be careful."

"Why?"

"Papa's OK with me dating single chicks, but not the married ones. He goes crazy."

"So, what's the code all about?"

"The woman's hot. She wants to get it on with me tonight. Problem is her husband's home so we can't do it at her place. Hand signal means change of plans; we have to go to our motel instead."

"I take it you've been with her before."

"Once a week for the last year, sometimes twice. The great thing is," he said, checking over his shoulder for his father, "she always pays for the room. I mean, how good is that, huh? Married chicks, ya gotta love 'em. The cougars are the hottest. Last fling before the menopause."

"You're going to wear yourself out, Nick. I don't want to have to come back for your funeral."

"Come back?" said Nick, frowning. "Where are you going?"

"I'm moving."

"Where to?"

"San Diego."

"Nah. You're kidding me, right?"

"No, I'm not."

"But you can't leave Toledo. I mean, you've eaten here so many times, you're almost Greek, for Christ's sake."

"Nicky," bellowed his father, waving a spatula in his son's face. "Watch your mouth."

"Papa, listen to me. The professor's moving away."

"What you mean, move away?"

"He's moving to San Diego."

The man frowned and turned to Howard, "Is true? You go to California?"

Howard nodded.

"Why you go there?"

"Too many memories, Spiros. You see, my wife—"

"Yes, yes, I remember now. She died in river." He thought for a moment, then spoke again, his voice full of compassion. "I understand, my friend. Too much sadness for your heart, yes?"

Howard nodded, and then looked away.

17

The man took off his apron and thrust it into his son's hand. "Here, help your mother in kitchen. Today I will eat with the professor."

"What do you want to eat, Papa?" said Nick.

His father shrugged as he stepped outside, "Surprise me."

Spiros put his arm around Howard's back and steered him to an empty picnic table.

"How your daughters these days?" he asked as the two men sat down.

"They're fine," replied Howard. "Tina's married and Lynn's a swimmer. She's still single."

"Ah yes, the swimmer. You bring her one time here, yes?"

"I can't believe you remember," said Howard. "That was a long time ago."

Spiros waved his finger at Howard. "If she single, you tell her to keep away from my boy. He's no good for your daughter."

"Oh, Lynn's a pretty strong-willed woman. I think she'd be more than a match for Nick."

"You know, professor, people give a name to my son."

"What name?"

"They don't say his Greek name, Nick Xenakis. They call him, 'Nick Xepenis.'"

"Really? Maybe they're just jealous he gets so many girls."

"No, no. It is because he has big one in his pants. Women talk to girlfriends. Next thing you know, another one want to see for herself."

Howard laughed.

"All Nicky want to do is make fuck with them. Married, single, don't make no difference to him. He thinks I don't know about the married ones, but I have eyes and ears. Someday, an angry husband gonna find out and shoot him."

"He'll settle down one of these days, Spiros. Most of us do. Someone will come along and he'll fall in love."

"Not my son," he said, shaking his head vehemently. "All the time I say to him, 'Nicky, why don't you marry a nice girl? I don't care if she Greek. Just marry and make babies for me and your mother.'"

"Well, he *is* a grown man, Spiros. He can do what he wants now that he's out of the nest."

"No, no," said Spiros, waving his finger for emphasis. "Nicky don't live by himself. I make separate apartment for him in the basement."

"You mean he's still living at home?"

"Yes," said Spiros, inhaling deeply, then letting out a wistful sigh, "still at home."

"How old is he?"

"Thirty-years."

"How come he's still living with mom and dad?"

"Because Helene don't want him to leave. She afraid."

"Of what?" asked Howard, noticing his friend's eyes filling.

"Of losing Nicky," he said, pausing to wipe spilled tears from his cheeks. "And I too am afraid."

"Why? Is he sick with something?"

He shook his head, then pulled a handkerchief from his pocket and blew his nose.

"Maybe I shouldn't have asked," said Howard, seeing the man's upset state.

"No, my friend. Is OK. I explain. You see, after Helene and I get married, we try right away to start a family. Helene lose the first two babies. Then we try again and get Nicky. We both happy and want more kids, but doctor say no more babies, or maybe next time *Helene* is the one who die. So, she go to the hospital and get the hys . . . hystect . . ."

"Hysterectomy?"

"Yes. After that, Helene is afraid that if we lose Nicky, she can't make more babies."

Howard touched the man's arm reassuringly, "I understand, Spiros. It must have been upsetting for you both."

"You know what upsets us, professor?"

"What, Spiros?"

"Nicky bring women to basement. We no see them come in. We no see them go out. He don't bring one upstairs to meet parents—not *one*. Why, I ask you? We are not bad people. We go to church. We pray to God. Why does Nicky do this to us?" He stopped for a moment and sighed deeply. "Helene and I hear Nicky and woman, sometime three o'clock in morning, laughing and fucking, bed going squeak-a-squeak. And the whole time we listen to this noise, my wife cries, and I cry, because inside our hearts we know, Nicky don't want to marry. Don't want to have children."

Howard looked up as Nick approached the picnic table with two plates heaped with steaming food. The young man was oblivious to his father's upset as a stunning blonde woman on rollerblades called to him. He called back, then stuck out his tongue and wiggled it lewdly. She threw her head back and laughed. He stood with a plate in each hand, watching her recede down the paved path, breasts swaying pendulously.

"Nicky," said his father, cuffing his son on the side of the head. "Where are your manners?"

"Sorry, Papa," he said, putting a plate in front of each man, then pulling cutlery and napkins from the pocket of his apron.

"You know what your problem is, Nicky?" said Spiros. "You're like a dog after a bitch in heat . . . always sniffing."

"But I'm young, Papa."

"What do you think Father Stavros have to say about that?"

"That's what confession's for, Papa," he said, laughing. "First you sin, then you confess and start all over again."

"See, professor," said Spiros, throwing up his hands. "What do I do with this boy?"

Howard brought out his wallet.

"No, no, you don't pay for lunch today," said Spiros, gripping Howard's arm. "Today, we eat like friends, not business. You like wine?"

"Yes I do."

"Nicky," he shouted to his son, "bring bottle of Xinomavro and two glasses."

"Sure, Papa."

They spent several hours drinking and laughing. The more they drank, the more each man opened his heart to the other: talking of their children, comparing the ups and downs of their lives, sharing regrets over lost opportunities, and about their mutual fears of impending old age. Spiros listened as Howard told him of his plans to teach high school in San Diego. When they had finished the bottle of wine, he had his son bring some ouzo. They sipped the licorice-flavored liqueur slowly, and snacked on a plate of olives and almonds.

"Does it worry you, professor to go from a place you know, to one that is strange?"

"Well, it *is* a big change, Spiros, but it's something I have to do. You understand don't you?"

"Oh yes. I understand. But change to a new place for you will be easier than for me and Helene. You see, when we come to America, we speak no English words . . . only Greek ones. No one could understand us."

"I don't have any trouble understanding you, Spiros," said Howard. "You leaned the language well."

"You know how I learn English, professor?"

"How?"

"One day I go to the market to buy bread. I meet a Greek man, Ikaros Antonopoulos. Ikaros helped me get job in construction. All the men I worked with speak English. They teach me. Every day, they say new words to me. Slowly I learn."

Howard smiled

"But for *you*, professor—for you it will be easy. Here you speak English, then when you go California, speak same language. And *here* you are teacher, then in California, same thing. No problem."

"You're right, Spiros," said Howard. "For me it will be easier."

"You are very smart man, professor. You have good education. That is like a pearl of great price. It will help you go far in California. You will see. Not to worry."

"Thanks, Spiros."

"And you know what else, professor?"

"What?"

"You are nice man. Make friends easy with people. You will not be alone."

The two men continued to talk long after the lunchtime crowd had dispersed. With the trailer closed up for the day, Helene and Nick sat at a distant picnic table, patiently waiting for Spiros, yet they put no pressure on him to leave. Spiros went to pour the last of the ouzo into their glasses.

"No more for me, thanks," said Howard, placing a hand over his glass, "or I won't be able to walk. I've got to be sober for tonight. Friends are taking me out for supper."

Howard got up and extended his hand. Spiros shook it, then embraced him.

"Today is very sad for me. California get new teacher, I lose friend. But . . . maybe someday you come back . . . yes?"

"If I do, this'll be the first place I visit."

"Before you go," said Spiros holding up his hand, "I got for you something."

The man walked to his truck, then returned with a gold St. Christopher's medal attached to a chain of flattened gold links. The three-dimensional piece was exquisitely crafted: the upper portion of the outer ring was inscribed with the words: *St. Christopher Protect Us*, the lower section embellished with two tiny crucifixes and an elaborate, bas relief design. Suspended in the center of the open ring was the figure of the saint in a flowing monastic robe, holding a staff in one hand, and carrying a young child on his shoulder.

"You like this?" he said, showing it to Howard.

"Of course I like it," he replied, wondering how he could gracefully decline the gift, "but you can't give me something like this, Spiros. I mean, it's too expensive, and besides, I'm not religious."

"It does not matter," said the man, hanging the chain around Howard's neck, and then gently patting the medal. "This will bring good luck to you."

"But, Spiros—"

"Listen my professor friend . . . this you wear each day, and I, Spiros Xenakis, will ask God to fix your heart and find you nice woman. He will do it. You will see."

For a long moment, Howard held the medal in his hand and pondered Spiros' words, spoken with such certainty—such unwavering faith. Then, he slipped it inside his shirt and briefly held it over his heart.

# CHAPTER 3

## *Send Off*

IT WAS MID-AFTERNOON BY the time Howard finished saying goodbye to the Xenakis family. The wine and liqueur had fogged his wits and turned his legs to rubber and he was unable to jog back to St. Martin's campus. Instead, he walked as quickly as his condition would allow.

When he reached the motor home, he unlocked the door after several stabs with the key. He went to his bedroom, collapsed fully clothed onto the mattress, and was asleep in minutes. Hours later the sound of loud knocking woke him.

"Howard," shouted Ken. "You ready yet?"

He gazed at his watch. Six thirty. Time to leave for Venezio's. The mirror beside his bed reflected a sorry image: bleary eyes, haystack hair, flushed face, and clothes rumpled more than usual, even for him.

"Be with you in a minute," he shouted back.

He filled the washroom sink with cold water, then dunked his head in the bowl.

"Sorry," he said, opening the door and seeing the shocked look on his colleague's face.

"What happened? You look like shit."

"I was drinking with a Greek friend."

"Surely not Spiros Xenakis."

"As a matter of fact it was. Why?"

"Good God, Howard, you're lucky to be alive. That man could drink a battalion under the table."

"How would you know that?" said Howard, stepping aside to let him in.

"Marsha and I have been to the Xenakis' banquet hall quite a few times," he said, dropping into one of the two captain's chairs. "We know the old guy."

"Careful," said Howard. "He's not much older than me."

"Are you in any shape to go out tonight?"

"I'll be alright after a cold shower. Sorry about this."

"Don't worry. We've got a small side room reserved for the evening. If we're late, nobody's going to give a damn. There's an open bar and—"

"Oh, don't talk to me about booze," said Howard, shuddering. "It's iced water for me tonight or I'll be down for the count."

"Well, no one's going to care if you want to lay off the booze."

There was another knock on the door. Howard opened it.

"Oh-my-God," said Marsha, staring at him.

"Long story," said Howard, motioning for her to come inside. "Make yourself at home. If I don't take a shower, I'm not going to make it out that door, let alone to the restaurant."

"No problem," she said. "We'll hold the fort."

"Try not to get up to anything sticky," said Howard, yawning. "I don't want to come out and find you locked at the loins like a pair of spaniels."

"Don't worry," she said, "I think I can keep my hands off him for a few minutes."

Howard entered the washroom and gasped as the jet of cold water raised goose bumps. After choosing an outfit from the closet, he dressed, then walked through to the front of the coach.

"There," he said, fastening the last button below his collar. "I'm ready. Let's go."

Marsha blocked his path.

"What?" said Howard.

"You can't go dressed like that."

"Why not?"

"Because for one thing, you've got a damned great stain on your shirt, and besides, the color doesn't go with those trousers."

"Ah, knock it off, Marsha. Let the man dress the way he wants."

"I'm only trying to be helpful," she snapped. "If Suzanne was here right now, I'm sure she'd want to help him, the same way I have to help you."

"When was the last time *I* needed help dressing?"

"Duh, like yesterday morning," she said, then turned to Howard. "Want me to pick out something else?"

"You really think this sucks huh?"

"Big time."

"Well, go ahead then."

She walked through to his closet and began taking inventory. Howard sat down with his colleague at the front of the RV. There was an awkward silence between them as they watched Marsha laying out clothing combinations on the bed.

"So," said Howard, "I hear you guys are going camping in New Mexico."

"Yeah."

"Any place in particular?"

"Nothing in stone at this point. We were thinking maybe the Las Cruces area. Take in some of the local sights. Why?"

"Suzanne and I were there a few times."

"Really? I didn't know that. Any suggestions?"

"Check out Mesilla. It used to be a part of old Mexico once upon a time. There's a lot to see there, like—"

"Here," shouted Marsha from the bedroom. "Come see what your valet picked."

"I didn't know I had that shirt," said Howard.

"It was hiding out of self-preservation. Didn't you hear it scream when I hauled it out of the closet?"

Howard, laughed at himself, "I'll never change, you know. This sort of thing used to drive Suzanne nuts."

"She told me many times. Now hurry up and put it on so we can get our asses out of here."

Minutes later, they piled into Ken's Volvo station wagon and sped away. At the entrance gates to the main campus, they swung onto the treed boulevard that ran along the front of the property.

St. Martin's College was a random collection of buildings scattered over several city blocks: research facilities, study halls, library, chapel, and a huge gothic-style building, Convocation Hall, the venue used to host most social events during the academic year including commencements. Ken turned into the circular driveway and stopped at the bottom of the stone steps that led up to the hall's imposing entrance.

"What're we stopping here for?" asked Marsha.

"Won't be a minute," said Ken, leaving the engine running, and stepping out of the vehicle. "Cal Summers set aside a few boxes of books for me."

"Need a hand?" asked Howard.

"No thanks," he said, opening the vehicle's rear hatch, and then bolting up the steps and through the front doors of the darkened building.

He made two trips, each time dropping a heavy box into the loading area of the Volvo.

"Sorry old man," said Ken, out of breath, "but there's one more box in there and unless I want a hernia, it's gonna take two sets of hands."

"Sure," said Howard, following his friend. When he reached the building's foyer, dimly lit by a single wall sconce, he looked around. "I don't see a box."

"It's in there," said his colleague, pointing to the main body of the building.

He opened one of two oak doors for Howard, who stepped into the hall. At that instant, all the lights came on and hundreds of voices screamed "surprise."

He felt a tap on his shoulder and turned; it was Marsha.

"*Now* do you see why I wanted to spruce you up?"

"Thanks for that," he replied, kissing her cheek. "You know me, I'd have turned up looking like an unmade bed."

"I'm going to save your ass again," she said, as people pressed forward to greet Howard.

"How?" he asked, as he shook hands with some old students.

"I'm going to put a drink together for you. One you can nurse all night if you have to."

"Better be non alcoholic."

"Trust me, honey, your liver will thank me."

"You're a lifesaver. What'd I do to deserve you?"

She winked at him as she headed for the bar, "You'll get my bill later."

The moment she left, Howard was enveloped by a throng of former students; they laughed and reminisced about past social events on campus, and recalled some of Howard's spirited lectures, the most popular and talked about learning events at St. Martin's. It was a hallmark of Howard's when introducing a famous figure from literature, to delve into the personal life of the artist as well as the times in which he lived. By doing so, he hoped to give his students the most three-dimensional experience possible.

The dance floor was already crowded with students, moving to the beat of the music. The five-man group was hot: a lead, rhythm, and bass guitarist, anchored by a superb drummer and keyboard player.

"Come on, Professor Munro, I love this song," said Carla Melini, one of his sophomore students, pulling him to the dance floor.

As they gyrated to the funky tune, an audience gathered. Other young women stood by on the perimeter, waiting their turn. Howard was the best dancer on the faculty with the fluidity of a Fred Astaire—light on his feet whether jitterbugging to fifties doo-wop, gliding to a big band tune, or losing himself in a heavy rock number. After a half-hour of dancing without a break, Howard's forehead was beaded.

"Don't burn yourself out," said Marsha. "Save a slow one for me."

"I will if these kids don't kill me first," he replied, extricating himself from the dance floor.

"You are an enigma," said Marsha, shaking her head. "I can't for the life of me figure you out."

"Really?" he replied, tamping his sweaty face with a bunched-up paper napkin. "In what way?"

"You're a dry cleaner's delight, always spilling stuff on yourself, yet you're so light and quick on your feet. I don't get it. The two don't go together."

"Dry cleaners *should* love me," he laughed. "I help them pay their mortgages."

The room belonged to Howard after his performance on the dance floor. His progress was slow as he worked his way through the hall; every few feet someone would buttonhole him for a chat. When people noticed he had finished his Perrier, they began to bring him drinks. He sipped each slowly, and then when no one was looking, he set it down. Eventually, his fifty-year-old bladder reached the critical point. He excused himself, and headed for the men's room.

He opened the door and approached the row of four unoccupied urinals. On the wall above, was the familiar notice board, a forum for the expression of views on any topic. He laughed at the current theme, a lampoon of the sitting president. Attached, was a digitally half-morphed portrait of George W. Bush and a pre-historic primate. The caption read,

"Leader of the Free World—*Australopithecus bozo.*" Beside the photograph were three Bush quotes:

> "Rarely is the questioned asked: Is our children learning?"

> "Families is where our nation finds hope, where wings take dream."

> "I'm the commander . . . see, I don't need to explain . . . I do not need to explain why I say things. That's the interesting thing about being president."

Howard was still chuckling when the door to the washroom opened. Bernard Lewis, one of his favorite students, stepped up to the next urinal.

"Isn't it great living in a democracy?" said Lewis, looking at the Bush photo. "Can you imagine posting something like this in a North Korean washroom?"

"If this was North Korea," said Howard, "there'd probably be a state-operated video camera watching us at this very moment."

"Not the kind of place for men with small dicks, huh?"

"Are you inferring that I'm hung like a tsetse fly, Mr. Lewis?"

"Isn't that an oxymoron, sir? You can't be hung like a tsetse fly. I mean, there must be a better simile to describe being under-endowed."

"I suppose you're right," said Howard, zipping up, and then pressing the flush lever. "And if there is a better one, you're just the man to find it."

"Speaking of our esteemed commander-in-chief," said Lewis, washing his hands at the sink, "did you see my editorial in the *Unicorn*?"

"I read it yesterday."

"And?"

"Great stuff as usual. Any plans to unleash that talent of yours on an unsuspecting world?"

"I've got a couple of submissions out there in different publications. Keep your fingers crossed for me."

"I will," said Howard, opening the door for his student and walking with him back into the noisy hall.

Howard grabbed a paper plate and made his way down a long buffet table, piling on cheeses, veggies, and sliced meats. As he went to leave the table, a baby carrot slipped from his plate and landed in a bowl of dip. Exasperated, he worked to extricate it with his plastic fork, hoping that no one was looking. But the more he dug at the carrot, the deeper it sank, until it disappeared altogether.

"What *have* you done now?" exclaimed Marsha suddenly appearing at the buffet table and interrupting his rescue mission.

"Don't tell anyone," he said, sheepishly, as he pointed at the bowl of onion dip, "but would you believe there's a carrot scuba diving in there."

"Oh, really," she quipped sarcastically. "I can't for the life of me guess how that might've happened."

"I think he must've run out of air," he said, laughing. "I don't see any more bubbles rising."

Howard found a chair and ate while balancing the plate on his lap. He looked around the room, so familiar to him.

The interior of Convocation Hall resembled the Great Room of a medieval castle. A travertine floor laid in a herringbone pattern anchored the rectangular hall. The lower wall sections were dressed with ten-foot-high oak wainscoting; the upper sections were of hand-worked stone, punctuated by leaded-glass windows recessed into gothic-arched openings. Support for the twenty-five foot-high wooden ceiling began half-way down the long walls of the rectangle; rows of symmetrically curved timber angled upwards and met at the center; wrought-iron chandeliers hung from the ceiling on long chains. Around the perimeter of the room were framed oil portraits of notable graduates of the institution. In a place of honor hung a huge portrait of the college's benefactor, Nigel Cooper, the wealthy industrialist from Canterbury, England. It was Cooper who had named the institution after St. Martin's Church, the oldest parish in Britain, the place where St. Augustine brought about the sixth-century conversion of the pagan King Ethelbert to Christianity.

The showpiece of the Hall was a massive oak panel, topped with the coat of arms of the college, and underneath, rendered in large calligraphic script, a quotation from English poet, John Milton's, *Areopagitica* of 1644:

Where there is much desire to learn,
there of necessity will be
much arguing, much writing, many opinions;
For opinion in good men
is but knowledge in the making.

Howard's reverie was broken by approaching footsteps.

"Having a good time?" asked Ken, on his way to the buffet table with Marsha for refills.

"Yes," replied Howard with his mouth full. "I take it you two had a hand in setting this up."

"Actually, no," said Marsha. "The student body put this together. We got the job of conning you through the doors."

"Well, you had my ass fooled," said Howard, not noticing he had just spilled a dollop of onion dip on the crotch of his slacks.

"Oh shit, Howard," said Marsha. "You've done it again."

"Done what again?"

"Look," she said, pointing to the white blob. "And after all my efforts to see that you'd show up here looking tidy for a change."

"Damn," said Howard, angry with himself. "I knew I'd never make it through the evening without a mishap."

"Well," she said, eyeing his pants, "given the location of the spill, you're on your own with the clean up."

"How the hell am I going to hide a stain? There of all places?"

"You could pull your shirt tail out," said Ken. "I mean, with your reputation, who's going to notice?"

"Don't do that. Not tonight," said Marsha handing him a napkin. "If you're careful not to spread it around, it might not show."

He was about to start work on the stain when he was asked to join the dean and key members of the faculty on stage.

The speeches from Howard's closest colleagues were short. Each one shared a favorite anecdote and conveyed the esteem in which he was held on campus. The last to speak was Celia Phillips. When she finished, she turned the podium over to the dean, Richard McKnight.

The dean spoke for ten minutes, sharing his own anecdotes and memories of working with Howard on faculty committees and research projects for the college. He concluded by presenting Howard with a gold watch engraved with his name and the college's crest.

After thanking the faculty and students for the gift, Howard stepped aside for the last speaker of the evening.

Bernard Lewis unfolded a prepared speech, and addressed the room.

"I'm sure many of us here tonight share a similar first memory of Professor Munro during our freshman year. He introduced us to *The Prophet* by Kahlil Gibran. It's a small book, less than one hundred pages, yet considered one of the literary and philosophical masterpieces of the twentieth century. Our assignment was to read it thoroughly, then discuss it in a group. At the end of our discussion, he reminded us that the poet held onto his manuscript for four years before releasing it for publication, because he wanted the book to be the very best that he had to offer. I'll always remember what Howard said to us afterwards. 'Whatever you write—whether it's an assignment for me, or something you put together after you leave St. Martin's—always carry Gibran's example with you. Strive for that same kind of excellence.'

I mention Gibran tonight for another reason. In *The Prophet*, Gibran said that the mark of a great teacher is one who does not invite the student into the house of his knowledge, but rather, one who leads the student to the threshold of his own mind. Howard Munro *is* such a teacher; he led us to that place within ourselves where we could discover our own potential, and in the process he left a part of himself in each of us."

"Here, here," shouted voices in the crowd, followed by a long round of applause.

He waited for the cheering to stop before continuing.

"And finally, on a lighter note," said Lewis, "I'd be remiss if I didn't mention another unique aspect of Professor Munro, his, shall we say, informal style. That said, I have a gift to present to him on behalf of the student body."

He pulled a gift-wrapped package from below the podium and handed it to Howard. The moment the paper was off, he burst out laughing and held it up for all to see: a spray bottle of stain remover. Waves of laughter mixed with applause and echoed through the large room. Then slowly a rhythmic chant began, "speech, speech, speech, speech!"

Howard stepped to the podium and adjusted the microphone, "Thanks for this," he said, still laughing. "Your gift couldn't have come at a better time. Only minutes ago, some onion dip had the gall to do a swan dive into my lap."

He pulled a paper napkin from his pocket, sprayed it, then dabbed at the stain that was obvious under the bright lights. The comic moment and its timing triggered riotous laughter and applause. Howard cleared his throat a few times, a nervous habit whenever he addressed a large gathering.

"I've been to a number of reunions in this room over the years, but this one is special for me. Thanks for coming here tonight. I always enjoy meeting former students and sharing memories. The best part for me is catching up on what you've been doing in your lives since graduating. I've met three people tonight who chose writing as a career. Two of you are print journalists; the other is a radio broadcaster in Cincinnati. As a professor of English that pleases me. But what pleases me just as much is to have one of you say that what you learned here helped you to deliver a better presentation in your workplace, or to make a point more effectively at a PTA or a town hall meeting. I can't think of a greater reward for my twenty years spent here."

He waited for the applause to finish.

"I remember the first lecture I gave. My knees were knocking as I looked out into a sea of faces and wondered how I was being judged as the newbie professor in an old, established college. It didn't take long for me to feel that I had been accepted. I think it was the nickname that did it: Colonel Ketchup."

Another long round of laughter and applause caused Howard to wait, and as he did, his eyes misted. He used the time to gather himself.

"Like you, I hate long speeches, so I'll share one last thing. The annual commencement ceremony was always a favorite time for me. I used to think of them as a kind of mass launching of ships, a chance to stand at the dock and watch my students sail away into their professional lives. For me, that's the best part of being a professor. Mr. Lewis has suggested that I have left a part of me in each of you, but I would argue that it works both ways. Mentors, if they are wise, learn from their students. I've certainly learned a lot from you, and it's been great fun. Thank you all."

An emotional Howard stepped back from the microphone, as the room erupted into a sustained and thunderous ovation. He stared out into a sea of smiling, approving faces, and wondered. Would he one day look back on this moment as the high point in his life? Or would it all be downhill from here? His future at this moment seemed so uncertain.

# CHAPTER 4

## *Departure*

HOWARD SLEPT ONLY THREE hours. It was the price he paid whenever he drank, which is why he seldom did. His head was fuzzy and his tongue thick, despite his best efforts to nurse the drinks people had bought for him.

He could not tell whether the light coming in the window was from the security light in the maintenance yard, or from the first hint of dawn, but the noise was unmistakable; it was raining steadily. He lay quietly in bed, listening to the rain beating against the roof and thinking.

His send off party at Convocation Hall had gone well, too well in fact, since it had not ended until two in the morning. By the time it was over he was tired from dancing and hoarse from talking. He recalled some of the conversations he had had over the course of the evening.

The grads were excited. In spite of the rocky state of the economy, many had found part-time jobs to tide them over until something permanent came along. A few, the offspring of wealthy parents, were going on junkets to Europe and enthused about their planned itineraries. And then, there were the faculty's lovebirds, Ken and Marsha, who planned to marry in the fall.

Although anxious to share the news publicly, they had decided not to announce it at the party. He was happy for them. Both were in their mid forties and had been on the faculty for five years; Howard and Suzanne had been friends with them ever since, attending many social functions together, both on and off campus. After Suzanne's death, they had been supportive to him through the grieving process, but the closeness of their relationship had been difficult for him at times; it only emphasized his own loneliness.

Howard flipped on his lamp and read, hoping to tire himself enough to drift off. But after twenty minutes, he gave up and set his book and glasses on the bed covers. He stared at the picture of Suzanne on the wall, taken on the front lawn of their suburban Toledo home, and it triggered memories.

He recalled how excited they were at the start of each year's summer break. Their routine was always the same: while he de-winterized the plumbing, Suzanne packed the motor home, shuttling armfuls of clothing and supplies from the house. On departure day they would leave before the morning's rush hour, find the nearest highway rest stop out of town, then have breakfast while listening to the Bob and Tom show. The distance covered each day varied depending on their mood or the weather. Often they left the interstates and chose secondary roads that took them through small towns. They enjoyed stopping for an ice cream or a coffee in a roadside diner and talking to the locals. At day's end, she would search their directory for the nearest campground and help Howard settle into a site in time for a barbeque and a walk around the park before turning in for the night. But that was past history. This trip would be the first he had taken without her.

It began to rain more heavily now. Reluctantly, he rolled out of bed. He had his usual toast and cereal breakfast, then donned his rain gear and went outside to connect the Jeep to the back of the motor home. He checked the running lights on both vehicles, hung his rain gear in the RV's shower stall, then slid behind the driver's seat and drove off the campus of St. Martin's College for the last time.

He glanced through the front windshield at a slate gray sky. The rain was in for the day. Even after rush hour, the traffic was bumper to bumper in the southbound lanes as he inched his way out of town. Finally he reached the cause of the slowdown; an overturned semi-dump truck had spewed gravel over the shoulder and the inside lane. Howard chafed at the delay. Once the rubberneckers had sated their curiosity, traffic began to move. A beat up Toyota with four male occupants passed him; the men were handing around a bottle of liquor. Typical, he thought, not a cop in sight.

Progress on Interstate 70 was not much better as Howard swung west toward Indianapolis. Motorists were driving slowly, peering through flooded windshields as wiper blades slapped double speed. Ahead, he noticed a dark-jacketed figure in blue jeans with a back pack standing beside the highway. When he had halved the distance he realized it was a woman, hitchhiking—illegal on interstate highways. A car abruptly left the pavement and approached her; it was the Toyota.

As he drew closer, he saw her talking with the occupants. Suddenly, a man in the back seat reached out and touched her; she stepped back instinctively. Howard veered onto the shoulder and leaned on the horn. It startled the man. He turned and made eye contact with Howard, gave him the finger, then hollered something to the driver. Quickly, the vehicle fishtailed back onto the highway. The woman ran toward him and opened the door.

"Thanks for stoppin'," she said, as she tossed her pack inside and then stood dripping onto the motor home's linoleum floor.

"I was hoping you wouldn't get in that car," said Howard. "They looked like a rough bunch."

"Jerks. They stunk o' booze. Must be alcoholics, startin' this early and all."

"So," said Howard, laughing and putting a thumb to his chest, "the old guy here looked a safer bet, huh?"

"No offense, mister."

"None taken," he said, easing the motor home back into the flow of traffic.

"Sorry," she said, looking at the puddle forming at her feet, "I'm makin' an awful mess o' your floor."

"I've got a washroom back there. Why don't you change into something dry?"

She looked hesitant. "Nah, it's OK."

They drove in silence for a few miles. He noticed the woman's lips were blue and that she was shivering and holding her arms around her torso for warmth.

"You're getting hypothermic," he said, concerned at her soggy state.

She relented and picked up her backpack, "Where's your washroom?"

"Behind that sliding door," he replied and pointed.

"Thanks."

"You'll have to flip on the pump first. The switch is over the range hood. There are fresh towels under the vanity."

The woman locked the door. Howard felt weird having a woman on board, especially a total stranger. The pump blipped as she ran water into the tiny sink. For the next half hour, he heard only faint sounds; the longer she stayed in the RV's washroom, the more uneasy he became.

"You OK in there?" he shouted and looked into the mirror that gave him a clear view down the inside of the coach.

The washroom door opened, "Fine. I gotta lot o' fixin' up to do, that's all."

A few minutes later, she came out. She had towel-dried her hair, applied lipstick, and was dressed in dry clothes: an old, gray sweat top with a Philadelphia Phillies logo on the front, blue jeans frayed at the bottoms and out at the knees, and men's work socks with her right, large toe poking through. On her feet she wore a pair of stained and matted terry cloth slippers.

"There's a rest stop coming up," he said, noticing a blue signboard. "Soon as we're in, I'll make a hot drink for you."

He pulled off the highway and drove down the long approach lane. Two signs appeared: cars to the right, RV's, trucks, and buses to the left. The lot was full of angle-parked commercial trucks. Halfway down the tarmac he found an empty space between two eighteen-wheelers.

"Would you like a coffee?" he asked, walking to the galley.

"Please."

After filling the kettle, he lit one of the propane burners and opened the jalousie window to let out the fumes. As he waited for the water to boil, he fanned the pages of the *Exit Guide* to check listings for I-70's exits on the highway ahead. The woman got up and changed to the lounge seat, directly across from the galley. As she glanced around the inside of the coach, he looked over the top of his book.

She had shoulder-length, mousy brown hair, and her frame, just over five feet in height, had the undernourished look of a stray dog. Her brown eyes and button nose were set in an oval, weary-looking face, and she had several inch-long scars on her chin. She had the pale, waxy complexion of an inner-city waif, perhaps a tenement dweller, someone who had lived most of her life indoors. He was not sure of her age, early thirties or late twenties, it was hard to tell.

"How do you take it?"

"Regular."

"Me too," he said.

As he fixed their drinks, he watched her scan the well-stocked shelves of the galley cupboards.

"Something wrong?"

"Mister . . . would you mind if I have a few o' those?" she asked, pointing to an unopened box of soda crackers.

"Course not."

Her hands were shaking as she took it from him. In her haste to open the sealed flaps, she dropped it on the floor. When she got it open, she grabbed a fistful.

"When was the last time you ate a decent meal?"

"A while back," she replied, embarrassed.

"Well, we're not leaving here till you've eaten."

"I don't wanna put you to any trouble. It's just that I'm so—"

"No trouble at all. Sit down and I'll whip something together."

Howard poured her a bowl of cereal, then dragged out a frying pan and cooked up hash browns, bacon, and eggs. She ate ravenously, and then wiped the plate clean with a slice of bread.

"Feel better now?" he asked.

"Lot better, thanks."

"Where are you headed?" asked Howard, cautiously sipping his scalding coffee.

"Malibu. To see my mother. You?"

"San Diego."

"Takin' a holiday?"

"No. I'm going there to live," he replied.

"Got a job waitin'?"

"Yes. At a high school."

"Oh, so you're a teacher, then?"

"A professor," said Howard. "Well, I *was* a professor."

"Did you get fired or somethin'?"

"No. I quit my job."

"Professors must make a lot o' money."

"How do you figure that?"

"You can afford a fancy rig like this. None o' the people I know could."

"I've owned it for a while," said Howard. "My wife and I used to travel a lot."

"How come she's not travelin' with you?"

"She passed away."

"Oh, I'm sorry," she said, looking sympathetic. "You must miss her a lot."

"Where's home for you," asked Howard, changing the subject.

"Philadelphia."

"Ever been to California before?"

"Nope. Never been out o' Pennsylvania. To be honest and truthful, I've hardly been out o' Philly."

Howard watched her dig into her backpack and pull out a package of cigarettes and a disposable butane lighter. "Don't worry," she said, noticing his concerned look. "I won't smoke in here."

She picked up her wet leather jacket to shield her from the driving rain.

"Take that instead," said Howard, pointing to a handle sticking out of a tubular holder beside the entrance door.

"Thanks," she said, stepping into the downpour and opening his umbrella.

She walked to the front of the motor home. The driver of a departing truck tooted his air horn and gave her the once over as he passed. After she lit up, Howard noticed the odd way she held her cigarette between her thumb and forefinger, the way most people toke a joint. Had she ever smoked weed, he wondered? She took deep drags and walked in aimless circles, as if at loose ends with her life. She tossed the half-finished butt onto the tarmac, then re-entered the RV. From her pocket, she pulled a square of gum and chomped noisily.

They sat for a few minutes watching a young woman walking her terrier in the designated pet area. The dog sniffed and walked back and forth over an imaginary grid, searching for the right spot. Then it squatted and its owner watched intently.

"Ever notice," she said, "how people always watch their dog take a crap? I mean they stare and stare till the whole thing drops out. Kind o' weird don't you think?"

Howard laughed. "I never thought about it really."

"And you know what else?"

"What," he replied, wondering what was coming next.

"Soon as that turd hits the ground, there'll be flies all over it in seconds. I mean, there must be whole squadrons o' turd-huntin' flies just zoomin' around and waitin' for one to drop."

"Look at that," she exclaimed angrily, pointing at the woman. "She never even picked up the turd. Just left it there to get smushed on someone's shoe. I mean, how ignorant is that? There must be a bazillion germs on that thing."

He carefully eased the motor home out of the parking space and accelerated onto the wet highway. The woman sat in the captain's chair beside him, drumming her fingers on the armrest, blowing bubbles, and popping them loudly. He began to wonder whether he had done the right thing in picking her up. She did not seem inclined to make conversation unless he started something, not like Suzanne, who loved to talk as they went down the road.

"By the way," he said, breaking the long silence, "my name's Howard Munro. What's yours?"

She reached over and shook his hand, "Miriam," she replied, then popped a bubble loudly. "Miriam Kovacs. But some people use my nickname."

"What's that?"

"Mimi."

"Cute."

"Thanks," she said, blowing another bubble.

"So . . . you said you were heading out to see your folks."

"No. Just my mom."

"Are your folks divorced?"

"Uh-uh. Dad died when I was eighteen, the year after I left home."

"Heart attack?"

"Highway accident," she replied, but offered nothing more.

"I'm sorry," said Howard, taking his eyes off the road and giving a sympathetic look.

Her silence signaled the need to change the subject.

"How'd your mother wind up living in Malibu?" he asked, swerving into the passing lane to avoid chunks of shredded truck tire.

"She remarried after Dad died."

"Must've married a rich guy. Malibu's a pretty exclusive address."

"Ever heard o' David Farnsworth?"

"No. Should I?"

"Mom met him when he was just a writer—"

"A novel writer?" asked Howard.

"Screenplays."

"For movies?"

"Yeah."

"That doesn't pay enough to buy a house in Malibu."

"He made his money on the stock market. Eventually, he became a producer."

"What movie is he working on now?"

"None. He died in L.A. havin' open heart surgery. Mom lives by herself now. David left her plenty o' life insurance and shares in a couple o' Hollywood studios."

"When you get out there, are you going to move in with her?"

She nodded, "Least till I find out what I'm gonna do."

"Got any plans?"

"Did have. Till I got pregnant that is. I stayed with some girlfriends in Philly for a few weeks, then called my mother and asked her if I could come out to California."

"How far along are you?" asked Howard, glancing at her midriff that as yet showed no signs.

"One month exactly."

"That's nice of your mom to help you out like that."

"Oh, that'll change. Haven't told her I'm pregnant yet."

"How do you think she'll take the news?"

"It's not the pregnancy part I dread."

"What do you mean?"

"It's tellin' her I want an abortion. She doesn't believe in that. But she's got connections in Hollywood. Knows people who do 'em for the stars."

"Is that what you're going to do?" asked Howard, turning to look at her. "Get rid of the child?"

She glared at him, chomping more aggressively on her bubble gum. "Don't look at me like I'm some kind o' criminal. I just don't wanna kid."

"You were smoking back there at the rest stop. Did you know that can harm a baby in the womb?"

"Hey, what the hell is this? Where do you get off givin' me a lecture?"

"Sorry," said Howard, lifting one hand from the steering wheel. "You're right. It's none of my business. I shouldn't have said anything."

"You're damned right you shouldn't have!"

Conversation ended abruptly. She swiveled her captain's chair and stared sullenly through the rain-splattered side window.

Traffic thickened the closer Howard got to Indianapolis. He took the ramp at the junction of I-70 and the southbound 465 beltway and kept to the center lane to avoid conflict with merging traffic. Local drivers familiar with the exits flew past on both sides; rooster tails of water flew up from their vehicles and made visibility difficult. His late-night going-away party was catching up with him now and the slip slap of the windshield wipers was becoming hypnotic. Occasionally he wandered out of the center lane. Passing motorists honked angrily.

"You're gonna nod off," she said, fear written on her face.

"Don't worry," said Howard. "I've never done that."

"Well," she said, "there's a first time for everythin'. Lemme out."

"Not on the beltway," he said. "It's too dangerous for me to pull over. Besides, look at the weather. You'll catch your death in this rain."

"How much longer we gonna be on this?" she asked, her voice a mix of apprehension and impatience.

"You mean the beltway?"

"Yeah."

"Fifteen or twenty minutes . . . that is if the traffic doesn't get any worse or there's an accident."

"Oh," was her only response.

The atmosphere inside the cab was strained now. She avoided conversation and leaned her head against the side window. Restless, she fidgeted and drummed her fingers on her knee. Howard was not used to traveling with a moody companion, so unlike Suzanne, who was always animated and upbeat. Still—at least the woman was company.

Howard was getting more tired by the minute as he plodded around the beltway, but he fought hard not to let it show.

"Soon as I'm clear of the city," he said, "I'm going to start looking for a place to camp for the night."

"Hey," she said, snapping her head sideways. "I'm grateful for the ride and all, but I'm *not* gonna sleep with you if that's what you're thinkin'."

"No, no," he said, holding up his hand, "nothing like that. I was thinking of something else."

"Like what?" she said, eyeing him with suspicion.

"Well," said Howard, taking a deep breath. "If I was to put you up in a motel and camp nearby, I could pick you up tomorrow morning. We could continue on and—"

"You mean you'd pay for my room?"

"Yes. All the way to California. I'll even make a detour and drop you at your mother's."

"What's the catch?"

"There is none."

"Look," she said with skepticism, "there's no such thing as a freebie."

"All right then. "Maybe I do have a motive."

"Ah, I thought so," she said, sarcastically. "Men are all the sa—"

"I didn't mean for sex."

"What then?"

"It's a lonely drive to California. I want someone to talk to. Is there something wrong with me wanting that?"

She stared out the window and mulled his offer, too good to be true. On the upside, it would mean guaranteed accommodation and a ride, plus less risk of getting busted for hitchhiking. But it was the downside that bothered her most. Would he stay on her case about the abortion, her smoking, or some other aspect of her personality he did not like? Would he look down on her? After all, he was an ex-professor and she was just a no account high school dropout.

"I have a confession to make," he said.

"What?" she said, cautiously.

"When my wife and I used to travel together, she always wanted to pick up a hitchhiker, to do something kind for someone. The thing is, it was me who wouldn't. Not because I didn't want to be kind, you understand, but because I wasn't comfortable with picking up a stranger. All I want now is to do something decent. No strings attached."

"Well," she said, "it *is* generous, and I guess if I have the room to myself—"

"Oh, you will," said Howard, emphatically. "I have no intention of taking advantage of you if that's what you're worried about."

"OK then . . . thanks."

He drove west out of Indianapolis for some distance before finding a suitable place, a small strip motel with a large parking area at the rear. It was plain-looking and dated, but clean.

Howard opened the door to the office. It was empty. Behind the counter was a door marked *Private*. He could hear a television playing. He hit a bell on the counter. A chair scraped and footsteps sounded on bare floor.

"Can I help you?" said a fortyish man in jeans and a black Harley Davidson T-shirt.

"Yes, I'd like a room."

"For how many?"

"Just one. It's for a woman outside, a hitchhiker who's traveling with me."

The man frowned.

"She'll be sleeping in here. I'll be in my RV out back."

"Room's fifty bucks. You can park your rig for free."

The motel keeper pushed a pen and registration card across the counter. Howard filled it out, paid the man, then took the key out to Miriam, now standing outside the RV, her pack slung over one shoulder.

"See you in the morning," he said, and then drove toward the back parking lot.

He parked the motor home, then turned off the ignition and sat behind the wheel for a few minutes. For the first time in ages, Howard felt a tinge of optimism. It was a long way to California. At least now he would have some company along for the ride.

# CHAPTER 5

## *Miriam*

SHE STEPPED INTO ROOM sixteen and tossed her pack and black leather jacket on a wooden chair. Then, she checked the dresser and night table drawers. They were empty, except for a Gideon bible, and a local telephone book: the essentials for salvation and pizza delivery. A peculiar odor hung in the room, a cloying, sweet smell of either air freshener or cleaning products, a cheap way to give the worn-out room a new feel. She flopped on the bed, lit a cigarette, and surveyed the room.

The scuffed walls were of low-priced wood paneling and the décor was 1970s, with shag carpeting, and shiny, polyester drapes, the hems of which sagged onto the window's air-exchange unit. She noted how the bed was reflected in the dresser mirror, a titillating arrangement. How many people, she wondered, had screwed someone else's spouse in front of it, turned on by their lewd reflections? Above her, a valentine heart with a cupid's arrow had been crudely scraped into the stippled plaster ceiling. How appropriate she thought. Love, or rather, the lack of it, had been the story of her life. She blew smoke rings, watched them rise, and daydreamed of her early life growing up in Philadelphia.

Compared to some families in her low-rent neighborhood, the Kovacs were well off. Her mother, Robin, worked as a bank teller to supplement her father's fluctuating income from trucking. Some months were better than others, especially if he got some lucrative long-distance runs.

Her father's nomadic life as a trucker, however, did little to create stability for the family. His migratory comings and goings made him seem almost like an intruder when he appeared at their door between runs to Alaska or Mexico. But when he was home, he tried his best to atone for the long absences. He brought small gifts for his wife and daughter, and took them out for supper, or on occasion, to the local bowling alley. And when the Phillies played a home game, he made sure they sat together as a family in seats as close to the field as he could afford.

She remembered her father with mixed emotions: sadness, bitterness even, over his time spent away from home, yet grateful for the quality hours they were able to spend together. There were two sides to Ray Kovacs: the macho image he maintained around his blue-collar buddies, and the softer, gentler side he reserved for her and her mother. He was an affectionate man, a man with simple tastes and needs, a hard-working, average Joe who lived life one day at a time and was content with his lot.

His hobby was collecting baseball cards which he organized by teams and kept in three-ring binders. Before she entered her teens, one of her favorite things to do was to sit with him on the sofa and flip through the collection; they would talk batting averages, player injuries and salaries, and about the history of the game including World Series trivia.

She made the most of their time together, knowing that after each brief visit, he would be out the door again, working to pay off the mortgage on his truck. And each time he was gone, Miriam did her best to mitigate her mother's loneliness by playing cards and doing jigsaw puzzles with her in the evenings.

But the farther she journeyed into her teens, the more they drifted apart. Her mother was strict, never more so than after Miriam reached puberty. She had all the phone numbers of her friends, and kept her on a rigidly enforced curfew and made unannounced searches of her room. Stripped of her privacy and under such scrutiny, Miriam developed a rebellious nature and devised clever maneuvers to cover her tracks, including the use of her bedroom's ventilation duct to conceal contraband. Fighting was a daily event: a concerned mother striving to protect her daughter, a headstrong girl, trying to establish her own beachhead of independence. They waged endless campaigns against each other, one skirmish at a time, taking ground one day, losing it the next, and then starting over. By the age of fourteen, Miriam was a regular user of marijuana and had her first sexual experience, a fumble fest in the back seat of a car.

She remembered trying to get a condom on the boy whose name she had long since forgotten, a boy whose eagerness for first coitus caused him to ejaculate before he got inside her. Her sexual relationships throughout high school followed a pattern; the boy pledged love to get sex, she dispensed sex to get love—a love that never materialized.

The sound of a large vehicle approaching drew her to the window. A diesel highway tractor towing a box trailer was swinging in off the highway. Smoke belched from twin exhaust stacks as the driver headed toward the back parking lot.

She walked to the bathroom at the rear of the suite and slid open the pebbled-glass privacy window. The driver had already made a large sweep through the lot and was expertly backing his rig between Howard's motor home and an eighteen-wheeler. She heard the familiar tsht-shhhh of the air brakes, followed by the dying rattle of the diesel engine. He wrote on a clip board for a few minutes, then jumped to the ground. After he had checked all the tires, he locked the cab and started for the motel office.

His looked nothing like the stereotypical trucker; he was trim, fit, and had the clean-cut look of an LDS missionary. He wore a white shirt tucked into neatly pressed beige pants that rested on polished cowboy boots. On his head was a straw cowboy hat with a deep valley in the crown. As he approached the rear of the building, she closed the bathroom window and stepped back onto the tiled floor.

She decided to use the toilet and removed the paper band that bound the lid and seat together. She grinned at the words printed across the top, "Sanitized for Your Protection." When, she wondered, had motels begun using these? Back when women thought they could get a dose off a toilet seat? She giggled to herself, as she recalled the lyrics to a song she had once sung in high school: "Don't Give a Dose to the One You Love Most." When she finished, she pressed the handle. The water made a lazy entry into the iron-streaked bowl and passed through the trap with a weak glug. She peeled the wrapper from the tiny bar of motel soap, washed her hands at the chipped porcelain sink, and returned to the room.

From the night table, she picked up the TV remote and aimed it. Nothing. She pried open the plastic case and found the batteries badly corroded. She was not surprised; people came to motel rooms like this to exchange bodily fluids, not to watch *Oprah*, or old re-runs of *Frasier*. She opened the flap below the TV screen to expose the manual buttons, selected a channel, and adjusted the volume low. She stared vacantly at the set, until the handsome young trucker walked past her window.

Through paper-thin walls she heard him open his door, toss his keys on the furniture, and listened to the floorboards squeak as he moved around the room. It was then she noticed the two units were joined by a set of back-to-back doors, equipped with thumb turn deadlocks. Only two thin slabs of wood separated her from the virile-looking man. A tingle of desire suddenly ran through her. She heard the shower running and the thud of him stepping into the tub. What did he look like in the nude, she wondered? Hard abs? A cute butt?

She rolled a joint, and stepped outside. She sucked the sweet smoke deep into her lungs, held it, and savored the buzz. Minutes later, the door to the next unit opened and the trucker emerged. His shirt was open and his bare chest exposed. She noticed he wore a wedding ring. He glanced briefly at her before walking around the building; minutes later he returned with a sheaf of paperwork.

"Ma'am," he said, nodding politely as he prepared to enter room seventeen.

"Hi there," said a smiling Miriam, anxious to engage him in conversation. "I saw your rig come in off the highway. It's a Peterbilt, isn't it?"

"Yep."

"Are you an owner operator?"

"Yep."

"So was my dad," she offered.

"Was?"

"Yeah. He's been dead a long time now," she said, then changed the subject. "What're you haulin'?"

"Farm supplies 'n' tractor parts."

"You got an Okie accent," she said, working hard to hold the quiet man's attention.

He eyed her with suspicion, then nodded.

"My father was born in Oklahoma."

"Where 'bouts?" he asked, brightening a little.

"El Reno. Small place just west o'—"

"Where I'm from," he exclaimed.

"Which is?" asked Miriam, trying to stall him from entering his room.

"Yukon."

"Hey, that's the home town o' Garth Brooks."

"Well I'll be dogged. Not many folks know that."

"I'm a country music fan. Garth's my favorite."

"Country's all I play," he said, opening up a little more. "Got a great sound system in that rig."

"How come you're stayin' in a motel, instead o' bunkin' down at a Flyin' J? You do *have* a sleeper cab in that truck."

"I need a break from truck stops every now 'n' then. Them places is too danged noisy, what with rigs pullin' in 'n' out at all hours."

"You a long distance trucker?"

"Yep. Done all the lower forty-eight."

"You don't look old enough to have traveled that much," she said, slyly probing for his age.

He dodged her question. "I spend a lot o' time on the road, ma'am."

"I thought it was only women that wouldn't tell their age," she said, laughing and toking her joint down to the roach.

He was upwind from her. She caught his scent, a mix of deodorant soap and spiced aftershave.

His cheeks reddened, "I turn twenty-four next month."

She smiled and gave him the once over.

"You ain't got no car," he said, glancing at the empty parking space in front of her unit. "How'd y'all get here?"

"Hitchhiked."

"Where you headed?"

"California . . . Malibu, actually."

As she appraised him, an idea formed. This man would make a better traveling companion. He was closer to her own social level, unlike the professor who was too high-toned for her liking, not to mention, judgmental. Plus, the trucker was much younger— appealing eye candy.

"Which way are you headed when you leave here?"

"West," he replied.

"Goin' far?"

"Three hundred miles. Why?"

"Think I could ride with you?"

"Well," he said, shifting from foot to foot and looking hesitant, "I don't reckon so. I mean—"

"But I've only got a small backpack. I wouldn't take up much room."

"You see . . . th' thing of it is, ma'am—"

"Please," she said, seeing her chance slip away.

"I'll be rollin' by six. You'll be asleep at that hour."

"No I won't. I'm an early riser."

"Well," he said, rubbing his hand on his chin, "since y'all are so persistent, I reckon I could make an exception."

"Thanks," she replied quickly, pointing to the opposite side of the secondary highway. "I'll be standin' over there when you pull off the lot."

The man nodded, then went to open the door to his room.

"By the way," said Miriam, "what's your name?"

"Troy."

"City in ancient Greece," she said, laughing.

"What's yours?"

"Miriam."

"Sister o' Moses," he said, smiling as he stepped inside his room.

# CHAPTER 6

## *Troy*

MIRIAM WAS WAITING BY the roadside at six the next morning. In the distance, she could hear truck tires whining steadily on I-70. Beside her was a rural mailbox belonging to a farm set back from the road. She wiped off the dew, set her backpack on top, then lit her first cigarette of the day. A rusted pickup with one headlight stopped beside her. The driver, a middle-aged farmer with a plug of chewing tobacco in his cheek, appraised her.

"Need a ride, honey?" he called through his half-opened window.

"No thanks, I'm waitin' for somebody."

"You sure?"

"Totally, but thanks for stoppin'."

"All right, then. Have a good one," he said, and drove off.

Minutes later she watched Troy leave room seventeen, lock the door, and walk to the office to put his key in the drop box. He waved to Miriam, then disappeared around the building and started the diesel in the big Peterbilt.

Five minutes later, the steel leviathan emerged from the side of the motel, engine rumbling. It crossed the highway and stopped astride the shoulder and the pavement. She opened the door, tossed up her pack, then climbed the metal steps to the cab. He moved the shifter into gear and let out the clutch. The engine torque lifted the huge cab as the truck left the shoulder of the road.

"Did y'all sleep OK?"

"Yeah. I lied though. About gettin' up early and all."

"I figured you was fibbin' to me. It ain't normal for folks to be up b'fore th' crack o' dawn. Early risin' is fer roosters 'n' truckers."

"I really appreciate you takin' me like this. I haven't ridden in one o' these since before my father died."

"Yeah. I recall you sayin' somethin' 'bout that yesterday." He reached over and turned on the truck's sound system. "There," he said, as a Garth Brooks CD started. "I b'lieve you said he was your favorite."

"Thanks for rememberin'," she answered, and buckled her seat belt.

She stared through the windshield and along the massive engine hood; at its front was a chromed hood ornament, an eagle with outstretched wings. When they reached the signboard for westbound I-70, Troy entered the ramp, and then jammed the accelerator pedal to the floor and up-shifted to highway speed. The merge was easy. At this early hour the highway had few cars, only eighteen-wheelers and a few pickups. Farms flew past the windows as the sun slowly peeked over the horizon behind them; it cast a long shadow of their truck on the pavement ahead. Troy concentrated on the road while Miriam glanced into the west coast mirror beside her door. The bullet mirror reflected the side of the trailer and the rapidly receding shoulder of the highway.

"You said you was headin' fer California," he said, breaking the long silence.

"Yeah, to my mother's in Malibu."

"I seen pictures o' that place one time. Right purty it was. Houses strung along the Pacific like pearls on a necklace. That be where she lives? I mean, by the ocean?"

"Not right on the ocean, but she can see it from the house."

"Is all your kinfolk out there?"

"Only Mom. She's widowed."

"Mus' be lonely 'n' all. Folks ain't meant to live by theyselves. Th' Lord intended us to have someone to warm our toes on."

"Yeah," she sighed, reflecting on the lack of a partner in her life.

"Hope you don't mind, but I like to put highway behind me b'fore I strap on the feed bag."

"Nope, that's fine."

He passed a Wal-Mart truck, then looked in his mirror and waited for the other driver to flash his lights.

"You ain't got no accent. Where you from?"

"Philadelphia."

"City o' Brotherly Love."

"The city that loves you back,'" she laughed cynically. "Might love some people, not me though."

"Got no feller in your life?"

"Did have."

"You done split up?"

Miriam nodded. "Dumped me when he found out I was pregnant."

He paused for a moment, thinking of something comforting he could say. "Well, I mean, it's nice when a baby's got a mama *and* a daddy. But lotsa women raise a child on their own these days. Better a child grows up bein' loved by one good parent, than in a house where both is fightin' 'n' cussin' at each other. Look at me. I turned out OK, and all I had was a mama. Didn't have a whole lot o' material things, mind you. Hand-me-down stuff and such, but it didn't harm me none."

Miriam said nothing about her plans for an abortion. He had made one reference to the Lord already, a good indication that he was pro-life. She did not need another lecture. Troy seemed to sense her mood and for a while concentrated on his driving. Fifty miles down the road, he flipped on the turn signals and eased onto an exit ramp.

"Pullin' in for breakfast, now?"

"Yep. The best eats this side o' th' Mississippi. Nobody leaves here on an empty belly!"

He stopped at the end of the ramp, looked both ways, and then turned left and crossed over the highway. Troy waved to a departing truck driver before turning into the diner's huge lot, packed with eighteen-wheelers.

After backing into an empty space between two gasoline tankers, they walked the oil-stained gravel parking lot toward the diner. Spinning ventilators on the roof pumped out aromas of bacon and home fries.

As they stepped inside, Miriam took note of the patrons: burly men in every shape and size, including a few women truckers, tucking into full plates of food. There was a congenial atmosphere about the place. Trucking was the life line of America and truck stops were the social oases where lonely drivers could stay in touch and renew acquaintances face-to-face, instead of over CB airwaves. There was no "wait to be seated" sign; they picked an empty booth and sat down.

While waiting to be served, they glanced at a woman trucker eating alone several booths away. She was short and morbidly obese. Her cellulite-riddled arms were bill-boarded with tattoos from wrists to shoulders, and except for the colored inks, her skin was a sickly white like flensed blubber. With her pendulous, apron-like belly wedged tightly in the booth, she resembled a stranded beluga washed ashore after a storm.

"Wouldn't want to meet her in a dark alley," whispered Miriam.

"You got that right. I'd rather wrastle a grizzly bear."

"And look," said a surprised Miriam, "she's wearing a wedding ring!"

"Lord have mercy," he exclaimed, looking at the woman again, then back at Miriam, "If she ever rolled on top o' her hubbie, why, he'd suffocate hisself to death."

"Hey, Troy," said a middle-aged waitress as she approached with two mugs and a pot of coffee. "Haven't seen your hide in here for weeks."

"Hey, yourself," he replied and tipped his hat. "Good to see y'all, Shirley."

"Brett not traveling with you on this run?"

"Brett's back in Yukon, lookin' after the store. This here's Miriam, my co-pilot for the next few miles. She's on her way to Schwarzenegger Land. Gonna visit her mama in Malibu."

"You be careful, sweetie. This boy'll charm the panties off you." She poured two coffees, and dropped down mini-containers of cream. "You want a menu, m' dear, or have you got something in mind?"

"I'll have the Number Four," said Miriam, pointing at the breakfast choices on the menu board.

"Make mine the Grand Slam," said Troy, "and don't forget th'—"

"I know, I know, grits 'n' gravy on the side," said the waitress. She turned and winked at Miriam. "This one can't live without 'em. I swear grits are the first solid food country boys eat after they're weaned."

Miriam smiled at the waitress' remark, and then scanned the diner. She thought of her father. This was Ray Kovacs' kind of life. A life spent pounding down the interstate highways of America. A life spent constantly on the move, where time was money, and pit stops had to be brief: a fill up at the diesel pumps, a quick rest room break, junk food grabbed on-the-fly, then back on the road to get to a freight terminal in time to unload. Eating a proper meal at a place like this was a luxury he had told her once—a chance to sit on a seat that did not move. She wondered if he had ever eaten here, maybe at this very booth. Trucking was a hard life and aged men before their time. She remembered her father's sunken eyes, weary from staring at endless miles of pavement.

"That was quick," said Miriam as their meals arrived.

Her eyes widened at the mountain of food on her plate.

"Didn't I tell y'all 'bout the food here? Good eats, 'n' plenty of 'em."

"I'll never finish all this."

"You gotta," he said, looking toward her midriff that as yet showed no visible signs of pregnancy. "Remember, you's eatin' fer two now. Here, try some o' these." He slipped some grits onto his fork, then leaned across the table. "If your little one takes a shine to these someday, why, you'll know who to blame."

Miriam gagged at the texture, smiled wanly, then started on her breakfast.

"Busy place," she said with her mouth full.

"They crank out meals right quick," replied Troy, nodding toward the open kitchen. "Wouldn't stay in business long if they didn't."

Along the upper edge of the serve-through window, a taut piece of wire and clothes pegs held meal orders. Two men worked the commercial stoves with lightning speed and efficiency: flipping pancakes, frying endless rows of sausage and bacon, cooking eggs according to preference, and buttering toast slices that issued from the conveyor wheel of an industrial toaster. Half a dozen Silex percolators ensured a constant supply of coffee.

When they were finished breakfast, Troy paid the bill and had the waitress package Miriam's uneaten toast and bacon in a doggie bag.

"Thanks for this," said Miriam.

"Glad to have the company."

"I don't know how you do it," said Miriam to the waitress. "I've worked a lot o' restaurants in Philly, but none as busy as this. You do a great job!"

"Well, thank you. Good luck in California, honey. If you're ever by this way again, drop in and see us."

"Here," said Troy, tossing Miriam the keys to the Peterbilt. "Would y'all open the rig and wait fer me? I gotta get somethin'."

He disappeared down the corridor that linked the restaurant to the general store that catered to truckers.

After settling herself on the air-ride seat, a photograph attached to the headliner caught her eye. It had been taken outside a church. In the center, Troy held a baby in a white christening outfit. To his left was a fine-featured blond girl in her late teens, and dressed in a minister's gown, was the preacher. Standing behind them were four older people, probably their parents. Now she understood his reluctance at taking her along for the ride. He was uncomfortable with a strange woman in his truck and did not want temptation sitting next to him, not with a wife and baby waiting in Oklahoma.

Ten minutes later she saw him striding across the parking lot. When he reached the truck, he stuffed a plastic bag behind his seat, then climbed aboard.

"So," he said, turning the ignition key and bringing the diesel engine to life. "Do y'all feel better now?"

"A lot better. And thanks for payin'. I don't have a lot o' money to get me where I'm goin'."

"My pleasure," he replied, then shot his thumb in the direction of the sleeper section of the cab. "If y'all wanna lie down, you're welcome to snooze for a spell. We got some hours on the road and stops to make b'fore I drop you off. Too bad I wasn't goin' up the PCH to Oxnard on this run. Coulda taken you all the way to Malibu."

Suddenly, she thought about Howard and felt guilty for spurning his generosity.

"I was lookin' at that photograph while you were gone."

"That's my kin," he replied proudly, tugging against the Velcro. He handed it to her and pointed, "Donna, my wife, standing with her folks, my mama 'n' daddy, and our pastor, Jim."

"Is your baby a boy or girl?"

"Girl. Charlene's her name. Our lucky child."

"Why's she lucky?"

"She was a long time premature. Just a li'l bitty thing, not much bigger 'n a squirrel. We didn't expect her to live. Never prayed so much in my entire life. Promised the Lord if He didn't take her back to heaven, why, I'd be the best daddy I knew how to be. He answered my prayer. Every day she growed a bit more. Next thing we knew, we had ourselves a healthy child."

"How old is she?"

"One-year-old next week. I'm fixin' to be home for her first birthday party. After that, I gotta long run to the coast. Be gone for some time."

"Humph," said Miriam, irritation showing in her voice. "Sounds like the kind o' life I had as a girl."

"Whatta you mean?"

"Dad spent forever on the road, or so it seemed. We never had a proper father/daughter thing. I used to forget what he looked like between road trips."

"Well," he said, lifting the brim of his cowboy hat, "I do try to make a phone call at the end o' every day. I get Donna to put baby Charlene's ear to the phone, so she can hear her daddy's voice."

"And you think that's enough, do you? Bein' a long distance dad?"

He looked uncomfortable.

"Because if you do, then you'd be wrong. Like I said, mine was hardly ever home."

"Well," he said, adjusting his hat again, "I reckon it's the best I can do under the circumstances. I mean to tell you, it ain't easy bein' on the road like this."

"I'm sure it isn't, but there's no substitute for bein' home with your family."

"I know, I know," he said, holding up his hand to fend off her criticism. "It's best for everyone. Besides, they's too many temptations away from home. I mean—"

"That's why you didn't want to pick me up, isn't it?"

"Yep."

He turned his attention to the sound system and changed to a new collection of Garth Brooks CDs. The soft notes of an acoustic guitar introduced the first song: *If Tomorrow Never Comes*. As the song played, the young trucker looked up at the photo of his wife and baby; the words of the tune moved him.

"Tell me 'bout yourself," he said, when the song had ended.

"Not much to tell. I've never traveled or done anythin' with my life."

"I know y'all like country music. What other kinda things do you like?"

"History," she said. "I like history."

"You mean of the United States?"

"Any history. This country, the world, whatever."

"Well, then," he said, laughing, "give me a hist'ry lesson."

She thought for a minute, and then said, "You're drivin' on a piece o' history?"

"Really?"

"The interstate highway system."

"How's that hist'ry?"

"President Dwight Eisenhower made this happen by signin' a piece o' paper."

"You don't say?"

"Back in '56. Long before I was born."

"Now ain't that the funniest danged thing," he said, slapping the steering wheel. "I seen some signs with his name on 'em, but never paid 'em much mind."

Miriam's morning with Troy passed too quickly; she enjoyed his company and good humor. They talked non-stop as he made long detours to deliver farm supplies to truck terminals.

They did not stop for lunch until almost mid-afternoon. It was a hasty affair as Troy grabbed takeout orders, and then raced the clock toward his last call of the day. But first, he had to drop Miriam off.

When he reached his exit, he stopped on the shoulder of the ramp. Miriam surveyed her surroundings. The view was not comforting: fields of crops, great living carpets, fanned out in every direction and the secondary road was devoid of traffic. The loneliness frightened her. How, she wondered, would she get her next ride in such an isolated spot?

"All the best to y'all," he said, reaching over to shake her hand. "I'm afraid this is where we have to say good-bye."

Miriam pulled out her backpack from the sleeper section, and opened the truck's huge door.

"Wait a minute," he said, reaching behind his seat and pulling out the plastic bag. "I bought this for yer new baby."

Miriam untied the knotted plastic. Inside, a brown teddy bear peered up with button eyes. She stared at it in her hand, overwhelmed by his generosity.

"Most of 'em had blue or pink ribbons. I didn't know if you was gonna have a boy or a girl, so I had the store lady tie a green one 'round its neck."

"Thank you so much," said Miriam, leaning across the cab's center console to hug the young trucker. "It's so sweet o' you."

He smiled. "Y'all have a safe trip, now. And don't forget, you cain't thumb a ride down there," he said, pointing to the highway. "The police don't take kindly to it. But they won't bother you none, long as you stay on th' ramp." He looked at Miriam for a moment before he spoke. "And by the way, I'll think on what you said."

"What's that?"

"About tryin' my hand at somethin' else. Somethin' that'd bring me home each night to Donna and the baby."

"That'd be nice. Don't be a stranger to that little girl o' yours. When she's grown up, she'll thank you for it—you'll see."

She slung her backpack over her shoulder, grabbed the teddy bear, and climbed down onto the gravel. As she went to close the passenger door, he smiled and tipped his hat.

"God bless y'all . . . sister o' Moses!"

She stepped back from the truck as it continued up the shoulder of the ramp, and then turned onto the secondary road. Tears stood in her eyes as she watched the rig fade into the distance.

She drew her windbreaker tightly around her. The air was damp with the threat of rain as a bank of black clouds approached from the west; underneath, long streaks of rain slanted toward distant cornfields. Farmers would be grateful for it. Miriam was not.

An hour later, only one car had appeared; the driver had averted his eyes as he drove by.

When the rains finally came, she carefully picked her way down the weed-infested, litter-strewn slope and took shelter where the inclined cement apron met the underside of the bridge. She noticed a sour smell and soon located the source, an empty Jack Daniels whiskey bottle lying on its side in a puddle of congealed vomit. As she stared in revulsion, a noise startled her. It was coming from a large potato chip bag. The bag was moving. She threw a small stone at it. A rat scuttled out and quickly disappeared into a gap in the concrete. For hours she sat on the damp apron with her knees drawn under her chin, battling waves of depression. Below her, vehicles hurtled past, dragging rooster tails of water behind them until the pavement under the bridge was as wet as the open highway. How long, she wondered, would it take her to get to her mother's? Worse still, what kind of reception would she get when she broke the dreaded news?

She dug into a plastic bag and scraped together enough weed to roll herself one last joint, something she hoped would ease the pain of her predicament. She filled her lungs, then lay back and stared at the underside of the concrete, covered in graffiti. There were the usual scrawled depictions of male and female genitalia and random names and phone numbers for sexual services, the same kind of ugliness found in places frequented by society's down-and-outers: the winos and the homeless, the chronically unemployed and the marginalized. Amid the filth and unsightliness, the desperateness of her situation weighed in on her. Even the marijuana could not dull the aching inside. She smoked the joint down to the roach clip, then put her head in her hands and wept. The sound of her sobbing echoed under the concrete, interrupted only by the drone of passing vehicles. She thought about the motorists, dry and comfortable inside their vehicles—the lucky ones heading to a warm home and a hot meal, to an affectionate setting where wives and children or lovers, anxiously awaited them. And the more she thought about them and the anchored, normality of their lives, the more lonely she felt and the more she cried.

When night finally came, she resigned herself to her grubby accommodations. She struggled to be optimistic, thinking that perhaps the rain would lift by dawn and that her prospects might improve. Surely someone would stop to pick her up. Surely.

She set her backpack below her feet, and tucked the plastic bag with the teddy bear under her head for a pillow. The traffic became white noise and eased her over the threshold into a restless sleep. Each time she awoke during the night, her throat was sore from diesel fumes. But what scared her most—what made her flesh crawl—was the squeaking and the scuttling of the rats.

# CHAPTER 7

## *Police Encounter*

WHEN HOWARD AWOKE, RANDOM patches of blue broke a cloud-tumbled sky that held more rain. But the threat of foul weather did not dampen his spirit; he was looking forward to having female company for the drive. He padded on bare feet to the center of the coach and scanned the frequencies until he found the syndicated Bob and Tom Show, then turned up the volume so he could hear it in the shower.

Once dressed, he searched the galley cupboards for a saucepan and mixing bowl. He would make Miriam a great breakfast today, Eggs Benny, the one he had made so many times for his late wife. With the butter melting in the saucepan, he whisked the eggs yolks steadily as he added the lemon juice, salt and cayenne pepper.

As he prepared the Hollandaise Sauce, he turned to look at their bed at the rear of the coach and remembered how Suzanne used to lie on her side and watch him as she sipped her pre-breakfast coffee. Conversation and laughter had always come easily to them and they would chatter away and tease each other. Even though a year had passed, she was still an indelible presence in his life. At least once a day he imagined he heard her voice, or the cadence of her footsteps.

He remembered looking up at a cloudless sky with her not long before she died. "It's easy to forget the stars are still out there in the daytime," she had said. "If I die before you do, Howard, that's where I'll be, out beyond the blue waiting for you."

He set the table, and then cut wildflowers on the edge of the parking lot. After filling a small vase with water he crushed the stems, immersed them, and placed the arrangement in the center of the dinette. With the meal completed, he covered the food with the lid of a warming dish and left the motor home.

At the front of the motel, he found a "Do Not Disturb" sign hanging from the door knob of room sixteen. He knocked anyway. As he waited for Miriam to answer, he watched distant vehicles entering the ramp for I-70. He knocked louder, thinking she might be in the shower.

Nothing.

Nearby a black housekeeper was offloading fresh towels and soaps from a cart to resupply vacated rooms. She was watching Howard.

"Problem, mistah?"

"I dropped off a hitchhiker yesterday. A young woman. Miriam's her name, and I'm trying to wake her up so we can get going. My motor home's parked out back and—"

"You don't say," said the woman, eyeing him suspiciously.

"You've got a master key to these rooms. Think you could open this one and see if she's in there?"

The woman shook her head.

"Why not?"

"How I know you not some jealous hubbie checkin' on his missus?"

"But . . . she's young enough to be my daughter. Why would I—?"

"Mistah, if I had a dollah for ever' time someone—"

"Is the owner in?" asked Howard, seeing he was getting nowhere.

Uh-uh. He gone to town. Pick him up a few things."

"Know when he'll be back?"

"Not long, I s'pose."

"Thanks. I'll have to wait then."

"Yes you will," confirmed the housekeeper, smugly enjoying her control of the situation.

As Howard walked toward the motor home, he glanced at the back of the motel. Room sixteen was the fifth from the end of the building. The pebbled privacy window to the washroom was open.

"Miriam," he shouted, "I've got breakfast on. Rise and shine."

"Mistah."

Howard looked toward the breezeway. The housekeeper stared at him angrily, a toilet brush in her rubber-gloved hand. "If you thinkin' o' breakin' into that room, I wouldn't if I was you—no, sir."

"Look, I'm not trying to do anything illegal. It's just that—"

"Maybe I bettah call the *po*lice. Have them guys sort you out."

Howard held up his hands. "That won't be necessary. I'll wait in my motor home. When the owner comes back, would you ask him to come see me?"

She paused before she answered. "Yes, sir. Long as they's no more funny business, y' hear?"

Howard started on his meal. This was odd, he thought. Yesterday, he had told Miriam that he would have breakfast ready for her. Was she a heavy sleeper? Had she forgotten his offer and instead, walked to the diner down the highway? There was a knock at the door. He opened it expectantly, thinking it might be Miriam.

"Housekeeper said you wanted to see me," said the motel owner.

"She tell you why?"

"Nope."

"Remember that hitchhiker I brought with me last night?"

"Yep."

"I couldn't raise her this morning. Your housekeeper wouldn't check the room when I asked her."

"That's right. We don't allow them to do that. Security reasons, you understand?"

"I hadn't thought of that. Would you check for me?"

"Come with me."

The man unclipped a cluster of keys from his belt, and inserted one into the door set, "Maintenance," he shouted into the room after knocking loudly.

Cautiously, he opened the door.

The room was empty.

He shouted again before checking the ensuite bathroom.

Empty again.

"Looks like she's gone," he said.

"I seem to remember seeing a diner down the road when we pulled in here last night."

"Paula's Roadhouse and Grill. They open early."

"Maybe she ate there, instead," said Howard.

"It's worth a try," said the man as he locked up room sixteen.

Howard made enquiries at the roadhouse; Miriam had not eaten there. Something had made her run off without telling him. What? Had she been that offended by his comments? Or was she uncomfortable with him for some other reason? The uncertainty nagged at him—angered him.

Although she was a grown woman and free to make her own choices, he could not bring himself to leave town until he had tried to find her; his sense of duty would not allow it. Besides, he thought, surely her mother would want him to look out for her welfare. It was the least he could do.

He drove the length of Main Street several times, hoping she might be in a store and see him passing. When she did not appear, he parked in the shade of a tree and waited. It was not long before his presence, the presence of a stranger in a small town, attracted attention; an elderly woman peered at him from behind lace curtains. Self-conscious, Howard moved on.

He dropped by the town's only police station attached to the municipal building. The on-duty officer made steady eye contact with Howard as he described Miriam.

"Sorry, sir," he said after running her name through his computer. "Can't find anything on her, and I haven't seen her round here."

"Any idea who might've?"

"Most transients passing through eat at Paula's. I'd check there."

"I already have."

"Well then, you might try the post office."

"The post office?" said Howard, frowning.

"Yes, sir. The Greyhound bus service picks up passengers there. The bus shelter's right outside the front windows. Someone might've seen her waiting for a ride."

"Any other suggestions?"

"The local church."

"She didn't strike me as the religious type."

"Sir, you did describe her as a down-and-out type. Maybe she was depressed and had need of a preacher's ear."

"I hadn't thought of that."

As Howard went to leave the station, he was asked to produce ID. The officer took down the particulars in his police notebook, but fixed him with a forensic gaze, as if trying to memorize his face. Then he allowed him to leave.

"Good luck," said the officer, breaking away to answer the phone.

He made more inquiries in town. No one at the post office had seen her and neither had the minister, a friendly sort who said he'd pray that Howard would find her.

Having drawn a blank, he returned to the RV to think. He could not dismiss from his mind the possibility that Miriam might still be in town somewhere. If that was the case and she came looking for him, she might feel that he had abandoned her. He decided to stay in the area for the remainder of the day; the motel was the most logical place. When he explained the situation to the owner, he charged him half rate to camp in the parking lot.

BY THE next morning he had accepted reality; she was gone. Depressed, he picked at his breakfast, then scraped it into the garbage.

He returned to the interstate and continued his journey west. It was raining again.

At mid-day, he saw the flashing strobe lights of a police cruiser parked under a concrete overpass. A trooper was standing on the passenger side of his vehicle, talking to someone. Rain obscured Howard's view, until he drove under the shadow of the bridge and recognized Miriam, looking even more disheveled than when he had first picked her up. He swung onto the shoulder, donned his rain poncho, and then walked back.

"Sir?" said the trooper, curious at Howard's sudden appearance.

"Is there a problem, officer?" he asked, glancing at Miriam who avoided eye contact.

"This doesn't concern you."

"I think it does. Are you arresting her?"

"Yes."

"What for?"

"Sir, would you please return to your vehicle."

Wary of Howard's motives, the officer appraised him closely and took a step backward, the palm of his right hand resting on his pistol.

"You haven't answered my question."

"Are you a lawyer, sir?"

"No."

"Then, this is none of your business."

"But, officer, I know this woman."

"I'm arresting her for vagrancy and soliciting a ride on the interstate."

"What do you mean, vagrancy?"

"She's got no I.D."

"Her name is Miriam Kovacs. She's from Philly and is heading for Malibu, California."

"How would you know that, sir?" said the officer checking the information in his notebook.

"She told me when I picked her up."

"Where at?"

"Just south of Toledo."

"So, she *was* hitchhiking on the interstate, then?"

Miriam looked to Howard and wondered how he would answer. She knew she had been beside the highway when he picked her up. Knew she had been breaking the law.

"No she wasn't, as a matter of fact. She was on the ramp at the junction of I-75 and I-70."

"Ramps are still considered part of the interstate, sir."

Howard turned to Miriam, "Were you thumbing a ride here beside the highway?"

"Uh-uh," she said, pointing to the top of the sloping concrete apron where it ended under the bridge. "That's where I spent the night. The reason I don't have any ID is because someone robbed me while I was sleepin'. They took everythin'. Even my damned cigarettes."

The officer was skeptical.

"She had a pack, when I picked her up, so she's not lying to you."

The patrolman let out an exasperated sigh.

Howard turned to Miriam, "You're lucky robbery is all that happened. You could've been raped."

"I know, I know. Spare me another lecture. If I had been raped, least I couldn't have gotten pregnant."

The officer frowned.

"That's because she's already pregnant," Howard explained.

The officer made another entry in his notebook, then pointed at the plastic bag she was holding. "What's in that?"

"A teddy bear," she answered, opening the bag for him.

The trooper grinned derisively, "You're a grown woman and you still sleep with a teddy bear?"

"Not usually," she replied, her face crimson with embarrassment.

"Lemme see that," said the officer, taking the bag. He pulled a flashlight from a leather holster and shone it along the plush seams, examining them closely. After squeezing its torso and extremities, he held it to his nose and sniffed.

"What're you doin' that for?"

"Checking it for drugs, ma'am."

"Oh, for God's sake. I may look like a vagrant to you, but I'm *not* a drug dealer, if that's what you're thinkin'. The trucker that dropped me off here yesterday bought it for me. Bought it for the baby, that is, after I told him I was pregnant."

"Was that the guy who parked beside me at the motel?" asked Howard.

"Yes."

"The one who left at six and woke me?"

"The same."

"Why'd you go with him? Wasn't my offer good enough? I was prepared to take you all the way to your mother's front door. Did you think I was some kind of danger to you? A dirty old man out to seduce you?"

"No, no. It wasn't like that at all. I made a bad decision on impulse. Story o' my friggin' life."

Howard explained to the officer how he had paid for her motel room to spare her the discomfort of sleeping in the motor home with a stranger, an arrangement he was prepared to repeat until he dropped her off in California. The trooper asked for Howard's driver's license and wrote down the particulars. Then he turned to Miriam.

"OK, ma'am," he said, tucking the notebook into his breast pocket and buttoning the flap, "here's the deal. I'm satisfied Mr. Munro has your best interests at heart. But, that's only my opinion. If you don't agree, I'll take you back to the station. You can get your mother to wire you some money so you can take a Greyhound. On the other hand, if you are comfortable with him, then be on your way. Just don't hitchhike on the interstate again. I'm passing the word to other agencies. If you're caught again, you'll be charged. Understand?"

Miriam nodded.

"So, what's it gonna be?" said the patrolman, hands on hips.

"I'll go with Mr. Munro."

The officer gave her a penetrating look, as if to detect deception.

"I'm sure and certain about it," she said, swallowing nervously.

"Fine. Have a safe trip, folks." he said, then returned to his patrol car.

Howard draped his poncho over Miriam and walked her back to the RV. The police car suddenly sped ahead of them with strobe lights flashing, crossed the center median, then raced eastbound to some distant emergency.

Howard slid behind the steering wheel. For a long moment, he fixed a penetrating gaze on Miriam, sitting beside him in the captain's chair.

"Why're you starin' at me like that?"

"I need to know something before I get back on this highway."

Miriam did not answer.

"Did you tell that cop the truth?"

"The truth about what?"

"About you coming with me?"

"No."

"So, you lied to him, then" said Howard.

"I had to, didn't I?"

"No. You could've been straight up with him."

"Look, I wanted to save my ass, OK. Keep from gettin' arrested. What I want is to take the cop's suggestion."

"Getting your mother to wire you money?"

"Uh-huh."

"Mind telling me why don't you want to ride with me?"

"I'm not comfortable with you, that's why."

"What have I done?"

"You look down your nose. Think I'm white trash 'cause I got shabby clothes and little money, and—"

"Because you're pregnant?"

"Especially that."

"Lemme tell you what I think," said Howard, his voice sharp with annoyance. "You're trying to make it look like I'm the one looking down on you, when the truth is, it's you who's not happy with yourself *or* your life. You're projecting your own feelings onto me, trying to—"

"I thought you said you were an English professor. You sound more like a shrink. Full o' psycho-babble."

"If that's what you want," said Howard, unwilling to argue any longer, "I'll find a bus depot and drop you off."

Howard eased back onto the highway, carefully avoiding a beer bottle on the shoulder. They did not speak or look at each other for some time. He concentrated on his driving, listening to the metronomic slap of the windshield wipers. She averted her eyes and watched rural properties flash past the rain-soaked windows. The farther they traveled, the more uncomfortable the silence between them. Occasionally, each stole a sideways glance at the other.

An hour later, Howard pulled off the highway and into the parking lot of an outdoor mall, anchored by a Wal-Mart Superstore.

"Why're we stoppin' here?"

"Because we have a few things to do before I drop you at a bus depot."

"Such as?" she replied, her voice defensive.

"First," he said, shutting off the ignition and sliding out from behind the wheel, "you need to eat. All I've heard for the last hour is your stomach rumbling."

"And then?"

"Then we go shopping."

"What for?"

"Clothes, a new backpack, and—"

"Why are you doin' this?"

"Because, when I do drop you off, at least my conscience will be clear. You'll have what you need to get to California."

She drummed her fingertips on the leg of her dirty jeans. "I don't deserve this, you know. Not after the way I've been."

"Never mind. Take a hot shower. My bathrobe's hanging behind the door. While you're freshening up, I'll put a meal together."

"Look," she said, pointing to the fast food restaurant at the end of the mall. "Wouldn't that be easier?"

Howard shook his head. "You don't need a belly full of grease."

He heard her step into the shower stall, then the steady chug of the water pump. He took a margarine container from the freezer, ran some water over it, then pressed out a frozen block into a saucepan. "I'm going to heat up some soup for you."

"Say what?" she hollered over the noise of the shower.

"Chicken soup. It's homemade. Want a sandwich with it?"

"Please," she shouted back.

The meal was ready when she came out. Howard noticed her eyes; she had been crying.

"Are you OK?"

She nodded, but suddenly brought both hands to her face and broke down, "I've been a damned fool. I feel so stupid."

"Eat," he said, pointing to her soup on the dinette table, "or it'll go cold."

Howard sat opposite her and took a few spoonfuls of hot soup; dribbles of it landed on the dinette table.

"I was thinking," he said, wiping the spill, "you might feel better with your hair done. There's a salon over there."

"I can't believe you're doin' all this for me," she said, dipping her sandwich in the hot soup.

"Would you or wouldn't you?"

"Well . . . sure . . . but . . ."

He crossed the parking lot and made an appointment for her, then returned to do the dishes while she went to the salon.

Afterwards, they walked to Wal-Mart's women's clothing department. They spent the afternoon choosing outfits, a new backpack, a nylon windbreaker, and grooming items. The check-out clerk totaled the purchases; Miriam winced at the tally as Howard swiped his credit card through the machine. On their way out, he approached the customer service desk.

"Excuse me, ma'am. Can you tell me if there's a bus depot in this town?"

"Yes, sir," said the service rep, a dark-haired Hispanic woman.

"Where is it?"

"Main part of town, across from the auto parts store."

"Would you mind jotting down the directions?" he said, then waited as she sketched out a crude map.

They returned to the RV; Howard helped her remove product labels and stickers. She unpackaged her grooming items and placed them in the outside pockets of the backpack.

"You'll never get all that stuff in there. I've got a drawstring bag you can have."

"No thanks."

"But, how are you going to carry—?"

"Does your offer still hold?" she said, giving him a sheepish look.

"What offer?"

"Takin' me to my mother's?"

"Sure," said Howard, relieved she had changed her mind. "I'll find a motel to get you into."

"Uh-uh," she replied, shaking her head. "I'll be fine in your RV. Sleepin' separate, o' course."

HOWARD BOOKED into a nearby RV park. The campground owner, a thin woman in her early forties, assigned him a site, processed his credit card, and then gave him a map of the park and a complimentary green garbage bag.

The park was occupied by only two units: a pickup truck/Airstream combination and beside it, a van conversion. Howard consulted the site numbers on the map and noted the woman had put them beside the Airstream.

"Dammit," said Howard, his voice impatient. "Empty sites galore and she puts us here."

"Why don't you pick another?"

"I'm going to," he said, pointing to one surrounded by trees.

"You gonna tell her you switched?"

"No. Odds are, if anyone else comes in here tonight, she'll set them close to those two."

Howard drove to the new site, hooked up the water, sewer, and electrical services, then disconnected the Jeep from the tow bar.

"It's a little late to make supper," said Howard, consulting his watch. "How about we find a decent restaurant and eat out?"

"That'd be great."

Howard headed for the men's showers, and left her the RV's washroom to freshen up in. She put on one of her new outfits, a pastel pink blouse and a pair of pleated grey slacks. She carefully applied her makeup and fussed with her hair; she liked what she saw in the mirror.

After getting a corner table, they silently perused the menu. When they did talk, the conversation was stilted as they worked to mend fences. Howard mused that this was the first time since Suzanne's death that he had taken a woman out for supper. With her new hairdo, clothes, and makeup, he had to admit, she was attractive.

He found himself staring at her as they ate, enjoying the look of her, yet he felt no sexual attraction; his libido had shut down, a condition unchanged since the death of his wife. Regardless, he was self-conscious of the age gap; it was drawing the attention of two people at a nearby table. Both talked in whispers and stole curious glances, as if they were witnessing a May/September affair.

Dinner had broken a little of the ice between them. On the way back to the RV, they talked more freely.

"See what I mean," said Howard, laughing as he negotiated the campground road. Four other campers had checked in since they had left for the restaurant. All were clustered around the original two units. "You'd think we were living in the 1800s for God's sake. Closing the wagon train to fend off the Apaches."

"Look at all the stars," said Miriam, pointing to a patch of sky as they got out of the Jeep. "I've never seen so many."

"I've got some folding chairs. Want to sit outside for a bit?"

"No thanks," she said, smacking a mosquito.

"Do you want to watch TV?" he asked, turning on a few lights in the motor home.

"OK."

He switched on the overhead set, then handed her the remote. "Watch whatever you like. Want a pop?"

"Sure . . . I mean, please."

Howard put some ice in a glass, and poured the ginger ale. When he turned around, she was inside his personal space.

"I feel guilty and ashamed," she said with a repentant look, trying to decide whether or not to hug him. "You've been so good to me and I've been a total shit. I'm sorry—*real* sorry."

There was a moment of awkwardness as they stood face-to-face, mere feet apart. Sensing his discomfort, she retreated, embarrassed by her impulsive gesture.

While she channel surfed from one of the captain's chairs, Howard stretched out on the sofa and immersed himself in the pages of a novel. When *Anderson Cooper 360* came on CNN, he put down his book and watched the news with her. Then she turned off the TV to prepare for bed.

The RV's layout was ideal for two people in need of separate space. The washroom with its toilet, small vanity, and full-sized shower stall, spanned the full width of the coach and divided the forward living area from the rear bedroom. There was a sliding door on each side of the washroom; it allowed either of them to enter it from their own sleeping quarters without disturbing or compromising the privacy of the other. Normally, Howard slept in his underwear, but with a strange woman on board, he used his track suit as pajamas and gave his bathrobe to Miriam.

He got ready first, then retired to his bedroom. He flipped on his reading light, and picked up his novel. Only feet away, Miriam brushed her teeth, peed, and then closed the sliding door on her side of the washroom. He heard the springs squeak as she got into the lounge bed he had made up for her.

"If you need to get up during the night, the light switch is beside you on the wall."

"Thanks," she replied, her voice muffled by the bathroom between them.

"And I put a glass of water on the ledge by your pillow. Save you getting out of bed if you're thirsty."

"Thanks again."

"Good night."

"Night."

Howard opened the slats of the venetian blinds; he could see the Milky Way meandering across an ebony sky, interrupted only by the canopy of trees on their campsite. Somewhere, a pair of owls hooted to each other.

Inside, two strangers thrown together by circumstance, lay awake in separate beds, each acutely aware of the other.

# CHAPTER 8

## *Visitation*

I N HOWARD'S BEDROOM, THE venetian blinds rattled softly. The cool air was fragrant and oddly familiar: a spicy mix of creosote bush, sage, and pinion bark with a trace of ozone that presaged an impending storm. He had a floating sensation and the feeling of a warm presence close to him. In the darkness, something touched his skin, then he felt soft breath on his neck.

"It's time," she said.

"Time for what?" he replied.

"Time to watch the storm come. It'll be here soon."

"You sure?"

"Yes, I'm sure."

"OK, then," he said. "Want me to bring rain ponchos?"

"Yes," she said, stepping outside and calling for him to follow.

He got out of bed and grabbed their vinyl raingear on his way to the door. It was overcast; there were no stars visible. In the blackness, he could not see and called to her.

"Over here," she shouted. "I found some shelter for us."

He followed the sound of her voice, and then stopped beside a rock monolith. It towered high overhead, silhouetted against the sky. At its base, was a hollowed out portion, an open-fronted cave that provided protection from the weather.

"Sit beside me, and lean your back against the rock." She took his hand and placed it against the volcanic stone. "Feel that. It's still warm from today's sun."

He draped the poncho over her shoulders.

"Look," she said, pointing toward the west.

Distances were deceiving across the broad plateau that separated them from the advancing storm. A low range of mountains reclined on the horizon, indistinguishable until backlit by sheet lightning. The storm was still many miles away, so distant that no thunder followed the slashes of light. Like the warp and weft in a loom, the lightning joined cloud to land and cloud to cloud. They could hear the faint rumble of thunder as the storm slowly advanced. The temperature plummeted as curtains of rain descended toward parched land.

Soon the storm was close and the atmospherics fierce; blinding flashes of light were followed instantaneously by a deafening cannonade. Rain pummeled the ground like lead shot and raised puffs of dust in the soil. At the height of the storm's fury, rapid flashes of lightning illuminated the vegetation: ocotillo, agave, and mesquite. They huddled against the back of the cave to avoid the torrents of water that cascaded from the rock above. A nearby arroyo filled with water and the rapid flow tumbled small stones. Then, slowly, imperceptibly, the storm moved on, and the sound of thunder trailed off to a faint murmur, like the growl of an empty stomach.

"Look at that," she said, pointing to a nearby outcropping silhouetted against the faint traces of light in the sky.

"What about it?"

"Don't you think it looks like an animal's head?"

"Yes, like a gorilla."

"Well then," she said, "let's call it Gorilla Rock." "It'll be *our* rock in case we ever come back here."

"Do you think we will?" he asked.

"Someday," she said, smiling at him. "Until then, let's make a pact." She made a hook with her little finger and held it toward him. He linked his finger with hers. "There now," she said, "that settles it. We'll come back to this very spot."

They sat together for some time and watched the storm make its retreat toward the east. Beyond it, a thin glow along the brow of the horizon heralded the beginning of a new day. They turned at a nearby noise and saw a coyote weaving between the sagebrush, heading for the open desert.

"You never were afraid of storms, were you?"

"Not as long as I had you beside me," she said, leaning into him.

He noticed the edges of her face were becoming blurred, and there was a hollow echo to her voice, as if she was speaking in an empty room.

"I'm sorry," she said, touching his arm.

"Sorry for what?"

"For going away so quickly . . . for making you sad."

He studied her features, luminescent and ethereal in the first light of dawn, shimmering like the pastel curtains of an aurora. She was beautiful: a cameo of exquisite loveliness, just as he had remembered. There was so much he wanted to tell her, but the words would not come.

She noticed him looking at her and held his gaze, "I have to go now," she said.

"But, I don't want you to," he said, reaching for her. "Stay a little longer with me."

"I can't," she said, pulling away from him.

"Why not?"

"Because I have to get back."

"Back where?"

"You *know* where. Beyond the blue."

"Will you come again?"

"Yes, but not like this," she said, touching her chest.

"How then?"

"Like that," she replied and pointed.

He turned to see a tiny canyon wren perched on the branch of a desert willow. The bird canted its head, and then burst into song—a descending scale of sweet, whistling notes.

"When will I see you again?"

"I can't tell you," she said, her voice trailing off. "I just want you to know that it's OK now."

"What's OK?"

"It's OK for you to—"

The white light suddenly intensified behind her, backlighting wisps of her hair into golden threads. Her lips were still moving, but no words reached his ears as she receded, as if being drawn back into a long tunnel. Finally, a mist enveloped her, and her once familiar features dissolved before his eyes. He reached out, trying desperately to hold onto her, but she had drifted into the ether—gone to a place he could not visit.

A wave of sadness washed over him, then confusion and a sensation of floating again. He heard the ticking of the quartz clock and opened his eyes. The details of his bedroom slowly registered and anchored him in the present. Through the window, he could see that it was not dawn. It was still dark. Above him, the stars of the Milky Way were shining. He was not in the desert. There had been no storm.

# CHAPTER 9

## *Remembrance*

HOWARD'S DREAM HAD SHAKEN his world and for hours afterward he was jolted awake by aftershocks. Each time, he instinctively reached for Suzanne's side of the bed. He remembered how for months after she died, the only way he could sleep was to arrange pillows beside him—something comforting he could touch in the night.

At dawn, he awoke for the final time and stared absently at the details of the room: the oak cabinets with their frosted-glass panels, the flowered border that defined the top of the walls, the roof vent above the bed with its fan whirring quietly. And on the wall beside the bed, he read the framed calligraphy he had given Suzanne on an anniversary long past:

> The value of life lies not
> in the length of days,
> but in the use
> we make of them.

As he pondered the irony of Montaigne's passage, he became peripherally aware of the sound of rushing water. Odd, he thought, he had not seen any river or stream nearby when he had registered. He turned on his reading lamp and reached for the campground map. There it was, running along the edge of the park, an un-named watercourse.

Eventually, the sound of water triggered a need to use the bathroom. Before returning to bed, he decided to check on Miriam.

"You up yet?" he asked, tapping lightly on the hollow door.

No answer.

"Miriam?" he said, rapping harder.

Nothing.

He slid the door open.

She was gone.

Still jangled from his dream, he was gripped by a terrifying sense of déjà-vu. It had been just like this the morning he discovered Suzanne was gone: the bed sheets turned back, the hollow on the pillow, the red light of the coffeemaker reflecting off the countertop, the rich smell of coffee lingering in the air.

Quickly he pulled on a track top, stabbed both feet into his running shoes, and dashed from the motor home.

He stopped first to survey the layout of the park and looked in the direction of the running water. A series of back-in sites ran along the edge of the park. Separating them from the adjacent woods was a double-railed fence. There was a gap in the fence and beyond it, the beginnings of a dirt trail. He bolted across the sites, dodging picnic tables.

As he entered the trail, the glint of moving water appeared between the trees. The sight that met his eyes chilled him: two shoes, neatly arranged one beside the other, and a few feet away, an empty ceramic coffee mug tipped on its side in the short grass by the riverbank; a small patch was flattened, as if someone had been sitting there. Beside it, lay an opened cigarette package. His heart pounded. His mouth went dry as cotton.

"Miriam," he shouted. "Where are you?"

The only sounds were the wind in the trees, and water tumbling over river stones.

"Miriam?"

Frantic, he paced the riverbank, pushing aside the overgrowth that clung to the shoreline, and repeatedly calling her name.

No answer.

The smell of cigarette smoke turned his head. She was barefoot and walking toward him on the trail. She saw his ashen face and shaking hands.

"What's wrong?" she asked, her brow creased into a deep frown. "You look like you've seen a ghost."

"Where'd you go?"

"Up to the office. There's a cigarette machine outside. I ran out o' smokes."

"I saw your shoes," he said, his voice shaky. "I thought . . . thought you'd drowned in the river."

"Nah. I'd never do that. I'm a good swimmer."

"So was my wife."

"Is that how she died?"

He glanced at her shoes in the grass, "Yes. It was just like this. Horrifying. I came looking for her, but she'd just disappeared into thin air as if . . ."

Miriam flicked her cigarette end into the river and came quickly to his side. "I'm sorry. I didn't know how she died"

"Course you didn't. I never told you."

"Wanna talk about it? I'm a good listener."

He slumped onto the grass and recounted the sequence of events on that terrible morning almost a year before and the painful ordeal of waiting for the searchers to find Suzanne. He described the days following her disappearance, days of mixed emotions, days of hoping beyond hope that she would be found alive, but knowing in his heart that the chances were slim to nonexistent. He spilled his grief and held nothing back, including the shock of seeing her decomposed body in the morgue and how he'd been unable to erase that image from his mind ever since.

"I'm so sorry. If only I'd known, I would've told you I was goin' for a walk. I've made a mess o' things again."

"It's not your fault. You didn't know."

"Can I ask you somethin' about your wife's burial?"

"Yes."

"You said you had her cremated after the autopsy."

"That's right."

"Did you scatter her ashes or bury 'em?"

"I scattered them."

"Where? In a place you could visit?"

"In a park we used to go to. Why?"

"Have you ever been back to the place where she died?"

"You mean the campground we stayed at?"

"Uh-uh. The spot by the river."

"No," he said, wiping his eyes on a shirtsleeve, "I never went back . . . couldn't."

"I think you should."

"Why?"

"Because it might give you some closure."

"Oh . . . I don't know," he said, sighing deeply. "I don't think it'd work."

"That's how *I* got closure after my father died."

"Highway accident didn't you say?"

"Yeah. He hit an abutment. Witnesses told police he just veered off the road and slammed into it. They figured he must've fallen asleep at the wheel."

"I'm sorry."

"Mom nearly went crazy with grief, and so did I. He was only a couple o' miles from home when he died. Never made it."

She stopped to light another cigarette, and took a few drags before continuing.

"Goin' back to where he died gave me closure."

"How?"

"I took some o' Dad's personal things to the scene."

"Personal things?"

"Baseball cards. Dad collected 'em. I just sat near the bridge, holdin' a few in my hand. Doesn't sound like much, but it helped . . . helped a lot."

"Strange you should bring this up," said Howard, "I mean, especially right now."

"Why's that?"

"Because we'll be crossing the Mississippi soon. The place where Suzanne and I camped isn't far off the highway. It's about an hour's drive from here."

"Well then, make a side trip and go there. If you wanna be by yourself, I'll give you space."

"Actually," said Howard, shaking his head, "I'd rather have you with me . . . if you don't mind."

"Course not."

Howard ran his fingers through his beard, "You know what's so weird about this?"

"What?"

"I thought of asking my daughters to go back there with me—just this spring, as a matter of fact."

"Why didn't you?"

"I didn't want to impose. They've got lives and careers."

"You shouldn't think like that. I'm sure they'd have gone if you'd asked."

"I can't help feeling how odd this is."

"What's odd?"

"Odd that I'm going back there with a stranger."

"A stranger maybe, but no stranger to grief. I've been there too. I didn't lose a spouse like you did, but my hurt was just as real as yours."

Howard consulted his map for the most direct route to the campground. He left the interstate and took a secondary highway that paralleled the river. Preoccupied with images and memories of Suzanne, he found it hard to concentrate.

One thought haunted him as he passed the trees that lined the banks of the great river. Which one of them, he wondered, had snagged her body as it floated downstream? In hindsight, he wished he had asked the police to take him to where the kayakers had found her. That was really where he wanted to go.

When he reached the entrance to the RV Park, he turned off the engine and stared at the office, the place he had run to that morning.

"This is difficult," said Howard, tightly gripping the steering wheel.

"I know. It was for me too. We don't have to stay long. Just go to the spot for a while, and then we'll leave."

"I'll drop in and see the owners first," said Howard.

There were no drapes at the office window. Miriam saw him approach the counter and tap on a paging bell. Moments later, a woman appeared, then immediately came around the counter and embraced him. She could not hear their conversation, but it was clear the woman was sympathetic. They talked for almost twenty minutes before he emerged.

"Problem?" asked Miriam as he entered the RV.

"No. She said to take all the time I needed. Even offered to ask the pastor of her church to come over and be with me."

"That was sweet of her. Sure you wouldn't prefer havin' a minister instead o' me?"

"Uh-uh."

Howard left the RV first. Miriam stuffed a fistful of Kleenex in her pocket, and then followed him across the campground.

Little had changed since he and Suzanne had pulled into the attractive park the year before. It was well-established, with sites separated by privacy bushes and nestled among mature trees. The layout was much like a small town, with paved roads laid out in a square grid. Most of the sites were seasonal, weekend retreats for families, or summer homes for retirees who preferred to spend prolonged periods out of the city. Some were double-wide models never meant to be towed, looking more like cottages with their shingled roofs and attached screen rooms. Others were travel trailers or fifth wheels, retired from active service and raised on blocks, then skirted with crisscrossed wood to keep out skunks and raccoons. Occupants personalized sites with their names or pithy sayings, and improved their leased sites with picket fences, water fountains, or whirligigs. One place still had its "redneck wind chimes"—four aluminum beer cans hung on string; in the light breeze, they clinked unmusically. A few seniors smiled at them as they headed for the trail that led to the river. Howard smiled back, but his smile was wooden. He envied them, long married to their spouses and seemingly content in their twilight years. It was what he and Suzanne had always envisioned for themselves, a quiet haven where they could relax and entertain grandchildren. But with Suzanne's untimely death and their daughters' decision not to have children, both dreams had gone unrealized.

"It's this way," said Howard, steering Miriam toward the entrance to the trail.

A broad expanse of river opened into view. Plying the muddy waters was a commercial barge, heavily loaded and low in the water. He looked around. The details of the spot were just as he had remembered: the clearing near the river's edge where he had spread a blanket and made love to Suzanne, the branch on which they had hung their clothing.

"It's very private here."

"Yes," he replied, and then explained the significance of the place.

After a few difficult minutes, he led Miriam to where the path ended at the muddy riverbank. Their arrival startled several mallards; they exploded into panicked flight and skimmed across the river in the direction of the passing barge.

Howard knelt and placed his hand on the ground, "This . . . is where I found her things . . . where my nightmare began."

"Here," she said, crouching beside him and handing him tissues.

"Sorry about this," he said, pausing to wipe his eyes, and blow his nose.

"Don't apologize," she replied.

He took a deep breath, "You know what made it so difficult? Losing her like that . . . so suddenly, I mean?"

"Yeah. I think I do. Not bein' able to prepare yourself for it. Missin' the chance to tell her things before she passed."

"Yes, that's it exactly."

"Did you tell her you loved her?"

"Hardly a day passed that I didn't."

"Well then, at least she died knowin' that. That's more than a lot o' women can say, especially those with husbands who only say it on Valentine's Day." She paused for a few moments. "Has it ever occurred to you that she might've been thinkin' o' *you* when she was sittin' here that mornin'?"

"No."

"I'll bet she was, considerin' you were on vacation and all."

"Funny, I remember thinking about her that morning, just before I went to join her at the river."

"Well, there you go. She was probably thinkin' the same. Thinkin' what a great guy she had."

They stopped talking and listened to the sound of river water lapping against the shore and watched another barge going upstream. The drone of cicadas in the treetops competed with the throb of the diesel engine.

"Tell me 'bout the good times you had with her, Howard. That is, if you're comfortable tellin' me."

"You really want to know?"

"Yeah I do. I think you said she liked the outdoors a lot."

He smiled as he recalled the memories, "Suzanne had this reverence for living things, no matter how small. When we canoed, she'd rescue dragonflies on her paddle and bring them aboard until their wings dried out. She admired the artistry and engineering skill of spiders; I never saw her break a web. Wherever we camped, the first thing she'd do was set out a bird feeder. When our girls were little, they and all their friends used to bring wounded creatures to our house, knowing Suzanne would do her best to fix them up. And it didn't matter whether it was a bird or a bat or a snake or a stray cat that needed a meal. It was the kindness that lived inside her, the sensitivity. That's what I remember most. It's what I loved so much about her."

"That's wonderful."

He cleared his throat, "And we had this tradition when we went on hikes. Whenever we came to a branch that hung over a trail, you know, like an arch, we'd stop under it and kiss. Silly I suppose when you think about it."

"Not silly at all. Most women would love to have a man do that."

She reached out absently and tugged at the stem of a wildflower growing beside the river, then stripped off the leaves.

"Suzanne loved flowers," said Howard, watching Miriam twirl the blossom between her fingers.

"Show me a woman who doesn't. All I know is, no guy ever picked 'em for me."

"Really? You've been dating the wrong kind of men."

"Tell me about it," she said, patting her stomach. "Story o' my dumb-ass life."

"Every spring, I always picked her lilacs."

"Ah, that's sweet."

"She loved the fragrance. And you know the best part?"

"What?"

"Even though I picked them every spring, she'd always act surprised, as if I was doing it for the first time. I remember how she'd bury her nose in the tiny petals and inhale. I can still see her doing that."

"Too bad lilacs aren't in bloom right now."

"Why?"

"You could pick some. Float 'em downstream like a remembrance. Course, there's other kinds growin' around here. You could always pick them instead."

"Yes," said Howard, warming to the idea. "Yes I could."

Miriam watched him comb the area. He unraveled the long stalk of a vine that was wrapped around a tree, and then cut off an eight-foot length with his pocketknife. He disappeared, and returned with fistfuls of different wildflowers. He sat close by, but kept his head angled away to hide his upsetness. She watched him coil the vine into a ring, then push in the stems of the flowers until it formed a wreath.

And all the time she watched, she thought of the final moments of Suzanne Munro's life, wading in the shallows of the great river. Had she had any prior warning of the heart attack that killed her? Did she have a lucid moment as she struggled to reach shore, perhaps calling for Howard, before collapsing into the muddy waters and losing consciousness?

"There," he said, as he finished the wreath, his eyes brimming.

"You want some private time?"

"Please."

She retreated along the trail, listening to Howard's expressions of tenderness as he spoke his wife's name. At the end of the trail, she looked back. She saw him bring the wreath to his lips, and then reverently lay it on the breast of the river. It bobbed in the waves, swept downstream by the same inexorable currents that had stolen Suzanne Munro's body. Twenty minutes later, he emerged looking preoccupied. Miriam was waiting for him, sitting at a picnic table smoking a cigarette.

"You were right," he said almost in a whisper as he sat beside her. "Coming here did help. I didn't think it would."

She took a deep drag on her cigarette, "Lemme tell you somethin'," she said, exhaling her words with the smoke. "Your wife died far sooner than she should've, but while she lived, she was a lucky woman."

"You think so?"

"I know so."

"How's that?"

"Because I'm gettin' to know the man who loved her."

# CHAPTER 10

## *Letting Go*

ALTHOUGH MIRIAM HAD SUGGESTED they only pay a short visit before moving on, Howard needed more time. He registered for another night at the campground office, but the evening was ruled by Murphy's Law.

The RV's water heater would not light, an irritating malfunction that took over an hour to fix. And when he tried to light a fire after dark, the damp wood produced nothing but smoke, sending people coughing and grumbling into their RVs. He became glum and quiet as they sat outside in their folding cloth chairs. The only sound besides the night bugs was the patter of rain on the foliage. When it became heavier, Howard adjusted the slope of the awning to shed the accumulating water. It streamed onto the soil and formed puddles at their feet. The foul weather only added to his gloomy mood. Finally, they cut their losses and moved inside.

While she settled herself in the captain's chair and channel surfed, Howard tried to read, but kept going over the same words; he gave up and shelved the book. He was not a TV watcher and became irritated with the programs she chose, especially the loud commercials that blared their annoying messages. Without saying goodnight, he retreated to the bathroom, brushed his teeth, and climbed into bed. Neither the double doors of the washroom nor the thin wallboard could muffle the sound of the television. Exasperated, he jammed wads of Kleenex, into his ears. Now, the only thing that he could hear was the internalized sound of his own breathing, the kind of white noise that often lulled him to sleep. But not tonight, held in the iron grip of insomnia. Repeatedly he turned over and adjusted the pillow. He got up and took a sleeping pill. An hour later he popped another, but nothing could push him over the threshold. At dawn he was still awake.

AT EIGHT o'clock, Miriam awoke. Water droplets still clung to the window beside her lounge bed, evidence of the previous night's rain. The sky was now clear with only a few random clouds.

Waves of morning sickness drove her to the washroom where she knelt in front of the toilet. Vomiting was something she had only done a few times in her life in spite of the many alcohol-soaked parties she had attended. It was the most disgusting bodily function she could think of, but now, with a baby growing inside her, she was powerless to stop the gagging that had plagued her since the beginning of her pregnancy. She remembered what a girlfriend had once told her; persistent morning sickness could be the sign of an impending multiple birth; the mere thought of it had her in a panic. Hunched over the bowl, she found her nausea even more humiliating, knowing that Howard was hearing every sound.

She waited an hour for him to get up. When he did not, she dressed and put on a pot of coffee, then went outside for her first cigarette of the day. The smoke felt good as she drew it deep. She sat on the rain-dampened picnic table and mused. Would he still be depressed? Had she done the right thing by talking him into coming here? Or had the experience been too painful for him? She tossed the half-finished butt into the fire pit and returned to the RV.

"Coffee's on," she said, knocking on his door.

There was no answer.

She knocked again and edged the door open. His bed was empty. He must have tiptoed past her, but when?

She poured two coffees, grabbed her cigarettes, and then headed across the campground in the direction of the trail. As expected, she found him by the riverbank.

"I made you this," she said, sitting beside him.

"Thanks," he said, wincing as the hot stoneware burned his fingers.

"Sorry to be so blunt and frank, but you look like shit."

"Never slept last night," he said, yawning.

"Not even a wink?"

"Uh-uh."

"You must be friggin' wasted," she said, sympathetically.

"My legs feel like jelly."

"Did I have the TV up too loud last night?"

"No," he lied.

Scalding coffee touched his lips. He spilled some on his shirt, and then berated himself for his clumsiness. "Why is it I can never eat or drink a damned thing without wearing it?"

Miriam laughed, "I'm gettin' used to you doin' that." She wet her hand in the river and rubbed at the coffee stain.

He felt comforted by her attentiveness as she knelt close to him.

"Want me to make you some toast to go with that?" she asked.

"No thanks. I'm not hungry."

"You sure?"

"Positive," he assured her. "Sorry about last night. I wasn't much fun to be around."

"Nothin' to apologize for. I had a feelin' I'd find you down here." She glanced at the river, then at him. "Too many sad thoughts?"

He nodded and carefully sipped his coffee.

"I feel guilty now," she said with a repentant look.

"What about?"

"Convincin' you to come here."

"Don't be. You were right to suggest it. I just had to stay a little longer."

"I understand," she said, lightly touching his arm.

"It's been a hell of a year for me," said Howard, setting his cup down and massaging his temples.

"I'm sure it has."

"After the initial shock, I was angry. Our girls were out of the nest and our time was finally our own. I mean, we'd made plans dammit . . . plans for our future. It's silly, I suppose, but I loved her for so long, I thought that love would keep her from dying on me. I figured we'd ride off into the sunset and get old and wrinkly together."

"Sounds like you were happy," she said, lighting a cigarette, and then exhaling twin plumes from her nostrils.

"Very. We had the usual scraps most couples have, of course. Small stuff, but overall, we got on well."

"You're lucky, then. Least you've got good memories. That's more than some can say."

"That's what I keep telling myself. I keep going over the good times in my head, but I just can't get over losing her."

"Somehow, you have to let go, Howard, because if you don't, you'll never move on."

"I've had that trouble before."

"Movin' on?"

"Yes."

"Who from?"

"A girl I was sweet on once."

"First love?"

He nodded. "We were in high school. I was nuts about her."

"Was she pretty?"

"She was to me."

"I take it you were goin' steady."

"Yes," he said. "We'd talked of getting married some day, once we were out of school."

"High school sweethearts?" she said, taking a deep drag on her cigarette.

"Yes," he said, picturing Lisa Crandall.

"Were you virgins?"

"Yes."

"What was it like . . . your first time together? Or am I bein' too personal?"

"It was very special," said Howard, recalling the experience, "but a little scary at the same time. I mean, it was a big step in our relationship, especially with us being so young. We both felt the same about it—that it was more than just sex. It was a very loving thing. We cared so much for each other and it brought us even closer together. The problem was though, she got pregnant."

"Holy George!" exclaimed a wide-eyed Miriam. "Didn't you use somethin'?"

"Yes," replied Howard, "but we were careless with the condom and it broke."

"Uh-oh. I'll bet her parents must have gone—"

"Apeshit," said Howard. "They were church people. The scandal made them leave town."

"Go on," said Miriam, incredulous. "You're kiddin' me—right?"

"No," he replied.

"That's friggin' extreme, don't you think?"

"Yes. I thought so at the time."

"Where'd they go?"

"I couldn't find out at first. Then I got this letter from Dubai."

"That's in Arabia somewhere isn't it?" Miriam asked.

"Yes. The United Arab Emirates."

"That's a long way from Toledo," said Miriam, taking a deep drag on her cigarette and exhaling a huge plume.

"Her father took a job supervising a long-term construction project."

"Did she have the baby over there?"

"No. She sent me a letter the day before her father took her out of the country to have an abortion."

"So," said Miriam, "by the time you received the letter the baby was dead."

"Yes," he said, sighing deeply.

"Well, at least now I know why you're so against abortion. I'm so sorry," she said. "You must've been so upset."

"We both were," said Howard. "We wanted the baby so much, even though it would have posed huge problems for us being so young and still in school. We'd even picked out names for the baby. But in the end, it didn't matter. We had no say in things. Her father saw to that."

"I know this'll seem like a dumb question and all," said Miriam, "because what's done is done, but what names *did* you pick?"

"Shawn if it'd been a boy."

"And a girl?"

"Holly."

"They're both lovely names," said Miriam, then she paused to choose her words. "It's probably not much comfort, but at least you did go on to have children with Suzanne. That's somethin' to be grateful for."

"You're right, and I *am* grateful," said Howard, "but it still hurts me to think that I might have had that child too. The way it turned out, I never even knew the sex of our baby, and although this might sound crazy, that bothered me to no end. Still does. It was as if the child I fathered was reduced to non-being status—to a nothing. No identity whatsoever. I couldn't even build an imaginary picture in my mind of what that boy or girl might have looked like. And I wanted to be able to do that—wanted it so badly."

Miriam held up her hand, "Dumb question number two. I know things didn't go this way . . . but . . . let's say you and your girlfriend had

*had* to put that baby up for adoption, would you have tried to find it at some point?"

"Absolutely!" said Howard without hesitation.

"But that's hard, isn't it?" said Miriam. "I mean, it takes a lot o' searchin' and money for private detectives and such."

"It wouldn't have mattered. I would have gone to the ends of the earth. Done whatever it took to find that child."

Miriam saw his clenched jaw and the expression on his face as he angled his head away: a mix of pain and anger, still raw at something that had happened over three decades before. She thought about her own situation and the plans she had for her abortion. The father of *her* child would not have cared like this, she thought. But what about her? What would happen after she had had the abortion? Years later, would she be this bitter? Have these same feelings of regret?

"I'm sorry," she said when he turned to face her. "I didn't mean to stir things up for you again."

He shrugged, but said nothing. There was, after all, nothing for him to say. The past was gone and he could not change it.

She waited a few minutes to gauge his mood before speaking again.

"I feel bad for you, Howard. For losin' this baby and for losin' Suzanne and all. But you're still young enough to move on. To make another life for yourself."

"Thanks for the thought, but really, who's going to want a train wreck like me?" he said, pointing to the coffee stain on his shirt. "I'm a disaster."

"You're sellin' yourself short. Haven't you dated since Suzanne?"

"Uh-uh," he said, shaking his head. "Lunch with female colleagues a couple times—that's all."

"So, in other words, I'm the first woman you've been around for any length o' time?"

"Yes."

She took a few short puffs, and then flicked her cigarette butt into the river. "Don't think I'm bein' disrespectful to your wife's memory—'cause I'm not—but there's a woman out there somewhere for you. I'm sure of it."

"Humph," said Howard, "I doubt it."

"You know what they say," she said, playfully poking the stain on his shirt. "It's not the packaging that counts, it's the person inside."

He squirmed uncomfortably, "I'm embarrassed to say this, but . . ."

"But what?"

"I don't have a sex drive anymore. I'd be reluctant to start anything with a woman. Afraid I couldn't get it up."

"You needn't worry about that. Makin' love's like ridin' a bike. When the right woman comes along, you won't forget how."

"I suppose you're right. It's just that—"

"Hey," she said, changing the subject, "did you know there's another trail in this place?"

"No."

She reached out with both hands and pulled him to his feet. "Come on. Let's take a walk—a happy walk."

"Thanks," he said, as they headed for the other side of the park.

"For what?"

"The pep talk. I needed that."

"You're welcome," she said. "Tell you what else I'm gonna do."

"What's that?"

"I'm gonna give you a new name. A nickname. One for your new life."

"Really," he said, laughing. "I always wanted one when I was a kid, but never got it till St. Martin's."

"What was it?"

"Colonel Ketchup."

"Yeah," she said, giggling, "I can see you gettin' that."

"It wasn't malicious," said Howard. "I got used to it."

"What was the one you really wanted?"

"Chip."

"Hey," she grinned and playfully punched his arm. "I like that."

They had walked only a short distance on the trail when she reached into the leaf clutter and picked up a small branch.

"Wilt thou kneel, sir," she said, giggling again.

Reluctantly, he complied.

"I dub thee, Chip Munro," she said, touching him on each shoulder. "It's what I'm gonna call you from now on."

Howard grinned. There was a guileless charm about this young woman. He was getting to like her—a lot.

# CHAPTER 11

## *Birds of a Feather*

H OWARD DID NOT TRAVEL far from the campground by the Mississippi. An hour down the road he approached the entrance to an RV park; clusters of helium-filled balloons swayed in the breeze. Beside them, a hand-lettered sign read: *Fifth Annual Rally. All Welcome.*

"We could be out of luck," said Howard as he turned up the paved drive.

"Why?"

"Campgrounds are often fully booked for these things."

"Are they common?"

"Fairly."

"What're they about?"

"Owners of the same brand of trailer get together."

"To do what? Kick tires and swap campin' stories?"

"That and seminars on different things: highway safety, equipment maintenance, stuff like that."

"Ever been to one?" asked Miriam.

"Uh-uh. Suzanne and I socialized with other campers, but never at one of these."

As they approached the office, a boy ran in front of the RV. Howard hit the brakes and the horn; the motor home stopped, but the horn did not work. The boy, wide-eyed with shock at the near miss, bolted away.

Ten minutes later he emerged, waving a camping permit. He handed the site map to Miriam and followed her directions along the interior roads.

It was a large campground with a mix of hardwoods and evergreens and in the center, a large lake. They passed an elderly man teaching a boy how to side cast a lure into a sheltered pool under the branches of a weeping willow. Two things united the campers: they owned the same brand of trailer, and wore the same uniform, a cotton vest adorned with pins and rally patches. Although it was well before sundown, campfires were already lit, some smoldering, others burning freely and launching fiery embers into the forest canopy.

"Turn here," said Miriam, pointing to their site in an empty section. "Looks like they've set us away from the main area."

With hand signals, she backed him into the site, then stepped aside as he hooked up the RV's shorelines. While plugging the electrical cable into the box, he noticed her looking across an open section of park.

Two boys were walking down the grassy slope that led to the edge of the lake. Each carried a fishing rod and a bait box. The taller boy was in his early teens, gangly and with oversized feet. The smaller boy was about eight-years-old, chubby, and animated. The sounds of their voices carried clearly.

"A humungous catfish hangs out by that log," said the older boy. "I've hooked him twice now. Both times he got away."

"Think we'll catch him?" asked the smaller boy.

"Hope so."

"How big is he?"

The older boy laid his rod and tackle box on the grass. "About this long," he said, spreading both arms as if measuring off a small whale.

"Awesome. I've never caught anything bigger than a sunfish."

"Tell you what," said the older boy, magnanimously. "Even if I catch him, we'll tell everyone that you did."

"It'll be our secret. Right?"

"Yeah."

Miriam turned to Howard with a wistful look, "I envy those two."

"How come?"

"They're havin' so much fun. Plus they're on a real vacation."

"Didn't you go on one when you were a kid?"

"No," she said, sighing deeply. "Not even a picnic. Dad was on the road a lot, and my mother—"

"What *did* you do on summer school breaks?" asked Howard.

"Played stickball in the streets. We used the manhole covers for bases and the storefronts for foul lines. Closest I got to water was when they turned on the hydrants for us inner city brats. I used to think that was the greatest."

"So," said Howard, "you never went to a lake?"

"Uh-uh."

"Camped out? Had a campfire?"

She shook her head.

"That's one thing Suzanne and I always made sure of. Our girls got a vacation every summer."

Her revelation took him by surprise. He leaned against the picnic table and thought for a moment.

"Are you in a hurry to get to your mother's?"

"Not really. Why?"

"Well, I'm in no rush. I've got a faculty meeting, but that's not until the week before school starts."

"What're you sayin'?"

"How would *you* like to have a vacation? Your first?"

"You mean on our way to the coast?"

"Sure. We could take side trips here and there. Suzanne and I visited lots of interesting places—places you'd like."

"But you've been so generous already. And besides, I don't deserve it, not after the way I've been."

"Ah, never mind that," said Howard dismissively. "What do you think of the idea?"

"But it'll cost money."

"Money's for spending."

"I gotta admit, it sure would be nice and all."

"Deal then?" asked Howard.

"Yeah," she replied, grinning. "Deal!"

"That's great," he exclaimed, then changed the subject. "How about we eat supper outside this time? Think you could brave a few mosquitoes?"

"I think I could do that."

Howard watched her enter the coach with a new lightness. He whistled happily as set up a portable barbeque on the picnic table. After buttering two baked potatoes and cobs of corn and wrapping them in foil, he slathered the burger patties in mesquite sauce, and then laid them on the hot grill. Miriam opened a can of pop and took the bench opposite him.

"Looks like we're gettin' a neighbor," she said, turning to watch a white delivery van drive onto a nearby site.

A heavy set man in his thirties lifted out a large plastic cooler, and set it on the table. Long strings of dirty black hair hung over his shoulders and his undersized T-shirt was stained and heavily creased. His blue jeans barely fit his bulging waist; they rode up to reveal bare ankles that protruded from a pair of shabby canvas runners. He lit a cigarette and opened his first beer. Then he sat at his picnic table, staring in their direction.

"He looks poor," said Howard in a lowered voice. "Think we should offer him some food?"

"Oh, I don't know about that."

"Why not?"

"Might make him self-conscious about his poverty and all."

"Never thought of that. Shows you how much I know about impoverishment, being raised in a wealthy suburb . . ." He stopped, suddenly aware of the look on Miriam's face. "Sorry, I wasn't thinking."

"It's OK," she said, glancing at the man. "Poor devil looks like he's homeless." She paused for a moment. "If it'll make you happy, I'll talk to him."

"Don't be long," said Howard, pointing to the food on the grill. "These'll be ready soon."

He flipped the burger patties again and turned the corn and potatoes. He watched Miriam stop at the man's site on her way back from the washroom. She shifted from foot to foot, trying to make conversation, but did not seem to be getting anywhere.

"I take it you didn't have much luck," he said when she returned.

"Uh-uh. To be honest and truthful, he creeps me out."

"Really?"

"Yeah."

"In what way?" said Howard, opening the hamburger buns and setting them on the grill to toast.

"I can't put my finger on it. Just bad vibes."

Howard served the food, and they sat down at the picnic table. At the first bite of his hamburger, a dollop of ketchup squirted onto the front of his shirt.

"Hey," said Miriam, laughing, "you're supposed to eat that, not wear it." She went into the motor home and brought out paper napkins.

"Thanks," he said, dabbing at his shirt.

"Tomato stains are hard to get out. Why don't you change out o' that? If I put it in to soak right away, it'll probably come out."

"Don't worry about it. Eat your supper before it goes cold."

"No. I insist. Lemme do somethin' for *you* for a change."

"Oh, all right," he replied, enjoying the fuss she was making.

He removed his shirt and handed it to her, then suddenly got self-conscious of his middle-aged spread. A few minutes later she returned with a replacement shirt. As he put it on, she noticed his tattoo.

"Funny, you don't strike me as a tattoo kind o' guy."

"Act of madness," said Howard, sinking his teeth into his hamburger.

"Looks faded. Had it for a while?"

"Got it when I was young and stupid."

"Somebody dare you?"

"It was because . . . of that girl . . . I told you about," he replied between bites.

"The one you got pregnant?"

"Uh-huh," he replied, wiping relish off his chin.

The sound of a vehicle engine starting cut conversation short. They watched as their neighbor drove to the washroom building.

"What a lazy turd," exclaimed Miriam. "A toddler could walk that distance."

Minutes later, their neighbor was back at his picnic table, drinking beer and staring once again at them as they finished their meal. Annoyed at the man's rudeness, Howard stared back. After what seemed like an eternity, the man dropped his gaze. He entered his van and emerged with a sheaf of papers. After sharpening a wooden pencil with a hunting knife, he began to write, gazing upward occasionally, as if for inspiration.

It was a beautiful summer evening, the air pungent with campfire smoke and vibrant with the sound of crickets, the setting sun glinting off the lazy ripples on the lake. The idyllic setting was marred only by the bizarre behavior of their neighbor, who talked to himself in a rambling and disjointed monotone.

"I am the serpent . . . all dead life is in me . . . they're in my sperm . . . Jews paid back the USA for nine eleven . . . hell can't hurt you . . ."

"If I listen to any more o' this guy's babble, I'm gonna go nuts. Feel like takin' a walk?"

"Yes" said Howard. "I'll grab a flashlight. Be dark by the time we're back."

"Better lock up your RV. No tellin' what this guy could do."

They walked the gravel campground road, now a ribbon of murky gray. Occasionally, their shoulders touched. At the sound of excited voices, they turned toward the lake. The younger boy had hooked a large fish; the rod tip was bent and twitched violently.

"Let's sit and watch," said Miriam, pointing to a bench.

"Holy crap," shouted the boy. "You think it could be the great catfish?"

"Might be," said his friend, adjusting the drag on the boy's reel. "Keep the line taut, but don't jerk it. You want to tire him out before you start pulling him in."

They watched the boy struggle to land the fish. He was tiring fast, but his older companion was not about to let him quit. When he finally dragged the fish onto the grassy slope, it was dark.

"It's the one," shouted the smaller boy. "I caught him. I actually caught him."

"Yeah, dude. "It's the one all right. Think your dad would gut him for you?"

"He's not here, but my mom will."

"How come? Are they divorced or something?"

"Yeah."

"If you want," said the older boy, "I could get my dad to clean him."

"Nah. My mom'll do it."

"Mom's don't do shit like that. Blood and guts make 'em puke."

"Not mine," he said, looking intently at the older boy. "She's awesome."

The boys dragged their prize toward the string of campsites. Howard and Miriam followed at a discreet distance, picking their way carefully along the dark road. They watched the young boy run onto his site, proudly showing off his catch to his mother and another woman, both in their mid-thirties, drinking beer at the picnic table.

"Hey, Mom?" said the boy. "Think you could clean it? Kevin's got this cool video game and said I could play with it."

"This is when I wish your father was around."

"He's *never* around," said the boy, contemptuously.

"Oh, all right," replied his mother, "I'll clean it."

"Ah, thanks," he said, giving her a high five. "You're the best."

The boys bolted from the campsite, oblivious to Howard and Miriam, still standing in the road.

"Your son looks pretty excited," said Howard. "We saw him land that monster."

"It's his first large fish," said his mother, taking a swig of Budweiser.

"So I gather," replied Howard, telling the woman of her son's boast to his friend.

"Oh my God," exclaimed the woman. "Did he say that?"

"Yeah," replied Miriam. "Said you weren't squeamish over blood 'n' guts."

"What am I gonna do now? I wouldn't know where to start. Cory always cleaned the damned things."

"Who's Cory?" asked Howard.

"My ex," said the woman, spitting the word contemptuously. "That knob is a waste of space. Only pays child support when he feels like it. He doesn't do squat with that boy."

"I'll clean it for you. Your son doesn't have to know it was me."

"Oh, thank you so much! By the way, I'm Karen," she said, smiling and extending her hand, "and this here's, Gwen, a friend of mine. More like partners in crime eh, girlfriend?"

The other woman laughed and raised her beer can, "I'll drink to that."

"I'm Miriam, and this is, Chip," she said, grinning at Howard's novel reaction to his new nickname.

"Nice to meet you," she said, then turned to Howard. "What do you need?"

"A sharp knife and a pair of pliers."

"Coming right up," said the woman. She opened a side compartment in her trailer and lifted out a toolbox.

Howard set about skinning and filleting the large fish, deftly separating the backbone and ribs. He cut the large fillets into meal-sized portions, wrapped them in aluminum foil, and then washed his hands. "There," he said. "You're good to go."

"You're a prince," said Karen.

"Glad I could help."

"Say, you folks had supper yet? I'll be putting lamb chops on the grill in a minute."

"Thanks," said Howard, "but we just ate."

"How 'bout a beer, then?"

"Wouldn't turn it down," he said, smiling.

"Make that a pop for me," said Miriam, glancing at Howard.

Conversation flowed easily. Karen sounded off to Howard about her divorce and delinquent husband. Gwen—a baseball fan and also born in Philadelphia—gossiped with Miriam about the Philly's star players. Miriam avoided mention of her pregnancy.

An hour later, both boys raced onto the campsite, breathless after a hard run.

"Hey Mom, did you clean it yet?"

"It's all divvied up and wrapped in foil."

"See," he said to his friend. "Told you she'd clean it." Then he turned to his mother, "Could Steve have supper with us?"

"Yeah, I'll be starting it in a few minutes, so don't run off again."

"Mom?"

"What?"

"Could you cook us fish instead of lamb chops?"

"Sure," she answered, grinning at Howard as she swigged the last of her Budweiser.

"Told you she was awesome," said the younger boy, beaming proudly to his friend.

"Thanks for the beer," said Howard, getting up from the picnic table with Miriam. "Nice talking to you."

"Have a safe trip to California, you two," said Karen. As they reached the road at the end of the campsite, she called out to Miriam. "He's a keeper, honey. Don't let him get away."

Miriam and Howard continued their stroll around the campground. Each time they passed a site, they looked in. Campfires reflected off the smiling faces of those gathered around flaming logs. Younger children were already in their pajamas, some cautiously holding marshmallows over hot coals, others scrambling onto the laps of grandparents. Burning softwood popped loudly, sending bright embers spiraling. The scent of wood smoke mixed with the stench of running shoes held too close to flames.

"I used to envy kids in my neighborhood," said Miriam, lighting a cigarette, her features momentarily illuminated by the flame of her butane lighter.

"What for?"

She exhaled before she spoke, "Goin' to summer camp. They'd talk about it each fall when we went back to school. Used to piss me off."

"Jealousy?"

"Yeah—big time. I'd lie awake at night, cryin' into my pillow, tryin' to imagine what it was like to be in such places, far from the inner city. I wish my parents could've sent me to camp—just once. I'd' have treasured that forever." She took a deep drag on her cigarette; the ember glowed brightly in the darkness. "You know what the worst part was, though?"

"What?"

"They'd tell me it was so dark at camp, they could see a million stars, and I hated 'em for tellin' me."

"Why?"

"'Cause they made me feel poor. Made me self-conscious that I never got out o' my shit-ass neighborhood. Couldn't see squat where I lived. Be lucky if I saw half a dozen stars. Anyway," she said, working the cigarette between her fingers, "I got even."

"How?"

"Started havin' sex with boys before they did."

"That's an odd way to get revenge."

"Maybe it was, but it worked. I'd watch their envious faces. Tell 'em the boys didn't want to screw 'em because they were so ugly. One girl, Jenny, she had this spinal deformity, sco, scolitis—"

"You mean scoliosis."

"Yeah, that's it. I told her the boys were callin' her 'The Pretzel.' She cried, but I didn't care. I'd find every girl's weakness and make up false gossip. I enjoyed hurtin' 'em, spiteful little bitch that I was."

"Did you ever feel sorry about that?"

"Not while I was dishin' it out. All I could think of was gettin' back at 'em. I was obsessed. It's scary the capacity kids have for bullyin'. Then, a couple o' years ago, I saw this TV program on it. People in their fifties were tellin' how they got picked on in high school. They were breakin' down in front o' the cameras. That's when the guilt hit me. Made me think about what a turd I'd been."

"Did you ever run into any of them after high school?"

"Couple o' times," she said, exhaling a long plume of smoke. "I just hung my head and walked on, I was so ashamed."

"You never apologized?"

"No, and I wish I had now," she said, grinding her cigarette butt vigorously with the heel of her shoe. "I owed it to 'em, but didn't have the guts. And who's the stupid one now? Miriam Kovacs, the pregnant loser with no man in her life. If those girls could see me now, they'd have the last laugh. They're probably all married with kids . . . livin' in the burbs with two cars in the garage."

"Well, what's done is done. You're older, and hopefully, wiser now."

"Hah," she exclaimed. "Not that wise. So far, I've done nothin' but make a big fat mess o' my life. I need to turn myself around. That's why I want this abortion and all. To start with a clean slate. Maybe if I'm lucky, I'll find a guy who *really* loves me."

"Has it occurred to you, that keeping your baby might be the start of turning your life around?"

"How?"

"Being responsible for another person might give you a sense of purpose—a reason to change."

"Think so?"

"Yes."

"But it wouldn't be easy though, would it? I mean, 'specially for someone in my circumstances and all."

"Nothing worthwhile in life comes easy. You wouldn't be the first single mom to raise a child. Thousands are doing it."

"Karen's doin' it."

"Yes, and she's got a jerk of an ex-husband by the sounds of it. At least that's something you wouldn't have to deal with."

Howard sensed her discomfort at his broaching the subject of her pregnancy; he quickly backed off.

In silence, they continued their walk through the campground. At an open section of the park, they stopped to look at the Milky Way. Miriam pulled a cigarette package from her jeans, went to light up, and then reconsidered.

"It's like a carpet o' diamonds," she said, staring into the night sky. Isn't it wonderful?"

"I've always thought so," he replied, happy that she had noticed, and recalling that the one thing he had never shared with Suzanne was his love of astronomy.

They resumed walking again. On the dark, uneven road, she clung onto Howard's arm to steady herself. In the faint light, he noticed her looking at him.

"Something on your mind?"

There was a long pause before she answered, "Yeah."

"What?"

"Can I ask you somethin' . . . you know . . . personal like?"

"Sure."

"You must think about your wife a lot—right?"

"Hardly a day passes that I don't."

"Do you ever get the feelin' there might be a place, you know, a place where people go after they die?"

"You mean, like heaven?"

"I dunno. Just some kind o' place—a place where they can see us from?"

"Yes, although I couldn't say exactly where. Suzanne used to say it was 'beyond the blue.' Why?"

"Well, it's been a long time now since my Dad died. And . . . what I guess I'm tryin' to say is that—"

"You still think about him?" said Howard, completing her sentence.

"Yeah."

"And you'd like to feel that wherever he is, he can see you?"

"Yeah. Yeah that's it. That's what I'd like. I'd like to know that for sure."

Howard sighed wistfully, "None of us know what's on the other side, or even *if* there's another side. It's life's biggest mystery."

"But, Chip, what if there's no such place? I mean . . . what if life here on earth is all there is?"

"Then there's still a place for your father," said Howard, as they stopped under a street lamp, a pseudo-sun orbited by moths.

As they stood on the road, bathed in a halo of amber light, he noticed to his surprise, that she was silently crying, tears coursing down both her cheeks.

"What place is that?" she asked, sniffling.

"Two places actually."

"Where?"

"In here," said Howard, touching his forehead, "and in here," placing a hand over his heart.

# CHAPTER 12

## *Psycho Camper*

WHEN THEY HAD FINISHED their circuit around the campground, the man was still mumbling incoherently on his site. The red ember of his cigarette—like the bloodied, malevolent eye of a Cyclops—glowed in the darkness.

Howard went inside first and flipped on the motor home's patio light. Just before she entered the RV, Miriam noticed the man staring intently at her. She stepped inside quickly and locked the door.

"That guy is freakin' me out! Good thing you've got a toilet on board. I wouldn't walk to the friggin' washroom if you paid me."

"He's probably harmless," replied Howard, dismissively. "Had one too many wobbly pops."

They watched a couple of TV programs, and then prepared for bed. While Howard showered and brushed his teeth, Miriam pulled out the lounge sofa and arranged her bedding. He read for his usual half-hour, then turned out his reading light and quickly fell asleep.

But she could not sleep, not with the unnerving presence of the strange man nearby. Although the sky was dark, the glow from the campground's security lighting gave a soft, eerie blush to the window openings. Nervous, she had shut the venetian blinds tightly so that no one could look in.

She had been awake for some time when she thought she heard a noise close to the RV. But it was so faint she dismissed it, thinking it might be the result of an overactive imagination, or an animal perhaps. But when she listened more closely, a shiver of fear ran through her. They were human footsteps.

After a brief pause, something brushed along the side of the motor home. Was it clothing she wondered? A hand perhaps? It was impossible to tell.

Metal steps squeaked, and then a shadow appeared at the window of the RV's door.

The door handle jiggled.

Shoes crunched on gravel.

The sounds stopped outside her window, inches from her bed.

Fingers grated on the aluminum screen.

Her heart pounded. Her mouth went dry.

Carefully, she peeled back her bedclothes, and tiptoed forward in the coach to another window. The floor creaked underfoot.

There was a grunt outside.

Had the person heard her?

She lifted a single aluminum slat and peered out. For a moment she saw nothing, until she realized that something was blocking her view. Inches away, on the other side of the jalousie window was the unmistakable shape of a human head.

Acrid body odor and beer breath wafted through the screen. He brought a cigarette to his mouth and took a deep drag. The ember brightened momentarily, casting a macabre glow on his face. His piercing eyes stared into her soul from the other side of the window. As she recoiled, her hand rattled the aluminum slats.

"I know you're in there," said the man in an eerily calm voice.

She froze.

"You've been waiting for me, haven't you?"

Miriam hands shook. She stepped back to the center of the coach, but the man remained at the window. Between the aluminum slats, she could see a faint pulse of light each time he dragged on his cigarette.

"Open the door and come outside," he said calmly, "I'm not going to hurt you. I would never do that to someone as pretty as you."

"G-go back to your site, or I'll c-call the police."

"No you won't," said the man, confidently. "You got no phone in there."

"I'm serious."

Instantly, the man's tone of voice turned sinister. "Call the police, honey, and I'll kill you deader 'n dog shit. I got a gun," he said, cocking the barrel of an automatic pistol to authenticate his threat.

"What do you want? M-money?"

"No."

"What then?"

"You, sweetheart. I want you."

He continued talking to her through the window screen. His voice had an impatient edge, angry that he was unable to entice her outside.

She retreated to the back of the coach and slid open the first washroom door; it squeaked loudly as the rollers moved in the metal track.

"Hey," said the voice outside. "What're you doing in there?"

Miriam opened the second door to the rear bedroom. Howard was reclined on his back, snoring lightly. She approached him in the faint light and shook his shoulder.

"Chip, w-wake up."

"Whuh?" he mumbled, startled by Miriam's intrusion.

"I'm scared."

"Scared of whuh?"

"That guy."

"What guy?"

"Our nutcase neighbor."

"Nah," he mumbled. "He'll be in bed by now."

"Uh-uh. He's been talkin' to me through the w-window for the past few minutes, t-tryin' to convince me to come outside."

Howard tore back the covers and leapt out of bed.

"He's got a friggin' gun."

"Hey bitch, get your ass back here. I'm not finished talking to you."

"Damn," said Howard.

"What?"

"My cell phone. It's in the Jeep."

"Oh shit," said Miriam, her hands shaking uncontrollably. "What do we d-do now?"

"Keep him distracted," he whispered. "Flatter him. Flirt with him if you have to. But don't open that door."

"What're you gonna do?"

"There's an emergency exit in my bedroom. A window that swings out. I'll have to squeeze through it without making a noise."

"Then what?"

The man at the window was getting angrier, "Look, if you're gonna jerk me around, I'll bust down this fucking door."

"Gimme a minute," she called, trying to stall him.

"I'll have to get my cell phone first," said Howard, "then go far enough from the RV so he can't hear me calling the police."

"B-but once you're outside, you can't c-come back in—can you?"

"No," replied Howard. "I'll have to stay outside. Wait for the cops."

"What if he . . . he gets in?"

"Then get a knife from the galley," he said, quickly donning his track suit and opening the emergency window in the bedroom.

"And do what?"

"Stab him."

"I can't do that."

"Why not?" he replied.

"What if I kill him?"

"It'd be self-defense."

"But—"

"No buts," said Howard impatiently. "Do it if you have to."

Miriam grabbed a knife and returned to the front of the coach. She kept the interior lights off, but opened the venetian blinds slightly. She changed her tone and began to sweet-talk the man. Occasionally, she coughed loudly to disguise the sound of Howard's struggles to exit the RV.

After a few minutes, she checked Howard's bedroom. He was gone. She was alone.

"What's your name?" asked Miriam, now back at the window.

"Stratton. Del Stratton."

"Say, isn't there a company by that name? Makes small engines or somethin'?"

"You mean Briggs and Stratton?" he answered.

"Yeah. You any relation?"

"No."

"I like your van," she said. "Do you camp a lot in it?"

"Now 'n' then."

"You got a bunk inside?"

"No," he snapped, his voice taking on a sharper edge now. "Don't get to go camping much."

"Why not?"

"I work long hours."

"Where?"

"At a scrap metal company."

"Oh yeah," she replied, feigning interest. "I never met a man in that line o' work before."

"Cut the crap," he said sharply, realizing that she was stringing him along. "If you don't come out, I'm gonna shoot the lock off the door."

"I w-wouldn't do that if I were you."

"Why not?"

"Everyone'll hear the noise. Somebody'll call the cops."

His laugh was menacing, "I've got a silencer on this gun. Nobody'll hear a thing."

How much longer could she stall him she wondered? Any moment now, and he could be inside.

She walked to the front of the coach and pressed the center of the steering wheel. The horn did not sound.

"Damn," she muttered to herself.

"Is that guy in there your boyfriend?" he asked, lighting another cigarette, and then puffing smoke through the screen.

"Yeah, you're my boyfriend . . . aren't you, Chip?" said Miriam directing her voice away from the window, hoping to convince the man that Howard was still inside.

There was a long pause. Miriam noticed the man trying to peer in.

"Why didn't he answer?"

"He's gone back to sleep, that's why."

"Then get him out of bed. Now!"

"But—"

"Stop playing games with me, bitch."

"You'll have to gimme a few minutes," she said, stalling for time. "He's got narcolepsy."

"What the fuck's that?"

"It's a condition. He goes into a d-deep sleep. I have trouble w-wakin' him."

"I don't give a damn what he's got. You tell him to get his chicken-shit ass out here right now, or I'm coming in."

"I will, I w-will," said Miriam.

She walked to the back of the RV, then spoke in a loud voice, "Chip, wake up. There's a man out here. Says he w-wants to see you."

Moments later, the man's anger boiled over. He smashed the window in the RV's door. A fist-sized rock thudded onto the linoleum floor.

Miriam rushed forward as the man stuck his right forearm through the jagged opening.

His fingers groped blindly for the release latch.

She brought a steak knife down with full force, burying it to the hilt in the man's arm.

"Cunt," he screamed, thrusting his other arm inside and fumbling to unlock the deadbolt.

Miriam rushed to the galley for another knife.

She yanked open the top drawer, and spilled cutlery to the floor. Her hands were shaking uncontrollably.

There was a slight delay, then a click. He had unlocked the door.

Suddenly the RV shook from a heavy impact.

The man's face slammed forward onto a triangle of broken glass on the window frame. Blood sprayed over her, and then he disappeared from sight.

She heard the sounds of men struggling and feet thrashing on gravel.

"Help me, Miriam," shouted Howard. "Quick!"

She opened the blood-spattered door.

At the base of the RV's steps, Howard had the man pinned face down against the ground. Even with the knife blade protruding from his right arm, he was fighting furiously and thrusting his left arm under the RV, groping for the weapon.

"Stop him," yelled Howard. "He's trying to reach his gun."

Miriam stomped her foot onto the knife handle in the man's forearm. He screamed and withdrew his left hand to clutch at his wound. She scrambled under the motor home and grabbed the pistol.

"Where the hell are the c-cops?" said Miriam, her hands shaking violently as she looked at the expanding pool of blood.

"I . . . called them," gasped Howard, in breathless bursts. "The dispatcher . . . said they'd be a few minutes . . . getting here."

"Where'd you go after you called 'em?" she asked. "I c-couldn't see you."

"Behind . . . that tree," said Howard, nodding toward a large oak at the edge of their site. "I . . . waited for my chance to rush him. Soon as he started trying to break in . . . I rammed his head into the door."

"Lemme go, you fuck!" screamed the man.

"Speakin' o' cops," said Miriam, turning at the sound of sirens.

"Get my flashlight . . . wave them over," said Howard, wrestling with the man who was desperately struggling to break free.

"W-where is it?"

"Shelf . . . inside the door."

Two police cruisers, light bars flashing, raced into the park. At the sight of the waving flashlight, they raced around the campground loop until they reached the motor home. Both officers exited their vehicles in combat stance with guns drawn. They approached cautiously, eyeing the pistol in Miriam's hand.

"That your weapon, ma'am?" asked the sergeant.

"No," she replied, pointing at the bloodied man. "It was his . . . t-till I took it f-from him."

Howard hung on tightly while the officers handcuffed and manacled their bloodied suspect.

"Car five to dispatch, over," said the sergeant into his portable radio.

"Go ahead, five."

"We're ten twenty-three here. Scene is secure. We got a white male in custody. Request you send an EMS unit."

"Ten four."

"Loosen the cuffs," pleaded the man. "They're cutting into my wrists."

The sergeant checked the man's wrists, but did not comply.

"Cocksucker," he screamed, spittle flying from his mouth. "I'll sue your ass for police brutality."

"Get the first aid kit," he said to the rookie, "and rubber gloves."

Both officers, equipped with safety glasses and latex gloves, knelt over the suspect. They applied a ring bandage around the knife wound and a pressure bandage to the deep gashes on the man's forehead. All the while the suspect howled obscenities and spat blood at both officers.

The sergeant dug into the suspect's pockets and produced a wallet. He flipped through glassine folders until he found a driver's license.

"Are you, Brant Wilson?" asked the officer.

"Eat shit," snapped the suspect.

The officer keyed his microphone, "Car five to dispatch, over."

"Go ahead, five."

"I'd like a ten twenty-nine on a Brant David Wilson, 1654 McAllister Road, apartment 204 in Topeka, Kansas. DOB 14 March 1974."

"Ten four on that. Standby."

"It's over now," said Howard, comforting Miriam who was shaking uncontrollably and crying.

"I can't believe t-this is happenin'," she replied. "I feel like I'm g-gonna be sick."

"Sit down," said Howard, steering her to the picnic table. "I'll be right back."

He entered the RV and returned moments later with his bathrobe and a facecloth; he wrapped her against the night air and sponged her face.

"Thanks. You know w-what I could to with right now?"

"What?"

"A smoke. I'm dyin' for a cigarette."

"Check the left pocket," said Howard.

"You're a mind reader," she said, pulling her package and lighter from his robe. "I really sh-should quit this you know. Go back to chewin' gum."

She lit a cigarette with shaking hands and took several deep drags. Howard sat on the bench with his arm around her.

"Look at the mess o' you," said Miriam, pointing at the blood. "You look more like, Colonel Ketchup than, Chip Munro."

Howard laughed.

"If it wasn't for you," she said, "there's no tellin' what would've happened. And you know what's even scarier?"

"What?"

"That creep might've picked me up when I was hitchhikin'."

Drawn by the sound of police radios and flashing strobe lights, campers began to arrive from distant sites, dressed in their nightclothes. They kept well back and talked among themselves as they watched the action. In the distance, the electronic wail of an approaching ambulance cut the night air.

The younger cop was taking statements from Howard and Miriam as the ambulance entered the campground.

"Dispatch to car five," crackled the radio.

"Go ahead," replied the officer.

"Your subject, Brant David Wilson, has prior convictions in Kansas for B & E, home invasions involving rape and assault, auto theft, and credit card fraud. There's an outstanding arrest warrant for him in connection with an armed robbery and homicide at a Seven Eleven in Amarillo, Texas."

"Ten four, out," said the sergeant.

"Holy George," said Miriam, bringing a hand over her mouth. "Did you hear that? He's actually killed s-someone. I might've . . . *we* might've been next."

After ensuring their suspect was strapped tightly to the gurney, the sergeant assigned the younger officer to accompany the paramedics to the hospital. He walked over to Howard and Miriam seated at the picnic table.

"You folks're lucky," he said. "That guy's a nasty piece of work."

"Guess he'll be spendin' a lot o' time in jail huh?" said Miriam.

"Worse than that, ma'am."

"Really?"

"Soon as he's fixed up, he'll be transferred to Amarillo to face charges."

"What'll happen if he's convicted?" asked Howard.

"Lethal injection most likely," replied the officer. "Texas has the death penalty."

# CHAPTER 13

## *The Midwest*

WITH THEIR FRIGHTENING ENCOUNTER miles behind them, they entered the bucolic spaciousness of the Midwest. It was an infinite land under an oceanic firmament of cerulean blue. A convoy of cumulus cloud ships—catboats and clippers, schooners and sloops—ghosted silently across its vast expanse and cast rippling, gray shadows that marked their passage over patchwork-quilted fields. Its immense acreage produced abundant cash crops and sustained huge herds of livestock, but it was not always so.

Before the arrival of the white man, it had been virgin grassland, part of the million-and-a-half-square-mile swath of open land sandwiched between the Rocky Mountains and the Mississippi River, populated by the many nomadic hunting tribes including the Comanche, the first to obtain horses from the Spaniards. It was a land of colossal dimensions, an undulating savannah over two hundred times the size of Africa's Serengeti Plain.

It began in the Canadian provinces of Manitoba, Saskatchewan, and Alberta, and swept southward into Texas and to the banks of the Rio Grande. The types of grass that grew upon it were determined by the amount of precipitation that fell. In the rain-shadow of the Rockies it was short grass prairie, a mix of blue grama and buffalo grass. In the wetter, eastern portion nearer the Mississippi River, the grasses were as high as a saddle horn: Indian grass, bluestem, switch grass and coneflowers. And in the center of the plains, was a mix of grasses—a region, that, once cultivated, would become the wheat belt.

It was Government grants that enticed the first farmers, among them, easterners of sturdy stock and strong faiths: Congregationalists and Quakers, Dutch Reformists and Ulster-Scots Presbyterians, hardworking souls, sturdy of back and stanch of will, determined to realize their dream of land ownership.

After braving the bone-jarring, cross-country journey from the east in horse-drawn wagons, they arrived at their destination, a vast and largely treeless expanse that offered scant resources to build a home. But they were resolute people, determined to triumph over any hardship. They cut rectangles of prairie sod and piled them row-on-row to make dwellings—insect-ridden, damp hovels that would shelter them from the fierce elements of the prairie. With their homes built, they set about tilling the soil.

But the soil, with its tough, deep-rooted grasses, obstinately resisted both hoe and plough. After a rain, it produced sticky, gumbo-like mud that caked onto, and quickly destroyed the early wooden ploughs. That changed when an Illinois blacksmith, John Deere, developed the steel moldboard plough, "the plough that broke the plains." It may have broken the plains, but it did not tame them. There were other trials to endure, each one heartbreaking and soul-crushing for those who had cast their lot with the land.

Families toiled through the growing season to produce a bounty, only to have it stolen from them before they could harvest it. On windless days under the sweltering prairie sun, when clouds loitered motionless in the sky, one cloud, independent of the atmosphere, moved over the crops. It was surreal as it advanced, shimmering diaphanously like a curtain of snowflakes. But it was an evil thing, a rasping, demonic thing that blotted out the sun and descended on the prairie with the apocalyptic wrath of a biblical plague: "*. . . and the sound of their wings was as the sound of chariots of many horses running to battle . . .*"

Locusts—trillions of them—advanced like a rampaging army, insatiable legions of tiny mandibles gobbling everything in their path with astonishing speed and efficiency. One by one, vanquished fields of crops fell before them, the foliage of each plant consumed within seconds. In a ravenous frenzy, they attacked fence posts and rake handles, curtains and clothing. When people tried to salvage what crops they could by covering them, the locusts devoured the blankets. Families, helpless to stop the hordes of insects, wept as they watched a malevolent, living scythe consume the fruits of their labors and drive them to the brink of starvation.

And there were prairie fires, roaring infernos of such intensity, that they created their own cyclonic winds as they scorched every combustible thing to charred and smoldering ash. Billowing clouds of choking smoke could be seen for miles as the leaping flames advanced, cremating terrorized farm animals and wildlife alike. And with their houses gone and their cattle gone, families were rendered homeless and destitute.

In summer, great atmospheric systems produced anvil-topped thunderheads that loomed ominously over the farms. The immense energy within them spawned tornadoes that tore swaths across the landscape, ripping buildings apart as if made of paper, scattering boards and shingles and household furnishings. They spawned hail of such size and quantity that livestock were battered to death in the fields, and men were pummeled mercilessly until they reached safe refuge under their wagons.

In winter, howling blizzards reduced visibility to zero. Mere feet away from the sanctuary of barns and the warm hearths of prairie homes, people died: their extremities frozen solid, their eyelids iced shut, their tracheas and lungs clogged by snow of flour-like consistency. In the infamous blizzard of January, 1888, rapidly plummeting temperatures and ferocious, wind-chilled air froze cattle to death where they stood, and killed scores of children, groping blindly through the white fury. Those who did survive were maimed for life after their frostbitten, gangrenous limbs had to be amputated.

But for all the vagaries of its weather, and all the sundry hardships it could mete out, it was, in the best of times, a fruited plain of such scale that it dwarfed everything that rested upon it: the farms and barns that hunkered behind sturdy tree breaks; the silver-domed silos and feed elevators that glinted brightly in the sun; and the pencil-thin roads that threaded their way across the great, agricultural tapestry toward distant hamlets and towns.

As they drove west, Howard concentrated on his driving while Miriam gazed at the large farms that flew past the window. At one point, a service road paralleled the highway. On it, a lone pickup kept pace with the motor home. At the wheel was a middle-aged man in bib overalls and a John Deere cap perched atop a shock of thick, gray hair. He drove in a casual manner, one hand resting on the top of the steering wheel, the other dangling limply out the window. When he glanced over, Miriam waved. The man smiled and waved back, then angled off toward a group of farm buildings.

"Town coming up," said Howard, glancing at his fuel gauge. "Better stop for gas."

He took an off-ramp, stopped at the rural secondary road, then turned toward the main part of town, busy with traffic. On the outskirts, he noticed an unmanned vegetable stand and a crude sign: "Payment on the honor system—make your own change." Howard passed a high school, then a New Holland farm equipment dealership. Parked vehicles, mostly pickups of assorted vintage, lined both shoulders. People were crossing the road toward a massive yard sale that was in full swing. Long, folding tables, the kind used in church basements, were set out on the lawns and driveways of three properties. Trees were decorated in red, white, and blue bunting. Every imaginable article was on display, from furniture to farm implements, salad bowls to sports equipment. A hopeful-looking boy about ten-years-old was examining a bicycle with high handlebars and a banana seat while two men were loading a set of kitchen chairs and a harvest table into the bed of a pickup.

When Howard reached the gas station, he had to wait for the driver of a small car to pay up before swinging the large motor home beside the pumps. A balding, overweight man wearing greasy mechanics coveralls walked to the driver's side of the RV.

"Premium or regular?"

"Regular," said Howard, turning off the ignition.

The man inserted the nozzle into the fill pipe, clicked the holding tab, then picked up a long-handled squeegee and began scrubbing dead bugs from the windshield.

"Check your oil?"

"Please."

He searched for a moment, found the release mechanism, then lifted the engine hood and drew out the long dipstick.

"You're down a quart, maybe two. Want me to top you up?"

"If you would, please," said Howard with a smile.

The mechanic lifted two plastic jugs from the oil rack and emptied them into a wide-mouthed funnel. He took Howard's credit card and went into the small office to process the sale.

"Parade comin'," said Miriam, pointing to the road ahead of them.

Approaching them was a uniformed high school band, marching two abreast down the southbound lane. At the head of the parade a young man carried a large baton, alternately slapping it against his chest. Behind him, a long line of musicians marched to the beat of snare drums. When the band neared the gas station, it swung onto the grounds of the community center.

"What's the occasion?" Howard asked the mechanic as he signed the credit card receipt.

"Charlie Davis is home from Iraq."

"Local guy?"

"Local hero," said the man, tearing off the customer copy of the gas receipt. "US Marine Corps, wounded in action. We're raising money for him today."

The man tucked the merchant's copy in his plastic clipboard.

"Say, are you folks in a hurry?"

"No," said Howard, looking at Miriam.

"Why don't you hang around for a spell and enjoy the festivities."

"Where can I park this?"

"Behind the station. Plenty of room back there."

"Would you have time to do a small repair for me?" asked Howard.

"How small?" asked the mechanic.

"My horn's not working."

"And you got a broken window as well," said the man, looking at the plastic film taped over the broken glass in the motor home's door.

"Any chance you could fix both while we're across the road?"

"Horn's easy; I can cannibalize one off an old Chevy Suburban I've got out back."

"What about the window?"

"Got no glass suitable for that," he said, lifting the brim of his cap and scratching his scalp. "But if you don't mind Plexiglas, I can make one up."

"That'd be great," said Howard.

As Miriam and Howard crossed the highway, they dodged large numbers of arriving vehicles, packed with occupants of all ages. Teenagers wearing orange safety vests were directing people to parking spaces on an adjacent field where the grass had been mowed and stakes set out to create rows. Members of the local Lion's club were selling raffle tickets on a red Chevrolet Corvette convertible donated by a GM dealership. The

Masons and Shriners—bedecked in their ceremonial aprons and fezzes were out in full force, some working barbeque grills, others taking people for rides in elaborately decorated golf carts. Volunteer firefighters were selling T-shirts and baseball caps and operating a face-painting booth for kids. It was clearly a community effort and the mood was upbeat and neighborly. Small groups gathered informally to chat and gossip. Howard and Miriam caught snippets of conversation as they mingled with the crowd. Two men, one chubby, the other, a string bean, were kibitzing.

"Hey bubba," said the thin man, dressed in baggy shorts and a wife beater. "I seen you paintin' that ol' tool shed o' yours yesterday."

"Oh yeah?"

"There was more paint on your britches than the gall-darned shed."

"Just doin' my civic duty, Randy," said the large man. "Tryin' to improve the neighborhood."

"It'll take more 'n a coat o' paint to do that. Hell, even the mice wouldn't move into it last winter."

"Think they would if I was to put a new roof on it?"

"Face it, bubba, that thing's beyond hope. You cain't make chicken soup out o' chicken shit."

Both men burst out laughing. Just then, a shapely, middle-aged woman approached. She stopped and placed both hands on her hips, then made bug-eyes at the thin man's skinny legs.

"Gee, Randy, I never seen you in shorts before. Are they your legs, or are you riding a rooster?"

When the second wave of laughter ended, the man got his own back.

"Well," he retorted, winking at his buddy, "least I'm not absent-minded like Carol here. I seen her running around in a fit with a tampon behind her ear. Couldn't figure out where she'd put her pencil."

The woman swatted the skinny man's ear good naturedly and moved on.

Howard bought hot dogs and drinks, and then walked with Miriam to the bleachers that were filling quickly. They had just taken their seats when he spilled mustard down the front of his shirt. She tried to wipe it away, but the napkin only spread the yellow stain. He said nothing, but was silently pleased; he enjoyed the fuss she made over him. It was a small intimacy, yet one he was comfortable with.

As they ate, two farmers dressed in peaked caps, coveralls, and rubber boots approached the bleachers; they took the bench in front of them.

Both appeared to be in their early sixties; one was six-feet tall, the other was short and walked with a limp. They were men of the soil, their bodies lean and sinewy from hard work, their skin inked a dark bronze from long days under prairie sun. They swapped local gossip for a few minutes before the conversation turned to farming.

"Say, Merle," said the tall man. "You gonna hire some help this summer?"

"I expect so," said the shorter man, working a toothpick between his teeth.

"Same kid as last year?"

"You mean that university student?"

"Yep."

"Hell no. I wouldn't hire him again—not as long as your asshole points to the ground."

"Why not?"

"Wilbur, that boy's as useless as tits on a tomcat. I thought he knew a thing or two 'bout farmin'—turned out he didn't know shit from shoe polish. He's a talker, not a doer. Shoulda looked at his hands b'fore I hired him. They was just as smooth as a baby's bum. Never done a lick of manual work in his *en*tire sorry-ass life. All he did was jabber on about book learnin' and diplomas and whatnot. I got sick to death of listenin' to his mathematical gobbledygook, like pie are square or some such crap. Hell, anyone with half a brain knows that cakes are square, not pies. Pies are round."

"You know something, Merle?"

"What?"

"You and me is gonna be plowing fields till the day they bury us. That boy'll have the world by the short hairs, just 'cause he's got a couple of degrees hanging on his office wall."

"Yeah, you're probably right," said the short man, sucking his teeth. "And I'll tell you what they'll be—a B.S., Ph.D—bull shit piled higher and deeper."

The venue was now filled. A man stepped forward to test the microphone. The high school band assembled on the field, and gowned members of a church group filed onto the stage. Minutes later, a black van equipped with a handicapped lift drove onto the grounds.

A low murmur ran through the bleachers. People craned their necks to see. The vehicle stopped, and after a slight delay, the sliding door opened. A uniformed man in a wheelchair was assisted to the ground by a hydraulic lift. Everyone in the bleachers cheered wildly for the man who had lost both legs below the knees. At his side, were his pretty wife and two-year-old son. The moment the man's wheelchair touched the field, he gave a sharp military salute to the cheers and whistles of the crowd.

Howard was deeply moved by the sight of the young man's war wounds—a lesser-seen facet of the ugliness of warfare. The evening news most often showed the flag-draped caskets of the dead returning from foreign wars—a terrible enough price to be paid. But it seldom showed the vast numbers of the wounded: the amputees, the paraplegics, the burn victims, the blind, or the men with invisible injuries, their psyches traumatized for life by having been witness to the bloody carnage of the battlefield—men who for years afterward, would be spooked by a sudden noise, like the crash of a falling object or the sound of a car horn.

"Ladies and gentlemen," said a man at the microphone. "Would you please welcome one of our own, Sergeant Charles Edwin Davis, United States Marine Corps."

When the long applause ended, the band played the intro and the choir's collective voice carried across the hushed field: ". . . O beautiful for heroes proved, in liberating strife, who more than self their country loved, and mercy more than life! America, America . . ."

Everywhere, people stood with their hand over their heart until the anthem ended. The master of ceremonies kept the pace moving and the mood upbeat.

"Your hometown's come out for you today, Charlie, and the band's got a surprise they've been planning for weeks. Take it away," he said with a wave of his hand.

The band broke into a medley of Gershwin and Cole Porter tunes. When it was over, the musicians got into the center of the field. While they played the melody and performed formation marching, the church choir sang the stirring lyrics of the Marine Corps Hymn.

When the performance ended, the crowd mingled. Townspeople formed a moving reception line and walked past Sergeant Davis to shake his hand. Howard handed a donation to one of the event organizers, then escorted Miriam through the large gathering and headed back towards the RV.

They were about to cross the highway when a voice called out, "Howard?"

He turned to see a tanned and fit young man coming toward him. He had the look of success: finely tailored slacks, expensive polo shirt, diamond-encrusted Rolex, designer sunglasses, and alligator loafers.

"I thought I recognized you, professor."

"Small world," said Howard, looking shocked to see Dave Morell, one of his less-than-favorite former students. "Are you living out here now?"

"God no," said the young man, reaching out to shake his mentor's hand. "I'm not the hayseed type."

"What brings you here, then?"

"My parents knew the Davis family, though I'm not sure how. They weren't able to make it for this. Asked me to come on their behalf."

"Looks like life's treating you well," said Howard, changing the subject. "What are you doing these days?"

"For business or pleasure?"

"Both."

"I'm an international marketing consultant," he said, inflating with self-importance. "Got my own firm, a BMW and a villa in Spain." He pulled out an embossed business card and handed it to Howard.

He glanced at it briefly, and then returned it. "What about the pleasure part?"

"I'm into diving."

"Into water or women's panties?" asked Howard, recalling the young man's shameless womanizing.

"Both. I'm a confirmed bachelor though. Too wily to get dragged to the altar." He turned and winked at Miriam who gave him an icy stare. "Besides," he added, "I'm not going to risk my seven-figure salary. No chick is getting her hands on that in divorce court."

"That's what pre-nups are for," said Howard appraising him for a reaction.

The young man ignored his remark.

"By the way, what are you doing in Butt Crack Corners?"

"Just passing through."

"Vacation?" he asked, casting a sideways glance at Miriam.

"No. I quit St. Martin's."

"You *what?*" said the young man, incredulous. "You gave up your tenure?"

"Yes."

"But, you had it made in the shade. I mean—"

121

"Suzanne died. I couldn't stay in Toledo anymore. Too many memories."

"When did this happen?"

"A year ago."

"How?"

"She drowned while we were on vacation."

"Sorry for your loss."

Howard cringed inwardly at the hackneyed platitude.

"Was it a boating accident?"

"You said you worked internationally," said Howard, anxious to steer the conversation away from Suzanne's death. "I guess you travel a lot, huh?"

"Yeah. Paris, London, Sydney, Dubai, and—"

"Dubai?" said Howard, suddenly jolted by old memories.

"You know someone there?"

"I used to, a long time ago. Back when I had hair," he said, laughing uncomfortably and rubbing the thin spot on his scalp.

"You said you were passing through. Where to?"

"San Diego. Got a new job waiting for me at a high school."

"That's quite a step down in the world isn't it? From classy St. Martin's to a lowly high school? Guess you'll be teaching wetbacks now. Will they be paying you in pesos or tortillas?" he said and laughed derisively.

Howard was stung by the man's remarks, but did not let it show.

"It's what I need, Dave. At least for now. After that, we'll see."

Howard caught the look on Miriam's face; she was fuming at the man's put down.

"Who's the little lady here?" he asked Howard, his tone condescending and judgmental, as if he thought his old professor had shacked up with a young tart, too soon after the death of his wife.

"Oh, sorry," said Howard, "I should've introduced her earlier. This is Miriam Kovacs, a friend of mine from way back. I'm dropping her off in Malibu . . . to visit her mother."

The smirk on the man's face conveyed his skepticism at Howard's explanation. Then he consulted his Rolex.

"Well, would you look at the time," he said. "Gotta run. Do some schmoozing and cruising. Good seeing you again, Howard. All the best with your new job."

Miriam watched Howard stare after his former student as he disappeared into the crowd.

"Did you ever think he'd be that successful when you taught him in college?" asked Miriam.

"Never doubted it for a minute."

"Really?"

Howard sighed, "When you've got parents like his, there's no way you can fail."

"What'd they do? Bribe the college to give him a passin' grade?"

"Oh, no," said Howard. "Nothing like that. He got through the academic part on his own, although not with outstanding grades."

"Was he a spoiled rich brat?"

"Completely. Never had to work for his tuition, or anything else in life, for that matter. Had everything handed to him on a silver platter. I'll bet his folks even bankrolled him after college. Set him up in the company he says he owns."

"Still and all, it must be nice, havin' parents like that."

"Not in his case."

"How come?"

"David's parents are nine tenths of his problem. Whenever he got into trouble they bailed him out, instead of forcing him to take his lumps. He's a walking testimonial to bad parenting."

"Were his parents rich?"

"I don't know about rich . . . more like comfortably well off. They're the ones who gave him his value system, warped as it is. To David, status symbols are everything. They're his testicles. Without them he's a eunuch, at least in his mind."

"But he looks so confident and self-assured."

"Maybe outwardly he does."

"You think it's all an act, then?"

"Yes. He laughs and flips things off like they don't bother him. But behind the cardboard façade is a painfully insecure man. Sad really."

"Tell you what I think," said Miriam.

"What's that?"

"I think he's an arrogant douche bag. He had no call to make a hurtful remark like that 'bout your new job and all. I hope he gets the clap and his pecker falls off."

Howard laughed at her remark as he checked both ways for traffic. Instinctively, he grabbed Miriam's hand and held it tightly as they ran across the busy highway.

"I might be a lowly English teacher," he said, still laughing when they reached the opposite shoulder of the road, "but you, Miriam Kovacs, are a poet."

As the traffic filed past, Howard realized he still had hold of her. She looked at their joined hands, then into his eyes.

"Sorry," he said self-consciously, quickly letting go.

"Don't be. No one's held my hand crossin' a road since I was a little girl. It was nice . . . *real* nice."

Howard stopped by the garage to pay the mechanic. The man made out a receipt, then traded small talk for a few minutes.

"If I were you," said the mechanic, "I'd have a tune up done on that motor home. The sooner the better."

"Anything serious?" asked Howard.

"Your rad hoses and fan belts look a mite tired. You'll get a bit more mileage out of them, but I wouldn't leave it too long."

"Thanks for the advice," said Howard, then he glanced at his watch. "Say, do you know where the nearest campground is? Time's getting on and I'd like to get us settled in."

"You're in luck. We got a municipal park nearby."

"How do I get there?"

"Keep to the main drag," he said, pointing up the road in front of the garage. "You'll see the sign at the far end of town. If you cross the railroad tracks, you've gone too far."

"Thanks," said Howard, "and by the way, we enjoyed the tribute ceremony. Very touching."

"I thought you'd like it," said the man, then changed the subject. "Where you folks headed?"

"California," replied Miriam.

"Have a safe trip," he said, then returned to the garage bay to service a vehicle on the hoist.

Howard started the motor home and grasped the gear shift lever. Miriam reached over and squeezed his arm.

"Chip?"

"Yes?"

"Thank you."

"For what?"

"For introducin' me as your friend, and not some raggedy-assed hitchhiker you picked up. That guy was lookin' at me like I was low-rent trash."

"Oh, don't pay any mind to David. That boy's got a lot of growing up to do. You're twice the person he is."

"That's sweet o' you to say, but I'll never be as successful as he is, with his fancy clothes and all."

"Like I said, don't be fooled by what you see on the outside. David's all show and no substance."

Progress was slow as Howard made his way along Main Street, but it gave him a chance to observe the town and its inhabitants.

The grid was as simple as a rose trellis. Three streets, including Main, ran the length of the town. All avenues that crossed at right angles were given the names of trees or birds. The utility poles were decorated with hanging flower baskets and small American flags, and the fire hydrants were hand painted in patriotic themes.

He noticed how often drivers waved to each other or to people on the sidewalks, and how courteously they stopped to let someone in or out of a parking space. In front of the post office, an elderly woman, her arms full of mail, stooped to admire a young woman's baby in a carriage. On the sidewalk in front of city hall, two boys with skateboards were jumping over imaginary obstacles, trying to impress a girl with their fancy footwork. There was a Norman Rockwell quality about the place, a laid back community full of honest souls, tucked away in the heartland and stalled in another era: where people did not lock their doors and where a man's word and handshake were all it took to close a deal.

At the edge of town, the sign for the RV park peeked from under the wispy branches of a weeping willow. On the door frame of the campground office was a buzzer and a small notice, "Ring For Service." Miriam pushed the button. While they waited, Howard glanced at a poem on a wooden sign.

> Who hath smelt wood smoke at twilight?
> Who hath heard the birch log burning?
> Who is quick to read the noises of the night?
> Let him follow with the others,
> for the Young Men's feet are turning
> to the camps of proven desire and known delight.

They turned at the sound of a screen door slamming. A tall, elderly man set out slowly across the gravel path that linked the owner's residence to the office.

"Door's open," he said as he climbed the two steps to the porch. "Go on inside."

A color-coded map on the wall showed all the campsites: pull-throughs, back-ins, water and electrics, full hookups, and un-serviced ones for tents. Occupied sites were marked with round tags hung on nails.

"I see you're almost full," said Howard, looking at the tags. "We'll need a site with full hookups."

"Fish hooks?" said the man with a confused look. "Don't sell 'em. Bait and tackle shop does though."

"No, no," said Howard, "I want a site."

"Not many sights to see 'round here."

"No, you don't understand. I need a campsite for that motor home out there."

"Say what?" said the man, cupping both hands to his ears. "I'm hard o' hearin', mister."

Howard picked up a pen from the counter and wrote his request on the back of a registration card, then held it up for the man to read.

"Why didn't you say so," said the man, indignant and embarrassed. He turned and pointed at the map. "You'll be needin' a pull-through for a rig that size. "Got two left. This one's next to the washrooms. That one's by a creek. Which do you want?"

"The one by the creek," replied Howard, putting his credit card on the counter and filling out the registration form.

The owner gave him a card to hang in the RV's window, then pointed to a shed beside the office. "We don't charge for firewood. Help yourself."

"Thanks," said Howard, then added, "I like your campground. You have lots of trees here."

"Cheese? Don't sell it. Grocery store does, though. It's back in town past the post office."

"It's OK," replied Howard, afraid to look at Miriam who was stifling a laugh. "I'll pick it up in the morning."

Before leaving the office, a wire rack of tri-fold brochures caught Howard's eye. He lifted one out and opened it. Written across the bottom were the words, "By Appointment Only."

"Hey, this looks like fun," he said, showing her the advertisement. "What do you think?"

Her face lit up, until she noticed the price. "It's expensive."

"Never mind," he said. "Would you like to do that tomorrow?"

"Well . . . yeah," she replied, surprised. "It'd be wonderful . . . great."

# CHAPTER 14

## *Dawn Ascent*

WHILE MIRIAM STUFFED THEIR sweaters and windbreakers into backpacks, Howard consulted the map on the company's brochure, then disconnected the jeep from the motor home. After a ten-minute drive on backcountry roads, they came to a sign and a gravel driveway that opened into a large field. At the edge of the property, a metal building topped by a bank of floodlights and an anemometer faced the rising sun. Minutes later, vehicles approached: a pickup towing a double-axel utility trailer, and a large window van; both bore the company's logo and name: *Burnett's Balloon Adventures.* A tall, graying man in his early sixties exited the pickup and made the introductions.

"Morning," he said, extending his hand. "I'm Rob Burnett and this is my crew."

"We've never been up in a balloon before," said Howard.

"Did you bring a camera?"

Howard tapped the pocket of his windbreaker. "How long will we be up there?"

"That depends," said Burnett, "but most times we manage an hour, a bit more if we're lucky."

"What about the landin'?" asked Miriam. "How do you know where to put us down?"

"Once I know the wind direction and speed, I can pretty much predict that." He turned to one of his crew, "Dwayne, how 'bout sending up a piball."

"What's that?" she asked as the man headed inside the building.

"A pilot balloon filled with helium."

The crewman released the white balloon, and then checked its direction with a hand compass. "A little north of due east," he said to his boss.

"Parnell's?" said Burnett.

"Looks that way," said the man, tipping the peak of his cap farther back on his head.

"There's coffee and doughnuts in the van. You folks help yourself while we set up."

One man opened the service building and turned on the powerful floodlights; a large section of the field lit up. After spreading out a giant groundsheet to protect the balloon, they connected the burner system to the wicker basket, and attached the balloon to the basket. Then, they started a gasoline-driven fan and began inflating the envelope. When enough air had been forced into the expanding envelope, one of the crew ignited the gas burner and directed the flame into the opening; the balloon began to take shape more quickly until it slowly lifted off the grass.

"How come that doesn't set fire to the balloon?" asked Miriam, nervously eyeing the nearness of fabric to flame.

"The skirt's fireproofed. Nothing to worry about."

When the balloon was fully inflated, a crew member tethered the basket to the vehicle.

"OK, folks," said a crew member. "Time to board."

Burnett climbed into the basket first, followed by Howard, then Miriam, who was assisted by the crew. At a nod from the pilot, the tether was released. When he opened the valve, a long tongue of flame roared into the rainbow-colored cavity. The basket did not move.

"Why aren't we liftin'?" she shouted over the roar of the burner.

"Takes about half a minute after I inject the flame," said the pilot, his hand still on the valve.

"Does this take a lot o' practice?"

"A fair bit."

"How long've you been doin' this?"

"Ten years."

His answer helped dispel her nervousness.

Except for the intermittent blasts of flame, the launch was gentle and silent—an out-of-body experience—a soul departing for the hereafter. They had barely risen above the field when they began to drift. The pilot fired the burner in long bursts; the ground crew grew smaller as the great balloon sailed upward and eastward.

The landscape looked different now, with irrigated crops standing out sharply against the drier prairie grasses. In the distance, tiny cars threaded country roads. School buses, their lights flashing, were already stopping at the end of rural driveways to pick up children. Trailing behind them on the ground below was the elongated shadow of the balloon and the tiny basket dangling from it. Miriam leaned over to look at a herd of grazing cattle. The pilot activated the burner, but this time the flame was weaker and the sound quieter.

"Somethin' wrong?" asked Miriam, alarmed by the abrupt change.

"Nope. I'm burning liquid propane instead of gas."

"How come?"

"Don't want to spook the livestock."

The longer the flight lasted, the more excited she became. As much as Howard was enjoying the flight, it was Miriam's unabashed enthusiasm and child-like sense of wonder that delighted him most. A grin never left her face as she waved and shouted to people on the ground and pointed out small features on the broad plain.

"Oh, Chip," she exclaimed, clapping her hands gleefully, "isn't this the most magical thing ever?" She closed her eyes and inhaled deeply, "Smell that cut hay. Air never smelled this sweet in Philly. And look at the leaves wigglin' on those trees. I've never looked down on a tree before. Everythin's so different from up here. So heavenly. So perfect. So orderly. We're seein' the world the way the birds see it, Chip. Seein' every little feature and detail."

"I'd say she's having fun," said Howard.

"Best of all," grinned the pilot, "she's not afraid to say so."

"It's *won*derful! Miriam continued. "This is the highest I've been since I climbed a tree when I was a girl. Funny, I was expectin' it to be windy up here, but I can't feel a breath."

"That's because you're drifting with the wind," said the pilot. "You only feel a breeze when you're standing still."

The pilot retrieved a bottle of chilled champagne from a plastic cooler, "Here comes the part that folks like most."

He popped the cork and a gush of foam shot out. Then he produced two glasses. He saw Miriam eye the bottle reluctantly, then glance at Howard.

"Something wrong?"

"Yeah," replied Miriam, then corrected herself awkwardly, "I mean, no . . . there isn't . . . the thing is . . . I shouldn't be having anythin' alcoholic. Do you have somethin' else?"

"Sure do," said the pilot. "I'll open you a pop, instead."

"It's . . . because I'm pregnant."

"Well, then," said the pilot, "all the more reason to celebrate. Here's to the happy couple and a healthy baby."

Miriam and Howard exchanged glances.

"Do you go to that balloon festival in Albuquerque?" Howard asked the pilot.

"Never miss it. You been there?"

"Twice."

"Take a ride next time," said the pilot. "Great views of the city and Sandia Peak."

"I've watched the mass ascensions, though," said Howard. "It's quite a sight. Six hundred balloons going up at the same time."

"My favorite is the balloon glow event at night," said Burnett.

Howard thought back to the times he and Suzanne had visited Albuquerque, one of their favorite places in the Southwest. They loved the adobe architecture and shopping in the boutiques tucked away on narrow streets and laneways in the historic Old Town section of the city, a ten-block area that fanned out from the central plaza. Over the years, they had shared many traveling experiences, but there were two things they had never done together: taken a balloon ride at the annual festival, or ridden the gondola to the summit of Sandia Mountain; Suzanne was only comfortable on terra firma.

Well into the flight, the pilot radioed to his ground crew. "OK, boys, I'm bringing her down."

"You're good to go," crackled a voice in the speaker.

The pilot pulled on a cord and opened the valve at the top of the envelope. Imperceptibly, the balloon began to sink towards the farmland. Burnett kept his eye on a property to the east as he pulled the cord at regular intervals.

"Is that the farm you're aiming for?" asked Howard, pointing.

The pilot nodded. "The Parnell's place. Sid runs the farm. Betty's our local vet. She's got a staff of five. They look after every critter for miles around."

The closer they came to the farm, the faster the land rose to meet them. Miriam leaned over the basket and watched as the ground crew drove the pickup and the van onto the Parnell property. Then, three men on foot chased the basket, trying to anticipate the moment of touchdown.

"Don't worry," said the pilot to Miriam, "I'll put this down gentle like," then added, "for mama and her baby."

Suddenly three sets of strong hands gripped the basket and held on.

"Bravo," she exclaimed, clapping her hands.

The crew helped Miriam and Howard exit the basket, then began deflating the balloon and pulling it onto the ground sheet.

"Burnett, you old rascal," shouted a voice from the nearby farmhouse. "If you keep dropping down on this property, I'm gonna have to start charging you landing fees."

The farmer, dressed in bib overalls, descended the porch steps and strode across the yard. A few steps behind him, a scrawny cat with a bobbed tail followed.

"Good to see you, Sid," said the pilot.

Moments later, the front door of the veterinary clinic opened. An attractive woman in her late fifties wearing a white lab coat appeared.

"Hey Rob," she shouted. "We've got no surgeries this morning. When you're done packing up, bring your passengers over for coffee."

Howard and Miriam wandered the grounds while they waited for the crew to complete their post-flight chores.

"Looks like a big operation," she said, pointing to a complex of metal-clad buildings.

Over the front entrance of the main building a sign read: Parnell's Veterinary Services. At the side, an unloading platform with a ramp led to a holding pen for large farm animals. A chestnut gelding plodded slowly toward the fence as they approached, its ears forward and relaxed. After resting his chin on the top rail, he chuffed, and swished his tail to dislodge flies. Miriam suddenly backed away. The horse reacted immediately.

"Are you nervous?" asked Howard.

"Yeah."

"He senses your fear."

"How?"

"By reading your body language," he said. "Horses are cautious. They spook easily."

"Why's that?"

"They're a prey animal. They see us as a potential threat."

"I don't get it," said Miriam. "They let people ride 'em. How does that work?"

"A horse has to be socialized in order to trust humans."

"Is that what horse whisperin' is?"

Howard nodded. "It's the new way. The old way was breaking a horse. Getting him to submit. It was traumatic for the animal."

"Have you been around horses before?" asked Miriam.

"I used to ride on a farm outside Toledo."

She reached up to touch the horse's face.

"Uh-uh," he said, grasping her arm. "Do this instead." He spoke softly and held out his hand, palm up and flat. "See how he sniffs."

"Yeah."

"This isn't threatening. It's a gentle introduction. When he's comfortable, reach out and stroke his neck and withers—then scratch him like this. See how he enjoys that?"

She nodded.

"Go ahead."

She mimicked Howard's slow movements and gentle manner. The horse responded well. "Think he'd take food from me?"

"Give him a minute to get at ease with you."

Howard picked a clump of fresh grass from outside the paddock and handed it to her. The gelding showed immediate interest. Howard took Miriam's hand and laid the grass in her upturned palm.

"Present it to him like that."

As Howard watched her feeding the horse, he recalled how he had done this with his daughters, Tina and Lynn. They were little then, eager to learn from their father. He thought on how quickly the years had flown by, and suddenly, he missed them.

"Coffee's on," shouted the vet.

They followed the balloon crew into the waiting area of the clinic. Betty Parnell introduced her staff and led everyone into the lounge; their voices and laughter triggered a round of barking from the kennels.

"Sounds like you've got a full house back there," said Howard, taking a doughnut from a box and lining up at the coffee machine.

"Four at the moment. Two boarding and two recovering from surgery. But not to worry, Nurse Bob is watching over them."

"You've got a male nurse?"

The assistant opened a door and Bob walked into the staff lounge. The scarred, gray cat was ugly, its ears split, and its tail—once long and willowy—amputated to the size of a human thumb.

"I get the feeling there's a story to go with him."

"Oh yes," said the vet, petting the cat that now rubbed itself affectionately against her leg. "He's been with us four years. Was close to death when we found him."

"Abused?"

"Terribly."

"Are those scars part of that?"

She nodded. "Far as we can tell, he was dragged behind a vehicle. We found a piece of binder twine still tied 'round his neck."

"He must've been one tough cat to have survived that. Where'd you find him?"

The vet pointed to one of her assistants, "Tammy discovered him on the shoulder of a back country road."

"I thought he was dead at first," said the young woman, taking a bite out of a doughnut, "till I saw him moving."

"It's a miracle he survived," said Miriam.

"He was badly dehydrated. We got fluids into him straight away."

"Did they catch the creep who did it?" Miriam asked.

"Never," said the woman, who then looked around the room, "but we have our suspicions, don't we girls?"

The veterinary assistants nodded and exchanged glances.

"Anyway, he's on the payroll now."

"Resident mouse catcher huh?" chuckled Howard.

"Much more than that," said the vet, reaching down to scratch the cat's back.

"Oh?"

"Bob's clairvoyant. We don't know where it comes from."

"Really?"

"Whenever we get a critically ill animal in here—one that's close to death—Bob knows. He'll stay beside its crate, or go into one of the stables with a sick horse and cuddle up to its face. He's just as devoted to an animal that's recovering from surgery. Bob'll stay with it till it's out of anesthetic. Won't leave a patient except to visit his litter box or to eat."

"That's incredible," said Howard.

"Oh, that's only a part of his talents. He'll stay with a pregnant female that's close to delivering. When she's ready to birth, he'll run out here, meowing like crazy."

The cat made the rounds, purring and enjoying the attention of everyone in the room. When he stopped at Miriam's feet, he brushed against her legs, and then jumped into her lap. She went to pet him, but he rubbed his face on her stomach, purring loudly. Staff members exchanged glances.

"Pardon me for being so personal," said Betty Parnell, "but . . . would you happen to be pregnant?"

"Yes," replied Miriam reluctantly, embarrassed at being the sudden center of attention.

"Bob's done that with every staff member here who's been pregnant."

"How does he know?"

"We haven't a clue. Anyway, my congratulations to you both. When's the blessed event?"

"Not for a while," replied Miriam, glancing sheepishly at Howard.

"First baby?"

"Yeah."

"What're you hoping for? Boy or girl?"

Miriam bit her lip and did not answer. She lifted the cat from her lap and placed him gently on the floor. When she looked up, every face was turned toward her. People waited for a reply or a look of joy from an expectant mother, but none came. Uncomfortable, the vet assistants glanced at their watches, then returned to work. The telephone rang, giving Betty Parnell her exit excuse.

Howard glanced at Miriam. She looked like a lost soul and would not return the eye contact. Instead, she fixed her gaze on her midriff. What, he wondered, was going through her mind? Was she still resolute about terminating her pregnancy? Or was she beginning to have second thoughts? It was hard to tell.

# CHAPTER 15

## *Heart to Heart*

AFTER DRIVING THROUGH KANSAS City, Missouri, they approached the bridge over the Missouri River; a blue signboard with a sunflower introduced its twin city in the neighboring state of Kansas.

As they drove west, the busy urban centers of eastern Kansas faded behind them, along with the hilly country and forests. The land gradually transitioned and became flatter and more featureless, like a vast expanse of unleavened bread. Evenly spaced rows of machine-planted crops ran out from both sides of the highway, ribs of living corduroy that shimmered as they passed. On the great, silo-studded farms, congregations of saffron-bonneted sunflowers genuflected under cathedral skies, all faces angled reverentially toward the life-giving sun.

"Chip?"

"Uh-huh," he replied, keeping his gaze fixed on the long ribbon of highway.

"Remember when you first said you'd take me on a vacation?"

"Yes."

"You said you and Suzanne had traveled a lot to places."

"What about it?"

"Well . . . I don't mean any offence or anythin', but . . . I'd like you to take me to different places . . . places you never took her. Would you be OK with that?"

He reacted angrily, snapping his head sideways and glaring at her. Why had she asked him that, he wondered? Was she not grateful? Did she not realize he was offering her an opportunity she would never have gotten otherwise? He had been planning to make side trips to New

Mexico, to drive Miriam around the Enchanted Circle and camp beside the Rio Grande at Questa. He remembered how he and Suzanne had sat near the edge of the gorge and watched the ravens riding the updrafts and doing barrel rolls along the rim. He wanted to show her red-rock country near Georgia O'Keefe's Ghost Ranch where searing sunsets tinged the sandstone with hues of gold and orange. Suzanne had always loved O'Keefe's paintings, especially those of el Pedernal, the artist's beloved mountain and final resting place. O'Keefe had once said: "It's my private mountain. God told me if I painted it enough, I could have it." Now, he could see the futility of suggesting places he wanted to see again, but this time through Miriam's eyes. They rode a long time in silence before she spoke.

"Sorry, Chip. I didn't mean to sound ungrateful."

"I know that. I guess I just wanted to share the places Suzanne and I had seen . . . that's all.

"But if we did that, you wouldn't be moving on with your life, would you?"

He sighed deeply, "I suppose you're right."

THEY PULLED into a rest stop and found a space in the parking area reserved for trucks and campers. Miriam stared at the broad landscape beyond the rest stop fence as they ate their lunch at a picnic table.

"Can you imagine," she said, brushing a wasp off her iced tea, "what it was like out here in the 1800s?"

"Must've been . . . an ordeal crossing this . . . in covered wagons," he replied between bites of his sandwich.

"I was thinkin' about the buffalo, actually. Fifty million, they say, before the white man came."

"That many, huh?" he replied, intrigued by her interest.

"Men used to gun 'em down from the trains for sport. No friggin' wonder the Indians hated us so much."

"I didn't know you liked history."

"Hey," laughed Miriam, putting a finger to her cheek, "this is more than just a pretty face you know!"

"What got you interested?"

"School, but I kept up my interest after I dropped out. Do you like history, Chip?"

"Yes. Suzanne and I had this tradition in our house. Before supper, we'd ask one of our girls to look up an historical figure in our encyclopedia, and then talk about the person at the table: their strengths and weaknesses, the role they played in history—that kind of thing."

"Cool."

"It was great fun and we all learned a lot."

"Was that a tradition you passed along from your own childhood?"

"No. My parents didn't do anything like that when I was a boy. They were both busy people, especially my father with his big medical practice."

"I've never asked you about your father. What'd he do for a livin'?"

"He was a doctor."

"Family doctor?"

"Specialist," said Howard, biting into an apple. "Orthopedic surgeon."

"What's that?"

"Bones, joints, muscles," he replied, as juice dripped off his chin.

"What was he like?" she asked, handing him a paper napkin.

He dabbed at his shirt, "You mean as a doctor?"

"Yeah."

"Dedicated. Pretty much what you'd expect a good doctor to be. A colleague of his told me he had a compassionate bedside manner. That surprised me."

"Why?"

"Dad was controlled with his emotions. Very pragmatic."

"What's that mean?"

"Practical. Results are what mattered most to him. He didn't put much stock in theories, unless there was proof."

"Was he a cold man?"

"No, just disciplined, and measured. People loved to get his opinion, because when he gave it, they could 'take it to the bank.' A buddy of mine buttonholed him once. Said he was thinking of going to med school. Dad asked him a lot of questions, and then suggested a career in corporate law."

"Did he change his mind?"

"Uh-huh. Today, Steve Corbett's one of the most successful corporate law attorneys in Ohio."

"What'd your dad do for fun?"

"Played chess mostly."

"Was he good?"

"Amazing. He could size up an opponent quickly, and then demolish him. Afterwards, he'd have that person's playing style committed to memory."

"Did you ever play him?"

"Yes."

"Beat him?"

"Couple times, but I know he let me win."

"What was he like with you?" she asked as they headed back to the motor home.

"I never doubted that he loved me," said Howard. "He just had an odd way of showing it."

"Such as?"

"If I made him proud, he'd give me a wink or a funny smirk."

"No hugs?"

"Uh-uh. He wasn't the affectionate type, but that was OK with me."

She looked him in the eyes, "I don't believe you."

Her abruptness startled him; he stared back, but said nothing.

"I mean it. You're tellin' me he was not affectionate, and you were *OK* with that?"

Still he did not respond.

"What about your mother?"

"What about her?"

"Was she a warm person? Loving?"

"In her own way."

"You must have felt lonely as a boy."

He nodded.

When she saw his pained expression, she let the matter drop.

"So, back to your father. What happened when you pissed him off?"

"Dad would slip me this subtle look," he said, imitating it for Miriam. "He'd give me that around a bunch of people without uttering a word. Nobody in the room would notice, but I'd get the message."

"What if it was just the two o' you?"

"He'd say something like, 'you disappoint me, Howard,' or, 'you can do better than that, son.'"

"That's it?"

"Yes."

"No yellin' or screamin'?"

"Didn't need to. He got his point across."

"What'd you do together?"

"You mean for fun?"

"Yeah. Father and son stuff."

"We went to a few baseball games . . . whenever he could drag himself away from his practice."

"You a fan o' the game?" asked Miriam.

"Yes."

"Hey, me too," she exclaimed, suddenly keen. "What's your favorite team?"

"Which league?"

"International."

"Toledo Mud Hens," he replied, sliding into the driver's seat and starting the engine.

"Got a Major League favorite?"

"Detroit Tigers. Guess you'd be a Phillies fan, right?"

"O' course, *and* I'm into World Series trivia as well."

"You're kidding."

"Try me."

"OK," said Howard. "What year was the first one played?"

"Boston Americans versus the Pittsburg Pirates in 1903. Best out o' nine. Boston took it five games to three."

"I thought it was always best-of-seven?"

"It has been except for that first game, and three others: 1919, '20, and '21."

"Was the series ever not held?"

"Twice. The boycott o' 1904 and the Major League strike in '94."

"Has it ever been won by a non-American club?"

"Toronto Blue Jays, two in a row. In '92 they beat the Atlanta Braves. The year after, they whipped the Phillies. Both times, they took the pennant in six."

"I've got a confession to make," said Howard, laughing.

"What's that?"

"You could've snowed me and I'd never have known the difference."

"Trust me," she said, grinning as she popped a square of bubble gum into her mouth. "You can 'take it to the bank.'"

"How'd you get into baseball trivia?"

"Talkin' the game with my dad, plus I'm real good with numbers."

"You mean with dates or mathematics?"

"Both."

"Really," said Howard. "I'm hopeless with math. I have to drop my pants to count to twenty-one."

She threw back her head and laughed heartily, "Never heard that one before."

"When you say you're good with math, do you mean doing figures in your head?"

"Yeah," she replied, blowing a large bubble and cracking it loudly. "Wanna call me on it?"

"Why do I have this feeling you're going to amaze me?"

"I'll try," she said, grinning. "Got a pocket calculator?"

"Top drawer of my night table."

"Here," she said, when she returned with it. "Fire away."

He started by giving her triple digit numbers. When she had done them without error, he increased to four digits; the result was the same whether adding or subtracting. Her answers always matched the calculator.

"You can go to five if you like," she said.

She was slower this time, but made only one error out of ten tries.

"That's amazing. Who taught you to do that?"

"Nobody," she replied, popping a bubble. It's just somethin' I do. Used to freak my teachers out."

"Didn't they encourage you to use that talent?"

"Uh-uh."

"How about percentages?"

"Oh sure," she said. "That's a snap."

He threw numbers and percentages at her and noticed that while making calculations in her head, she closed her eyes and touched her thumbs and fingers to the tops of both legs. Curious, he asked what she was doing.

"In my head I work the answer out in shortcuts. In blocks, like. And with my fingers and thumbs, I carry over numbers. It's a system I figured out. Works like this—"

"Don't' even try," he said, holding up his hand. "I'll take your word."

"Did you know numbers follow patterns?" she said, her eyes sparkling with enthusiasm.

"Really," said Howard, squeezing into the left lane for a short construction zone. He waited for the road to widen before continuing.

"What kind of patterns?"

"Take any number and multiply it by nine. The sum o' the digits in the product will always add up to nine."

"Always?"

"Every time."

"Show me."

She picked up the calculator, "If I punch in, say, 548 x 9, you get 4932." She held out the display screen. "Add 'em up."

"Eighteen," replied Howard. "One plus eight."

"Cool, huh?"

"Humor me," he said. "Try a bigger number."

"All right. Let's try 8953 x 9." She punched in the numbers, and held up the answer: 80,577.

"Twenty-seven," he replied, and laughed.

She smiled, and then blew a large bubble that popped and stuck to her nose.

Howard laughed as she picked the gum off her face. What an unlikely person to have such a skill, he thought. Here was an inner-city kid that had fallen through the cracks of a flawed education system—a girl probably written off as a hopeless case, something that might have caused her to drop out of school. If only she had been a student of his, back before St. Martin's when he had taught high school, he might have been able to help her.

"Ever heard of a repeatin' number?" asked Miriam, eager to draw his attention back.

"No."

"Punch in 142857," she said, handing the calculator back to him.

"OK," he said, pressing the calculator against the hub of the steering wheel, "now what?"

"Multiply it by two."

He punched in the multiplier and smiled at the result: 285714.

"See how the answer is a rearrangement of the original numbers?"

"Yes. That's amazing."

"It keeps doin' that till you hit seven Then it spits out six nines. After that, the pattern starts comin' apart somewhat, but you can still see it in the product."

The exercise broke an invisible barrier for Miriam. All her life, men had looked down on her, but now, she was able to impress a man whose education far exceeded hers. Howard's admiration made her feel that she was not some no account high school dropout. For the first time in years, she felt pride in herself.

"I got one more math thing for you," she said.

"Shoot."

"Bob says he'll pay you a hundred bucks an hour for a forty-hour week. Tom says he'll pay you one cent for the first hour, and then double it every hour till quittin' time on Friday. Who you gonna work for?"

Howard thought for a minute, "Tom."

"Good answer," she said, clapping her hands gleefully. "You'd be one o' the richest dudes in the world—a multi-billionaire."

"No kidding," he said, enjoying her enthusiasm. "That much huh?"

"Your calculator will max out. You'll end up havin' to figure out the last of it on paper."

He drove for a few more hours, and then pulled into a rest stop near Junction City, Kansas. While he made coffee, Miriam picked up his dog-eared Rand McNally Road Atlas.

"Think we could camp there tonight?" she said, putting a finger on the page. "We're not that far away."

"Abilene?" he said.

"Yeah."

"Suzanne and I passed by there once, but we never drove into town."

"Good," she said. "We'll both be seein' it for the first time."

"What's in Abilene?"

"History," she replied.

LATE IN the afternoon, he left the interstate. With Miriam calling out directions from his campground directory, he followed a series of secondary roads that led to a private park, miles off the highway.

It was a small place, no more than fifty sites, a well-kept oasis of trees in an otherwise open expanse of prairie. Pull-through sites were situated in the center, with back-ins arranged around the perimeter. All were perfectly level and graveled with timber edging to set them off from the neatly clipped grass. Howard parked the RV, and then walked with Miriam to the office.

The building was gray, board-and-batten with a flower box anchoring each lace-curtained window. On the covered porch, hanging

143

baskets overflowed with petunias. A small plastic sign read, "Wi-Fi for Campers."

An overhead bell tinkled as they entered. The store was well stocked with canned goods, cereals, bread, condiments, and hamburger buns, and an upright cooler full of dairy products and cold cuts. A wire stand held wooden plaques with pithy sayings:

"When did my wild oats turn to prunes and All-Bran?"

"Some days you're the dog—other days you're the hydrant."

A prim, matronly looking woman appeared, drab as day-old pudding. Howard smiled inwardly, thinking how much she went with the corny sayings.

"Can I help you, sir?"

"Yes," said Howard. "We'd like a site for that motor home out there."

"How long will you be staying with us?"

"Couple nights," he said, and then looked at Miriam. "That OK with you?"

"Yeah."

"Will you want a campfire?"

Howard turned to Miriam again who nodded enthusiastically.

"Yes. Do you have firewood for sale?"

"Five dollars a bundle, but you'll have to take a back-in site. We don't allow fires on the pull throughs."

"That's fine," said Howard, laying his credit card on the counter. "We'll take a back-in and five bundles."

"No charge for newspaper and kindling. They're in a box inside the wood shed. If you need light to see, the fixture has a pull string."

"Thanks," said Howard as he filled out the registration card.

"I have four other sites occupied right now. Would you like me to put you and your wife close to them, or would you prefer something more private?"

"On our own, if you don't mind," he replied, then added, "Thanks for asking. Most places don't."

Howard stopped to get wood on the way to their site. Miriam helped him detach the Jeep from the tow bar. Without any direction from him she hooked up the water, sewer, and electrical services.

While she made supper, he laid kindling and logs in the metal fire ring: the rusted rim of a truck wheel.

After supper they walked to the west end of the campground and sat on the fence to watch the sunset. Miriam fought the urge for a cigarette and instead, chomped noisily on a double wad of bubble gum. The cool air of late evening was sweet with the bouquet of the surrounding fields. Cloud fingers reached across the sky, forming a spectacular palette.

"That was beautiful," she said as they walked back to their site.

He set out two folding chairs, then stuck the wand of a butane lighter under the paper and lit it. When the flaming newspaper died down, the kindling still needed help. He got down on his hands and knees and blew repeatedly on the wood. A loud pop launched a flying ember onto Howard's shirt, burning a pea-sized hole in the fabric.

"*You* are a friggin' disaster," said Miriam, laughing and shaking her head.

"I know, I know," said Howard, disgusted as he assessed the damage.

He returned to the RV for a new shirt, and then came back with a wire-handled aluminum container of popping corn and two cans of pop.

"Gimme that," she said, grabbing the container, "before you set yourself on fire."

"Just what I need. A guardian angel to protect me from myself."

"A new woman in your life," she said, pointing her finger at him, "is what you need."

He watched her hold the pan over the fire, jiggling it often as the kernels popped; the foil cover slowly expanded into a silver ball. When finished, she tore open the top and offered it to him. He took a fistful. On the way to his mouth, he dropped buttered pieces onto his lap, leaving greasy stains. They both laughed this time.

"I'm gonna get you your own bowl," she said, heading back to the RV.

"Get one with high sides," he said, calling after her, "and bring a bib while you're at it."

He heard the sound of dishes as she searched the cupboards. Then she appeared in the doorway. "Mind if I play a Willie Nelson CD?"

"No, so long as you don't drown out Mother Nature."

He burst out laughing when she returned with a long strip of paper towel. "I didn't think you'd take me literally."

"You ought to buy one o' those plastic jobs you tie around your neck," she chided. "The kind they use in nursin' homes."

"I'll get to my dotage quick enough, thanks. A flatulent old fossil dribbling into his feeding tray."

"No you won't," she said, playfully cuffing his ear. "You'll still be travelin' around the country in your RV."

"I'd better be," he said. "Can't imagine going on one of those senior's bus trips."

"I hear that old folks have a good time doin' that."

"I'm not ready to ride the Incontinent Express, wearing a plastic name tag: 'My name is Howard. If I get lost, please call Varicose Valley Nursing Home.'"

"Oh, be quiet and let me fuss over you," she said. "You know you want me to."

She grinned as she tucked the paper into the open collar of his shirt and arranged it over his chest. With her face now inches from his, he noted the amber speckles around her irises that gave intensity to her eyes, the tiny crease where the tip of her nose made its upward turn, the dimple in her right cheek that gave an asymmetrical quality to her face. And as he appraised her features, his mind wandered . . .

"Chip?" she said, breaking his reverie.

"Yes," he replied, getting up to add wood to the fire.

"Thanks."

"For what?"

"For takin' me on this vacation."

"Enjoying yourself?"

"Loads," she replied, "except for the crazy camper, o' course."

"Me too," he said, settling back in his chair, and then edging it closer to hers until their arms touched.

They laughed and talked and ate popcorn and watched embers pop and flames probe the inky firmament. He glanced at her from time to time when she was looking at the fire. The glow reflected off her cheeks, highlighting her expression, warm and wistful. From the RV's stereo, the grass-sweetened prairie breeze carried the crisp notes of an acoustic guitar and the singer's wavering, whiskey-throated lyrics.

On such an exquisitely perfect night, and sitting beside this lovely young woman, Howard mused that not since the death of his wife, had he ever felt so happy.

# CHAPTER 16

## *Trailside Revelations*

T HE FOLLOWING MORNING, ALL sightseeing plans were on hold. They had both slept fitfully and were exhausted. Miriam had beaten a path to the washroom during the night, suffering persistent bouts of nausea. Howard had been up as many times, putting cold compresses on her forehead, preparing a concoction of hot water spiked with cider vinegar, and feeding her dry crackers to keep her strength up and curb the churning feeling in her stomach.

Over her protests, Howard had switched their sleeping arrangements. He moved her personal things to the rear bedroom and put fresh sheets and pillowcases on the queen-sized bed. When he had finished shifting his items to the lounge, Miriam took a shower, and then climbed under the sheets.

"Feel better now?" he called from the galley as he poured himself a coffee.

"Yeah. Thanks for doin' this. You didn't have to, you know. I would've slept on the lounge up front."

"Any idea what set you off? That was your worst session so far."

"I dunno . . . the oil in the popcorn maybe."

"Sorry," he replied, stirring in the sugar and cream, "I didn't think of that."

"Did Suzanne have mornin' sickness?"

"Yes, both times."

"Did it last long?"

"Not that I recall."

"Do you remember what worked?"

"Diet I think," he said, sipping his coffee.

"I don't know how the frig she went through this. Twice and all. Least when you barf from bein' drunk, that crappy feelin' is pretty much over."

"Well," he replied, "I'm sure we can beat this thing."

"How?"

"First, I'm going to check the internet."

"Then what?"

"Then I'm heading into town to shop for foods that'll sit better with you. Can you think of anything you'd like?"

"Sherbet."

"What flavor?"

"Lime if they have it."

"And if not?"

"Orange'll be fine."

"Anything else?"

"You know those little fruit cup things they put in kid's lunches?"

"Sure," he said, making a note. "I'll probably be a couple hours. Try to get some sleep."

He tore a blank page from the pad and tucked it into the window frame beside the bed, "If that's still there when I come back, I'll know you're snoozing."

"You're a funny guy, Chip," she said, glancing at the paper.

"What do you mean?"

"I mean, one minute you're spillin' stuff on yourself, and the next, you're thinkin' o' somethin' like that. The two don't go together."

"You forget, "I've already raised two girls. You get used to being protective."

"Lucky for me you came along in Toledo: an experienced dad."

Howard laughed, "Just call me your knight in ketchup-stained armor."

His first stop was the park office. After re-registering for a longer stay, he surfed the internet for information before heading into Abilene.

He drove the tree-lined side streets, a contrast to the vast, open spaces that surrounded this middle-American center. The plat of the town had a commonsense orderliness to it: north/south streets were named, east/west ones were numbered, all of which were divided into compass-designated quadrants, making addresses easy to find. At the Visitor Center, he picked up brochures on local sights and attractions. The townspeople and store clerks were friendly, unhurried folks, generous with their time. Howard quickly found what he needed and was back at the campground before noon. The paper was gone from the window.

"How come you're awake?" he said, carrying in the shopping bags. "I thought I'd find you snoozing."

"I did a bit. Enough to feel better anyway."

"I got your medicine."

"The sherbet?"

"Ta-dah," he said with a flourish and lifted a container from the insulated bag. "Lime!"

WITH A change of diet and rest, Miriam got her morning sickness under control. They spent four days in Abilene touring the town's historic buildings, including the Eisenhower Center, and taking a ten-mile train excursion to the town of Enterprise through the Smoky Hill River Valley.

Howard made some local enquiries and picked up supplies at a co-op for a surprise day outing. The night before, he made lunches and loaded the Jeep for an early morning departure.

"Aren't you gonna tell me where we're goin'?" asked Miriam as they followed a John Deere tractor out of town.

"No," said Howard as the farmer pulled onto the shoulder of the road to let him by. "It's a surprise."

Consulting a crude map, Howard zigzagged his way across the grid of backcountry roads. At the entrance to a large property, he drove under an arch of logs and a wooden sign: Sky View Ranch.

Miriam grinned, "You're takin' me horseback ridin' aren't you?"

"Here," he said reaching into a bag and producing a straw Stetson. "Put this on so at least you'll look the part."

The Jeep shuddered and crabbed over the metal rails of a cattle guard. When he topped a rise in the gravel driveway, they looked down on a white clapboard farmhouse and several metal-clad stables. Inside a paddock, horses were pulling tufts of hay from a livestock feeder; they lifted their heads to watch the vehicle as it passed. Howard parked against a fence near the stables. As they climbed out, a mare slowly ambled toward them and put her nose over the top rail.

The screen slammer to the farmhouse opened and a middle-aged man headed toward them. He had the look of an experienced rancher; except for white squint lines around his eyes, his face was leathery and darkly tanned, and his cheek bulged with a plug of chewing tobacco.

"You, Chip Munro? Feller what called yesterday?"

"Yes," said Howard.

"How do," said the taciturn man, giving Howard a bone-crushing handshake, then turning to Miriam and touching the brim of his hat, "ma'am."

"Nice and sunny," said Howard, trying to break the ice.

The man angled his head away and ejected a stream of tobacco juice onto the parched soil. "Been bone dry for weeks," he said, hooking both thumbs in his waistband. He studied them briefly, and then nodded toward the tack room. "This way."

The moment they entered, they were enveloped in the musky scent of leather. The two longer walls held the tack: bridles and reins on wooden pegs, folded saddle blankets on deep shelves, saddles suspended from wooden racks, and a wall cabinet with neat's-foot oil, buffing cloths, and brushes. In the center of the room was a wooden saddle horse.

The man had them try a couple of saddles, then called in his stable hand, "This here's, Shane," he said, introducing a young man in his late twenties. "He'll get your horses ready."

They followed him into the stables, pungent with the odor of horseflesh. At the sound of their footsteps, heads curiously protruded from the stalls. One animal whinnied loudly and kicked its stall door. A bug zapper crackled as a bluebottle landed on the electrified grid and sizzled momentarily.

"You folks ridden before?"

"I have," said Howard, "but not for a while."

"How 'bout you, ma'am?"

"Never."

He picked out Miriam's horse first, "This here's, Suzie," said the man, leading her from her stall.

"Is she gentle?" asked Miriam, presenting her upturned palm to the animal.

"Gentle as a lamb."

He secured the mare in cross ties, brushed her back and picked out her hooves, then tacked her. Miriam stood close to the horse and gently scratched its flank. Immediately, the mare lifted her tail.

"Ah, look at that. She's raisin' her tail. She must like me doin' that."

"No, ma'am," he said, chuckling as a load of manure plopped onto the stable floor, followed by a powerful jet of urine.

"Silly me," she said, looking at Howard, who was bent over with laughter.

When the man had finished saddling Howard's horse, he walked each animal for a short distance, and then stopped to re-tighten the cinch.

"How come you do that?" asked Miriam.

"Horses puff themselves up so the saddle stays loose on their backs. If I didn't do this it'd slip round and dump you."

The man hung a leather bag with their water bottles and lunches on Howard's horse, and then said, "You might want to stop by the cabin. It's by a grove o' cottonwoods. Got a stove and running water and basic fixin's. There's a water trough out back for the horses."

"We'll be sure to water them," said Howard. "We should be back by late afternoon."

"I'll be here," said the young man, tipping his hat back on his head.

Slowly, they rode off the property into sparsely treed land that gently rolled to the horizon in every direction. They could see each puff of wind as it came, rippling the grass like a line of incoming ocean surf. As they rode through the swales, grassy hummocks on either side cut off their views and shielded them from the wind. In the sheltered pocket, they could hear the creak of saddle leather, and the muffled tread of hooves on soft soil.

An hour later they arrived at the cabin, a small log building with a gabled roof covered in cedar shakes, and a covered porch out front. They rode around to the back, watered the horses, and then tied them to the hitching rail.

Howard lifted the iron latch on the Z-slab door. The faint odor of stale wood smoke and creosote greeted them as they entered. The unvarnished floorboards creaked underfoot as they walked to the center of the cabin. Years of winter frosts had shifted it slightly on its makeshift foundation, putting the building a degree or two out of level, and causing the chinking between the logs to separate, so that they admitted tiny slivers of daylight. Sash windows let in more light that revealed a woodstove with a dented stovepipe that passed through a metal collar on the pine ceiling. Beside the stove, a rusted tub provided an ample supply of quarter-split logs and pine kindling: two-by-four cutoffs and random lengths of thin strapping. Perched on top, a box of wooden matches leaned against rolls of old newspaper editions: *The Abilene Reflector-Chronicle*. While Howard checked out the cabin, she unfurled one and flipped the pages.

The community calendar listed various events and dates: a quilt show, a Gideon prayer breakfast at a local restaurant, bingo nights, and meetings of various service clubs. While scanning the ads, she noticed contact numbers of support groups for victims of domestic violence and sexual assaults. After her bucolic trail ride through such tranquil surroundings, she found these last entries hard to fathom. In her mind, she associated such strife with housing projects in inner city neighborhoods. Oddly, she found the obituaries more comforting.

She noticed that many of the deceased had lived into their late eighties and early nineties, country people, most of whom had spent their entire lives in the country, doing honest labor on the land, and breathing hay-scented air. Some were survived by numerous children and grandchildren. Miriam envisioned them gathered together for special occasions—Christmas and Thanksgiving and Easter—laughing and feasting on sumptuous turkey dinners and eating home-made apple pies.

She read that one woman had been a shopkeeper in town for almost twice as long as Miriam had lived. Another had been a school teacher, probably in a one-room schoolhouse, with wooden desks and inkwells and an iron stove, like the one in this cabin, for warding off the marrow-chilling prairie winters.

But what intrigued her most, were the references to the deceased persons' sons and daughters, rural youngsters who had been brought up on family farms, kids who had raised chickens, tended their own vegetable plots, and in the fall, entered their prize pumpkin at a county fair; kids who had milked cows and then, when they were old enough, had driven tractors at harvest time. How she envied these people she had never met. They had lived lives so different from hers in Philadelphia. The kind of life she fantasized about, especially now that she had seen what existed outside the only world she had ever known.

"Cozy," said Miriam, tossing the newspaper onto the wood box, and then surveying the log chairs and small tables. "Imagine bein' out here in the winter with a toasty fire to keep you all warm and comfy."

"Stove's been well used," said Howard, noting the buildup of ashes below the grate.

Against the rear wall was a sink and a crude drain that ran out through the wall. A painted cupboard held instant coffee fixings and a collection of mismatched mugs. When Miriam opened a tap, the pump clicked on.

"Man was right about runnin' water," she said, putting her finger into the cool stream. "Wanna coffee?"

"Sure," he said, looking at his watch. "It's a bit early for lunch, but I brought some cookies."

She struck a wooden match and lit one of the burners. Through the window she watched as Howard approached his horse and opened the saddlebag.

"I thought the balloon ride was pretty cool," she said when he returned, "but this is amazin'. It's like someone's turned the clock back to the Old West."

"Different than Philadelphia, huh?" he said, laughing.

"No kiddin'."

When the kettle whistled, she made their coffees as Howard set up two folding chairs on the porch's sun-bleached boards. They sat with their feet propped on the railing, and dipped into the cookie bag. A puff of wind suddenly swept into the small grove of cottonwoods; it tickled the leaves and caused the horses to whinny nervously behind the cabin.

"What a gorgeous sight," said Miriam, pointing to the endless vista of prairie grass. "From now on, whenever I get upset about somethin', I'm gonna imagine myself back on this porch."

Howard appraised her as she stared wordlessly into the distance, the edges of her profile creamy in the dappled light, her eyes fixed as if preoccupied.

"You OK?" he asked, sensing her pensiveness.

"Yeah," she said, taking a cautious sip of scalding coffee. "Just thinkin'."

"Good thoughts?"

"Uh-huh," she said, smiling at him.

"Like what?"

"I'm thinkin' that this vacation I'm havin' with you . . . is the best thing that's ever happened to me in my entire life."

"You've never told me much about that," said Howard.

"About what?" she asked.

"Your life," he replied. "You know a lot about mine, but I don't know much about yours."

"It's been a train wreck mostly," she said, biting her thumbnail. "I made a lot o' mistakes."

"Who hasn't?" he replied.

She swirled her mug and flung the dregs onto the dry soil beyond the porch.

"I'm a loser, Chip."

"No you're not."

"I am when it comes to pickin' men. Lived with three since I left home. Not one of 'em worth a damn. Course, doin' drugs didn't help."

"When did you start that?"

"Long before my father died. Did drugs *and* had sex when I was young—too damned young. It's all I lived for through school: good sex and good weed."

"How old were you when you first lived with someone?"

"Eighteen. Same year Mom took her lucky vacation to California and met David. Her life got better. Mine went down the toilet after I met Jason."

"Where'd you meet him?"

"In a pool hall."

"Do you play pool?"

"Uh-uh, but my girlfriend did. Sherri was a waitress at Hooters. Every time she bent over the table, guys'd be starin' down her top. Jason was one of 'em. He tried puttin' the make on her, but she wouldn't have anythin' to do with him. I should've been smart like her."

"What was he like to live with?" asked Howard, finishing his coffee.

"Charming at first. Thought I'd landed myself a winner till I got to see his other side. By then it was too late."

"How long did you stay with him?"

"Ten years."

"Why didn't you leave?"

"It's complicated, Chip. Sure you wanna know this?"

"Only if you want to tell."

She let out a long sigh. "Jason was a control freak. Took over every aspect o' my life. Didn't want me to work. The odd thing was, I never knew what he did for a livin'—least not at the start, anyway. But the bills got paid and we always had money for booze and drugs."

"What kind of drugs?"

"Marijuana, hash, cocaine."

"Anything stronger?"

"Uh-uh. I wasn't a heavy coke user, but still, I was hooked."

"What was your boyfriend like?"

"A time bomb. When somethin' set him off, he'd blow. Smash things and get verbally abusive. He told me if I ever left him for someone else, I was as good as dead."

"That must've terrified you."

"It did 'cause I believed him. It was his on-again-off-again behavior that wore me down."

"Like what?"

"He'd treat me good for a while, and then turn nasty all of a sudden. Tell me I was a no good piece o' shit. Said I should be grateful he loved me, because I was too ugly for any other man to love. I was like a dog that gets petted one day, then kicked the next."

"I suppose this is a stupid question, but did he ever hit you?"

"Lots. Mostly in the body where my clothes'd hide the bruises."

"Did he give you those?"

Self-consciously, she touched the scars on her chin, "He threw a beer bottle at me once."

"And this relationship lasted ten years?"

"Yeah, and for ten years I was a prisoner. I wanted to escape, but was too terrified to leave."

"How did it end?"

"The day two cops came to my door. They asked me to come down to the morgue and identify a body."

"Was it him?"

She stared at Howard for a moment, and then answered with a nod.

"By who?"

"The cops figured it was someone connected to the drug trade in Mexico. They beat him to death, probably with baseball bats; his head and neck were nothin' but pulp."

Howard shook his head.

"I never wanted a live-in arrangement after Jason."

"What changed?"

"I met Aaron."

"How?"

"Through Sherri. 'Clean cut and sweet' was how she described him. Thought he'd be good for me 'specially after bein' with a knob like Jason.

Anyway, she arranged this double date. Four of us went out for Chinese. He was pleasant, but shy. Didn't do a thing for me. Not even a flutter."

"If he was that boring," asked Howard, "how did you wind up living with him?"

"I'm gettin' to that," said Miriam. "At one point, Sherri and her boyfriend decided to go out for a smoke and leave the two of us alone. We were sittin' there fumblin' with our chopsticks and makin' small talk. I found out he was five years younger than me, and that he hadn't dated much. Don't ask me why, but I got this weird idea. I asked him flat out if he'd ever been to bed with a woman before. He shook his head. I nearly flipped. I mean, what guy in this day and age is still a virgin at twenty-four?"

"That's rare," said Howard.

"I'll say," she exclaimed. "So anyway, I figured, what the hell, I'd have a fling, show him the ropes, then find a humane way o' dumpin' him."

"Let me guess," said Howard, "he fell in love with you."

"Uh, uh," she said, shaking her head. "It was the other way around."

"What happened?"

"He adored me, that's what. He was kind and considerate and talked real nice to me. And I fell for him."

"What did he do for a living?"

"Fixed computers for a small electronics outfit. A few times he talked about quittin' and workin' for himself, so I surprised him and put together a work area in the apartment: tables, shelves, and whatnot. I was hopin' it'd encourage him, you know, to take the plunge."

"And did he?"

"Uh-uh. Turned out he was a dreamer, not a doer. He wasn't motivated or confident enough to follow through."

"Is that what went wrong between you?"

"No."

"What was it then?"

"Religion."

"Yours or his?"

"His. I am *so* not into that stuff. I stopped believin' in fairy tales when I was a kid."

"Fairy tales?" said Howard, stunned by her flippant remark. "That's a pretty harsh assessment, don't you think?"

"Not to me it isn't . . . it's how I feel."

She noticed his lingering look of shock at her disclosure.

"Look, Chip, I may not be the sharpest cheese on the cracker, but even I know a tall tale when I see one. Religion is way too farfetched for me to believe in."

"But, millions of people believe in a God of some kind," said Howard.

"And good luck to 'em. Whatever floats their boat. It just doesn't float mine!"

"Sorry to interrupt," said Howard, still pondering her comment. "You were saying?"

She paused to pick up the thread "Anyway, I didn't realize it at first," she continued on another tangent, "but religion was the reason he'd never been with a woman before."

"How did he deal with having sex if his beliefs told him otherwise?"

"He didn't, that's the thing. He was very prudish. Had loads o' sexual hang-ups."

"Sounds like that part of your relationship was pretty dull."

"Dull as dishwater. I was naïve when I think back on it. I thought that over time I'd be able to help him get more relaxed about sex, but I couldn't do it. He never changed."

"I didn't think anyone in this day and age would be that hung up," exclaimed Howard. "Sex is supposed to be fun."

"What you gotta understand is, Aaron was brow-beaten by religion. Sared out o' his wits with all its 'shall nots' and its burn-in-hell-for-eternity-punishments. Plus, he was obsessed."

"What kind of things did he obsess about?"

"Convertin' me was numero uno on his list! At first, he was low key about it. He'd leave his Bible open on the kitchen table with certain scriptures flagged. But after we'd been together a while, he got more aggressive. That's when the arguments started. He was determined to convert me, and I was just as determined he wouldn't. Whenever he'd start one o' his Bible rants, I'd start askin' questions."

"How did he deal with that?"

"He came unglued. Said it was sinful to question the Bible 'cause it was a hundred per cent true. He'd pop out all these scriptures on this, that, and the other. The one that bugged me most was about the man bein' the head o' the household and havin' to be obeyed."

"Whoa," said Howard.

"Whoa is right. I told him if he expected me to obey him, then he could kiss my butt."

"Sounds to me like he was a fundamentalist," said Howard.

"Oh, he was mental with it all right. Stark ravin' cuckoo."

"No, I mean, fundamentalists are people who take the Bible word-for-word."

"Yeah, that was Aaron all right. To him, everythin' was black or white, good or bad. Nothin' in between. The weird thing was, when religion wasn't in our conversation, he could be as nice as pie and we'd have happy times together. But as soon as it was, his intolerant side came out. He'd start attackin' science, evolution, gays, same-sex marriage. You name it. Anythin' that contradicted the Bible."

"What church did he go to?"

"I dunno. Holy Rollers 'R' Us or some such. I met a few of 'em once. Never wanted to run so fast from a bunch o' people in my friggin' life. They turned Aaron into a zombie. Controlled him like a puppet. Problem was, they weren't just controllin' him, they were affectin' our relationship as well."

"How long did you live with him?"

"Eight months . . . till the final straw."

"And that was?"

"Money. When he first moved in with me, we planned to save for a condo. A place we could call our own. We opened a mutual bank account and started saltin' money away. One day I found out the account was empty. I nearly shit a brick. At first I thought someone had ripped us off, you know, like identity theft or somethin'. Never thought it could be him."

"Was it?"

"Yeah. He'd tithed away our money. Every damned cent we had to our name!"

"To who?"

"To TV evangelists. He told 'em he'd tried his best to bring me to Jesus and failed. He asked for their help, and naturally, they stuck out their greedy hands for money. Those people are like a bunch o' hyenas, preyin' on the weak and needy. And all the while, they're rakin' in the dough, hand over fist and tax free, to buy their thousand dollar suits and fancy mansions. Friggin' scumbags—they're lower than toe jam."

"How did it finally end?" he asked, after she had finished her rant.

"I realized if we stood any chance of a healthy future together, Aaron needed psychiatric help. But when I suggested it, he flipped out. Accused me of attackin' his faith and bein' in cahoots with the devil."

"He believed in the devil?"

"It was as real to him as a buzzard sittin' on his shoulder, just waitin' to peck its way into his brain. Anyway, by that point, I'd had enough. I told him to pack his stuff and get out."

"Did you feel relieved when it was over?"

"Big time! Aaron's intolerance scared me more than anythin'. He was so full o' anger at people who didn't see the world his way, I used to wonder how long it'd be till he bought a gun and shot someone comin' out an abortion clinic or a gay nightclub."

"You actually thought he'd go that far?"

"I was never sure. When a person's mind is that taken over by somethin', it's like they lose their ability to think straight. You never know what they're capable of. But mostly, it was the constant prayin' and scripture quotin' that pissed me off in the end. I just couldn't take it anymore. After we broke up, I went to a woman shrink, Pat, to get my head together."

"Did she help?"

"A lot. She asked questions about Aaron and ran over a list with me."

"What kind of list?"

"Symptoms o' religious addiction. Turned out he had most of 'em."

"I've never heard of that," said Howard.

"Neither had I. Seems it's the one addiction people don't wanna talk about. She said it was the same as other addictions though—one sickness coverin' up another."

"And what was that?"

"Chronic depression. Pat said if he stood any chance o' beatin' it, he'd have to confront his habit, the same way an alcoholic has to."

"Do you think he could have done that?"

"Not a chance. He was too much in denial to go for therapy. He'd have been worried that the devil would get inside his head. For Aaron, the only safe territory was the Bible. Scriptures were the one-size-fits-all solution. He'd rather cling to 'em like a shipwreck survivor than get into the lifeboat—get professional help."

"Well, I think you were smart to go for counseling," said Howard.

"I think so too. I didn't realize how much he'd screwed up my head. Plus I had a lot o' guilt."

"Over what?"

"Feelin' like I'd given up on him."

"What did your counselor say about that?"

"She said I did the right thing by lettin' go, else I'd have become a victim too. That it was like me holdin' Aaron by the wrists to keep him from fallin' off a roof. If he wouldn't help in his own rescue, then he'd just keep gettin' heavier and heavier, till I'd either have to let go, or be pulled down with him. She said that religious addicts eventually get disillusioned when their faith doesn't produce the results they expect. At that point, they start lookin' for somethin' else. Another 'feel good' fix. Another band-aid solution to their problems instead of tacklin' them head on."

"Well, at least you had some happy moments together."

"More than with any other man," she said wistfully. "Deep down, he was a kind man with a good heart, and I know he loved me, yet we couldn't make it work. I still feel bitter about how he was taken from me. Aaron was like a fly that got killed by a spider. First, he got tangled in the web, then stung, then wrapped up so tight he couldn't get away. After that, his insides got sucked out till all that was left was a shell. In the end, it was the spider—his addiction—that won. There was nothin' left for me."

Howard thought back to her impious remarks. Did her angst stem from genuine contempt for religion per se? Or was it the result of Aaron's addiction and the fact that it had destroyed their relationship? Or was it a bit of both?

"Anyway, I'm grateful to him for gettin' me off cocaine. Funny isn't it? He helped me beat *my* addiction, but couldn't beat his own."

Suddenly Miriam went quiet. She had said as much as she was prepared to say. Emotionally drained, she stepped off the porch and leaned against the trunk of a cottonwood.

"Fancy another coffee?" he asked.

She was preoccupied and did not answer.

"I said, do you fancy—?"

"Yeah . . . yeah, that'd be nice."

He put another kettle of water on the propane stove. As he waited for it to boil he watched the horses behind the cabin, switching flies with their tails.

"Careful, it's hot," he said, handing her the mug. "How about we say hello to the horses? They're looking lonely back there."

Together, they walked behind the cabin and sat on the edge of the water trough. When their legs touched, neither of them pulled away. For a long while they watched the horses eat and studied the pencil-thin contrails of jetliners as they made cat's cradles in the sky. Neither of them felt the need to fill the void with idle chatter. Then, unexpectedly, Miriam dropped her head onto his shoulder and broke down; he hugged her as she sobbed.

"Thanks," she said, when she had composed herself.

"What for?"

"Listenin'."

"That's OK," he said, kicking at the dust with the toe of his boot. "You leant me *your* shoulder when I needed it."

She sighed deeply. "I'm scared o' my future, Chip. I'm thirty-five. Assumin' I live to eighty, my friggin' life's almost half over and I got squat to show for it. No job, no man, a kid I don't want—and worse still—the guilt I carry for *not* wantin' it."

She slipped her arm through his and pulled herself close to him. There was nothing sexual about it, just a need on her part to take comfort from the closeness. Again, there was a long lull in conversation before Howard spoke.

"Suzanne used to say that if we all put our troubles in a pile, and we saw what others have to deal with, we'd grab our own and run like hell."

"Yeah, that makes sense . . . sorry."

"What for?"

"For doin' a 'poor me'," she said. "You're already carryin' your own bag o' nails."

"No need to apologize. But if I had any advice for you, it would be this: wait till you get to California and have a chance to catch your breath. There may be new opportunities waiting. You never know."

"I suppose you're right. I'm always crossin' bridges before I get to 'em."

"Come on," he said, changing the subject. He dipped a bucket into the water trough. "Let's give them a drink."

Miriam followed him and fussed over the animals as they drank.

"You know somethin'?" she said, as she scratched her horse's withers.

"What?"

"I've never told a soul the stuff I told you this afternoon. Not my closest girlfriend. Not even my mom."

"I'm a good keeper of secrets. What you told me stays in here," he said, putting a hand over his heart.

"You should be flattered," said Miriam. "I don't trust easily."

"I know what you mean. Unloading your feelings with the wrong person can be a mistake."

"Tell me about it. I got girlfriends that'd spread that faster than a dose o' herpes. Others that'd flip it off with a joke. Either way, I'd be left feelin' that I'd pulled down my panties and bared my butt in public."

She shifted away from him momentarily and rooted through her pockets.

"What are you looking for?"

"Tissues to wipe my face. I forgot to bring 'em."

"Here," he said, lifting his arm. "Use my shirtsleeve. I've got enough spilled food on it to open a supermarket."

She laughed as she wiped her cheeks, "I've never met anyone as casual as you."

"Hey, what's a little snot and tears between friends, huh?"

He returned to sit on the water trough while Miriam remained with the horses. She had lost her fear of them now. He felt good as he watched her interact with the animals, touching her cheek to theirs and talking softly to them.

After the long ride to the cabin, Miriam was saddle sore. Instead of going any farther, they spent the remainder of their day lounging on the porch and talking. In her own time she told him about her last live-in lover, a lothario, who, after getting her pregnant, quickly moved on to other conquests. But in the telling, she did not speak his name. It was as if she wanted to expunge every trace of him.

As they talked, he thought back to when he had first picked her up in Ohio. Seeing her bedraggled state at the side of the road, he had been tempted to drive on. Even after picking her up, he wondered whether he had done the right thing. She seemed so different from him, is if she had come from some other world—certainly not his world. He remembered thinking that her lack of sophistication would mark her for ridicule at any cocktail party, and that her grammar would never earn her a high SAT score. But now, on this trail ride, he had gained a better understanding of the woman and the events that had shaped her. There was an authenticity about her that he liked. He did not always agree with her opinions, but he admired her honesty.

In his years of academia he had had his fill of the scholarly, the witty, and the pretentious. He had learned to meet and greet and make all the appropriate clucking noises within his social circle and in the halls of St. Martin's. Now, for the first time in his life, Howard realized that he had finally shed the standard of measurement he had inherited from his father. Dr. Cameron Munro had judged people by the loftiness of their achievements and by the number of framed degrees on their office walls. The fact was, Miriam Kovacs would never attain any of these, and maybe, he reckoned, that was not such a bad thing after all. She was an uncomplicated woman whose only desire in life was to achieve a modicum of happiness. In that respect they were both alike. It was all that Howard wanted too.

# CHAPTER 17

## *Blood*

IT WAS THE FIRST thing Howard noticed when he went to the RV's bathroom in the morning; crimson speckles of it dotted the linoleum beside the toilet.

"Miriam?" he said, tapping on the rear bathroom door.

There was no answer. He slid it open. The covers on the bed were turned back. She was gone.

He dressed quickly, and then dashed across the campground until he stood outside the door of the women's washroom. Through the screen, he could hear faint crying. He knocked first, before entering. His eye traveled to the center of three cubicles that lined the opposite wall. Under the privacy barrier the ruffled fabric of pajama bottoms rested on a pair of familiar slippers.

"Miriam?" he said, his voice echoing against the concrete walls.

"Yeah," she replied, her voice breaking.

"I saw blood in the RV. Why didn't you wake me?"

"Because . . . I wanted to deal with this by myself. I think I might be havin' a miscarriage."

"Are you bleeding a lot?"

"No. I'm just spottin'. I've never been pregnant before, so I'm not sure what this means."

"Why don't you come back to the RV?"

"I've got blood on my robe. I was gonna wash it out in the sink first."

"Never mind that," he replied. "I'll get you mine."

He returned a minute later and flipped his robe over the top of the cubicle divider along with a green garbage bag to put her robe in. She emerged looking pale and shaken. He put his arm around her shoulder and led her toward the door.

As they left, a woman and her young daughter approached the washroom building.

"What was that man doing in our washroom, Mommy?"

"Shush," said the woman, smiling apologetically, then quickly steering the curious girl inside.

No one else on the campground was up yet. They reached the motor home unnoticed. Immediately, Miriam entered the RV's washroom.

"Oh, no," she exclaimed.

"What's wrong?"

"I left a mess in here."

"It's *me* who messed up," said Howard, angrily stabbing the keypad of his cell phone. "I took you horseback riding when I should've known better."

"What're you doin'?" she asked.

"Calling 911. I'm getting you to the hospital."

"No, Chip."

He ignored her and waited with the phone to his ear.

"But I've got no medical insurance," she protested.

"Police, fire, or ambulance?" asked the dispatcher.

"Ambulance," said Howard, glancing at Miriam who had now emerged from the washroom.

"Please don't," she said, holding up her hand. "To be honest and truthful, I'm more scared than anythin' else."

He ordered the ambulance, and then began putting personal things together for her, insisting that she remain seated until the arrival of the paramedics. Soon the EMS unit brought the curious to the windows of their campers. People watched the crew blanket and secure Miriam to the stretcher, collapse the supports, then slide her into the vehicle.

Howard followed in the Jeep. After getting a parking space outside the Emergency entrance, he rushed inside. Miriam had already been taken into the ward. He had to wait for an admissions clerk who was busy with a middle-aged couple. The man's hand was wrapped in a blood-soaked motel towel. His wife was politely answering questions.

"How will you be paying, ma'am?" asked the clerk.

"We've got out-of-country travel insurance," said the smiling woman, proudly laying her documents on the counter. "We bought the deluxe package. It covers everything."

"That's fine," said the clerk, barely glancing at the policy, "but you have to pay up front."

"I have to *what?*" snarled the man's wife, her demeanor instantly changed.

"Do you have a credit card, ma'am?" the clerk asked.

"Well, of course I do, but that's to cover other expenses."

"It's hospital policy ma'am. We'll give you an itemized receipt you can submit to your health care insurer when you return to Canada."

"But this guarantees you'll get your money, now" said the anxious woman. "I just have to call this 1-800 number first, and they'll approve everything."

"I'm sorry, ma'am."

The more the woman complained about payment arrangements, the more impatient Howard became.

"Would you look after this gentleman?" said the clerk, turning to a colleague. The girl got up from her desk and came to the counter, "Are you with the young woman the EMS just brought in?"

"Yes."

"How will she be paying, sir?"

"Credit card," he replied, laying plastic on the counter.

The Canadian couple looked on curiously as Howard explained Miriam's medical situation.

"Do you have any identification for Ms. Kovacs, like, say, a birth certificate or driver's license?"

"I'm afraid not," said Howard. "She had her purse stolen recently and hasn't been able to get replacement ID yet."

"Are you a relative of hers?"

"No. Just a friend."

"Do you know if she's allergic to any medications?"

"No I don't," he said, "but I do know she's pregnant."

"How far along is she?"

"A month or more I think."

"Very well then," said the girl, picking up a clipboard. "I'll get some basic info from her."

Howard picked through the pile of magazines in the waiting area, but could find nothing worth reading, only dog-eared gossip magazines and pulp tabloids—idiotic pap. He shook his head; no wonder reading skills were plummeting across the nation.

He re-focused on his surroundings. The Canadian woman had finally calmed down, having resigned herself to the hospital's payment policy. Beyond the glassed entrance to the emergency ward, he noticed a bald woman in a wheelchair, probably a cancer patient. She was hooked to an IV drip on a wheeled stand. She lit a cigarette, held it to her tracheotomy, and smiled with pleasure as the jag of nicotine took effect.

"Ms. Kovacs is asking for you, sir," said the admissions girl, nodding in the direction of the ward. "See the charge nurse first."

"Over here," called Miriam at the sound of Howard's voice.

"Knock, knock," he said, outside the privacy curtain.

"It's OK. I'm decent."

"Hello, doctor," he said as he stepped into the examining cubicle. "How's my friend doing?"

"I'd like to run a few tests first," the doctor replied, preparing to leave.

"Is it OK for me to eat?" asked Miriam. "I haven't had breakfast yet."

"I'll have Dietary put a tray together for you."

"How are you feeling?" asked Howard after the doctor had left.

"Better now that you're here," she said, taking hold of his hand.

"I could kick myself for taking you horseback riding," said Howard."

"Well, if I don't get to do it again, least I did it once."

A ward nurse arrived and after releasing the wheel locks on the bed, pushed Miriam out of the emergency ward and down a tiled hallway.

Howard grabbed a drink from a vending machine in the lobby, and then went for a long walk. When he returned to the hospital an hour later, she had finished breakfast. They talked until the doctor returned with the test results. Howard got up to leave.

"Don't go, Chip."

"The news is good," said the doctor, smiling at Miriam. "I have no reason to believe your baby is at risk."

"But what about the spotting?" she asked. "That can't be a good sign."

"Spotting within the first trimester is normal for many women. Yours was light and not accompanied by abdominal pain or cramping, so there's no ectopic pregnancy—"

"What's that?" she asked, interrupting him.

"A pregnancy that occurs outside the womb, for example, in the fallopian tubes. I also checked for a cervical polyp and any growths. There were none. No signs of Chlamydia or bacterial vaginosis either."

"If everythin's OK, will I be able to go horseback ridin' again?"

"I'd give that a miss till after you've delivered."

Miriam glanced at Howard, then at the doctor, her face registering no joy at the happy prognosis for the baby. "Couldn't you gimme a D and C?"

The doctor's forehead creased in a deep frown, "I get the impression," he said in a disapproving tone, "that you don't want your baby. Are you considering an abortion by any chance?"

Miriam bit her lower lip and again glanced at Howard. Her silence spoke volumes.

"I have a question, doctor," said Howard, trying to lighten the atmosphere.

"Go ahead," he said, his warm, bedside manner having chilled.

"Do you think our trail ride might have brought this on?"

"Possibly," replied the doctor, his face devoid of expression, "but not necessarily. Women can experience spotting after a variety of activities, or for no apparent reason."

"Am I in any danger?" asked Miriam.

"No, but I'd advise you to see an obstetrician as soon as you get to California."

"I'm planning for us to go four-wheeling when we get to Colorado," said Howard, changing the subject. "Is it safe for her to do that?"

"I can't see why not. Nothing too strenuous though."

The doctor forced a smile, parted the privacy curtain, and left.

THEY SPENT the rest of the day relaxing on their site; Howard kept the mood upbeat and did not mention the encounter with the doctor. The weather was hot, but instead of staying inside with the air conditioning on, Miriam wanted to sit in the shade of the awning. Howard fussed over her and insisted she lie down on a chaise. He brought her cold drinks and did everything possible to make her comfortable. After preparing a pot of home-made spaghetti, he set it on simmer.

They had a late supper and dined al fresco. At the end of the picnic table he put out a cereal bowl filled with sunflower seeds. Chickadees snatched the seeds, then fluttered into the cottonwoods to hammer open the husks.

"There's somethin' you haven't done yet," said Miriam, picking at her food.

"Oh?" he said, as a dollop of pasta sauce landed on his shirt.

"Your girls are probably thinkin' you're in San Diego by now. Don't you think you should call 'em?"

"I suppose you're right," he said.

"You don't sound keen."

Howard wiped his chin, "You don't know my girls."

"Oops. Did I touch a nerve?"

"No," but you *are* right. I should call them. It's just that they can be pretty judgmental at times . . . Lynn especially."

"What's to judge? You're headin' for California and decided to see some sights along the way." For a moment she was puzzled by Howard's reluctance, and then the penny dropped. "Are you worried what they're gonna think about havin' me along for the ride?"

"Yes."

"Then don't tell 'em," she said.

"I can't do that."

"Why not?"

"Because, I don't like lying," he said, then changed the subject, "You want some sherbet for dessert?"

"Please."

He cleared the table and headed for the RV with his arms full.

"Need any help in there?"

"Uh-uh," he called back, and then dumped the dishes noisily into the galley sink.

While she waited for him to return, she put sunflower seeds in the palm of her hand. The first bird hopped onto her thumb, stole a seed, then flew off. Others quickly mimicked the first, landing on her arms and shoulders.

Juggling two bowls of dessert, Howard approached quietly, and slid onto the bench beside her. The birds were not deterred by his presence and kept feeding.

"Never had a wild bird land on me before," she grinned as another diner perched on her thumb. "They're trustin' little souls, aren't they?"

Howard nodded and smiled as her watched her. She was as enchanted as a young child at the novelty of the interaction.

"Chip?" she said, as the bird flew off.

"Yes."

"I don't wanna be a nag, but think about callin' 'em. Please. They need to know you're OK."

When they had finished dessert, he entered Tina's number and waited. A man's voice came on the line.

"Hi, Gerry, it's Howard."

The man called to his wife over the sound of the TV. "Tina, honey, it's your dad."

In the background, footsteps advanced quickly.

"Hey, Dad, how's sunny San Diego?"

"I'm not in California yet."

"Why not? Have you had an accident?"

"No, no. Nothing like that. I'm in Kansas."

"Gerry, turn the TV down," she shouted, then spoke into the receiver. "You should be at the coast by now. Why aren't you?"

"It's a long story . . . sort of."

"What do you mean long story? Is there something you're not telling me?"

"I decided to take my time. Take a vacation on the way out."

"Oh? Last time we talked you couldn't wait to get out there. What's changed?"

Howard paused, not sure of how to break the news, "I, uh . . . picked somebody up . . . not long after I left Toledo."

"Surely not a hitchhiker. Oh, please tell me not a hitch—"

"Yeah . . . I did."

"Oh my God, Dad! What were you thinking? You've never done anything like that. Who is it? Some runaway kid with tattoos? A drifter? A fugitive?"

"None of those."

"Who then?" she asked. "You've got me scared to death now."

"A woman."

"What kind of woman hitchhikes across the country with a total stranger?" she said, derisively. "Certainly not a decent woman."

"You're wrong there. She's a very nice woman actually. We get along well. I wish you could meet her."

Miriam watched Howard's pained expressions as he tried to explain her to his adult daughter. She motioned with hand gestures, suggesting she retreat to the RV and give him privacy, but he shook his head.

"How old is she?" asked his daughter.

"Around your age I think, but—"

"What if she's a drug addict or something," said Tina, her voice trembling. "She might have a gun. Might decide to rob you, or—"

"Look, will you calm down. She's not a druggie and she doesn't have a gun."

"But what if—?"

"Dammit, Tina, I'm fifty-years-old. Give me some credit for being a good judge of character. If I thought she wasn't fit to ride with me, I'd have dumped her long ago."

Miriam motioned for him to hand over the phone, but he resisted. She waited until he was not looking, and then quickly grabbed it.

"Hi, Tina . . . it's Miriam . . . Miriam Kovacs."

There was an awkward silence at the other end.

"I know you must be worried about your dad pickin' me up and all. But, to be honest and truthful, he's been a prince. Don't know where I'd be without him. I was on my way to California to see my mother when your dad stopped for me. When I left home I didn't have much money, and so I decided to hitchhike. And he's been so good to me . . . takin' me to places along the way, sightseein' and such . . . 'cause I've never seen anythin' outside o' Philly, and—"

"Thanks for getting on the phone," said Tina, her tone a little friendlier. "I feel better now."

"I'm so sorry to hear about your mom dyin'. Chip told me what happened to her. It must've come as such a shock."

"Chip?"

"Oh, it's this thing o' mine. I give people nicknames, 'specially people I like. And your dad, well, he'd always wanted that particular one ever since he was a boy and so I thought that it'd be nice to—"

"Miriam?"

"Yeah."

"I know this is an odd thing to say, because it's really none of my business. I mean, you're both adults. But the thing is, Dad's still raw right now. Vulnerable I guess is what I'm saying. It's only been a year since Mom died and God knows he must be lonely as hell. Oh, shit, I'm making a total mess of this aren't I?"

"No you're not. It's OK, Tina. I understand what you must be thinkin' what with us bein' on the road together and all. Especially livin' out o' the motor home. But I can tell you for sure and certain that there's no hanky panky goin' on here."

Howard was embarrassed now and tried to grab the phone back, but Miriam quickly moved away.

"No, Chip," she said, sharply. "You're not gettin' the phone. Not till your daughter and I have had a woman-to-woman."

Although they were not face-to-face, it was obvious to Miriam that she was speaking to the daughter of well-educated parents. Tina was articulate and confident, whereas, Miriam was self-conscious of her limited schooling. She tripped on her words as she tried to explain how she too had lost a parent to an untimely death and had struggled for closure, how she had convinced Howard to return to the scene of Suzanne's death, and how she had tried to comfort him. She explained her own situation, being unemployed and pregnant, but said nothing of her planned abortion. Mostly, she told Tina about Howard's many kindnesses.

"Hey, Dad," she said as her father got back on the line. "I'm sorry. You were right to pick her up. Enjoy the rest of your trip. Call me when you get to San Diego."

"I will," he replied. "Would you do me a favor, honey?"

"Of course."

"Will you call Lynn and explain all of this? I'd rather you did it, especially after talking to Miriam."

"Sure, Dad, but I'm going to ask a favor back."

"What's that?"

"Give that woman a hug for me."

# CHAPTER 18

## *The Accident*

I T BEGAN AS ONE of the happiest days they had shared on the road. After leaving Abilene, they continued west toward the Colorado border. Excited at the prospect of seeing the Rockies for the first time, Miriam studied the horizon with the zeal of a mariner straining for the first sight of land. But the mountains were still a long way off and she passed the miles by singing along to Garth Brooks CDs that Howard had bought her.

She was a Brooks fan to the bone, enthusiastically mimicking each song lyric-for-lyric and without missing a word. With the volume of the RV's stereo cranked up, she mesmerized Howard as she kept up with the fast paced, *Ain't Goin' Down Till the Sun Comes Up*. Lost in the music and angled forward in her seat, she tapped the floor mat with her heels and drummed the dashboard with flying hands. When Howard began to laugh, she turned in her seat and used his shoulder as a drum.

After a leisurely lunch at a rest stop, they were on their way and traveling again, this time behind a cluster of westbound vehicles that included an eighteen-wheeler. As the group approached an exit, a small, dilapidated car entered the off-ramp. Moments later, the driver had a change of mind and tried to re-enter the stream of traffic. The truck driver swerved to avoid the car. Wheels dug into the soft soil of the median strip. The tractor regained the pavement, but then flipped onto its side, pulling the fifty-three-foot trailer over with it. The rear doors opened, spilling its cargo onto the road. The small car was the first to collide with its underbelly, followed by others that piled into it with the sickening sound of grinding metal.

"Oh my *God*," screamed Miriam hysterically, bringing both hands to her face. "It's awful. There's gonna be people hurt—people killed. Oh, no. Oh, please no!"

The scene was one of total carnage. Windshields exploded. Radiators burst. Coolant spewed onto hot engine blocks and generated clouds of steam that swirled about the wreckage. Air bags had saved drivers from impalement on steering wheels, but not from shock or broken glass; the stunned faces of bloodied occupants gazed through shattered windows. And above the fray, like a macabre one-note version of taps, a stuck car horn blared loudly.

Howard pulled the motor home onto the shoulder of the off-ramp, his heart pounding and his mind racing, trying to put together a plan of action.

"Quick," he said, thrusting his cell phone at Miriam. "Call 911. Tell them to send police, fire, and ambulances."

Westbound traffic stopped quickly. Impatient motorists stepped out of their vehicles and peered ahead to assess the cause of the holdup. Howard asked two men to help him; they ran from vehicle to vehicle comforting drivers and making note of injures. The air reeked of diesel fuel; one of the saddle tanks of the tractor was leaking onto the pavement; Howard hollered a warning to people at the scene.

"I'm an off-duty firefighter," shouted a man emerging from his pickup truck. "Somebody help me contain the spill."

Two motorists volunteered, using hubcaps to scrape dirt from the shoulder of the highway and carry it to the spill site.

"I called 911," said Miriam, breathless as she rejoined Howard on the highway.

"Quick," he said, pulling her toward the small car pinned against the undercarriage of the trailer. "Nobody's checked this one yet."

Together, they scrambled over the twisted hoods and trunks of other vehicles to get to it. The Hispanic driver, a domestic cleaning woman, was alive and conscious. Her face was splattered with blood and her hair packed to the scalp with cubes of broken auto glass. Both her arms were pinned by crumpled metal and her right ankle had a compound fracture. The woman wailed hysterically.

"Mi hijo está muerto. Mi hijo está muerto."

Howard checked the interior of the vehicle. No air bags had deployed; it was too old to have them. The impact had torn the passenger seat from the floor; still strapped in it was an unconscious boy about ten-years-old, his head and face bloody, and shards of broken glass embedded in his swarthy skin.

"Oh por dios, estas muerto," screamed the woman.

Howard climbed onto what remained of the car's trunk. There was no glass left in the rear window.

"I can't get in," said Howard after his second failed attempt to squeeze through the opening.

"Lemme try," said Miriam. "I'm smaller than you."

She lay on her back, and then inched her way into the car, wincing as broken glass tore her blouse and cut into her skin.

"Does he have a pulse?" asked Howard.

"I can't reach his wrists."

"Try his neck."

"Where?"

"Beside his Adam's apple."

"Oh por dios, estas muerto. Mi hijo está muerto."

"He's got a pulse!" shouted Miriam excitedly. "He's got a p-pulse!"

"Is he breathing?"

"No."

"Open his mouth and check his airway."

"W-what do you mean?" she asked.

"I mean sweep your fingers through his mouth. He might have a blockage."

There was a long pause before she answered. "He had food stuck in his throat."

"Is he breathing now?"

"B-barely."

"Quick. Give him mouth-to-mouth."

"I don't know how," she exclaimed, her voice a mix of panic and fear.

Howard issued basic pointers, and then turned his attention to assessing victims.

The accident scene was getting more chaotic by the minute. Crowds of onlookers hemmed in around the smashed vehicles, getting in the way of people who were trying to help. Gawkers snapped photographs with their cell phones and iPods. Tempers flared. In the distance, emergency vehicles advanced along the shoulder of the highway, strobe lights flashing and electronic sirens wailing.

"Hey, buddy. You need help over there?"

"Yes," said Howard, turning to see the off-duty firefighter again, this time peering over the wreckage.

"Whataya got?"

"Woman and a boy trapped and badly injured. My friend's doing mouth-to-mouth on the boy."

"Our trucks are almost on the scene now . . . I'll be right back."

"How's he doing in there?" asked Howard, peering inside the wrecked car.

"Better now. I got him b-breathing."

"They're over here," said the familiar voice, leading four men in bunker gear and helmets.

"Do any of you speak Spanish?" asked Howard.

"I do," said the fire captain.

"Can you tell the driver that the boy's alive?"

While the captain consoled the crying woman, two firefighters began cutting the roof posts with a set of power shears while a third man stood at the ready with a charged hose line. The moment the roof was off, a paramedic relieved Miriam and checked the boy's vital signs. In minutes, both victims had been stabilized on backboards and were on their way to waiting ambulances.

The injured woman called out to Miriam, "Dios te bendiga, senorita!"

"What'd she say?"

"She said 'God bless you, Miss,'" replied the fire captain.

"Was the boy her son?"

"Her only kid."

A state trooper approached them as they stood talking to the fire captain. "I'm the investigating officer. I'll need you folks to come over to the cruiser for a few minutes."

Miriam gave her statement first, and then while the officer took Howard's, she listened to the police radio playing inside the car—a faceless dispatcher directing other cruisers to distant scenes. She noticed a bunched up McDonald's bag on the floor of the cruiser, evidence of a meal eaten on the fly by a busy officer trying to serve and protect an indifferent public. Outside the cruiser, people were still milling about the scene, staring at the wrecks and taking photos.

"Don't these people have friggin' lives?" said Miriam, as they prepared to leave the cruiser. "Got nothin' better to do than stick their noses into other people's misery?"

"It's like this at most accidents," said the officer.

"Must drive you nuts."

"You get used to it, ma'am."

Howard kept the motor home parked on the shoulder of the off ramp while he bandaged the cuts on Miriam's back. But the emotional turmoil of the accident had taken a greater toll. The upbeat, joyful mood that had characterized their morning was gone now.

"Let's call it a day," said Howard, as they drove back onto the highway. "I'm not in the mood to drive much farther."

"You must've read my mind," said Miriam, her hands shaking from the trauma of the event.

Howard drove for fifty miles with no luck. Frustrated, he decided to stop for fuel. As he pulled up to the pumps, the bored attendant put down her cigarette, pushed open the glass door, then shuffled toward the motor home.

"Fill it?" she asked in a monotone.

"Please. Low octane."

She selected the fuel grade, inserted the nozzle in the fill pipe.

Howard leaned out the driver's window, "My campground directory doesn't list anything around here. Any idea where there's an RV park?"

"Yes, sir. Go up this here road to the third crossroads and hang a left. It's the first farm on the right."

"Farm?"

"That's right. Henderson's Farm. Not a traditional farm, mind you. They've all kinds of stuff for families to do. At the rear of the property is where the campground's at. It's real quiet back there, if quiet's what you want."

"As a matter of fact," said Howard, "that's exactly what we're looking for."

# CHAPTER 19

## *Frank*

H OWARD FOLLOWED THE WOMAN'S instructions and drove
north into the Plains, then turned onto the gravel concession road
bordered on both sides by cornfields. At the entrance to the farm, two hay
rolls painted with yellow smiley faces framed a sign:

Welcome
Henderson's Family Farm
Proprietors: Ken & Maureen Henderson

The recreational farm had something for everyone besides RV
camping: a petting zoo with goats, sheep, calves, and rabbits; a mini put; a
stocked fish pond; horseback rides and lessons; and a farmer's market that
sold pies, homemade preserves, bread, and fresh produce.

"How many sites have you got?" Howard asked the woman at the
registration desk.

"Twenty-four. Only three are occupied at the moment."

"I know you like your space, Chip, but do you mind if we camp near
someone tonight?"

"Sure, but why?"

"After bein' at that accident, I need people around me."

The woman's interest piqued, "You talking about that big highway
wreck east of here?"

"Yes," said Miriam. "It was awful."

"Nobody killed though, thank the Lord."

"How do you know?" asked Miriam.

"Heard it on the radio."

"Oh, that's wonderful," said Miriam. "I was worried someone would've been killed back there. So worried."

"We'll take a site close to one of the other RVs," said Howard.

"I'll put you on number eight," said the woman. "There's an older couple from Canada next to you. Pulled in not twenty minutes ago."

Howard drove the single road that wound its way through the farm. Site eight was next to a fifth wheel with a Canadian flag decal on the front. Howard hooked up the shore lines, but did not detach the Jeep from the motor home. When finished, he set out two chairs and mugs of iced tea. Miriam toyed with her drink, still upset after the accident.

"I can still see the terror in that woman's face," said Miriam.

"I know it's difficult for you," said Howard, "but try to think positively. If you hadn't done mouth-to-mouth on that boy, he'd be dead now."

They turned to see a man in his late seventies walk beside his camper, butane lighter in hand. He lit the water heater; a blue flame shot into the heat exchanger.

"Hi there," said the man, looking over.

Howard waved. "Where are you from in Canada?"

"Ontario. How about you?"

"I used to live in Toledo, but I'm—*we*—are on our way to California."

The man glanced from Howard to Miriam, as if assessing the relationship.

"I'm just about to put supper on the barbeque. We'd be pleased if you'd join us."

"That'd be great," Miriam answered quickly. "Wouldn't it, Chip?"

"Yes," he replied, sensing her eagerness for company.

"Can we bring dessert?" asked Miriam.

"Sure," said the man.

"We'll be over shortly," said Howard, following Miriam into the RV.

"You don't mind visitin' these folks do you?"

"Course I don't mind," he replied, pulling a frozen apple pie from the freezer and defrosting it in the microwave.

Miriam wrung her hands anxiously. "I'm so sorry, Chip, but I just can't get that injured boy out o' my head. I can still see his poor face."

"Tell you what," he said. "How about I call the hospital in the morning and ask how he's doing?"

"Oh, would you?" she said, hugging him. "I'd feel so much better if I knew he was OK."

Supper was a social affair with plenty of laughter and conversation. If traveling kept people younger, then the Watsons were living proof. Both in their late seventies, they were full of vitality and anecdotes of their travels at home and abroad. Marjorie was an attractive woman and possessed of an inviting smile. But of the two, Frank was the most gregarious; his voice was gravelly and resonant, and his face deeply lined, suggestive of a hard life.

"When did you start traveling?" Howard asked, after splashing a dollop of mustard into his lap.

Miriam shook her head as she handed him a napkin.

"Oh . . . a long time ago," said Frank hesitantly, glancing at his wife. "Guess you might say it was circumstances that put me on the road . . . eh, Hon?"

Howard noticed the way he had looked to his wife and the pregnant paused that followed.

"Frank's life is quite a story," she said to Howard, then turned to her husband, "isn't it, dear?"

"Yes . . . I suppose it is."

"Feel like tellin' it?" asked Miriam.

"He glanced at his wife again, then suggested everyone move from the picnic table to the folding chairs. He waited for Marjorie to pour cups of hot tea and set out a plate of cookies before he began.

"My real father died in 1934 when I was two. His death changed my life."

He paused to sip his tea.

"Were you an only child?" asked Miriam.

"No. I had a brother and a sister by my original parents."

"Did your mom remarry?"

"Yes," he said with a look of distaste. "She married a drunken son of a bitch, if you'll pardon my language."

"Did she have any more children?"

"Five, and it wasn't a good time to be having kids. Millions were out of work. My stepfather had work, mind you, but after what he spent on booze, we'd barely enough to keep the wolves from the door. Anyway, the long and short of it was: I hated him and he hated me. That's what sealed my fate."

"What'd he do?"

"Trumped up a false story for the Children's Aid Society. He told them I'd stolen a pocket watch from the next door neighbor's house. I was a nine-year-old little boy for God's sake, and he had me taken away to a foster home. To make matters worse, he stripped me of the name I'd been born with and gave the CAS people a false one. For years, that's what my official name was because I had no birth certificate to prove otherwise."

"Where was your mother in all o' this? Why didn't she stop him from sendin' you away?"

The man stared and blinked at Miriam, unable to find words.

"What were your foster parents like?" asked Miriam, changing the subject.

"Which ones? I had so many."

"The first ones."

"Mean. Didn't give a damn about me. I was just an extra pair of hands. They made me milk cows, clean barns, and peel vegetables and pretty near everything else. When I did something I wasn't supposed to, they beat me with an oxen whip in front of the other foster kids." He lifted one leg of his trousers and pointed to scars still visible after seven decades. "These are the scars you can see. The others are in here," he said, placing a hand over his heart.

"You said you were in lots o' foster homes. Did you ever try to escape?"

"I escaped from every one. And each time they caught me I got sent back, except once when I rowed across the Annapolis Basin."

"Isn't that near the Bay of Fundy?" asked Howard.

"It opens into it."

"Sorry. Go on."

"Anyway, after my rowboat adventure at age fourteen, I was sent off to reform school. Punishment there was far worse. I got beaten with a leather belt and put in a cell by myself for days at a time."

"Did you escape again?" asked Miriam.

"Yes, and for four years I managed to dodge the people who were looking for me."

"Till you were legal age?"

"Yes."

"Where'd you go?"

"I hitchhiked to Truro, Nova Scotia and met two bootleggers in a pool hall. They gave me a job running illegal booze. In between delivering whiskey, I worked in a hat factory. When I'd had enough of both jobs, I bicycled to Woodstock, New Brunswick, and wound up in a Salvation Army hostel. One day when I was trying to sell my bicycle, a farmer offered me a job at a saw mill he operated. He and his wife had no kids and they took me in for a few years. They were kind people. Salt-of-the-earth types and treated me like their own son. I left them eventually and hitchhiked to Toronto, but I stayed in touch over the years until they died."

"What'd you do in Toronto?"

"I worked a couple of jobs for a while. Then I got an itch for adventure. That was the start of my rail-riding days."

"You mean like hoppin' freight trains?"

"Yes."

"How old were you?"

"Sixteen and green behind the ears. I didn't know a damned thing about how to board a moving train, but I soon learned."

"Who from?"

"Older men. Guys who'd been doing it since the Great Depression and couldn't give up the lifestyle. Sometimes I'd get tips from rail yard workers. They'd tell me what freight trains were leaving and where they were headed. I learned to steal food from grocery stores and outfit myself with a traveling kit. I found the best places to catch a few winks and still be within running distance of an outbound train. Smart young bugger I was. One time I slept in a building used to store sand for the railroad, but I was always one step ahead of the bulls."

"The bulls?" asked Miriam.

"Railroad police. They'd arrest you for trespassing. Never caught me though."

"Weren't you afraid o' fallin' off the train?"

"Not once I got into the boxcar. I was more afraid of getting locked inside."

"How come?"

"You could be trapped till the car reached its destination, which might not be where you wanted to go. Sometimes a boxcar would get dropped off at a marshalling yard and might sit for days until it was picked up by another train. By that time, you could be out of food and water, and have no way of getting any till they opened the door. In winter, you could freeze to death. In summer you could die of dehydration and heat stroke. If you did survive, the minute they opened the door, they'd turn you over to the bulls."

"Did you get to see many places?"

"Plenty. I rode the rails clear across Canada from one town to the next. I'd work a job for a while, and then move on to another city or town, wherever I could find a job. One time, I rode to Calgary, Alberta, on the water tender of a steam locomotive. Those things belched out lots of soot and cinders. By the time I got there, I looked like a raccoon with blackened eyes. The last job I had before I turned legal age was on a cattle ranch in London, Ontario. Somehow, the people at the Children's Aid Society found out where I was, but I gave them the slip. Once I turned eighteen, they couldn't touch me anymore. That's when I took up trucking for a living, hauling machinery and supplies to Alaska and into some of the northern mining camps over the ice roads."

"Never heard o' ice roads."

"Frozen lakes," he said. "When the ice gets thick enough, you can take a fully loaded eighteen-wheeler on them."

"Isn't there a danger o' the truck fallin' through?"

"There is if you go too fast. It starts a wave rolling under the ice that can break it."

"So," said Miriam, changing the subject, "when did Mrs. Watson here come into the picture?"

"After I divorced my first wife. Marjorie and I married when I turned thirty-five. She was the one that convinced me to start searching for my family."

"Did you find them?"

He nodded. "It took some doing, mind you. I went back to my home town and searched the public cemetery for names. I found my grandparents' headstones, as well as my father's, but not my mother's. After that, we drove the streets one by one, looking at names on mailboxes. I went up to this house and knocked on the door. It turned out to be my uncle's place. He invited me into his living room. Told me my real name wasn't Frank Watson—it was Charles McInnis. Good thing I was sitting down when he told me. I'd gone all those years as Frank Watson. So long, my real name had kind of blown away in the wind. He told me my brother, Sid McInnis, was living in Maine. Then he asked if I'd seen my sister or my mother yet. When I shook my head, he took me to the front window and pointed to two houses up the street: my sister's and my mother's."

He stopped talking and took a tissue from his wife to wipe his eyes.

"When my sister opened the door, I asked her if she knew who I was. She said, 'you're damned right I know. What took you so long?'"

He paused to blow his nose

"Before I left my sister's, she called mother and told her she'd be getting a visitor, but didn't say who."

"I'll never forget the moment. We just cried and hung onto each other. Cried over those lost years. All thirty-one of them. It hit us both hard. First thing she did was bring out my birth certificate. I just stared at it and ran my fingers over the name—Charles McInnis—the first proof I had of who I really was. Mom had been searching for me for years, but under my birth name, so of course, she never found me."

"How come you still go by Frank Watson?"

The man cleared his throat, "Because it's what everyone knew me by. It didn't make sense to change it back. Not after that long."

"I guess news must've spread fast in your town," said Miriam, "about you bein' back and all."

"Yes, they all came: neighbors, family, townspeople. They dropped by for a visit and a cup of tea. I remembered listening to them reminisce about me. That was hard for me to listen to. They might as well have been talking about a stranger."

"Did you ever find out why she let your stepfather, send you away?"

He shook his head, "She passed away twelve years after our reunion. It was the secret she took with her to the end."

There was a long, awkward pause after he finished. No one seemed to know how to restart the conversation. The only sounds were the rasp of crickets in the cornfields and the whine of the occasional mosquito. Marjorie Watson broke the silence.

"Well, hon," she said, squeezing his hand, "at least your life's a lot better these days. Better than it was."

"I'll say," he replied. "Still . . . I'll never forget how I felt as a kid . . . knowing someone didn't want me."

Howard immediately looked at Miriam. If Frank's comment had touched her conscience, it was impossible to tell from her facial expression—it was inscrutable. But when he dropped his gaze, he noticed the thumb of her left hand, absently tracing tiny circles on her abdomen.

# CHAPTER 20

## *Toward the Divide*

H OWARD AWOKE TO THE music of laughter and conversation;
Miriam was having her first coffee of the day with the Watsons. He
glanced at his watch. It was eight thirty. Odd he thought, most retired RV
travelers would already be a hundred miles down the highway by now.

He recalled how much retirees used to irritate the hell out of him
and Suzanne wherever they camped. The gray-haired geriatrics—blessed
with the least harried of human agendas—were always up with the birds,
fouling the air with noxious diesel exhaust and shattering the tranquility
with their idling engines, chattering loudly to each other as they packed
up, and then pulling out of campgrounds at the most ungodly hour,
waking all the campers because of their obsessive need to get off to an
early start. These were the same inconsiderate people, who, instead of
doing their banking transactions during mornings or afternoons, always
waited until the noon hour, when working people were trying to bank on
their limited lunch breaks.

As he rubbed the sleep from his eyes, he recalled how they had all
savored the glorious sunset on the High Plains, then sat late into the evening,
listening to Frank's storytelling: of his roving adventures through boreal
forests under the neon glow of northern lights; of highway confrontations
with moose, anxious to escape the springtime hordes of mosquitoes and
black flies that plagued Canadian forests; of fishing for pickerel and pike
and muskellunge in the dark, cobalt waters of glacial-carved lakes; and of
the soul-stirring tremolo of loons on silken, summer nights. But what he
remembered most about the evening was Miriam's interaction with the
Watsons—her need to connect with them.

"Tell me 'bout the history, Frank," she had asked. "Tell me 'bout Canada."

And Frank Watson had been happy to oblige. She had sat in rapt attention as he told her: about the first Europeans on Canadian shores, the Vikings, who settled at L'Anse aux Meadows, on the northern tip of Newfoundland, five hundred years before Columbus arrived in the New World; about how the indigenous people gave the country its name, *Kanata,* "the settlement" in the Iroquois tongue; about *les couriers du bois,* the runners-of-the-woods, hardy French fur traders who paddled and portaged their birch bark freighter canoes into the interior of a vast, rich land, then returned, loaded to the gunwales with a fortune in furs—the pelts of beaver and muskrat and mink and wolf; about the forming of the Hudson's Bay Company, the oldest and largest corporation in North America and its network of early trading posts that helped supply those who opened the country; and about the founding principle of the country—compromise—that attempted to accommodate the diverse cultures of First Nations aboriginals, as well as the first European settlers, the French and the English. And he talked of his nation's heroes: her soldiers who fought to topple tyrants, and afterwards, distinguished themselves on the world's stage as peacekeepers, so that tyrants could not rise again; the Royal Canadian Mounted Police, who maintained law and order in a burgeoning country and kept it from having gunfights in the streets, and a lawless frontier; and of more recent heroes, like, Terry Fox, the selfless teenage boy who, having lost his leg to cancer, attempted to complete his solitary mission—The Marathon of Hope—a cross-country run to raise money for cancer research, only to die with his goal half-finished when the disease returned to claim him.

Howard rolled out of bed, yawned, and stood at the window eavesdropping on the Watson's site.

"How do you cope with those long winters up in Canada?" asked Miriam, sipping her coffee.

"Oh," said Marjorie, laughing, "you get used to the cold, dear."

"No, I mean the long months o' total darkness when the sun never comes up. Must be weird and all, tryin' to figure out when to sleep and when to stay awake."

The couple exchanged surprised looks. When Marjorie went to answer, her husband placed his hand on her arm.

"Well now, Miriam," he said, his eyes twinkling, "I'll tell you a thing or two about Canada's Great White North. Our winters are cold—so cold your shadow'll freeze to the ground. Every once in a while someone goes missing in a storm. They don't find them till the snow melts in spring."

"Really? You get that much huh?"

"Yep," he said. "Some years, it's fifty feet deep by the end of March. So deep you can't see the telephone poles or the street lamps. But it's the cold that kills most Canadians. Sure does. Freezes them to the marrow."

"No kiddin', said Miriam.

"Oh yes," he said, gathering momentum. "In Toronto, people have frozen to death while waiting for a bus. Why, I remember one winter it got so cold you couldn't even light a match. I saw a guy toss a glass of water up and it froze in mid-air and fell to his feet in little crystals. Birds were dropping dead on the wing and falling into snow banks . . ."

"Frank *Watson*," exclaimed his wife. "Don't you be telling fibs to that girl. You'll have her thinking we live in igloos."

"But you do *have* igloos in Canada," said Miriam nodding emphatically. "I know 'cause I saw pictures of 'em in a book one time."

"Not where we live," said Marjorie.

"A girlfriend of mine went to Niagara Falls once," Miriam continued, "and you know what she told me?"

"What was that, dear?" said Marjorie, again exchanging glances with her husband.

"She said there were miles and miles o' vineyards, and orchards full o' peaches and pears and plums. I never knew you grew fruit in Canada. That surprised me, what with the cold winters you get up there and all."

Marjorie brought a hand up to stifle a grin just as her husband was ready with another round of tall tales.

"Don't you say another word, Frank," said his wife.

Miriam started laughing. "Ah," she said, playfully slapping Frank's arm, "I had a feelin' you were pullin' my leg, but I wasn't sure."

"This husband of mine is an awful teaser, Miriam, but I'm gonna tell you two things you can tell your friends, and they're both true."

"Oh yeah?"

"Did you know there's a place in the United States where you can look south and see Canada?"

"Where's that?" asked Miriam, popping a piece of gum in her mouth.

"In Detroit. When you look south you can see Windsor, Ontario."

"Really," said Miriam, chomping vigorously. "What's the other?"

"There's a little piece of land in southern Ontario on the shore of Lake Erie called Point Pelee. It's on a level with northern California."

"Wow!" exclaimed Miriam, then blew her first bubble that broke over her lips.

"And what a climate it has," said Frank, deadpan. "Next time you're in a supermarket ask the grocer if he has any Point Pelee bananas. They're delicious."

The Watsons were in no hurry to leave and they invited Howard and Miriam to join them for breakfast. While Frank flipped pancakes on the griddle and stacked them on a plate, Howard sat beside him and made small talk. Miriam glommed onto Marjorie and the two women chatted and laughed together over cups of coffee. Every now and then Howard caught snippets of their conversation; but after a time, he noticed them talking in hushed tones.

"Would you mind if I have a word with you, Marjorie?"

"Of course not, dear," she replied, gesturing toward her trailer.

Ten minutes later the two women emerged carrying dishes and cutlery. Miriam wore a brave smile, but her eyes were red and puffy. With the table set, everyone tucked into a mound of pancakes and the conversation turned lively. Once again, Frank Watson was in high form, joking and teasing.

By mid-morning both couples had packed up and stood around saying their goodbyes. It was always an awkward time. Howard remembered how he and Suzanne had played out this same ritual, exchanging addresses and promising to stay in touch. Howard noticed how affectionately Miriam clung to the Watsons, a couple old enough to be her grandparents. She had only known them for hours, yet seemed unable to let go, especially of Marjorie, who she held in a vigorous embrace.

"Good luck with everything, dear," said Marjorie, kissing Miriam's cheek.

They watched the Watsons tow their trailer off the campground, and then made their own last minute preparations to leave. Miriam did a final outside check of the motor home while Howard went inside to pack out the trash. As he gathered the corners of the bag to tie a knot, he noticed the last items on top: two unopened packages of Miriam's cigarettes, still in their cellophane wrappers.

AFTER GETTING off to a late start they decided to skip lunch and try to reach the Colorado border by suppertime. It was a monotonous drive across the remainder of Kansas, an endless vista cleaved by the arrow-straight band of asphalt that joined them to the western horizon. Miriam was comfortably ensconced in her captain's chair, her bare feet propped on the dashboard. He noticed how the grasses swayed by the roadside and in the fields that flanked the highway. He had crossed the Great Plains many times with Suzanne and could not remember a time when there was no wind, when dust devils did not twirl and twist over open land like dervishes. Howard glanced occasionally at the altimeter on the dashboard; they were climbing ever so slowly toward the eastern slope of the Rocky Mountains.

"What's that, Chip?" asked Miriam, pointing to a long, metal framework set above a series of A-struts with balloon tires.

"A center-pivot irrigator. You'll see a lot of them out here."

"But the land looks so dry. Where does the water come from?"

"Underground. The Ogallala aquifer."

"Is it big?"

"Humungous," said Howard, pulling out to pass a slow-moving car towing a U-Haul trailer.

"Spindly looking things," said Miriam, as they passed another rig. "Looks like they'd fall apart in a strong gust."

"They might look flimsy, but there's plenty of engineering in them. Have you noticed the wind out here?"

"Yeah. I've been watchin' the dust swirlin' around."

"Wind is the enemy of these irrigators."

"How come?"

"If the water droplets coming out of the sprinklers are too small or the discharge is too far above the crops, the wind evaporates the water before it can reach the roots of the plants."

"How come you know so much about 'em?"

"I worked out here on a farm one summer."

"Must've been hard work."

"It was healthy work," said Howard. "I never ate or slept so well in my life."

"Where'd you stay?"

"With the McCallum family."

"Good people?"

"The best. Plain living folks with big hearts. The kind that make you feel like family, even when you're working for them. Ever hear the expression, 'the bread basket of America'"?

"Yeah."

"Well, you've been driving through it," he said, with a wave of his hand. "Some of the food you ate in Philadelphia was grown out here."

"Speakin' o' food, I'm gettin' hungry," said Miriam, late in the afternoon. "We got any snacks on board?"

"Pretzels," said Howard, checking his rear view mirror.

Miriam unbuckled her seatbelt and made her way to the pantry. She tore open the bag and dumped the contents into a mixing bowl, then pulled two cans of iced tea from the fridge.

"Here," she said, cracking the aluminum tab on Howard's drink, and setting the bowl between them on the console.

"Thanks," he said, transferring the can to his drink holder.

"Chip, can I ask you somethin'?"

"What?" said Howard, reaching into the bowl.

"Do you think it was silly o' me exchangin' addresses with the Watsons?"

"No. Sometimes people stay in touch."

"You mean like pen pals?"

"Uh-huh," replied Howard, "except people use email mostly. Letter writing's a lost art these days."

"I'd *have* to write a letter."

"Why's that?"

"Can't use a computer."

"You've never used one?"

"Not a proper computer," she said, taking a swig of iced tea. "Just the ones in the restaurant that tally up people's bills."

"Would you like to write to the Watsons?"

"Sure," Miriam replied, "but I don't know if they'd write back."

"What makes you say that?"

"Oh, I dunno," she sighed. "They might not wanna bother."

"I'm sure they would. You'll never know till you contact them."

"Did you and Suzanne meet a lot o' people on the road?"

"Quite a few. Why?"

"Did you stay in touch after?"

"Not that I remember."

"Oh," she said, and then went quiet.

"Is there something you're trying to tell me?" asked Howard, taking a swig of iced tea.

"Yeah . . . I guess," she said, absently rotating the aluminum can between her fingers.

"What is it?"

"I been thinkin' that once this trip's over, I'd like to stay in touch."

"Well, like I said, send the Watsons a letter and I'm sure they'll—"

"No, Chip," she said as they crossed the Colorado state line. "I meant with you."

# CHAPTER 21

## *Breakdown*

N O LONGER THE AWKWARD strangers they had been in Ohio, they stood with shoulders touching, facing the first light of a new day. At over 6,000 feet they were on the high shelf of the Great Plains, the grassy plateau on which the Rockies sat. Yet the mountains seemed to elude them, as if the closer they got, the farther they retreated.

The air had a different quality here than that of the Midwest. In the rain-shadow of the mountains it was more arid and drew the moisture from their eyes. It was thinner too, with less oxygen for lungs and bloodstreams accustomed to the richer air of the East's lower altitudes. And it was steeped in something mystical that beckoned: the promise of aspen and spruce and pine-forested slopes, of ancient, silver-laden rock and of gold-flecked icy streams, of snow-crowned alpine peaks towering above sweeping meadows carpeted with Rocky Mountain wildflowers: columbine and blue bonnet, fairy slipper and sky pilot, Aspen daisy and lupine.

"Look there," said Miriam, suddenly jabbing a finger toward the western horizon. "Is that them?"

Howard squinted ahead. They were deceptively small, but unmistakable: a purple, bumpy spine that stretched from north to south under a bank of vanilla clouds.

"Yes," replied Howard.

"Oh my God," she squealed. "We're here. We're actually here."

Howard found a place to pull over. The moment Miriam was outside she jumped excitedly. "Get your camera, Chip."

"I won't get a good picture," he protested. "They're too far off."

"I don't care. I want a souvenir o' this very moment."

"I'll do better than that," grinned Howard, buoyed by Miriam's contagious euphoria, "I'll take *our* picture."

He set his camera atop a tripod, armed the timer, and then rushed into the picture. They laughed and smiled and hammed it up for the lens with silly faces, arms wrapped unselfconsciously around each other, and cheeks pressed tightly together—May/September moments.

Back in the RV they scrolled through the photos, "This one's my favorite," she said. The picture showed a smiling Howard standing behind Miriam, his hands gently squeezing her shoulders, his bearded chin resting on the top of her head.

"Mine too," he replied.

"I like it, 'cause it shows exactly how I feel."

"And how's that?"

"Happier than I have ever been *and* with the man who made it all possible." Then she surprised him by suddenly kissing his cheek. "I can't wait to tell my mom about this."

"Speaking of your mother," said Howard, steering back onto the road, "when was the last time you called her?"

"Just before I left Philly."

"You should've been at Malibu by now. She'll be worried."

"Nah. I don't think so."

"Why not?"

"She's got plenty o' things goin' on in her life, country club, volunteerin', and whatnot."

"Still," he insisted, "you should call and put her at ease. We've got more to see before we get to California."

"I suppose you're right. Soon as we find a phone booth somewhere I'll call her."

"No," he said, handing her his cell phone. "Do it now before you forget."

Miriam opened an iced tea and popped a fresh wad of gum in her mouth, then keyed in her mother's number. The line rang four times: "I can't come to the phone right now, so please leave a message after the tone and one of us will get back to you . . ."

One of us? Was she living with someone new and had not told her yet? Or had she forgotten to change the message since David died?

"It's Mimi, I'm just callin' to let you know that—"

"Mimi . . . honey," said a breathless voice.

"Mom, are you OK?"

"Yes . . . just got in the door . . . where *are* you? I've been worried sick."

"I know, Mom. Sorry I didn't call before this, but guess what?"

"What?"

"I'm at the Rockies. The Rocky Mountains. In Colorado—"

"What's that noise in the background, honey? Sounds like you're calling from a vehicle."

"I am," she replied, excitedly. "From a motor home."

"What are you doing in a motor home? Only transients and lowlifes drive those things."

"Oh, Mom, you are *so* out of touch with life outside Malibu."

"You haven't answered my question, Mimi."

"I hitched a ride just south of—"

"You *what?*"

"Hitched a ride."

"With who? Some drifter?"

"No," replied Miriam, taking a deep breath. "This guy picked me up."

"What kind of guy?"

"A decent guy, Mom. His name's, Chip."

"How old is he?"

"What difference does it make how old he is?"

"Sweetheart, you don't know a thing about this man."

"You're wrong, Mom, I know a lot about him, and what I know, I like."

"Honey, I hate to say this, but you're not a very good judge of men."

"Mom, would you listen to me. I'm not out to marry the guy. He's givin' me a ride, that's all. Makin' sure I get to your place safely."

"Oh my God!" shouted her mother in a panicky tone. "He's dropping you here? Driving that thing into *this* neighborhood?"

"Uh-huh, and he's goin' out o' his way to do that. He's headed for San Diego."

"But," said her mother, "why is it taking you so long to get out here?"

"He's been takin' me places. We've been horseback ridin' and flyin' in a hot air balloon, and he says we're gonna—"

"Mimi, honey, men don't do things like that without wanting something in return, and you know what that thing is: you're sitting on it."

"Mother, don't be so crude."

"Put this man on the phone, Mimi. I want to talk to him."

"No."

"Why not?"

"Because he's drivin' at the moment."

"Then you tell him to pull that damned thing to the side of the road and talk with your mother."

"I'm not doing that," said Miriam, her tone defiant.

"Don't be angry with me, honey. You know I have your best interests at heart."

"Yes, Mom, but I'm not a kid anymore. I can look after myself."

There was a long pause.

"Mimi."

"Yeah."

"I love you, sweetie. You know that's why I worry, don't you?"

"Yes, Mom, but you gotta stop this worryin' stuff. Chip's an OK guy. He really is. He's gonna be takin' me to a few more places before he drops me off."

"What kind of places?"

"I dunno. We're just wingin' it as we go."

"Oh, Mimi, I don't like the sound of this. Don't like it one bit."

"Don't like what, Mom?"

"You riding with a stranger. Things happen to women. Bad things."

"But, I've told you, he's a very likeable guy."

"Have you got any next-of-kin information, honey? If something happened, I'd have no way of knowing."

"Yes, Mom," she replied impatiently, not telling her mother she had already been robbed under a highway bridge.

"Promise me you'll be careful, dear."

"I will, Mom," said Miriam, and ended the call.

"I'm going to pull over and call her," said Howard. "She must be worried half to death about you."

"No, Chip," said Miriam, massaging her temples.

"I'm a parent too. I know how she feels."

"It's more than that," said Miriam. "Mom's always had this need to control me. She pisses me off with it."

"Is she clingy?"

"Very. Never been able to cut the apron strings."

"Why? Doesn't she trust you?"

"Oh, I dunno. It's like she's got an empty space inside her that nothin' can fill."

"Nothing but you?"

"Yeah."

"I get the impression," said Howard, "that you've never been to her house in Malibu."

"You're right."

"Why's that?"

"I couldn't afford the time off. Afraid I'd come back and find myself unemployed."

"So," said Howard, "are you telling me you've hardly seen her since you left home at eighteen?"

"Oh, no. I see her every summer when she flies out to visit her friends in Philly. She always stays a couple days."

HOURS LATER after a long, slow climb through the San Isabel National Forest, Howard reached the parking lot at the summit of the continental divide, the rocky spine from which all water drained to the Atlantic, or the Pacific. Two signboards provided information to travelers: an appeal for caution on the steep, downhill grade, and the FM radio stations that gave out weather data. Beyond the parking lot, great swaths of clear-cut forest marked the ski runs. The slopes near timberline were patchy with fir trees, a contrast to the thicker forests at lower elevations. On the treeless peaks, remnants of winter snow pack remained.

When they stepped outside, gusty, altitude-chilled air swirled parking lot grit against their ankles. Miriam, grinning like a Cheshire cat, posed for photographs in front of the summit sign: Monarch Pass, Elevation 11,312 feet.

At the thunder of motorcycle engines they turned to see a long line of machines enter the parking lot. It was a club outing and members were warmly dressed in leathers. The rowdier Harley riders obnoxiously revved their engines. The more sedate ones glided in quietly on Hondas. Members gathered in small groups to talk and have a cigarette; their drifting tobacco smoke gave Miriam a sudden craving.

Beyond the parking lot she noticed a building with large letters on its side: *Scenic Ride*. Smaller print advised people to take a camera and allow fifteen minutes for a round trip, or a chance to get off at the observation room at the top. A neon sign in the window announced it was open for business.

"Look," she said, pointing to a descending gondola car. "Think we could take a ride?"

"Don't have time," said Howard, casting a serious glance at his watch. "It's a long drive down the other side of this mountain."

"Oh," said Miriam, crestfallen.

Howard winked and smiled.

"You are wicked!" she said, punching his arm. "For a moment I thought you were serious."

"We'd better take jackets," he said, chuckling. "It'll be even colder at the top."

Miriam beamed as Howard bought tickets. They waited only briefly until their gondola entered the building. The operator stopped the cable hoist, and helped steady the tiny car while they entered. As they made their slow climb to the summit, the wind whistled through the door crack and broadsided them into a disarming sway. Howard pressed both hands against the inside walls to steady himself. But Miriam was oblivious, and pointed out features on the ground below. When they reached the first support tower, the gondola's connecting arm rumbled over the cable pulleys and sent a shudder through the car.

At the summit they disembarked at the observation building. The view across the peaks was dazzling in the bright sunlight, and they spent their time enjoying the panorama and chatting with other tourists. On the outside deck, the wind was gusty and cold. Soon, they retreated inside.

"Ugh," said Miriam, suddenly slumping onto one of the benches.

"What's wrong?"

"I've got a headache."

"Bad?" Howard asked.

"A whopper," she groaned, massaging her temples. "It's not like me. I rarely get 'em."

"Altitude sickness. It'll pass."

"What do I do in the meantime?"

"For openers, we'll go down to the parking lot."

They took the next gondola car off the summit. Once again, the car swayed in the wind, but his concern for Miriam overrode his nervousness. When they emerged at the base, he kept his arm around her as they walked back to the RV.

"I'm going to get us off this mountain," he said as he slipped behind the driver's seat and started the engine.

Only a few cars remained in the parking lot when he wheeled the motor home toward the roadway. As he made the wide turn, he glanced into his mirror. There was a large stain on the ground where he had been parked.

"Somethin' wrong?" asked Miriam, frowning as the RV stopped.

"I'll tell you in a minute."

He walked to the front of the vehicle and peered underneath. Fluid was leaking from the engine area: the radiator hose was split.

"Is it serious?" she asked, seeing his concerned look.

"Serious enough I can't drive it off the mountain."

"But we've got the Jeep if we have to go somewhere for help, right?"

"I don't want to leave the rig up here. Once the gondola shuts down, there'll be nobody around till morning. Be too easy for someone to break in."

"Maybe the ride operator can get someone to tow us. It's worth askin'."

"You stay put. I'll be right back."

He was winded by the time he reached the operator, busy helping passengers embark from a gondola car.

"Which way you going?" asked the man.

"West. For the San Juans."

"Well," said the man, scratching his head, "I can get a licensed mechanic up here from Salida, but that'd put you back east of the mountain. You'll have to climb the pass all over again."

"Is there anyone west of here?"

"Harry Kimball, but he's unlicensed."

"Unlicensed, huh," said Howard, mulling the idea.

"I wouldn't let that put you off. He's been fixing things around here forever."

"Is he good?"

"Better than good."

"Beggars can't be choosers I suppose," said Howard, shrugging with resignation.

"Want me to call him?"

"Sure. Do you think he could get us off the mountain before dark?"

"I doubt it, but I'll ask him."

The man stopped the cable for an elderly couple, and then restarted the machinery and placed the call. He laughed and bantered for a few minutes, then got to the point. The person at the other end spoke loudly enough for Howard to hear; the tow truck would not be up until eight o'clock the following morning.

"What's the verdict?" asked Miriam when he returned.

"Looks like we're up here for the night."

"You mean campin' out . . . in the parkin' lot?"

"Afraid so. Sorry I didn't get things fixed before this, but I figured it'd hold together till California."

"It's gonna be cold after dark. We got enough warm stuff on board?"

"Plenty. By the way, how's your headache?"

"Still got it. Not nearly as bad though."

"Good," he replied. "I'll fling supper together. Baked beans on toast OK?"

"Fine," she said, laughing. "We'll need our farts to keep us warm tonight."

He fired up the gas stove and boiled water to make a hot compress for Miriam's forehead. By the time they had finished their meal and washed the dishes, he appraised the cloudless, pre-sunset sky.

"If I promise to make you warm enough," said Howard, "do you feel well enough to stargaze with me?"

"Sure. If we're stuck up here we might as well make the best of it."

"Remember how your school friends bragged about seeing lots of stars at summer camp?"

"Yeah."

"Well, you're going to see a whole lot more."

"How come? You got a telescope or somethin'?"

"Uh-uh. Binoculars with big lenses."

They dressed warmly, took chairs and blankets outside, and then sat in the lee of the motor home. Even without clouds the sunset created its own high-altitude magic. Around them, Englemann spruce stood at attention, their spear-like tips making a ragged border against the evening sky. The moment the sun dropped below the treetops, the air temperature plummeted.

"Look," whispered Howard, pointing to the edge of the spruce.

"What? I can't see squat."

"At the opening in the trees."

It took a moment for her eyes to adjust to the deep shadows. "Oh wow . . . it's a deer . . . two deer."

"Sshh," said Howard, holding a finger to his lips.

The animals stood motionless on the opposite side of the highway, blending seamlessly into their surroundings. All their prey-detection senses were on high alert: eyes watching for the slightest movement, noses probing for the scent of predators, ears swiveling to amplify the faintest sounds. When the aluminum frame of Miriam's chair creaked, they turned in unison and stared in her direction. Once satisfied they were in no danger, both does stepped cautiously onto the pavement and crossed the road. They angled through the parking lot, hooves lightly crunching on gravel. Suddenly, they froze again. In the distance, the groan of a diesel engine announced the approach of an eighteen-wheeler. When the headlights appeared, both animals bounded to safety and melted into the forest.

After reaching the summit of the pass, the driver engaged the jake brake and shifted to a lower gear to begin the long descent toward Salida, Colorado. Gradually, the retreating growl of the engine was absorbed by the mountains, until all they heard was the sigh of the wind through spruce needles.

As the eastern sky darkened in the advancing twilight, brighter magnitude stars appeared first. While they waited for total darkness, Howard talked about his field trips with members of St. Martin's Astronomy Club and how sometimes a professional astronomer was invited along to make a presentation.

"Did Suzanne ever go with you?" asked Miriam.

"No."

"Why not?"

"She needed dimensions she could grasp. Peering through a telescope overwhelmed her. She couldn't fathom the distances."

"How far away are they," she said, pointing to one of the brighter stars.

"Astronomers measure them in light-years."

"What's that?"

"The distance light travels in a year at 186,000 miles per second."

She paused to do a mental calculation. "Holy George," she exclaimed, "That's over eleven million miles a minute. They must be at least a couple light-years away."

"Try billions of light-years," said Howard, "for some of the farthest ones."

"Go on," said Miriam, with a disbelieving look. "You're kiddin' me, right?"

"Scout's honor."

"No wonder that blew Suzanne's mind."

"It's dark enough now," said Howard, handing the binoculars to her. He pointed to a small section of sky with few visible stars. "Have a look there."

She took a moment to adjust the focus wheel, "Oh my, *God*," she shrieked. "There's thousands."

"See the dark spaces in between?" asked Howard.

"Yeah."

"If we aimed a big telescope at them, you'd seen thousands more."

Despite the motor home's mechanical problems, and whatever repair costs lay ahead, Howard Munro was having the time of his life. Miriam gazed in awe at the night sky as she moved the binoculars. Hyper with enthusiasm, she bombarded him with questions and listened intently as he explained black holes and quasars, the red and blue shift of stars, the differences between comets, asteroids, and meteors, and how the eruption of solar flares on the surface of the sun threatened spacecraft and produced auroras. He took her on an imaginary voyage across the universe, traveling through time, to visit hypothetical worlds in other galaxies. He found her hunger to learn and her exuberance intoxicating. With each discovery, she was agape with astonishment, like a pauper seeing the riches of a sultan's palace.

"Look, there," she pointed and squealed with excitement. "One is actually movin'."

"That's a satellite," he replied, watching it with her as it journeyed through the constellations.

"Oh, Chip," she exclaimed and squeezed his hand. "This is the most magical thing I have ever done, but I feel guilty for sayin' it."

"Why?"

"Because we wouldn't be doin' this if the RV hadn't broken down."

"That's my fault. I should've taken that mechanic's advice and got things fixed."

He noticed Miriam staring at him. She wore an expression he had not seen before.

"What?" he said.

"Do you believe in destiny?"

"In what way?"

She pointed skyward, "You know . . . like there's some kind o' force up there that makes things happen for a reason? That brings two people together."

"I don't know," he replied, quickly cutting her off. "I never think about stuff like that."

She sensed his discomfort and said no more. Instead, she turned her attention back to the night sky. Howard continued pointing out features in the heavens, but now he wondered what she had meant. Was she falling in love with him? Did she think he was falling in love with her? Perhaps there was nothing to her remark, just something she had blurted out in the moment. Regardless, he could not dismiss it from his mind.

"You know," she said, wrapping her hands around the warm mug and holding it against her chest, "I wish I'd finished high school. Gone on to a place like St. Martin's."

"Why?"

"Because I might be a whole lot smarter. Be doin' more than just waitin' on tables in some greasy spoon."

"You could always take a correspondence course, you know," said Howard. "Lots of people do."

"In your dreams," she said, in a self-derogatory tone. "I'm too stupid."

"Don't say that. You're smarter than you know."

"You think so?"

"Yes," he said. "I wish I was half as smart as you are with math."

"Well," replied Miriam, "I just wish I was smarter, period, to be honest and truthful."

"You know what?"

"What?"

"I wouldn't change a thing about you, Mimi," said Howard, realizing he had used her nickname for the first time. "Not a single thing."

She reached out and touched his arm, "That is the sweetest thing any man has ever said to me!"

# CHAPTER 22

## *Josh*

IN THE OXYGEN-STARVED AIR of 13,000 feet, sleep had been difficult for them. Adding to their discomfort was the fact that the RV's battery had run flat, disabling the furnace, the only safely vented appliance they could use to keep the chilled mountain air at bay. Their only consolation came at dawn with the realization that they would soon be off the summit and breathing easier at a lower elevation. Still, in the early morning light, they saw evidence of how cold it had been; a crescent-shaped bib of thick frost lay across the top of their bedclothes, an icy by-product of their exhaled breath.

"You awake?" Howard called from the lounge bed.

There was no answer. He looked at the wall clock. It was 6:05 a.m.

"Mimi?"

"Whuh?"

"I think we'd better get up."

"Got lots o' time," she mumbled. "It's just turned six."

"Yes, but we've got breakfast to get and—"

"I don't wanna get out o' bed. It's too friggin' cold in here."

"It won't be so bad," he said, "once we turn the stove on. How'd you sleep?"

"Don't ask."

"Not good I take it?"

"Kept wakin' up. But thanks for givin' me the duvet and the hot water bottle."

"I'll bet you didn't have to get up once during the night."

"Nope."

"I did," he confessed.

"I know. I heard you. You must've worn a path to the toilet."

"It was all that coffee I drank."

"A likely story," she said, laughing.

"Coffee's a diuretic, you know," he said, defensively. "Makes you pee more."

"Sounds more like ol' man's bladder syndrome to me."

"Hey," shouted Howard in mock protest, "that's elder abuse."

"We should've bought you some adult diapers at Wal-Mart," she said, giggling loudly. "Then you could've peed without gettin' out o' bed."

"Wait'll you're my age," he said. "You'll be up more during the night."

"Speakin' o' senior citizens, how would you like breakfast in bed this morning?"

"You *owe me* breakfast in bed after a cheap shot like that."

Miriam got out of bed and shrieked twice: once as she tip toed to the washroom on the glacial floor, again when she sat on the frigid toilet seat. Now it was Howard's turn to tease her, and he did so without mercy. Moments later, she stormed from the rear of the coach giggling and swinging her pillow at Howard's head. He quickly retreated under the covers and between fits of laughter, issued muffled shouts of protest as she straddled his cocooned form and battered away. The exchange did not last long until both were gasping for air from all their exertion.

When she had recovered, she bundled herself in Howard's terry bathrobe then turned on one of the stove's three propane burners.

"Open a window," he warned.

"Can't we wait till it's warmed up in here?" she protested.

"We'll be dead from carbon monoxide before that happens."

She made coffee, then cooked bacon and eggs on a Teflon griddle, all the while blowing warm air on her fingertips.

As Howard sipped his coffee, his mind replayed the events of the previous year. He realized that in all that time, a period dominated by a visceral feeling of loss and sadness, he had never laughed out loud, never shaken from a hearty belly laugh: not till this morning. The laughter and the teasing and the thought that someone cared about him was the warm light that drove away the cold, polar darkness of his grief. The morning's revelry had been another milestone for them; they now joked more easily with each other and talked about some of the places they might visit between Colorado and the coast.

Howard glanced at the wall calendar and realized this was only his seventeenth day on the road with Miriam. He marveled at how quickly they had become comfortable with each other. A kind of mutual intuitiveness had developed between them, to the point where they could almost anticipate each other's thoughts, much the same way as it had been with him and Suzanne. He had been careful to keep the topic of her planned abortion out of their conversations, something that had contributed to the growing harmony between them. Still, he wondered, had she changed her mind?

At the sound of a large vehicle, she parted the venetian blinds, "Tow truck's here."

Howard looked at his watch. It was 7:45 a.m. The man was early.

"I'll clean up," she said.

"There's no time for that. Just toss everything in the sink and fling yourself together."

The heavy-duty recovery truck stopped alongside the motor home. Two men jumped to the ground from the high crew cab. The driver was a lanky, leather-skinned man in his seventies wearing denim bib overalls and a checked shirt. His assistant, dressed in mechanic's coveralls and work boots, was a blonde-haired man of medium build, about six feet in height. Howard noticed the man's pronounced limp and the facial scars that ran from his forehead into his scalp. For a fleeting instant he saw something odd in the man's expression.

"Good morning," said Howard.

"Morning," said the older man.

The young man only nodded, and then quickly got chains and tow bars in place to secure the motor home for the long descent off the mountain.

"Thanks for coming up here, Mr. Kimball," said Howard.

"We go by first names around here. It's Harry."

"Do we have far to go?" asked Howard as a loud diesel truck drove past on the road.

"Say again," said Harry, cupping his ear.

"Your garage? Is it far?"

"About an hour's drive."

"Think you'll have the parts to fix it?"

"If not, I'll have them delivered."

Minutes later, as Miriam left the RV, she tripped on the door threshold and toppled forward. The young man caught her in his arms before she hit the ground. For a fleeting instant, their faces were inches apart. She fussed with her hair and clothes, trying to salvage her dignity.

"You OK, ma'am?"

"Yeah," she said, and smiled. "Thanks."

"I'm Josh . . . Josh Woods," he said, shaking her hand.

"Miriam Kovacs . . . Mimi, for short."

"Come on folks," said Harry, walking toward the truck.

Progress was slow on the winding road as the tow truck and its long cargo snaked its way toward the base of the mountain. A scanner in the cab crackled with the voices of police dispatchers and officers somewhere in the ether. In the front seat, the two men found common ground and discussed sports. In the back, all was silent. Josh sat with arms crossed and his work gloves neatly folded over one knee. Occasionally, he stole a glance at her. When she noticed, he smiled, and then quickly looked away. She sensed shyness in the man and realized that unless she started the conversation, they would be making the journey in silence.

"So, where do you live, Josh?"

He brightened a little, "On Harry's property. Out back."

"In a house?"

"In the barn. The old tack room."

Miriam smiled, recalling her Kansas trail ride with Howard.

"I turned it into an apartment," he said. "It's got everything I need."

"What kind o' work do you do?"

"Different things."

"Like what?" she asked, struggling to draw him out.

"I help Harry tow cars . . . whenever he needs me."

"What else?"

"I'm a wood carver," he said, almost inaudibly.

"Really," exclaimed Miriam. "What kind o' things do you carve?"

"All sorts," he replied, warming to her interest in him. "Animals, people, chair and table legs, plaques and what not."

"How do you sell your work?"

"Got a sign out by the highway. Folks stop and buy now and again."

"This nephew of mine," said Harry, looking into his rear-view mirror, "is one modest man. Folks drive all the way up from New Mexico to buy from him. If you ask me, he don't charge near as much as he should."

"Would you gimme a tour o' your shop?" asked Miriam.

"Sure." he answered hesitantly.

"Best carvings you'll ever see," said Harry, making up for his nephew's reticence.

As they came near the base of the mountain, Josh suddenly went quiet. She watched him anxiously wring his hands. He had retreated to his own interior world.

A half-hour later, two professional-looking signs appeared: "Kimball's Garage" and "Images in Wood." Harry Kimball made a wide arc onto the far shoulder of the road, and then swung the motor home and Jeep through a gate and up the long, dusty driveway. There were three buildings on the property: a two-story clapboard house with a covered porch that faced the driveway; then, beyond the house where the driveway split into a Y, a barn on the left and a large repair garage on the right. Harry tooted the horn as he passed the house. He stopped in front of the garage and jumped down from the driver's seat.

"Be back in a few minutes," he said, striding toward the house. "Better check my answering machine."

Miriam watched as Howard unhooked the Jeep from the motor home. Josh separated the tow truck and drove it into the high grass beside the garage. He limped into the building and returned with a wheeled mechanic's crawler and a trouble light on a long extension cord. He unlatched and propped open the hood, then held the light in one hand while he poked inside the engine compartment. When finished, he lay down on the crawler and shimmied under the RV until only his work boots protruded.

Howard turned his attention to the metal-clad industrial garage. Outside, forty-five gallon oil drums overflowed with an assortment of rusted auto parts. Inside, benches were covered with random pieces of fabricating metal, works in progress. Dangling from an overhead chain hoist was a V-8 engine block, cylinder heads removed and pistons exposed.

"Bit of a mess in there," said Howard under his breath.

Miriam nodded, "Hope this Harry guy knows what he's doin'."

"He knows," said a testy voice from under the RV.

Miriam whispered into Howard's ear, "Nothin' wrong with *his* hearin'."

Josh slid from under the RV just as Harry Kimball returned.

"What'd you find?" asked Harry.

"Rad hose is busted. Fan belts are near wore out. RV battery's dead. Plus, there's a couple wonky springs. Could fail any time soon."

"When was the last time you had major servicing done?" asked Harry.

"About a year ago," replied Howard, feeling negligent.

Harry glanced at the RV's Ohio plates, "I imagine you're due for a lube and oil."

"Yes," said Howard. "Go ahead."

"Can I make a suggestion?"

"Sure."

"How about I do a bumper-to-bumper inspection first? That way, if there's a list of things, you can decide what you want me to fix."

Howard agreed but looked concerned that the list might be long. He had not used or maintained the motor home since Suzanne's death.

"I charge forty bucks an hour. That's a whole lot less than you'd pay at a dealership. And if I go fifteen minutes past an hour, I charge you for the quarter hour, not a full one. Fair?"

"Very," said Howard, relieved. "Do you take credit cards?"

"Uh-uh. Cash only. Keeps the IRS out of my pocket."

"Are there any ATMs nearby?"

"In Gunnison, a few miles down the road."

"How long do you figure it'll take?"

"Depends what I find."

"Of course," said Howard. "Dumb question."

"Tell you what. You folks are gonna be here at least overnight, which means you'll be living out of this thing, right?"

Howard nodded.

"Well then, let's get you backed up close to the garage. I'll run out a water hose and an electric cord. Then you can come and go as you please."

Josh emerged from the garage, wiping the last blobs of mechanic's soap from his hands with a paper towel. He had slipped out of his mechanic's coveralls and was dressed in a western shirt and blue jeans.

"Thanks for your help, Josh," said his uncle.

"Will you be needing me anymore now?"

"I don't think so."

"Fine," he said, tossing the bunched up paper in a waste barrel.

"Hey," said Miriam. "Do I still get my tour?"

"Tour of what?"

"Your shop," she said, wondering how he could have forgotten his promise so soon after making it. "You said I could—"

"Oh yeah," he said, putting a hand to his forehead. "Sorry, ma'am, I forget stuff if I don't make a note to myself."

"It's Miriam, not ma'am," she said. "Actually, you can call me, Mimi."

"OK then, Miriam."

She shook her head.

"What's the matter?" asked Howard with the young man standing only feet away.

"I just told him to call me, Mimi," she said, her voice full of irritation, "and he calls me Miriam. Must have a head like a friggin' sieve!"

Stung by her remark, the young man limped across the yard, into the barn, and slammed the door.

Harry Kimball had also prickled at her comment. He noted her look of confusion and motioned for her to join him on a wooden bench out of sight of the barn. Howard leaned against one of the metal barrels. Harry took a briar pipe and a tin of tobacco from his pockets. He loaded the bowl and tamped it with his thumb. Then he drew the flame from a wooden match down into the sweet-smelling blend.

"Let me . . . tell you something . . . 'bout that nephew of mine," he said between puffs.

"Uh-oh. I've said somethin' to make you angry, haven't I?" said Miriam, looking sheepish.

"You didn't know."

"Is there somethin' wrong with him?"

He puffed a few more times, and then set his pipe on the bench. "Did you notice how quiet he went when we came off that mountain?"

"Yeah . . . I figured he was shy."

"Oh, he's not shy. Not when you get to know him."

"Was he upset about somethin'?"

Harry cleared his throat. "Five years ago, he was airlifted off that road, barely alive. Thirty-years old he was. Had his whole life ahead of him."

"Was it a car accident?" Miriam asked.

Harry nodded, "One of the worst around here for years."

"What happened?" asked Howard.

"A truck was coming off the summit, same as we did today, except at night. It was loaded with livestock—hogs to be exact. Somewhere on the downhill run the driver lost his airbrakes. For a while he kept the vehicle under control, but eventually he started hitting cars coming up the pass. Josh's was the last one he hit before the rig jackknifed and came to rest across the highway. Truck driver was killed outright. Josh's air bag went off, but he didn't have his seatbelt on for some reason. He got thrown out of the vehicle. Investigators said his body hit rocks, which is why he got smashed up so bad. Broke more bones than I can count—except for his hands—thank the Lord."

"What was he doin' on the mountain after dark?" asked Miriam.

"Going home to Denver."

"Oh, so he wasn't livin' here at the time?"

"No. He'd taken a few vacation days. Came down for a mental-health break after his divorce. We had horses on the property back then. Josh spent most of his time riding into the high country. Anyhow, he stayed later than usual that evening. I wanted him to stay overnight and leave the next morning, but he was impatient to get going. He was a different man back then. A workaholic. Always on the go."

"What'd he do for a livin'?"

"Chartered accountant. He'd been smart as a whip with figures ever since he was a boy. Had some of the biggest accounts in Colorado: ski resorts in Vail and Aspen, construction companies, mining conglomerates, and whatnot."

"Sounds like he was doin' well," said Miriam.

"Making money hand-over-fist."

"You said he was divorced."

"His job brought that on. Carol couldn't handle his work schedule, the schmoozing parties, the ladder-climbing crap. Josh was like that Energizer bunny on TV. He never stopped."

"Did they have any kids?"

"No," replied Harry.

"How come?"

"No room in his life," he said, picking up his pipe from the bench.

"Didn't he like them?"

"Oh, I don't think it was that so much," he said, tapping out the burnt tobacco on the ground. "He was too busy for kids."

"How'd his wife take that?"

"I think Carol wanted 'em, although it was more to keep Josh at home than any other reason. She wasn't the mothering type. Least I never thought she was."

He pulled a penknife from his pocket and reamed the charred bowl of the pipe, rotating it slowly in his hand. When he had finished, he reloaded it and lit up, this time inhaling a lung full before exhaling a long plume that curled around Miriam.

"So, to come back to the accident," she said. "How'd you find out about it?"

"I got a tow request from the police dispatcher. We've had plenty of mishaps on that pass for years, but it's always some city slicker passing through. You never think it'll strike close to home."

"What was it like when you got there?"

"Armageddon. Spilled diesel fuel. Trapped hogs a-squealing inside the livestock trailer. Dead hogs on the road. Injured ones running around with their guts hanging out. Cops trying to control the chaos and deal with injured motorists."

"Where was your nephew's car?"

"Couldn't see it at first. The impact had knocked it off the road like a tenpin."

"How'd you find it?" asked Miriam.

"I found him before I found the car. Saw a group of people standing over a body. I went over for a look see. Couldn't believe it was Josh. I mean, he'd been hugging us goodbye only minutes before. Seeing him lying there put a chill through my heart. He was covered in blood. Limbs twisted every which way like a broken string puppet."

Harry Kimball's eyes filled and he looked away.

"You said he was airlifted."

"Yes," he replied, pulling a handkerchief from his pocket and blowing his nose. "I was there when the helicopter took him. They say he'd never have lived if he'd gone by ground ambulance. That's how bad he was."

"Where'd they take him to?"

"Denver Trauma Center."

"Good hospital?"

"Very good. Still, he was a long time getting better. His ex-wife, Carol, bless her heart, stuck by him through the whole ordeal."

"What happened when he got out o' hospital?"

"He couldn't work again as an accountant. Something happened to his brain. That's when the lawsuit started."

"For medical expenses?"

"Nope," said Harry, pausing to re-light his pipe. "Loss of career and future income. His lawyers proved negligence on the part of the trucking company. He wound up with a good settlement in the end—real good."

"How'd he wind up living here?" asked Howard.

"Josh had trouble coping with city life afterwards. I offered him a quiet place on the property. He jumped at it. I moved the horses out of the barn and boarded them over in Gunnison. He made the old tack room into his living quarters and the barn into a workshop and showroom."

"Does he do well?" asked Miriam.

"He doesn't make a fortune, but he earns enough to buy whatever he needs. He's a lot happier out of the corporate rat race. Turned into a genuine country boy."

"So, the accident didn't affect his ability to carve, then," said Miriam.

He shook his head, "I swear he received a miracle that night. Today, Josh can do the two things he loves best: carve and ride horses."

"Does he ride a lot?"

"Three, four times a week. Those horses are his babies. Fusses over 'em like you wouldn't believe."

"I am *so* sorry I said what I did. I had no idea."

"I know you didn't," replied Harry, placing a reassuring hand on her shoulder. "I just thought it'd be best if I told you his story. If he has a lapse of memory, at least now, you'll know why."

There was a pregnant pause.

"Well," said Harry, glancing at his watch. "If I'm going to get you folks back on the road, I better get my butt in gear."

"Is there a place we can go while you're fixing the RV?" asked Howard.

"Sure is," replied Harry. He disappeared into the garage and returned with a dog-eared map. "Keep this if you like. It'll show you all the back roads."

"Thanks," said Howard.

"By the way," said Harry. "Will you be doing any four wheeling in the high country?"

"Yes. We're planning to go to the San Juans."

"Ouray and Silverton?"

"Yes."

"You be sure you keep that thing fueled and stocked with survival stuff. The high country shows no mercy to the unprepared."

"Thanks," said Howard. "I'll keep that in mind."

WHILE HARRY Kimball worked on the RV, Howard threw blankets and water bottles in the Jeep, and then struck out for Gunnison. From the moment they left the property, Miriam was unusually quiet.

"Something bothering you?" asked Howard.

"Yes."

"What is it? Are you feeling sick with the baby?"

"No. I feel ashamed."

"Surely not over your faux pas?"

"Yes. I had no idea he'd had an accident. Suffered brain damage."

"Of course you didn't," he said, trying to reassure her.

"Did you sense there was somethin' wrong with him?"

Howard hesitated.

"You did, didn't you?"

He nodded.

"Was it his limpin'?"

"No."

"What then?"

"It doesn't matter," he said, dismissively.

"But, it does matter. How come you noticed somethin' and I didn't?"

"Because I knew a guy once who'd had a brain injury. He had this expression. It was very subtle, a sort of momentary zoning out. Josh has it."

"Really?"

"Uh-huh. But don't beat up on yourself for what you said. I'd be rich if I had a dollar for every time I put my foot in my mouth. I did it shortly after we met."

"Oh?"

"It was after I picked you up . . . remember? I let my feelings show."

"You mean about me wantin' an abortion? My smokin'?"

"Yes. I expressed opinions I should've kept to myself."

"I don't hold that against you, Chip. Not after you tellin' me about that girl you were sweet on. About her havin' an abortion. I understand now why you feel the way you do."

Howard nodded. "Anyway, I haven't mentioned it lately."

"I know you haven't, and I thank you for that."

When Howard reached the outskirts of Gunnison, they parked at the small airport to watch planes take off and land. Then they found a parking space in the main part of town and got the last table-for-two in a busy restaurant.

"I hope the food's good here," said Howard, after their waitress had left with their orders.

"Lots o' customers," said Miriam, "is a good sign."

They people-watched as they ate. The noontime chatter and the sound of cutlery on plates ebbed and flowed. Louder snippets of conversation rose above the din: ranchers lamenting the high cost of feed, fishermen bragging of trout caught in mountain streams, old women evaluating the new pastor in town, and a couple of burly men in camouflage outfits already planning their annual elk hunt. The ambience in the restaurant and the mode of dress made it clear they were in the West, where clothing was manly and casual and preferably scuffed so as not to look out-of-the-box new: faded blue jeans held up with hand-tooled belts and saucer-sized buckles, cowboy boots with pointed, "nose-picker" toes, and Stetsons in every shape and color. Dining styles were casual: elbows propped on tables, and hats worn while eating.

""This is where you belong, Chip," teased Miriam.

"What do you mean?"

"A place where you can spill stuff on yourself and no one notices."

"I haven't done that lately," he said, defensively.

"Not in the last five minutes, anyway," she said with a laugh, and then changed the subject. "It's pretty here in the mountains. Think we can go for a short drive before we go back to the RV?"

Howard looked at his watch. "I don't see why not. It might take the sting out of the repair bill."

"You really think they're gonna find that much wrong?"

"I have no idea. I'll have to wait and see."

"I don't think he's out to fleece you, if that's what you're worried about. He seemed like an honest guy to me."

"Yes," he said. "I got good vibes."

On their way back to the Jeep, they passed a diesel pickup with a large horse trailer. The animal's head was protruding over the sidewalk. She stopped to pet it.

"I wish I could go ridin' again," she said, wistfully. "Especially here in the mountains."

Howard raised his eyebrows, "Remember what the doctor said."

"I know, I know. Just thinkin' how nice it'd be, that's all."

# CHAPTER 23

## *Alice*

THEY ARRIVED BACK AT Harry Kimball's garage by late afternoon, and were greeted by the hiss of a cutting torch.

"Helloo," shouted Howard, peering inside.

"In here," came the reply, then a caution. "You've got no goggles on. Don't look at the flame."

They stepped inside to see a hunched figure in coveralls wearing a welder's shield over his face. He was cutting through a slab of quarter inch plate. The oxy-acetylene torch spouted a sharp tongue of fire and sent a torrent of sparks cascading onto the cement floor. Miriam jumped in alarm when the severed piece hit the floor with a loud clang. Immediately he shut off the torch and threw his head back to lift the shield.

"How'd it go?" asked Howard.

"I replaced all your belts and hoses and did a lube," replied Harry, taking off his leather gloves and setting the cutting torch aside. "Put in a new battery as well."

"That's great. Are we good to go?"

"Technically, yes."

"Uh-oh," said Howard. "That sounds ominous."

"There are a few things you should consider fixing."

"You mean the springs that Josh found?"

"Yes. Worn shackles, bushings, and a broken leaf spring."

"I forgot about that."

"If I were you," said Harry, removing his face shield and hanging it on the portable welding rack, "I'd have them seen to, especially if you're gonna be driving in these mountains."

"Do it," replied Howard without hesitation. "The last time somebody told me to fix stuff, I put it off, and this is where it got me."

"That's not all."

"You found more?"

"Yes."

"Should I be sitting down for this?" asked Howard with a look of concern.

"No. Come take a look."

He plugged in a mechanic's trouble light and ran it under the motor home.

"See those brackets and fittings near your waste tanks?" he said, aiming the light for Howard.

"Shot are they?"

"Yes, and you've got two choices if you want me to repair them."

"Like what?"

"I can fabricate them, or I can order proper replacement parts from your RV manufacturer."

"What do you think is best?" asked Howard.

"If it was me, I'd go with factory-made."

"How long will it take to get them?"

"Depends whether they're in stock. The place is in Indiana, so there'll be a shipping delay even if they do have what we need."

Howard looked at his watch, "They'll be closed by now."

"I'll call first thing after breakfast."

"Guess we might as well go back into town for supper," Howard said, turning to Miriam.

"You're more than welcome to have supper with us," said Harry. "In fact, I'd prefer it if you did. By the time you're done eating it'll be close to dusk. There's too many deer roaming around here just itching to become hood ornaments."

"You sure about us comin' for supper?" said Miriam. "That'll be more trouble for you."

"No trouble. The wife's cooked roast venison with trimmings. She's made lemon meringue pie for dessert."

"Sounds great," said Howard. "Do we have time to freshen up first?"

"Sure. I'll go ask Gladys to put out three more place settings."

"Three?" said Miriam.

"Yes," said Harry, heading for the front porch. "Josh'll be joining us."

Miriam bit her lip nervously as he disappeared into the house.

"Don't tell me you're still worried?" said Howard.

"Yes. He's not gonna be happy sittin' down to supper with me."

"I think you're wrong."

"What makes you say that?"

"Intuition."

"That's a woman's domain," said Miriam.

"If you ask me, Harry's set this up so you can put things right."

"You think so?"

"Just a hunch."

Half an hour later, they knocked on the front door.

A woman in her mid-seventies greeted them. "Come in," she said, smiling warmly, "I'm Gladys."

The aroma of cooked food enveloped them as they followed the woman down the creaking hallway into the rustically decorated home. The furnishings were plain and set against painted walls with a mix of family photos and Remington prints. In the dining room were two prominent objects on the end walls: a regulator clock in an oak case with a swinging brass pendulum, and a mounted deer's head with an impressive rack. There were six place settings on the pine harvest table and in the center, a long trivet with china serving bowls.

"Your home's lovely," said Miriam.

"Thank you," she said, and then turned at the sound of uneven footsteps advancing along the hall. "Josh, honey, is that you?"

"Yep," he said, limping into the dining room.

"I believe you've already met our nephew," said Gladys, giving him a warm hug.

Miriam nodded and smiled at the young man.

"It's . . . Mimi . . . isn't it?"

"Yes," she replied, pleased that he had remembered.

"Well, then," said Gladys, looking at everyone, "let's eat, shall we."

"Mom," shouted Harry. "Supper's ready."

"Be right there, dear," a voice replied from deep in the house.

Everyone took their seats: Harry at the far end of the table, Howard and Gladys to either side of him, and Miriam and Josh opposite each other near the vacant chair at the head of the table. Moments later, an elderly woman with coiffed, white hair appeared in the doorway. She was dressed in slacks and an open-necked blouse and wore full makeup and jewelry. She smiled at everyone, then, with the elegance of a swan on a millpond, she glided to the table and pulled out her chair.

"Folks," said Harry, "this is my mother, Alice."

"Alice Louisa Kimball," said the woman, formalizing the introduction, her eyes twinkling. "I'm pleased to meet you both."

Howard nodded and smiled; Miriam reached out and gently shook her hand.

"You're a lovely girl . . . and such warm hands too."

"Thank you, ma'am."

Harry cleared his throat and joined his hands prayerfully. All heads bowed on cue.

"Make it short," said Gladys. "We're hungry."

"Yes, son," added Alice, for emphasis.

Harry exchanged a quick glance with his wife, and then began. "Bless us, Lord, and this food which we are about to receive from your bounty. We thank you for bringing these folks safely to our home and ask that you watch over them as they travel on their journey, through Christ, our Lord, amen."

The moment the lids were lifted from the serving tureens, rich aromas flooded the room: garlic-scented meat, home-baked cheese bread, rich bouquets of onion and tomato and basil-flavored vegetables and of oven-roasted potatoes. For a few minutes, the eagerness to fill plates halted conversation. The only sounds were the clink of serving spoons on plates and the steady tick of the regulator clock.

"This is wonderful," exclaimed Miriam at her first taste of wild venison. "So tender."

"Thank you, dear," said Gladys. "Twelve hours in the crock pot."

"Hey," shouted Harry. "Don't I get credit for hanging the meat properly?"

"Yes, my love," said his wife, "you certainly do."

"It's Josh we really have to thank," said Harry, spreading butter on his potatoes. "He shot this deer right here on the property."

"Oh yeah?" said Miriam, looking across the table.

"Yep. Saw it from my shop window. I just opened the door and fired."

"Do you do a lot o' huntin' out here?"

"Yep," replied Josh. "Most years we get something."

"Depending on luck," added Harry with his mouth full.

"Don't you find that hard to do?" said Miriam. "Killin' an animal?"

"They die instantly," said Josh. "It's more humane than dying in the wild."

"Guess I must sound like a wimpy Easterner, but back in Philly we go to the supermarket for our meat."

"It's different here," said Harry, spearing a piece of roast potato with his fork. "We depend on hunting to put fresh meat on the table. And Josh is one of the best hunters around—not to mention a great rider."

"Ever ridden a horse, Mimi?" asked Josh, pouring more gravy over his venison.

"Only once."

"Did you like it?"

"Uh-huh," she replied, glancing at Howard. "Chip took me ridin' in Kansas. My butt got sore."

The young man smiled, but said nothing more.

"You're not saying much tonight, Mother," said Harry, looking down the length of the table.

"Just paying mind to what's being said, son. No one can say I suffer from the disease of not listening."

"Shakespeare," exclaimed a startled Howard, suddenly looking up from his meal.

"Excuse me?" the old woman said.

"That saying, ma'am. It's Falstaff's line from Henry IV: 'it is the disease of not listening, the malady of not marking, that I am troubled withal.'"

"Well, I'll be darned," she said, wiping her chin with a dinner napkin. "I've used that expression for years and never knew where it came from." She paused for a moment, "May I ask how you know that?"

"Yes, ma'am, I'm an—"

"That's twice you've called me that, young man. I may have snow on the roof, but I don't want you deferring to me on account of it. Call me Alice," she said and winked at him.

Howard smiled. "I haven't had anyone call me 'young man' for a long time."

"Well, I reserve the right," she said, her eyes twinkling. "And by the way, I like men with beards."

He laughed and self-consciously brushed a hand across his face, "It has a tendency to collect things I'm afraid. Hopefully not venison or gravy."

"I can assure you, it's free of both at the moment. It gives you a professorial look."

"Funny you should say that, Alice, I *am* a professor. At least I was."

The conversation shifted toward Howard, beginning with an explanation of his tenure at St. Martin's and the reason for his leaving to start a new life in San Diego. In the process, he told her how he had met Miriam and how much he was enjoying her company on their trip west. But he told no one about Miriam's pregnancy.

The woman turned to Miriam, "And what about you, Mimi, dear? Are you enjoying the journey?"

"Yes, ma'am, I mean, Alice," she said. "Chip's been takin' me places."

The old woman smiled, "Soon as we've had our pie, you can tell me all about them."

When he had finished his dessert, Josh excused himself from the table; he thanked Gladys and kissed her cheek.

"Not staying for coffee?" asked Harry.

Josh shook his head.

There was an awkward moment as the young man tried to extricate himself from the room. Conversation stopped and all heads turned.

"I don't wanna miss gettin' my tour," said Miriam, noting the man's anxiousness to leave. "Think I could come over in a while?"

"I'm a mite tired . . . Mimi. How 'bout tomorrow?"

"Tomorrow's fine," she replied, but looked disappointed.

The dining room remained quiet. Everyone listened to Josh's uneven gait as he limped from the house. Through the dining room window they watched him, head down, cross the dirt driveway in the direction of the barn.

"Did I say somethin' wrong again?"

"No," replied Harry, shaking his head. "Josh has times when he needs to be on his own. This is one of them. Don't take it personal."

Miriam looked unconvinced.

"Couple things I didn't tell you yesterday about Josh," said Harry, glancing at his wife, then back to Miriam.

"What's that?"

"The accident affected him a lot. You see—"

Gladys interrupted him, "Can I say something here?"

Harry deferred to his wife.

"I guess what Harry's trying to say is that Josh is sensitive around strangers about his limp and the way his memory gets muddled. Not with local folks mind you. They've known him since he was a tad."

"And I didn't help yesterday with my comment . . . did I?"

"You didn't know, dear. That's why Harry invited Josh to supper, so you could have a chance to put things right."

Miriam, glanced at Howard.

"And you did," continued Gladys. "In fact, I noticed something tonight . . . a change in him."

"Oh?" replied Miriam, looking surprised.

"Did you see how quick he got onto horses when Harry brought up the subject?"

"Yeah."

"Did Harry tell you our horses are on a ranch over in Gunnison?"

"Uh-huh."

"We don't ride anymore," said Gladys. "They're Josh's horses now. His babies."

"He'll be going there first thing in the morning," said Harry. "Why don't you ask him if you can tag along? If you like horses, you'll have a friend in Josh."

Miriam looked at Howard, "You OK with that?"

He hesitated before answering, "Of course," he said. "That'd be fine."

For an instant, Miriam caught a look in Howard's eyes. It was a pained look, as if he was losing her to another man. Impulsively, she leaned over and kissed him on the cheek, but the expression on his face remained unchanged.

"Tell you what," said Harry. "Why don't you and I go for a stroll? I always like walking off a big meal."

"Sure," said Howard, getting up from the table.

"I'll do the clean up, Mother," said Gladys, starting to clear the dishes. "Why don't you and Mimi sit where it's soft and have that talk?"

# CHAPTER 24

## *Life Lessons*

MIRIAM FOLLOWED ALICE INTO the living room. The woman moved with economy as she straightened the crocheted afghan on the sofa, and then lifted her tiny feet onto a petit point stool with hand-carved, ball and claw feet.

"Did you make that?" asked Miriam, pointing to the intricate design.

"The stitching's mine. The woodworking is Josh's handiwork."

"It's beautiful."

"I did the design from a photograph," she said, momentarily shifting her feet so Miriam could see.

"Is that your work too?" said Miriam, pointing to a slender doll with a crocheted white dress."

"Yes. But that's enough about me. I want to hear about this journey you're making. To California isn't it?"

"Uh-huh."

She made a small adjustment to her hearing aid, and then said with a self-deprecating laugh, "Go ahead, my dear, I'm wired for sound now."

Miriam began with Howard's roadside rescue of her in Toledo, about her decision to travel with Troy, and how she reunited again with Howard and the places they had visited together, including the scene of Suzanne Munro's drowning.

"I think you left something out of your story, dear," she said, placing an age-spotted hand on Miriam's stomach.

"How did you know?"

"I've lived a long time—seen the signs."

"What signs?" said Miriam, baffled by the woman's intuitiveness.

Alice smiled, "You don't have to be showing for me to know."

"But—"

"I've been watching you."

"You have?"

"You've been doing something all evening. In fact, you did it just a moment ago."

"Really? What?"

"Protecting your unborn child."

"How?"

"By placing a hand on your belly. You're probably not aware you're doing it."

"Well . . . I guess there's no foolin' you is there?"

"No, dear, and if you'd rather not talk about it, I'll understand. Not all women want it known."

Miriam hesitated.

"Tell you what," said Alice, offering a box of Belgian chocolates. "Let's have us a nice after-dinner treat. There's no brandy centers in them. Nothing to hurt that baby of yours."

"Thanks," she said, lifting one from its plastic pocket.

"Mmm. Now *that* is divine," said Alice, biting into a soft center and catching a dribble of syrup on the back of her hand.

"They're almost sinful, aren't they?" said Miriam, taking a second one.

"The best kind of sin, dear. One that requires no trip to the confessional."

Miriam ate her third chocolate slowly, trying to decide whether or not to open up. She wanted to, but felt reluctant; the family had already said grace and Alice had just mentioned the confessional. Was she a devout Catholic? Would she deliver a harangue on the evils of abortion?

"Here," said Alice, offering another before closing the box.

"I feel like such an oink," said Miriam, eyeing her next selection.

"They're my chocolates, dear. We can eat as many as we want."

Conversation lagged as both women savored their choices. Miriam slowly found her voice.

"Alice?"

"Yes, dear."

"Do you believe some sins are unforgiveable?"

"I don't know. I'm not religious."

"Oh? Somehow, I thought you were a churchgoer."

"That's Harry's thing, not mine. I haven't been religious since I was a girl."

"That's a relief," said Miriam.

"I get the feeling you want to tell me something, but you don't know where to start. Is that right?"

"Yes."

"She patted Miriam on the knee, "I think I know what it is."

"You do?"

"You're not sure whether you want to keep your baby," she said, making eye contact. "Am I in the ball park?"

"On home plate."

"I thought so."

She picked up Miriam's hand, "Look, dear, at one-hundred-years-old, nothing shocks me. I've seen it all, and heard it all. I learned long ago not to sit in judgment of other people's circumstances."

"Can I tell you them?"

"Of course, but I think my room's a more private place for something like that. The men might come back and interrupt us."

Miriam followed Alice into her bedroom and closed the door. In the center of the small room was a single bed, neatly made and without a wrinkle. Around the room were tiny keepsakes and photographs in frames. She eased herself onto the settee, and then invited Miriam to sit beside her.

"There now, Mimi dear," said the woman, "tell me what's troubling you."

Miriam took a deep breath, "The father of my child dumped me when he found out I was pregnant. To be honest and truthful, I'm afraid to go through with it. That's why I'm headin' to California. My mother's got enough money to pay for an abortion."

"How far along are you?"

"Into my second month."

"First pregnancy?"

"Yeah."

"Is it because you're afraid? Most women are. Especially the first time."

"It's more than that. I've made a mess o' my life so far. Havin' a kid is just gonna make things worse."

"Afraid of being a single mother?"

"Terrified. All I know is waitin' on tables. I dropped out o' high school. Don't have the education to get the kind o' job I need to support a child on my own. Suddenly, she broke down. "I just don't think I can do it," she sobbed. "I'm not strong enough."

Alice pulled a fistful of tissues from a box and handed them to her, then waited.

"I'm sorry, "said Miriam, wiping her eyes.

"Don't be. There's nothing like a good cry to clear the air. It's what makes us so much healthier than men—poor creatures—they keep things so bottled up."

"It's good o' you to listen to me," said Miriam, stuffing soggy tissues in her pocket.

"Why don't you get my chocolates from the living room? More comfort food is what we need."

Miriam was returning to Alice's bedroom when Howard and Harry entered the house.

"What's up?" asked Howard, seeing the box in her hands.

"I'm havin' a talk with Alice . . . in her room."

"A private talk?"

"Yeah. Can you find somethin' to do for an hour?"

"Sure," said Howard. "Is everything all right?"

"Fine . . . really!"

She settled into Alice's room and for a while made small talk. They discovered a mutual love of baseball. Alice was a Toronto Blue Jays fan and gave her opinions of favorite players. Miriam entertained the woman with her recall of baseball trivia. It was Alice who drew the conversation back.

"Now . . . your education. Wasn't that where we left off?"

Miriam nodded.

"I got less than you did, my dear. Only four years of public school. Barely enough to read and write and do basic sums. The rest came from what I taught myself."

"But how?" asked Miriam.

"I had to become my own teacher. Learn from books. Talk to other people."

"What'd you do to make a livin'?"

"I had different jobs throughout my working years. I learned to adapt, you see. I caught on quickly to new things."

"What about havin' kids?"

Alice smiled, "Perhaps it'd be best if I tell you what the times were like when I got married and had my family."

She held Miriam's hand, parted the curtains of time, and led her back to one of the bleakest episodes of the twentieth century: the Great Depression.

"I married Stan in 1929, the year the stock market crashed. I was nineteen-years-old."

"How'd you meet him?"

"At a fairground near the amusement rides," she said, her eyes glistening at the memory. "He'd gone there with his girlfriend. I got knocked to the ground in a crowd. Stan picked me up and it was love at first sight. After that, he dumped his girlfriend and I was his girl. He used to take me to the movies, and then out to supper. A fish 'n' chip dinner cost twenty-five cents back then. Can you imagine? You can't buy much for a quarter these days."

"How long were you married?"

"Forty-eight years. He died when I was sixty-seven."

"And you never remarried?"

"No. He was the love of my life."

"Do you miss him?"

"Every day, dear," she said, glancing at his framed photograph on her wall.

"Sorry I interrupted," said Miriam. "You were gonna tell me about your kids."

"Oh yes. I had Ethel in '31, Harry in '34, Joyce in '37, and Bernice in '39, the year the Second World War started."

"Did your husband have a job?"

"He had several. He harvested grain out west. When he *was* home, he made money driving the local doctor around to make house calls. Stan even hauled coal and ice to people's homes."

"Ice?" said Miriam, looking confused. "You mean fridges didn't come with automatic icemakers back then?"

"No, dear," said the woman, smiling at Miriam's generational naiveté. "In those days a lot of people used iceboxes to keep their food cold.

Domestic fridges weren't in every home back then . . . and none had automatic icemakers, I can assure you!"

"Were you working during the Depression?" Miriam asked.

"Yes."

"If you were both workin', who looked after your kids?"

"Stan took them in the truck while he made his deliveries. There were no child daycare centers in those days."

"No daycares?" said Miriam, incredulously.

"None. And even if there had been, we'd no money for babysitting. Just enough for basic necessities."

"That must've been tough."

"Everything was tough back then, dear. I was making thirty-five cents an hour in a radio assembly factory. We decided to go on strike for more money, but we didn't have the backing of a union."

"What happened?"

"The Depression wasn't a good time to go on strike. We got fired. The company knew there were thousands desperate for work and willing to take our jobs, even if they didn't pay well."

"But . . . how'd you feed yourself?"

"The grocer advanced us credit till we had money to pay. One time, we were so broke I had to sell my alarm clock to pay off what we owed on our food bill. We lived on soups and stews and swapped food vouchers with neighbors so we could get the items we wanted. Stan and I used to stand in front of the bakery store window and play a game: 'which cake would we buy if we had money.' Now and then, the owner of the corner store would make up twist bags of penny candy. They tasted like they'd been swept off the floor, but we didn't care. We were grateful just to have something sweet. One summer we pooled our pennies with the neighbors and had a community corn roast in a big field. Someone brought records and a wind up gramophone. After we'd finished eating, we danced in the tall grass. Oh, how wonderful that was," she said, her eyes misting at the memory. "The glorious, delicious joy of it all. Dancing under that clear, blue sky, and for a short while, forgetting all our troubles."

Every so often she would pause to retrace the labyrinth of her memory, searching for an event further back in time than most people have lived. To Miriam, the task seemed daunting, like a movie editor hunting for a single frame in a mile-long strip of film. Alice would summon the memory from decades past, then, with the picture fully formed in her mind, she would begin her story and it would emerge, fresh and vibrant in the telling.

"Winter was an especially difficult time. Why . . . I remember walking along railroad tracks with a straw basket . . . grateful at finding chunks of coal that had dropped from the freight trains. Anything we could burn in our furnace. And even after we'd finished burning things, I'd sift through the ashes for any bits we could burn again. You scrounged without shame in those days. You had to live by your wits to survive."

"What were your Christmases like?"

She pulled a tissue from her pocket and blew her nose. "Simple. No hundred dollar gifts. Not like today. In fact, it was a feat just to put something green in the house. One year we had no money for a tree, so Stan made one."

"*Made* a tree?"

"He cut the bristles off a corn broom and drilled holes around the handle, then stuck it in a bucket of sand. Late at night, he went to the vacant lot where they sold Christmas trees. Now, this is back in the days when trees didn't come wrapped in netting. They looked just as they did before they were cut, all bushy like. The men selling them would prop the trees against a fence or the wall of a building. Branches would break off and get scattered on the ground. Stan would gather up as many as he could carry, bring them home, and together, we'd push the stubs of the branches into the holes in the broom handle."

"What about decorations?"

"I made paper chains and hung photographs of our family—black and white, of course—and fashioned garland by piercing lima beans with a sewing needle and arranging them on a string."

"I don't know how you did it," said Miriam in disbelief, "livin' with so little."

"I've wondered that many times, dear. I was a different person when it was all over."

"In what way?"

"I was a timid girl in my teens. But as life got tougher, I had to get tougher. The Depression came as close to breaking me as anything I'd ever been through. There were days when I felt I simply couldn't go on anymore. I wanted to go back to live with my parents."

"What stopped you?"

"My wedding vows and the look in my kids' eyes. I had to be strong for all of them. Besides, there were so many more families like us. We were all in it together. I don't know how I found the strength, but I did. I had no other choice, really. I had to make the best of things. Ride it out till it was over. Had to have faith."

"Faith in God?"

"Nope. Faith in myself. You've got to have faith in something, dear," she said with a laugh, "even if it's an old toothbrush."

As they talked, Miriam studied the diminutive woman. After a century of living, her face was deeply lined, especially around the corners of her eyes, yet there was character in the lines—brushstrokes of artistry in well-cared-for skin. She was a tiny wisp of a creature, light enough to be blown away by a gust of wind, but possessed of an unassailable spirit. Despite the harsh episodes that had been written into the early chapters of Alice Kimball's life, she was a living monument to grit and determination. She reminded Miriam of the "survivor tree" in Oklahoma City, the century-old American elm so badly damaged by the blast of a terrorist's bomb that no one thought the tree would survive. The following spring, the tree bloomed and became a symbol of survival.

"Today," continued Alice, "I'm grateful for every material thing I have, no matter how small. We learned to be happy with less during the Depression. I saw a lot of charity shown back then. People sharing what they had with others. The use of a car or a telephone . . . a lot of things, really. And you know what else?"

"What?"

"Most of the dire things I worried about never happened. I fretted for nothing."

"I'm a worrier," said Miriam.

"Show me a woman who isn't," said Alice, laughing. "It's in our genes."

"Alice?"

"Yes, dear."

"What's your secret?"

"Secret?"

"To livin' a long life."

She thought for a moment, "Luck mostly," she replied, and then laughed. "I suppose that's why I survived pneumonia when I was four.

The doctor told my mother to buy a dress to bury me in, but I fooled them."

"Did you party a lot when you were young?"

"I've done my share."

"Did you drink or smoke?"

"Never smoked. Just a glass of wine at Christmas."

"Any other secrets?"

"You mean to staying young in here?" Alice said, tapping an arthritic finger on her forehead.

"Yeah."

"Carpe diem."

"What?"

"It's from the Latin. Means 'seize the day.'"

Miriam wore a blank look.

"It means to live in the moment . . . to make the best of each day. You see, dear, some folks live in the past. They dwell on the memories of the way things used to be. But the past is gone, and even if it *was* good, they can never get it back."

Miriam nodded.

"And some folks pine for the future, but the future's uncertain and may not come at all, especially if they come to an untimely end."

"So what you're sayin' is—"

"Find joy in the life that surrounds you right now: in a lover, in friends, in the fragrance of a flower, by dipping your toes in a creek, by catching snowflakes on your tongue . . . so many things, really. And the more joy you look for, the more joy you will find. I found joy in my children—and grandchildren of course."

"How many have you got?"

"Seven grands, sixteen greats, and six great greats."

"Holy George."

"But you asked me my secret to a long life . . . I think my parents contributed to that."

"In what way?"

"They kept me on the straight and narrow. Steered me away from trouble. Dad was the boss in our house. He demanded obedience from us kids *and* my mother."

"You had siblings?"

"Three brothers. One died at fourteen months."

"You said your father was stern. Did you have a curfew?"

"I'll say. Eleven o'clock and not a minute more! One night I was out with a boyfriend and we got a flat tire. He offered to put me on a bus, so I'd make it home before curfew. Instead, I decided to stay and help him fix it. I got home at midnight and tried to explain, but my father would have none of it. I made the mistake of talking back to him and he slapped me across the face. I didn't talk to him for a whole year after that."

"My mother was the strict one in our house," said Miriam. "She tried to keep tabs on me all the time, but it didn't work. I got into trouble with this and that. And look at me now. Pregnant and on my own. How stupid am I?"

"Not stupid, dear. You made a mistake."

"But," said Miriam, "you sound like a saint compared to me. Someone without vices."

"Oh, I wouldn't say that."

"You have vices?"

"One," she said, her eyes twinkling.

"What?"

"My lips are sealed," she teased.

"Oh, don't be mean. Tell me. Please."

Alice paused to heighten the drama. "Gambling. I started when I was a young girl, pitching pennies with the boys in my neighborhood."

"Do you still gamble?"

"Every chance I get. I take the bus to Vegas or Laughlin."

"To play the slots?"

"Slots, craps, blackjack, poker, and keno. Keno's my favorite."

"Have you ever won big?"

"A few times. But I'm careful not to get hooked."

"I'm sure it's easy to get carried away," said Miriam.

"Yes it is," said Alice. "One time when I was in Vegas, I remember two suicides by bankrupt gamblers. One gal hung herself in the ladies' washroom, the other jumped from the seventh floor of one of the hotels . . ."

Suddenly, the story-telling had taken its toll. Alice's eyes grew heavy and her head began to nod. Miriam helped her to the bed, removed her slippers, and draped a blanket over her tiny figure. She was asleep in moments. Miriam brushed strands of white hair from her forehead, and then kissed her cheek. Quietly she closed the bedroom door and left the house.

The sun was low and cast long pewter shadows in the yard. A gray tabby emerged from the shade of the garage and trotted toward her. It rubbed itself on her legs and purred. She picked it up and cradled it between her breasts. Content with the closeness, the animal drew in its paws and settled in her arms. She carried it across the yard toward the rear of the barn where an abandoned tractor sat half-buried in the tall grass.

Inside the barn, Josh was at work on a carving. Bent over his work table, he guided the whirring tip of a Dremel tool over the piece, scattering fine chips onto his shop apron. For a split second something cut the beam of light coming through the window. He looked up to see Miriam walk past.

She slid onto the tractor's seat to watch the sun and stroke the cat. When she looked back toward the barn, Josh's face was framed in the window. He raised his hand and waved. A good sign, she thought. Had he forgiven her tactlessness? She smiled and waved back. Perhaps if she played her cards right tomorrow, he would take her to see his horses.

# CHAPTER 25

## *Mountain Interlude*

MIRIAM ATE HER BREAKFAST in silence while Howard perused the pages of the *Denver Post.* He wondered whether her private talk with Alice was over her plans for the abortion. If so, he avoided raising the issue. He had grown to like her too much to jeopardize their relationship, even though at this point, he did not know exactly where she fit into his future life.

There was a knock on the RV door. He put down his newspaper.

"Got good news 'n' bad," said Harry," dressed in mechanic's coveralls and puffing on his pipe.

"The good?"

"They've got the parts."

"And the bad?"

"UPS can't get 'em here till tomorrow."

"That means we'll have to camp in your driveway another day," said Howard. "Is that a problem?"

"Not at all," said Harry. "If you're worried about filling your holding tanks, you can use our shower and washroom. We'll leave the porch light on for you and the front door unlocked."

"Thanks. That's good of you."

"You folks got any plans today?"

Miriam looked at Howard. "I was gonna ask Josh if I could go into Gunnison with him to see the horses. That OK with you?"

"Sure," he said, but did not mean it.

"If she's going with Josh," said Harry, "how'd you like to ride with me?"

"Where to?"

"Little place called Tincup. Guy up there wants me to do some welding. It's a pretty drive. I think you'll like it."

"When are you leaving?" asked Howard.

"Right now," said Harry, consulting his watch.

"I'll grab my jacket," he said, then closed the RV door.

"Sure you don't mind me goin' with Josh?"

Howard hesitated.

"Oh, you *are* upset, aren't you?" she said, and touched his arm.

"Well," he said, looking disappointed, "I was hoping we could drive around the countryside. See some mountain scenery."

"We can do that tomorrow," she said. "Just you and me. I promise."

Wearing a somber expression, Howard left the RV and climbed into Harry Kimball's waiting tow truck.

Miriam stood at the window and watched the big wrecker go down the dirt driveway and swing onto the highway. She poured a second coffee, and then stepped into the cool mountain air.

Barn swallows were flying sorties from their nests inside the garage. The tabby cat joined her as she ambled across the yard toward the barn and a decrepit 4x4 Dakota pickup. In the truck's open bed were bales of straw and bags of animal feed. The door to the barn opened. Josh, dressed in full western gear and cowboy hat, limped across the threshold.

"Mornin'," said Miriam.

He lifted his hat politely, "Morning to you."

She took a deep breath to quell her nervousness, and then exhaled slowly, "Harry said you're headin' into Gunnison today . . . to see your horses."

"Oh?" he said, unclipping a fistful of keys from his belt loop. "He told you that?"

"Shouldn't he have?"

He shrugged.

"I hear they're very pretty," she said, hoping to make up for his indifference.

"I think so," he said, climbing behind the wheel and keying the ignition. "Course, I'm biased."

She stepped closer to the truck and placed her hand on the side mirror. "Harry said if I asked you, you'd take me along."

"Did he now?"

"Uh-huh," she replied, and waited with baited breath.

He paused for a long moment as if to think it over. She steeled herself for the rejection she was sure was coming.

"Well then," he said, "I guess you'd better jump in."

Miriam ran around and opened the truck's creaking passenger door. Before she could seat herself, the cat leapt into the cab.

"Should I put her outside?"

"Uh-uh," he said, putting the truck in gear then heading down the driveway. It's a him, by the way."

"What's his name?"

"Coggy."

"Odd name for a cat."

"This guy's half dog," he replied, affectionately scratching the animal's ear. "Aren't you ol' friend!"

For much of the drive to Gunnison, Josh spoke little; getting conversation out of him was like pulling teeth for Miriam who found it difficult to break the ice. But the ride was anything but quiet.

The truck was a battle-scarred veteran of rough, rural service, dented and scraped and rusted through at the fenders. Like an orchestra tuning up, discordant squeaks of different pitches issued from the jiggling body and frame, and loose items clattered in the glove box. The dust-covered dashboard was littered with remnants of hay and binder twine, and the rear-view mirror had a Parkinson's shake. A couple of times Josh recognized the drivers in oncoming vehicles. He lifted an index finger from the steering wheel—an understated greeting. Yet despite the man's taciturn nature, he had an easy-going, good-humored nature. He smiled easily and after accepting a wad of bubble gum from Miriam, competed to see who could blow the biggest bubble. He won, and laughed when a sticky balloon burst in his face.

When they arrived at the boarding stables, he wheeled up a gravel driveway that ended in a small parking area. He lifted a bale of hay from the bed and limped toward the long building; beside him, Coggy walked to heel. Miriam followed with a metal coffee can full of sliced apples and carrots.

When they entered the stables, Josh yodeled. Immediately, two heads appeared from the stalls. The quiet man suddenly transformed into a gushing sentimentalist, showering the animals with terms of endearment.

He kissed their cheeks, held their faces in both his hands, and exhaled softly into their huge nostrils.

"Never seen a man kiss a horse before," said Miriam, clearly taken with the man's tenderness.

Josh grinned and stepped back, "You're next, Coggy."

In a single jump, the cat landed on the top ledge of the stall's half door. The horse lowered its huge head for the cat to rub against its muzzle.

"Want to give them their treats?" he asked.

"Sure," she said, then moved forward cautiously with the coffee can.

The animal raised its head at her approach and took a step backward.

"Becky doesn't know you," said Josh, taking the can from her. "She's spooked."

"By what?"

"Your body language."

"Well . . . maybe I shouldn't."

"No, no," he said. "Do this." He approached the door of the stall in a lowered posture and leaned against the door. "See that?" he said, as the animal stepped forward to sniff him.

"Yeah."

"My gestures are non-threatening. That's why she lowered her head. A sign of calmness and trust."

"OK then, lemme try," said Miriam, putting a few treats in her pocket and passing him the can.

"Uh-uh," he said, handing it back. "Never keep food in your clothing."

"Why not?"

"She'll nip you trying to get at the food."

Miriam mimicked his attitude toward the horses; both readily took treats from her hand. With her confidence boosted, she helped him walk the horses to the paddock, and then returned to muck out the stalls and set out fresh hay. Then they brought each horse back to the stable, secured it on the cross ties, and groomed it. He demonstrated each action, and watched her as she repeated it. When she got it right, he smiled; when she did it wrong, he patiently guided her through the steps again. Her interest in his horses brought the quiet man from his shell. She watched him at work, noting how tenderly he talked to the horses and how lightly he touched them. He glanced at her often, enjoying her interaction with the animals and her eagerness to learn. It was close to mid-day when the stable was cleaned and the horses were back in their stalls.

"You hungry?" asked Josh, checking his watch.

"Starved."

"There's good eateries in town."

"Is that a formal invitation?" she asked, grinning.

"Close as I get to one."

They jumped into the old truck and drove into Gunnison. This time it was Josh who did most of the talking. He was more animated now and talked horses all the way to the diner. He picked a different place to eat than the one she had been to with Howard; it had the same western-friendly atmosphere with patrons dressed mostly in ranch clothing.

"I owe you an apology," she said when their food orders arrived.

"What for?"

"For sayin' what I did yesterday."

"Ah," he said, dismissing it. "Wouldn't be the first time someone took me for a retard."

"I didn't think that about you."

"Yes you did," he said, touching Miriam's arm to temper his remark, "but I don't hold it against you."

"I hope not."

"See, I had this accident a few years back and—"

"I know. Harry told me."

"He did?" he replied with a look of surprise.

"Yeah. He was just tryin' to explain how it affected you. So I'd understand."

"It's natural you thought what you did," he said. "You see a guy limping, and then he zones out on you."

"Do you have trouble concentrating?" she asked, warily.

He paused to wipe his chin with a napkin. "You know when you walk into a room and flip a light switch?"

"Yeah."

"Know how the light comes on right quick?"

"Yeah."

"With me, there's a delay sometimes."

"Does it affect your carvin'?"

"No," he said, and went back to his food.

Miriam changed the subject, "Harry said you used to be married. That you lived in Denver before you moved down here."

"That was my other life. The one before the accident."

"Were you born and raised there?"

"Yes."

"So, you've always lived around mountains then?"

"Uh-huh. It's the best place to live. If I had a choice of desert, ocean, or mountains, I'd pick mountains."

"How come? I mean, I know they're pretty and all, but—"

"Mountains humble people and . . ."

Suddenly she realized that he had lost his train of thought. She took another mouthful of food and waited. The mini-trance dragged on as he tried to pick up the thread.

". . . and we need to be humbled once in a while. Does us good to be cut down to size."

Before she could answer, a metallic sound turned her head. A young cowboy wearing spurs and chaps entered the restaurant. She glanced at his scruffy appearance, clothing layered with dust, cheek bulging with a wad of chewing tobacco. He asked for two coffees to go, then sauntered toward their table exuding a pong of hay and horse dander that made Miriam's eyes water.

"Hey, Josh," said the man, through a jaundice-toothed smile. "Who's the pretty lady?"

Josh made introductions, this time remembering to call her Mimi.

"You live around here?" asked the cowboy, eyeing her lecherously.

"Uh-uh," replied Miriam. "Just passin' through."

"Pity," he said, sucking his filthy teeth.

Josh quickly steered the conversation to horses until the waitress called the man to the cash register.

"Nice meeting you, Mimi," said the man, touching the brim of his Stetson, and then shuffling from the restaurant with spurs jingling.

"Whew," said Miriam, fanning a hand in front of her nose. "Wonder when he last had a bath?"

Josh laughed, "The horses love him. Whenever Tim's around he keeps the flies off them."

"Is he a ranch hand?"

"Ranch hand, rodeo rider, rascal-about-town."

"Surely not with the ladies?"

"Not with women you'd call 'ladies' that's for sure," said Josh chuckling. "No local gal in her right mind will go near him. The only nookie he gets is when the 'lounge lizards' are in town to make some 'mattress money.' And even *they* won't service him till he scrubs up. You can always tell when Tim's getting it—it's the only time you ever see him clean."

"That is gross," exclaimed Miriam.

"You think that's gross?" said Josh. "Rumor has it that in between his human romances he diddles ewes in the high country. Must be some truth to it, 'cause that's when he stinks of fleece instead of horse flesh."

"Ooo," said Miriam, shuddering and making a grim face. "That's too disgustin' to even imagine."

"I was wondering," said Josh, putting his cutlery down, "now that we're done eating, would you like to go riding with me?"

"Sorry . . . can't."

"Why not?" he said, looking at his watch. "You don't have to get back to the RV yet. Harry and your friend will be a while in Tincup."

"No, it's not that . . . I'm . . . pregnant. Last time I rode a horse was in Kansas . . . with Chip. I started bleedin' after."

"Sorry to hear that," he said, disappointed. "How 'bout we just walk them on halters instead? I know it's not as much fun as riding but—"

Miriam smiled, "I'd like that very much."

They returned to the boarding stables and took Becky and Orion for a number of circuits around the large property. Josh was more relaxed with Miriam now, enough to open up about his failed marriage to Carol Woods, his former job as a chartered accountant, and finally, the accident on the mountain. Miriam talked about her childhood in Philadelphia and about her past relationships including her current predicament.

"So," he said as they turned at the corner of the fence, "what're you gonna do when you get to California?"

Miriam kept walking her horse with her head down, unsure of how he would react to her plans.

"I said—?"

"I heard you," she said, looking uncomfortable. "I'm . . . thinkin' o' havin' an abortion."

He raised his eyebrows, "Would I be stepping over the line if I asked why?"

"No," she said. "To be honest and truthful with you, I'm worried about raisin' a kid on my own."

"You mean financial like?"

She nodded, "I don't make much as a waitress."

"Couldn't you take some kind of training? You know, like a night course or two at a community college?"

"I'd need a lot more than two," she replied.

"How come?"

"I dropped out o' high school. Anyway, I'm not even sure I'd *be* a good mother when push comes to shove."

"How do you figure that?" he said.

She shrugged. "I just believe it."

"Why?"

"I dunno," she replied, feeling cornered and flustered with his persistent questioning. "Right now I'm all over the place . . . emotionally that is. Feel guilty too for even thinkin' o' doin' it."

"Wish I'd had kids," said Josh.

"Then why didn't you?"

"My job was my world."

"What about now?" she asked.

"I missed my chance. I think Carol would've had them, but she's out of my life now."

He took the halter from Miriam's hand and tied her horse, then his, to the lower fence rail. "Why don't we sit here and enjoy the view for a bit?" When she went to climb the fence, he put both hands on her waist and shifted her sideways. "If you're gonna sit on a fence, sit near the post. It's more steady there."

"You'll have to excuse me," she said, laughing awkwardly. "I'm a city girl. Don't know squat 'bout country ways."

He smiled at her, "Bet you'd be a fast learner."

"Think so?"

"Yes I do," he said, hooking the heels of his boots behind the lower rail, "and I never say anything I don't mean."

Miriam grinned and shot him a sideways glance. "Would you tell an ugly woman she was pretty?"

He thought for a moment. "No, but I'd find something nice to say that'd make her feel good about herself."

"You missed your callin'," said Miriam, laughing.

"Oh?"

"Yeah. You should've been a diplomat, or maybe even a gigolo."

He smiled at her teasing. "Diplomat maybe. But gigolo? I don't think so."

"Why not?"

"Because," he said, melting her with a smile, "I'm a one-woman man!"

"Good answer, cowboy."

Suddenly, he slipped his arm around her waist. "I'm not trying to be fresh," he said, "but I don't like the way you're perched on this fence. You're not wearing boots with heels. Try tucking your toes behind that rail. I don't want you falling off."

She put her hand on his shoulder to steady herself, then anchored her feet to the fence. They sat for a while, just staring across the valley at the mountains. A mare and her colt were grazing in a field of knee-high grass, slowly working their way toward them. Josh made a clicking sound with his tongue. Both animals looked up, and then ambled over. Before they arrived, he jumped from the fence. He lifted her by the waist and set her down gently in front of him—close enough to kiss her. He held her for several seconds before letting go. She felt her heart pound.

"I'n't she a pretty little thing?" he said, turning toward the colt.

"Boy or girl?"

"Girl. Her name's, Juniper. I was here the night she was born."

"No kiddin," said Miriam, surprised.

"When the vet said the mare was getting close, a buddy and I slept on cots outside the stall. My hands were the first to touch her when her little head appeared. I cleaned her face with a towel and made sure she was breathing properly. She was the most precious thing you ever saw. The mare took it in her stride, but Kirk and I . . . well . . . I mean to tell you . . . we were teary-eyed wrecks."

"Must've been special."

He nodded, "It was the most exciting thing that's ever happened to me. It took a lot of convincing afterwards on my part, but I eventually talked Kirk into selling her to me."

"Why another horse? You've already got two."

He smiled. "Juniper's the closest I'll ever come to having a kid. Besides, I think being at her birth had a lot to do with it. We made a connection-of-the-heart you might say."

They spent some time fussing over the colt before climbing back on the fence. He told her about his life growing up in the mountains and how he had hiked alpine peaks—the roof of Colorado. He talked about his love of animals, a love that had spawned an early passion for wood carving. They led the horses back to the stable and put them in their stalls, then sat on the tailgate of his truck, talking.

In late afternoon they arrived back at the barn. Josh turned off the ignition. In the long, awkward pause, the only sounds were heat pings coming off the hot engine.

"Well," she said, breaking the silence. "Thanks for everythin'."

"By the way, I haven't forgotten," he said, pulling a slip of paper from his shirt pocket and handing it to her.

It was a page from a memo pad with a tiny letterhead: "Images in Wood." She smiled at the scribbled message: Supper & studio tour for Miriam Mimi.

"What's a good time?" she asked, tucking the note in her jeans.

"Six o'clock. Bring a good appetite."


SHE WAS waiting in the RV when the tow truck swung in off the highway. She opened the door and stood waiting for Howard. He looked angry as he crossed the yard.

"Whoa," she said. "Who peed in *your* cornflakes?"

"Just look at me," he said, pointing to his pant legs peppered with tiny holes. "I'm hopeless—you know that—hopeless!"

"How'd you get those?"

"Standing too close when Harry was welding."

"You gotta admit, it makes a change from spillin' mustard and ketchup."

He shook his head in disgust as he stepped inside the RV.

"What was that town you went to?"

"Tincup. A little fart-squeak of a hamlet in the middle of nowhere. Sits in a valley with mountains all around. Used to be a mining town way back when. It's a ghost town now, except for a few diehards."

"Tincup, eh? Cute name."

"Cute place," he replied. "I'd like to take you there tomorrow for a picnic lunch. The guy that Harry did the welding for said he'd loan us his canoe. He told me there was a big reservoir nearby."

"Sounds wonderful."

"How was your day," he asked, "as if I needed to ask."

"What do you mean?"

"That grin hasn't left your face. Let me guess—Josh?"

"He's asked me to have supper with him tonight . . . over at the barn . . . six o'clock."

"That doesn't surprise me."

"Really?"

"I saw the way he looked at you across the supper table last night."

"You did?"

"Yes. Especially when the topic of horses came up. Harry did say you'd be Josh's friend if you liked horses."

"Friend? I hardly think so. We're only here for another day at most."

"At any rate," said Howard, consulting his watch, "you better start getting ready soon or you'll be late for your dinner date."

He slumped onto the lounge sofa and hid behind the pages of the *Denver Post*, but could not concentrate. Instead, he stared blankly at the justified columns. In the background, Miriam hummed to herself as she rooted through the bedroom closet for an outfit to wear. When she climbed into the shower; her bare feet padded softly on the bottom of the tub. Over the sound of the water, he heard her singing. There was a different lightness to her now that he had not seen before.

As he listened to her singing in the shower, he had a moment of déjà vu. Suzanne used to do the same thing, break into song unselfconsciously as she showered, shampooed her hair, and then shaved her legs. He lapsed into a reflective mood and began thinking about their RV trips across the country—the miles traveled, the meals shared, the historic places visited, the many languid evenings spent watching sunsets together. He recalled the times on this trip that he had felt her presence in the coach. It had been so real that his skin had prickled, as if she were standing right next to him, and that at any moment he would feel the loving touch of her hand.

Then suddenly, irrationally, he resented Miriam being on board the motor home, as if she were somehow usurping Suzanne. Would he ever be set free from the pain of losing her he wondered? Now, his feeling of aloneness was amplified even more so by Miriam's impending date with Josh. His emotions made no sense to him. He did not love Miriam, but felt like she was about to abandon him. It was then he knew he had to leave.

He tapped softly on the bathroom door, "Mimi."

"Yes," she replied, turning off the water.

"I'm going out for a drive. I'll see you later."

"OK!"

"Enjoy yourself."

"Thanks, Chip."

On his way to the Jeep, he passed the RV's open window. She was singing again.

# CHAPTER 26

## *Rendezvous*

IT HAD BEEN A long time since Miriam had dated anyone. With care, she laid out several outfits before choosing a pair of pleated slacks and a pastel blouse—clothes that Howard had bought for her. She preened at a mirror, critically examining every minute detail of her face, and applying foundation makeup to hide tiny blemishes, especially the scars on her chin. When satisfied, she crossed the dusty yard toward the barn and knocked on the door marked, "Tack Shop." After a long pause, it opened.

"Yes?" said Josh, staring vacantly at her.

"Hi," replied Miriam cautiously, wondering if he had forgotten their dinner date.

"Can I help you, ma'am?"

Miriam's face fell. She stared back with a bewildered look. About the same time she noticed his change of clothes and the scent of aftershave. Then, she saw an impish smile form, followed by a laugh.

"Don't worry, Mimi," he said, reaching for her hand, "I didn't forget. You look beautiful."

"Thanks," she replied and started breathing again.

"Make yourself comfortable," he said, and motioned her toward the leather sofa, set out from the wall of the open-concept room. "Can I get you something to drink?"

"Got anything fizzy?"

"Yes, but nothing alcoholic." Then he remembered she was pregnant and apologized for forgetting.

"You a non-drinker?"

"Yes," he replied.

"Wow! Never met a teetotaler before."

"Disappointed?"

"Not on your life," she replied and smiled.

"Club soda with a slice of lemon be OK?"

"Sounds fine."

As he stepped to the small kitchenette, she glanced at the room's masculine theme, devoid of a woman's frilly touches. Table lamps cast the rough texture of pine wallboards into high relief. Two hunting trophies dominated the décor: deer's heads with full racks that seemed to survey the room with their glass eyes. The walls were taken up with grouped collages of black and white photographs in matted frames: spruce-carpeted mountainsides in early-morning mist; alpine-fed streams tumbling over glistening rocks; abandoned ranch buildings immersed in tall grasses, a refuge for birds and field mice; and close-up portraits of Josh's horses, including Juniper, the youngest addition. The furniture was ranch-style that included a glass-topped coffee table in the center of a fringed rug. A small part of the room was set aside for dining, just enough for a circular table and four chairs. She broke her focus with the surroundings and watched Josh slice a wedge of lemon on the countertop, squeeze the juice into a tumbler, and then fill it with carbonated soda.

"Thanks," she said, taking the glass. She noticed a light on inside the oven. "Somethin' smells good."

"Hope you like Mexican."

"Love it. What're you makin'?"

"Chicken enchiladas."

"Do you cook a lot or do you eat with Harry and Gladys?"

"Once in a while . . ."

He had lost his train of thought, momentarily looking bewildered and embarrassed. She sipped her drink and waited.

"Once in a while," he continued, "Gladys invites me over, like yesterday, but mostly I like to cook for myself. Fancy stuff when I'm in the mood, or when I have company, which isn't too often."

"A non-drinker *and* a chef," exclaimed Miriam. "How rare is that!"

"Hardly a chef."

"I like the rustic look," said Miriam, glancing around the room and beyond to the single bedroom and washroom that adjoined the main living area. "Did you have a lot o' fixin' up to do to get it like this?"

"Yes. I had to tear out the old walls and expand into the barn. But I've still got enough room out there for a studio and showroom."

"The photography yours?" she asked, glancing back again at the framed prints.

"Yes, it's a sideline hobby of mine. I use it as a basis for my carving."

When they reached a lull in conversation, Josh turned his attention to preparing the meal. As he took condiments from the cupboards, she noticed yellow post-it notes stuck to the insides of the doors. She was curious. Were they to jog his memory on larger issues, like paying bills or keeping appointments? Or were they to remind him of day-to-day incidentals?

"You mind havin' a nosy woman in your kitchen?" asked Miriam, getting up from the sofa and hovering.

"Not at all," he said. He donned oven mitts, and then lifted out a steaming glass casserole dish and two pre-heated plates. "Do you like cooking . . . Mimi?"

"Uh-uh. I'd rather have a root canal without freezin'."

"That bad, huh?"

"Oh, I can throw somethin' together when I have to. I'm pretty basic when it comes to cookin'."

With two spatulas he lifted out each enchilada, stuffed with chopped chicken, peppers, onions and cheese, and topped with sliced Jalapenos, and set it on a plate. He spooned out a portion of black beans and Spanish rice, then picked up a squeeze bottle and drizzled a zigzag of sauce over each enchilada.

"That sauce isn't hot by the way. I just put it on there to be fancy."

"Hey, I'm impressed."

He donned the oven mitts again and carried their meals to the table, "Watch your pinkies. The plate is hot!"

"Mmm," she exclaimed, taking her first bite. "This is *won*derful." She pointed to the tortilla on her plate. "What holds the fillin' together?"

"Cream of chicken soup and shredded Monterrey Jack," he replied.

"If," she said with her mouth full, "I ever open a Mexican restaurant, you're hired."

"If I ever give up wood carving," he said and winked, "I'll keep that in mind."

As they ate, she appraised him. Aside from facial scars, and the occasional lapse of memory, there was nothing that marked him as different from the average man. But the more they talked, the more she sensed something pleasing about him. He seemed grounded and content.

"It's just a hunch," she said, working some rice and beans onto her fork, "but I get the feelin' you're satisfied with your life. Are you?"

He rested his forearms on the table for a moment before speaking, "Yes, I'd say so, all things considered."

"You hesitated there," she said.

"Well . . . at times I have mixed feelings."

"Oh?"

"Don't get me wrong, I like carving. It allows me to be more in charge of my life than when I was working for the firm. But there's a part of me that still misses the ego rush that goes with the corporate life: the big money, the competitiveness, the thrill of closing a deal. All those things used to factor big in my life. I felt more important back then—that what I did for a living counted for something. I mean, let's face it, it's the movers and shakers that make the world go round, not wood carvers."

"But you must have more freedom now," said Miriam. "Isn't that better?"

"It is," he said, then finished a mouthful of rice before continuing. "I take on projects that interest *me*, not someone else. If the weather's good, I saddle up and make a day of it. Ride up there with a packed lunch and my Nikon. Then, when I'm back, I'll start on a carving. I still put in a good eight-hour day, but without the stress I used to have. So, yes, that part's good." He paused for a moment to reflect. "Funny thing is, for years I was chasing something and never found it, no matter how hard I worked or how much money I made."

"And what was that?" asked Miriam.

"Contentment. I had to lose my marriage and almost lose my life in the process. In a way, my accident was a blessing in disguise. If it hadn't been for that, I'd have probably died of ulcers or a heart attack."

They finished their dessert, sopapillas drenched with honey, then retreated to the sofa. She noticed the way he leaned toward her when she talked, as if he was genuinely interested in what she had to say. When his knee accidentally brushed the top of her leg, she felt her heart race.

After the sun dropped below the treetops, the temperature in the building began to fall. Josh laid a fire with newspaper and kindling and lit it with a wooden match. Tendrils of smoke rolled along the roof of the firebox, and then curled up into the flue. Soon, the resin in the spruce popped loudly, and the sweet fragrance of burning wood filled the room. When the flames had spread throughout the firebox, he closed the metal door. The room quickly warmed.

"Hope you haven't forgotten your promise," she said, after they had finished their coffee. "You did say you'd give me a tour of your studio. I want to see the maestro's creations I've heard so much about."

He got up and limped into his bedroom. She heard a dresser drawer open and close; moments later he returned with a sweater.

"Here," he said, draping it over her shoulders. "It'll be getting cool out there in the showroom."

He took her hand and led her through a door into a small anteroom, "I built this to keep sawdust out of my living quarters," he said, then opened the far door into his workshop and flipped on the lights.

It was the heady scent of the place she noticed first, a perfumed mix of wood shavings, resins, and polishes. The room held an assortment of power tools and was equipped with a dust-collection system of pipes and exhaust blowers. A U-shaped work bench hugged three walls, with the main carving area situated under a north-facing window.

"Now," she said, leaning closer to him, "tell me how all this works."

"Each piece starts here in the prep area," he said pointing to a storage rack laden with blocks and slabs of wood in various sizes. "I rough cut the wood on that table saw, then sketch out the shape with a pencil and trim off the waste with the band saw."

"What's that gonna be when it's finished?" she asked, pointing to an angular block covered with pencil lines and saw marks.

"A merganser."

They moved to the carving area by the window, equipped with chisels, files, and small shaping and sanding machines. Miriam slid onto the high-backed stool and peered curiously through a magnifying lens at a partially finished carving. A Steller's jay startled her as it flew past the window to a feeding station.

"What a pretty place to work," she said, watching the blue, crested bird grab a peanut, and then flit into the branches of a spruce.

"It beats having to commute to an office."

"What's in those jars?" she said, pointing toward the finishing area against the far wall.

"Wood stains. I make up my own. I've got over a hundred shades and colors."

"I don't see any finished pieces."

"The last one went on display yesterday."

"Can I see it?"

He led her from his workshop into the large showroom; when the lights came on, she gasped. Dangling from the ceiling on spidery strands of monofilament line were raptors in full flight: different species of owls, an osprey, and a peregrine falcon diving on a sparrow. The centerpiece of the collection was a life-sized bald eagle, its massive wings outstretched with primary feathers extended like splayed fingers. In the vice grip of its talons was a salmon, glistening as if it had just been plucked from an icy stream. She moved closer to study the fine details of his work: each feather delicately carved, each scale on the legs and the curve of the talons rendered with frightening realism; the head, fiercely noble, crowned with white feathers and possessed of all-seeing eyes and a razor-like beak. It was as real as if it had just swooped in through the building—a raptor in all its predatory perfection and primal majesty.

She circled the room to view pieces set out on cloth-covered tables. The variety of his work was extensive and neatly arranged in groups: predators from timber wolves to weasels; prey animals from marmots to field mice; and reptiles from rattlesnakes to lizards like the Gila monster which was not only carved to perfection, but colored with semi-transparent stains and dyes to replicate the pink and black tones of its skin. Many of the wildlife carvings were integrated with natural materials: chunks of rock, smoothed river pebbles, hand-worked iron, and blown glass. The human figures were as diverse: lovers holding hands on a park bench, clowns with oversized feet and painted faces entertaining children, and a blacksmith in a miniature leather apron at an anvil, hammering a piece of metal into a horseshoe. But one piece in particular captured her imagination; she went down on one knee to examine it.

On the table cloth, a folded card introduced the carving: *Gift from the Sea*. The large, oval base was covered in rippled beach sand and sprinkled with an assortment of tiny seashells. In the center was a much-enlarged shell about eighteen inches long, and hinged in the open position. Cradled inside the scalloped base of the shell, a sleeping baby lay in the fetal position, its head resting on a large, opalescent pearl of hand-blown glass. Clutched in the baby's tiny fingers was a starfish. Except for the pearl, the entire carving had been rendered in woods of different hues. The piece had been varnished to a lustrous finish and dusted with patches of sand and imitation sea froth, as if the ocean had just deposited it on the beach.

"It's absolutely magical," whispered Miriam, awed by the realism. She ran a finger over the contours of the baby's face: the rounded forehead, the button nose, the crescent shape of each eyelid, the tiny chin and bubble cheeks. "Just look at that peaceful expression. Oh, Josh, you've made a piece o' wood come alive. Given it a heartbeat. A soul."

"Thanks," he replied, delighted by her compliment.

"Where'd you get that pearl? It's in perfect proportion to the head."

"I made it."

"Made it?" she said, with a look of surprise. "I'm totally impressed."

"I dabble," he said, modestly. "A bit of metal work . . . some glass blowing now and then. Otherwise, I harvest from nature: pebbles, pine cones, and such."

"I don't mean to be rude or anythin', but—"

"But what?" he said.

"I've been lookin' at some o' the price tags. You should be chargin' way more than you are."

"That's what Harry keeps telling me."

They returned to his living quarters and sat on the sofa again, but closer this time, and looked through photo albums, snippets of his life lived entirely in Colorado. One shot caught her eye: a smiling boy in hip waders, fly casting into a mountain stream. The backlighting from the sun outlined the lyrical curve of the fishing line as it reached toward a quiet pool by the bank. She studied the pictures of his Denver wedding to Carol. He looked handsome and confident in his tuxedo. Pages later, she came to newspaper photos of hideously mangled vehicles on a darkened highway and news clippings tucked behind plastic. She noticed one of the headlines: **Miracle on Monarch Pass.** The article described the accident and Josh's life-saving flight by helicopter to the Denver trauma center.

"Is that your car?" she asked, pointing to a badly crumpled vehicle.

"Uh-huh."

"They certainly got the headline right," she said.

He quickly flipped the pages of the album, anxious to focus on happier moments in his life.

After the photo albums, it was her turn to dazzle Josh with her grasp of trivia and history and numbers. He admitted he could no longer do calculations in his head since the accident, but he enjoyed Miriam's prowess with mathematics and had fun testing her answers against a calculator.

Despite their closeness on the sofa, he had made no move toward deeper intimacy. By now, the kind of men she had dated in the past, would already be trying to grope her, anxious to 'score.' His gentlemanly reserve stoked a fierce burning in her, a sudden longing. But it was more than a physical thing. It was his uncommonly gentle nature and steadiness that attracted her. For the entire evening, she had sensed there was something different about him. He was, she thought, the kind of man she could feel safe with. A man who could be tender, yet not be self-conscious of tenderness—not like other men she had known who kept their feelings buried and related to her with a pseudo self.

Conversation and laughter flowed more easily between them the longer the evening progressed. And the more she got to know him, the stronger her attraction became. For hours, they sat close to each other on the sofa, their shoeless feet propped on the glass coffee table; occasionally, he brushed the side of his foot against hers. The effect on her was electric; her skin tingled and she felt an intense stirring. Never before had she experienced such a physical longing for a man. Finally, she meshed her fingers with his and looked intently at him.

"Josh?" she said, her voice shaky with nerves.

"Yes."

"I don't want you to think badly o' me for askin' you this, but . . ."

"But what?"

Her heart was pounding now with anticipation.

"Would you . . . ?"

"Would I what?"

"Make love to me?"

He blinked, taken aback by her forwardness.

"Don't you want to?"

"Well," he replied, "I wasn't expecting it, to tell you the—"

"Are you turned off 'cause I'm pregnant?"

"No."

"Am I not attractive to you?"

"It's not that."

"What is it then?"

"I'd have thought it was the other way around," he replied.

253

"Why?" she said, her forehead creased in a frown. "Do you think your accident has somehow made you less attractive?"

"Sort of . . . plus . . . I'm just not the old me."

"And who was that?"

"The more confident Josh. The guy who was up for it all the time."

"Don't be offended," said Miriam, "but can I ask you somethin' personal?"

"Sure."

"What kind o' lover were you back then?"

"You mean with Carol . . . before the accident?"

"Yeah."

"Aggressive," he replied, laughing nervously. "Slam bam I guess you could say."

"Funny, that's not how I see you at all."

"Oh?"

"I've just seen what you do for a livin'."

His face was a question mark.

"It takes a sensitive man to breathe life into wood the way you do. It's one o' the things that makes you attractive to me."

"Really?"

"Uh-huh. I saw your tender side when you were around your horses. That gentle touch you have . . . it's so sweet . . . says a lot about who you are."

"But . . ."

Suddenly a troubling thought crossed her mind, something she had not considered. Did his reluctance to make a romantic move have any connection to his accident? Had his injuries been so damaging that he was impotent? He had just told her that he was once 'up for it all the time.' What about now? Had that changed? If so, she had just boxed him into a corner with no way for him to save face. Carefully, she couched her words, terrified of offending him again.

"Look, Josh, I didn't mean to be so bold . . . so forward. I'm not normally like that. It's just that . . . well . . . I want to spend the night with you. I'd be happy to bits, just to have you hold me in your arms . . . to kiss and cuddle me close in bed. If that's all you do till mornin', then that'll be fine with me. And if it leads to other things . . . well . . . that'll be fine too."

WHEN SHE opened her eyes in the morning, Josh had left the bed. She smelled coffee percolating and heard bacon sputtering in a pan, then the metallic pop of a toaster. Her eyes scanned the bedroom. Hanging on the back of the door, she noticed his terry robe. She put it on and padded on bare feet to the kitchenette. She found him standing at the counter, dressed only in track pants, bare-chested, and buttering slices of toast. He flashed a broad smile.

"Sorry," she said, yawning and running fingers through her disheveled hair. "I look a fright first thing."

"You beat me to the draw," he said, pointing to a large wooden tray, already set out with food and condiments. "I was about to bring us breakfast in bed."

She came up behind him, slipped her arms around his waist and kissed his deeply scarred back. "Well then, don't let me spoil your plans."

She was waiting for him in bed when he limped into the room with a towel draped over one arm, playfully mimicking a waiter in a fine restaurant. He set the tray in the center of the bed. They talked and laughed and kissed as they ate. And the kissing led to shared delights and self-discoveries: he was no longer the failure he believed himself to be, the once bright star fallen from a corporate sky, relegated by circumstance to the humble lot of a wood carver; and she was not, as she had come to see herself, a no-account high school dropout, a tenement waif from Philly's inner city who was good for nothing more than waiting on tables in a skid row greasy spoon.

When they had finished making love, he left for his showroom and returned with a decorative gift box.

"Here," he said. "Something for you to remember Colorado by."

"Oh, you've already given me that," she said with a smile.

"Go ahead," he said. "Open it."

She removed the lid and lifted out the bunched tissue paper. Mounted on a polished wooden base was a single columbine blossom, the state's flower—a delicate, cupped cluster of five alabaster petals carved to wafer-thinness from fine-gained wood and airbrushed with a blush of transparent, colored stains. A cluster of yellow stamens reached up from the center of the white blossom, as if enticing bees.

"Oh," she gasped and brought a hand to her mouth. "It's gorgeous . . . so real . . . and look how the wood grain shows through the colors."

When it was time for her to leave, they stood awkwardly at the door, talking and holding hands. Neither wanted to let go and end the perfectness. He cradled her face tenderly in his hands, and softly kissed her eyelids.

"I've enjoyed this," he said, pulling her close and pressing his cheek against hers, "more than you know."

"So have I," said Miriam. "Everythin' was lovely . . . so very lovely."

"Take care of yourselves," he said as he released her.

"Yourselves?"

"You and—"

"Oh, yes," she replied, then instinctively touched her belly.

She stepped into the morning light, cut by the erratic flight of barn swallows as they snatched insects on the wing. The field grasses were drenched with dew, and the droplets in the seed heads split the sunlight into rainbow-hued spectrums. As she crossed the yard, the only sounds were her footsteps on gravel, and the rasp of crickets.

When she reached the steps of the motor home, she paused for a backward glance. She smiled at Josh, who was standing in the open doorway, watching after her. Her tryst with this man, she mused, had been a brief and impulsive act—a one-night stand by common definition to be sure. But to Miriam, it had not been a tawdry affair at all. For the first time in her life, she had been made love to by a sensitive, caring man—a man, who, through circumstances not of his making—had been rendered vulnerable. Her intimacy with him had restored her lost faith in men and she dreaded having to leave him behind as they pushed on for California. But even more so, she dreaded facing Howard.

# CHAPTER 27

## *The Leaving*

WHEN MIRIAM ENTERED THE RV, Howard was at the galley sink washing dishes with a tea towel draped over one shoulder. He kept his back turned to her and said nothing. She glanced at the dinette table. Her place was set and the hot breakfast he had cooked for her had gone cold.

"Sorry, Chip," she said, placing a hand in the hollow of his back. "You've got every right to be mad at me. I should've let you know I was stayin' the night with Josh. I didn't plan it that way. It just sort o' happened."

He made no response, and kept his back turned.

"Are you upset I went to bed with him?"

"Your sexual escapades are none of my business."

His tone and the use of the word *escapades* seemed to confirm it for her; Howard was jealous. But why, she thought? Nothing sexual had passed between them. Their physical contact had been chaste to a fault, at least up to this point. Was that about to change, she wondered? Had he secretly harbored romantic feelings for her? Feelings he was reluctant to act upon because of the age gap between them? Because of residual feelings he still had for Suzanne? Or was it impotence? He had already admitted that his libido had shut down. Could that be the reason?

She stepped closer and placed a hand on each of his shoulders, massaging the muscles, tight as knots. As she did, she wondered about her own feelings for Howard. Like Josh, he too was a gentle and sensitive man. Had she been kidding herself? Would she, if Howard had made sexual advances toward her, succumbed and taken things further? Gone as far as she had with Josh?

"Talk to me, Chip," she said in a pleading tone.

"What do you want me to say?"

"I don't care. Read the friggin' cereal box to me. Anythin' at all. I just want to hear the sound of your voice—the voice I'm so used to hearin'. You freezin' me out is the cruelest thing."

He turned to face her. "You want to know cruel," he said, his face flushed with anger, "I'll tell you cruel. The way you've used me is cruel."

"How have I used you, Chip?"

"Sneaking off with that trucker after I'd offered to take you all the way to your mother's."

"You're right. That *was* cruel and thoughtless of me. I said I was sorry and I meant it—meant it with all my heart."

"I care about you, Mimi, goddammit," he blurted out. "There. I've said it. Ever since I picked you up in Toledo I've cared. Worried about you when you ran off. Wanted to give you the vacation you never had as a kid. Wanted to protect you—"

"Is that why you're so pissed at me goin' to bed with Josh? You thought you needed to protect me?"

"Howard just stared at her and blinked.

"It is, isn't it? You thought he was takin' advantage o' me. Admit it."

Reluctantly, he nodded.

"Answer me somethin', Chip," she said, pointing a finger at him, "and don't you *dare* bullshit me."

"What?"

"Have you fallen in love with me? Is there some kind o' sexual attraction thing goin' on here that you haven't told me about?"

"No," he said emphatically, "and that's the truth. I just care about you one helluva lot. I care what happens to you, care about your future—"

"And it's sweet that you do. No one's *ever* been as good to me as you've been, Chip, but there are some things I don't need protectin' from. Things I'm capable o' doin' without you watchin' out for me. I may seem like a kid to you at times, but I'm a grown woman. You gotta stop treatin' me like a child. For years, that's how my mom used to treat me."

"I know, I know," he said. "I'm sorry. I stepped over the line again, first with your abortion plans, and now with this."

"Look, I don't have to tell you this, but I'm gonna tell you anyway. Josh wasn't the one who made the move. It was me. I needed to feel loved romantically, even if it was only for one night, even though I'll never see him again. He did that for me. For the first time in years, I felt like a woman who was cherished and accepted for who I am."

"And today we'll be leaving here," said Howard.

"Oh, don't remind me," she said, putting up her hands. "I can't bear to think o' that. Not after last night. Anyway, enough talk o' leavin'. I said that today we'd do somethin' together—just me and you. And I still want that very much."

"I'm sorry for the upset," he said, contritely.

"It's OK," she sighed. "Let's forget it."

"I've picked out a place I think you'll like."

"That's nice," she replied, "but first I want somethin' from you."

"What's that?"

"A hug."

AFTER STOPPING in the hamlet of Tincup, they arrived at the Taylor Park Reservoir with their borrowed aluminum canoe. It had more dents than a demolition-derby car and the cheap paddles were split and moldy from neglect. But the scenery that back dropped the man-made lake, more than made up for their derelict craft. Wide, grassy areas led back from the water's edge before giving way to rolling stands of evergreens that melted into the lower slopes of the distant mountain range. A scattering of fisherman's vehicles and ATVs ringed the water's edge. Anglers were already ensconced in lawn chairs, beer coolers within arm's reach, as they kept silent vigils over fishing rods anchored in tubes and lines cast into the deeper water.

They shoved off into mirror-smooth water under a cloudless sky. Miriam dipped her fingers in the frigid, mountain-fed lake, and then quickly pulled them out. She paddled leisurely at the bow while Howard steadily J-stroked toward an unoccupied stretch on the distant shoreline. Once ashore, they used the overturned canoe as a back rest, and their lifejackets as cushions to insulate then from the cool ground. They had barely unwrapped their lunches when the magpies arrived, waiting for an opportunity to swoop off with a sandwich. Howard poured steaming coffee from a large thermos flask. As they sipped their drinks, a pair of wet-suited operators on personal watercraft carved figure eights in the lake.

"Damned crotch rockets," said Howard, watching the daredevils playing chicken with each other and harassing the fishermen. "Is there a lake in this country that isn't plagued with them?"

"I'm not sure they're allowed on this reservoir," she said, pointing to a sheriff's patrol car that was cruising the perimeter of the lake.

The watercraft operators eventually tired of the novelty and sped off toward the marina. Suddenly, the water calmed and the lake was quiet again.

The mirror-smooth water doubled the nearby mountains and triggered a pensive mood in Miriam. She left Howard sitting by the canoe and meandered down to the water's edge. For a while, she sat back on her haunches and watched the minnows as they darted among the rounded stones. Absently, she lifted a few large pebbles from the lakebed, and then tried without success to make them skip the surface. At each attempt, they plunked clumsily into the chilly mountain-fed water.

"Do you know how to do this properly?" she said, looking over her shoulder at him.

He grinned.

"Don't give me that look o' yours, Chip. I need a coach real bad. Get your butt down here and show me."

AFTER SEVERAL leisurely hours spent walking the shoreline, talking and skipping stones, Howard pulled the cell phone from his backpack and called Harry Kimball. The parts had arrived shortly after they had departed for the lake. Repairs would be completed by late-afternoon.

"Where are we goin' after Gunnison?" she asked when he got off the phone.

"To the San Juans," he replied, "but there's no way we'll make it there today. How would you like to camp tonight by a reservoir just like this?"

"You mean there's another one between here and where we're goin'?"

"Yes. I've seen it on my road atlas."

"All right then," she replied, her voice having suddenly gone flat and her mood, melancholy.

They paddled back across the lake, put the canoe on top of the Jeep, and returned it to its owner. On their way back, Howard stopped at an ATM in Gunnison and took out cash to pay Harry Kimball.

"You're good to go," said Harry, when they arrived.

"I can't thank you enough," said Howard.

"I've checked her over well and done a test drive. You shouldn't have any more problems now. I'd go easy on the big climbs though. She's got quite a few miles on the clock."

"Where's Alice?" asked Miriam.

"In the house baking pies with Gladys," replied Harry.

While Howard settled up his bill, Miriam went inside to say her goodbyes. Minutes later she returned, her eyes puffy.

"You OK?" asked Howard.

She nodded, but could not find her voice. Just then she turned at the sound of a door opening. It was Josh, wearing a workshop apron as he headed over from the barn. Quickly, she wiped her eyes on her sleeve.

"Looks like you're ready to go," said Josh, his face a portrait of disappointment.

"Yeah," she said. "I was . . . just about to come over to say goodbye."

They hugged each other tightly. Miriam slipped a square of folded paper into his apron pocket.

"Good luck," he said, his eyes brimming.

"Thanks," she replied, but said no more, afraid she might break down.

The whole family gathered in the yard to see them off. Howard aimed the motor home down the long driveway toward the road. Miriam looked into her side mirror and smiled. Josh's head was bowed; he was reading her note. As they swung onto the road, she glanced back toward the Kimball property. Everyone but Josh had gone inside. She rolled down her window to wave to him, but it was too late. A stand of tall spruce suddenly cut off her view.

The farther they drove from the Kimball's property, the deeper she plunged into a depression; the atmosphere between them became strained. When he tried making conversation with her, she lashed out.

"I wish you'd never picked me up in Toledo," she shouted.

"You'd have probably come to harm with those drunks."

"So friggin' what if I had," she hissed. "Maybe they would o' killed me at some point . . . they'd have been doin' me a favor."

"You don't know what you're saying."

"Don't I? If they had killed me, least I wouldn't be hurtin' anymore. And I'm sick to death o' hurtin'. Sick o' pickin' men who are losers. Sick o' bein' alone. Sick o'—"

"Look," said Howard, trying to calm her down, "I understand you're upset right now. I mean, you're pregnant and you've probably got hormones playing hell with your emotions."

"Oh, is that what it is?" she retorted, her voice dripping with sarcasm. "Besides bein' a goddamn teacher, you're a friggin' hormone expert too!"

"Mimi," said Howard, ignoring her tirade and speaking calmly, "is it leaving Josh that's upset you?"

"Duh," she blurted out, and then dissolved into tears. She unfastened her seatbelt, disappeared into the washroom, and slammed the sliding door. He could hear her sobbing.

"I figured you'd say that to me," she said when she returned, eyes puffy and still angry. "Chip Munro, alias Dr. Phil . . . expert on romance and relationships. Comin' from you that's a joke."

"How do you figure that?" said Howard.

"Because you've got neither," she shouted, then dropped her head into her hands and sobbed again.

The remark stung Howard, but he let it pass. It was clear that she was stressed and needed to lash out. She raged in cycles: citing hurts from childhood, anger at her pregnancy, bitterness over her failed relationships. She blamed him for their breakdown at the summit of Monarch Pass, saying that it would delay her arrival in California and worry her mother even more. But he saw through the veneer. Her angry outbursts continued, but he curbed his tongue and let her vent. Exhausted, she eventually calmed and gazed catatonically at the passing scenery.

He turned off the highway at a camping sign and chose a site. The location was beautiful, beside a long, blue reservoir in mesa country, carpeted with acres of knee-high sagebrush and back dropped by scenic cliffs that swept dramatically down to the water's edge. There were no hookups for RVs so there was nothing for him to do but level the motor home. The moment he stopped, Miriam retreated to her bedroom at the rear of the coach and did not come out either for supper or to sit with him beside the lake and enjoy the evening. He stayed outside until well after dark, grappling with feelings of loneliness until the chill drove him inside.

Howard made up his bed on the lounge sofa, but lay awake staring at the ceiling. Far in the distance, coyotes yipped as they gathered for the night's hunting. Inside, Miriam tossed in bed and cried into her pillow.

When her upset was over, she came into the kitchen to get a can of iced tea. Then she retreated to her bedroom where she remained until morning.

SHE WAS still sullen at breakfast and avoided eye contact with Howard. When he reached across the dinette table and touched her arm, she pulled away.

"I've packed my things," she said resolutely. "When we get to the next town, I want you to drop me off. I'll make my way from there."

"Please don't do that," he said.

"I need to travel on my own now, Chip. You've been good to me so far—better than I deserved—but I gotta move on."

"But why?"

"Because I can't do this anymore."

"Do what anymore?"

"Travel with you."

"Why? Have I said something to piss you off?"

"No."

"I don't understand," he said.

"Travelin' means meetin' people on the road. And just when I get to like 'em, I've gotta say goodbye . . . never to see 'em again. It's too difficult for me. I need to travel alone. Anonymously."

"What can I say to make you change your mind?"

"Nothin'. My mind's made up."

"But I'll worry about you, Mimi. You know damned well I will. I'd go nuts if anything happened to you, especially now."

"What do you mean, 'especially now'?"

"Because you're not the stranger I picked up in Toledo."

She made eye contact for the first time.

"You're a friend now—a good friend. The kind of friend I want to stay in touch with once this trip's over."

Her eyes darted away as she tried to process what he was saying. She could count on the fingers of one hand the people who had genuinely cared for her. Would she regret setting out on her own? Would she experience other hardships and dangers? Already she had looked at Chip's road atlas. Beyond the mountains, there were miles of desert to cross before she reached California and the coast. What would happen if she could not get a ride? What if she had to tough it out in the open? She ran her hands nervously through her hair, trying to think. Maybe the worst part of all would be leaving Chip. Once he dropped her off and drove away, she would miss him—deep down she knew she would.

"Can I ask you something?" said Howard.

"I guess."

"Besides having to leave Josh, exactly what is bothering you at the moment?"

"Plenty," she said, absently shuffling pieces of spilled cereal. "I've been through all this before with you. Gettin' pregnant. Facin' a shitty future. Havin' no money and no job. Havin' to depend on my mother's charity."

"Is that the worst part?"

"Yeah. Bein' a grown woman who's a walkin' screw up. I feel like a child . . . so maybe I *am* a child, Chip. Someone who never really grew up."

"Does riding with me make you feel like a child?" he asked.

"Partly."

"What part?"

"Bein' dependent on you."

"What about the vacation part?"

"No. That makes me feel special."

"Listen, Mimi, if I *was* to drop you off at the next town as you suggest, then I will literally fall apart."

"Oh, that's not fair," she shouted. "Not fair at all . . . layin' a guilt trip on me."

Howard took a deep breath, and then exhaled through pursed lips, "You're right. I'm sorry. It's just that, in my own pathetic way, I'm trying to tell you how much you mean to me. How much you've helped me on this trip by being a friend. The loss of Suzanne has brought me as close to a mental breakdown as I've ever come. Do you know how scary it is being that close to going nuts?"

"Yeah," she replied in a barely audible whisper. "Yeah, I do."

"Well, you've kept me sane is what you've done."

Miriam suddenly brought both hands to her face and dissolved into tears; Howard slid beside her on the dinette bench and put his arm around her.

"I gotta confession to make," she sobbed.

"What?"

"Remember the night I slept under the highway bridge?"

"Yes. What about it?"

"I was . . . was so depressed, I wanted to kill myself. I lay awake starin' at the underside of that bridge. Listenin' to the traffic flyin' past. Thinkin' of how I'd do it . . . that I'd run out into the path of a truck and end it all. But when push came to shove, I chickened out."

"I'm glad you did," said Howard, shocked at her revelation.

"When you came along the next mornin' . . . you know . . . like when the cop had me and all."

"Yes."

"I just couldn't believe it was you again. Ever since then, I haven't thought of doin' that . . . committin' suicide, that is. You see, it's worked both ways. You've kept *me* from goin' nuts too. To be honest and truthful, maybe it was meant to be that way . . . that you'd pick me up again so we could help each other."

She went to the bathroom to wash her face. When she returned, she sat quietly gazing at her reflection in the window superimposed over the view of the high cliffs. Then her eyes fixed on Howard's side of the dinette table, littered with toast crumbs and grains of sugar that had missed his cereal bowl.

"Oh frig," she said, laughing as she wiped the debris with a dishcloth. "I can't leave now. Who's gonna look after you . . . you damned great lump."

THEY PACKED up and left their site by the reservoir, then headed west toward Montrose and the road that would take them south into the San Juan Mountains. As they approached the outskirts of town, Howard pointed to a sign: "AUCTION SALE TODAY! THE MORRISON ESTATE."

"Never been to one o' those," said Miriam.

"Want to?"

"Sure," she replied. "Long as you don't mind stoppin'."

Howard turned off the highway and followed signs to a metal-clad building on one of the backstreets. The parking lot was full and both sides of the street were lined with vans and pickups. With Miriam's help, he maneuvered the RV onto the wide shoulder some distance away. As they walked toward the building, they fell into step behind two locals.

"I'm glad that ol' cow's finally dead," said a man to his buddy. "Never did like that Ellie Morrison woman."

"Wasn't she a piece a work?" said his friend. "No wonder Wiley died so gall durned young. Can you imagine the naggin' he must o' took for all them years. Why, it'd be enough to put anyone in an early grave."

"Wiley's gonna be some pissed off though."

"What do you mean, pissed off? He's fucking dead."

"What I mean is, Ellie is now buried right beside him."

"So?"

"So, think about it. He's gonna be cheek-by-jowl with that cranky ol' bitch for eternity. Even in death he ain't gonna be free of her naggin'."

"I reckon you're right. Never thought on it like that."

Miriam giggled at the men's banter. Minutes later, she and Howard entered the building. He lined up at the registration table and showed his ID. One woman entered his particulars in a laptop computer, while another pulled the cap off a felt marker and wrote a bold number on a white card—259.

The rectangular room was ventilated by overhead fans, and lit by tobacco-yellowed fluorescent lights, their reflective plastic panels dotted with dead flies. At the end of the room, a raised stage held two people: the auctioneer, and a matronly woman at a table who recorded each sale on a laptop. Articles were laid out on tables down both sides of the room and in the area below the stage. Two assistants held the smaller items high overhead so the crowd, seated in metal chairs, could see. On stage, the auctioneer used a hands-free microphone so he could acknowledge bidders more easily. Some nodded. Others held up their numbered card. One woman, busily knitting, never looked up at all; she placed her bids by shouting "yip."

Howard and Miriam cruised the room eyeing the sea of items for sale that attracted the attention of collectors. One man, a Coca Cola aficionado, was thrilled to find half-a-dozen classic, small bottles in the original carry pack. A fat, fiftyish woman picked through boxes of trashy romance novels while her husband, a farmer dressed in denim coveralls and a dirty railroad cap, fingered a stack of Lawrence Welk and Mitch Miller vinyl albums. As he studied the album covers, he sucked noisily on his teeth. Howard felt a tug on his shirt.

"Look," said Miriam, as the auctioneer's assistant picked up the next item.

"Want me to bid for it?"

"Oh, would you?" she asked, bubbling with excitement.

It was a deep, shadow box containing autographed baseball cards, a miniature baseball, bat, and catcher's mitt. In the background was a replica of a baseball diamond complete with raised pitcher's mound. Around the perimeter were tiny, colored pennants representing all the major league teams.

"Here's a nice one-of-a-kind item, folks," hyped the auctioneer. "Ideal for the sports fan in your family. It's packed with priceless baseball memorabilia. An heirloom you'll treasure for years to come."

Predictably, he tried to start the bidding at twenty-five dollars. Predictably, the audience waited for him to drop the price to entice the first bid. Soon the action picked up.

"Five dollar bid, now ten, now ten—at ten, now twenty—at twenty bid, now thirty, now thirty . . ."

Howard nodded.

"Thirty bid, now forty, now forty—at thirty make it forty . . ."

Another man held up his card

"Forty dollar bid, now fifty, at forty bid, go fifty . . ."

"Yip," shouted the knitting lady.

"Fifty bid, now sixty—at fifty, now sixty . . ."

The old farmer raised his railroad cap, followed quickly by other eager bidders. The auctioneer, smooth and experienced, never missed a beat, keeping up his rapid-fire spiel as he moved his hands to acknowledge bidders scattered throughout the sea of people in the large hall.

"Sixty dollar bid, now seventy, now seventy—at seventy bid, now eighty—at eighty bid, now ninety . . ."

Howard showed his card.

"Ninety bid, now a hundred— at ninety go a hundred, go a hundred . . ."

The auctioneer worked the room, but could not drive the price any higher. Miriam looked on as Howard winked at her.

"Buy it for yourself, buy it for your grandson. A bargain at twice the price, folks . . . at ninety dollars, going once—at ninety, going twice—all done and last caaall," said the auctioneer scanning the room for one last bidder, "*sold* for ninety dollars to number 259."

Howard took the item from the auctioneer's assistant, handed it to a delighted Miriam, then made his way to the registration table to pay and turn in his card.

Miriam was beaming as they left the building with her prize, "Thank you," she said, kissing his cheek.

"Feel better?" he asked.

"Much better."

"Will you do something for me now?"

"What's that?"

"I don't want to hear another word about you hitchhiking to California on your own. Deal?"

"Deal!" she replied.

"Good," he said. "Now let's head for the high country."

# CHAPTER 28

## *The San Juans*

HOWARD SWUNG SOUTH TOWARD the snow-capped peaks of the San Juan Mountains—a landscape for the heart and mind where the rural air was crisp and the alpine views enticing. They seemed even deeper into cowboy country now; pickup trucks continued to be the vehicle of choice. On the road ahead, one of them towed a beat up horse trailer piled to the roof with hay bales. They laughed at the bumper sticker: "A Hard-on Doesn't Count as Personal Growth."

He did not need to consult his altimeter to know they were climbing; the motor home's engine labored as they made their way toward the jagged range. The views got more spectacular with each mile and bend in the road, until they drew close to their destination campground.

Two descending mountains, one on either side of the highway, plunged to create a deep V. Framed in the notch was the pyramidal peak of Mount Abrams, crowned with an ermine mantle of snow. Its imposing presence dominated the head of the valley, a monument to the colossal forces that had created it, a spectacle of supreme beauty in all its geologic majesty. Sphinx-like, the great mountain seemed to gaze up the valley as if demanding homage from every mortal who dared to stand before it.

At the campground sign, Howard turned off the highway and crossed a narrow bridge; rushing under it was a torrent of milky, mineral-laden water, snow runoff from the surrounding mountains. They registered at the office, and then drove to the rear of the park, an expansive area ringed by groves of quaking aspens. All around were views of rock and spruce and steep, mountain slopes. Deer grazed warily on the fringes of the campground with a watchful eye on them as they disconnected the Jeep and set up their site.

Afterwards, they hiked a trail out of the campground and across a high ridge. The vegetation was a mix of small trees and shrubs, interspersed with lurking clusters of prickly pear, like so many pairs of praying hands.

"Watch your step," he cautioned. "You don't want one of those stuck in your ankle."

"I'm watchin', believe me."

They found a fallen log to sit on. Above the ridge, they watched a hawk circle, then glide in to investigate one of the pocked slopes. Suddenly, it angled its body and dived into the trees. Moments later it emerged with a squirrel dangling from its talons.

"I wonder if anyone from Kansas ever sat here?" said Miriam.

"Why Kansas?"

"I was thinkin' how hemmed in they might feel, you know, after those endless horizons and all."

"You're not feeling claustrophobic are you?" asked Howard.

"No. It's wonderful. Better than anythin' I could've imagined in my wildest dreams."

They spent the remainder of their day in the town of Ouray—The Switzerland of America—browsing the shops and posing in nineteenth century costumes to have their photo taken in an old-time studio. On the sloping main street they talked to locals who told them of conditions in the high country. In spite of considerable amounts of residual snow, the high-altitude roads were now passable.

EARLY THE next morning, they drove south out of town in the Jeep and immediately entered a dramatic, rock-walled gorge. The scenery was savagely beautiful—haunting and primordial—as if they were back in the Cretaceous Period and expected to see the shadows of pterodactyls pass over them, or see the head of a tyrannosaurus lunge out to devour them. Although the sun was up, it was hidden by the high peaks as they drove through the bottom of the deeply shaded valley on a narrow, paved road—the Million Dollar Highway—one of the most scenic drives on the continent.

"Oh my *God!*" shouted Miriam, shocked at the scant, ribbon of asphalt that hugged the canyon wall, barely wide enough for two-way traffic. "Look at the friggin' road! I think I'm gonna be sick."

"Better get used to it," said Howard. "This is going to be our route out of here when we leave for California."

"I'm scared to look," she said, peeking between her fingers.

It was a white-knuckled ride not for the faint-of-heart, certainly not for cell-phoning or text-messaging while driving, unless the driver had a death wish. Only passengers could enjoy the luxury of gawking at the mind-blowing scenery, and even then, it was a tense affair. Sitting close to the outside edge of the road, Miriam swallowed nervously as she peered into the bottom of the gorge, a stomach-churning view of fallen boulders that were once part of the mountain. On the inside of the road cut, sheer rock faces dropped to the edge of the pavement; small piles of fallen rock were ever-present reminders of the constant erosion. On the outside—the side they were on—there were no guard rails, just a painted white line on the asphalt, then inches beyond that, oblivion. Even northbound motorists with another lane between them and the abyss, hugged the wall for security. In places where the road had once collapsed, concrete retaining walls had been constructed, and then backfilled and the highway re-surfaced.

"Oh my God!" she croaked again as they approached what looked like the end of the pavement.

At the last second, Howard cranked the wheel for a sharp left turn as the road went around a shoulder of rock. At that moment, an oncoming gasoline tanker filled the northbound lane and squeezed them close to the edge. When she opened her eyes, she saw they were on a long horseshoe-shaped loop going east up a side gorge. Thousands of feet to her right across the yawning gap, was the continuation of their road on the far side of the loop. An eighteen-wheeler was slowly crawling along the ledge with a long line of automobile traffic behind—a beetle leading a parade of ants.

Despite the terror of the drive, the scenery was worth the racing heartbeats. They marveled not only at the exquisite views, but at the engineering feat of hacking out a road through such impossibly tortuous country. Bridal veils of crystal water tumbled down glistening, ebony fissures in the cliffs, passed under the road, then leapt outward for the long, misty drop into the gorge below. Evergreens stood tall and defiant, their roots set tenaciously into cracks in the cliff walls; others clung precariously to sloping fields of tumbled boulders. Occasionally, they passed windowless mine buildings, tin-roofed, weather-streaked survivors of the gold and silver heydays of the 1800s.

When he found a safe place to pull over, Howard consulted his map. His finger traced a meandering route up the side of the mountain on an old mining road.

"This is it," he said, folding the map and tucking it above the visor.

Miriam swallowed nervously, "You mean . . . we're goin' up *there*," she said, pointing to the higher reaches of the trail.

"Not to worry. The guy at the campground told me lots of people drive this road."

"Road? Looks more like a friggin' donkey path to me."

He engaged the Jeep's four-wheel drive and started up the rocky slope. He picked his way carefully to avoid hanging up the undercarriage on larger rocks. They saw no other vehicles as they worked their way toward snow-covered peaks. En route they passed massive patches of snow in the shadier places and ran through pools of silt-laden water, snow melt from the higher elevations. Occasionally, he had to dodge wash-outs and move onto loose rock along the edge of the road. Some sections were so steep that the trail ahead disappeared, replaced by views of the engine hood and blue sky; Howard had to hold open the driver's door and lean out to see.

Above tree line the air grew chillier. Marmots peeked shyly from the rocks and watched them as they passed. Miriam became nervous as the camber of the road tipped the vehicle. Frightened they would roll over, she shifted her weight in the seat, and hooked her arm over the window threshold.

As they neared the upper reaches of the mountain, their starting point at the base of the trail seemed part of some lost world, invisible and deeply buried in the bewildering maze of valleys. At the summit, they were alone as they stepped out into the cold and blustery altitude-thinned air. Their view was sensational and unobstructed—a 360° sweep of jagged, snow-capped "fourteeners" that formed the roof of Colorado. They took photographs, then sat on the warm hood of the Jeep and checked a map of the surrounding terrain.

"Oh damn," she said, at the sound of an approaching vehicle. "There goes our solitude."

The driver, a strawberry-complexioned, middle-aged man smoking a cigar, parked away from them. His blonde, female companion was first out of the vehicle. She took a short pull from a hip flask, and lit a cigarette.

Wisps of smoke drifted toward them. Miriam fought the sudden nicotine urge and dug for a wad of gum. The couple looked in their direction. Only the woman spoke.

"Nice day," she said, exhaling a toxic plume.

"It is so," said Howard, raising his hand in greeting.

"You're from out of state," she said, eyeing the license plate. "First time up here?"

"Yes," said Howard. "You?"

"Uh-uh."

"You live around here?"

"In the valley," she replied.

"You must know this place like your hip pocket, then."

"Pretty much. I was born and raised in this county."

The woman's grizzled companion stared mutely and puffed on his cigar.

"My map shows a lot of roads through this country."

"You're smart to have one. Some folks don't bother. They underestimate the dangers."

"I guess there's plenty," said Miriam.

The woman nodded as she dragged deeply on her cigarette, "Getting lost. Dying of hypothermia, Falling."

At a sudden clicking noise, they turned toward a rock-strewn slope.

"What's that?" asked Miriam.

"Scree," said the woman.

"Scree?"

"Broken rock. Bits are always coming down. You rarely see them."

"Dangerous," exclaimed Howard.

"Very," said the woman, raising her eyebrows for emphasis. "Never drive on that stuff. You can roll over easy. Trigger a slide. Next thing you know, you're upside down and buried alive."

Miriam swallowed nervously and glanced at Howard.

"Thanks," he said. "I'll keep that in mind."

"Where you headed from here?" she asked, then took another swig of liquor from her flask.

"California."

"I meant once you're off the summit," she said, screwing the cap on and slipping the flask into the pocket of her windbreaker.

"We were thinking of trying out some other roads. Got any suggestions?"

"Sure. Let's have a look," she said, taking the map from Howard.

She spread it across the Jeep's hood and ran her finger across some recommended routes. At the same time she gave pointers on mountain traveling and a bit of local history about the old mine sites. Then she rejoined her standoffish companion and the two drove off the summit.

They took one of the routes the woman had suggested, stopping often to enjoy the views. On the opposing face of the next mountain, they saw movement—a long crooked string. Howard brought out his binoculars and adjusted the focus wheel.

"Sheep," he said, then handed them to Miriam.

"Must be hundreds of 'em," she said, peering through the lenses. "I can see guys on horseback and dogs."

He took the binoculars from her and looked again. Two Hispanic-looking shepherds on horseback—each with a lamb hooked behind his saddle horn and draped over his lap—stood out from the huge flock. Border collies dodged and weaved constantly as they rounded up stragglers. They took turns watching them, then climbed into the Jeep and moved on.

At mid-afternoon they spotted a 4x4 pickup parked beside a rushing stream and decided to stop for a late lunch. Two men in rubber waders were digging in the creek bed with shovels and panning for gold. The older man looked to be in his seventies, thin and stooped at the shoulders. The joints of his fingers were swollen and his hands grotesquely misshapen with arthritis. His colleague was a younger man, fiftyish, heavy set and swarthy, with dark beard stubble. Both wore fleece bush shirts and camouflage cargo pants.

"Havin' any luck?" asked Miriam, taking a bite of her sandwich.

"Not yet," said the older man. "We jus' got here."

"Mind if we watch?"

"Nope."

"You been doin' this for a long time?" she asked, curiously peering over his shoulder.

"Since I was knee high."

"Looks like tryin' to find a needle in a haystack," said Miriam.

"It ain't if ya know where to look."

"What're the best spots?"

"Wherever th' water slows down. Th' inside bend of creeks, under boulders, in large crevices."

"Why there?"

"Gold's heavy, ma'am. Gets pushed along by th' water till it comes to rest. After we dig, we screen out th' coarse gravel first, then slosh th' finer grit in th' pan."

Miriam looked at one of the empty pans, "What're those ridges?"

"Them's riffles. Th' idea is to catch th' fine gold on 'em while you sweep away what ya don't want."

"Oh," she replied, and then wandered downstream with Howard.

For a while, they sat on a large boulder by the edge of the creek and watched the prospectors busy at work, their voices muffled by distance and the wind. Soon Miriam grew restless and wandered the creek bank on her own, gaze lowered, her attention focused. Howard watched her retrieve something from the frigid water. She turned it in her hand, then, excited, rushed back to show him.

"I think this is what they're lookin' for," said Miriam, handing Howard a nugget the size of a pea.

He examined it closely. "I'd say so, although I'm no expert on gold. It might be fool's gold for all I know."

"I'm sure they'll know if it's the real deal," she said, glancing toward the prospectors.

"You might want to think first whether or not you want to show it to them," said Howard.

"Why?"

"Because they may have staked a claim on this creek. If so, that nugget belongs to them."

"Never thought of that," she said, slipping it into her pocket. She paused for a moment then exclaimed, "I know what I'll do with it."

"What?"

"Have it made into a pendant. A souvenir."

"Claim jumper," teased Howard.

"Sshh," she said, holding a finger to her lips.

They said goodbye to the men, then continued their excursion through the high country, stopping to examine old mine buildings, but paying more attention to the sights than to the time. Shadows were lengthening now, and the air was taking on a deeper chill. They needed to get off the mountain and begin heading back to the campground. Howard did not relish driving the highway in the dark with its hideous drop-offs. He stopped to consult his map, trying to decide on the quickest way down.

"That looks like a short cut," he said, pointing across an open section of mountainside.

"But . . . isn't that scree? The stuff the woman told us not to drive on?"

"Yes, but it looks stable to me."

"Why don't you get out and walk on it first," said Miriam, nervously biting her lip.

"We'll be OK," Howard assured her. "It's only about a quarter mile across, and the slope doesn't look so bad."

"Chip?"

"Yes."

"You know that St. Christopher medal you wear?"

"What about it?"

"Hang it on the mirror."

"Ah," he said, dismissing the notion.

"Do it for me," she said, her voice trembling. "Please!"

"I don't get it," said Howard. "Back on our trail ride, you said religious stuff was 'fairy tale' stuff."

"Guess I'm just superstitious," she said, looking sheepish.

He lifted it over his head and draped it on the mirror, "There. Feel better now?"

"Barely," she said, fearfully eyeing the scree field, which seemed to cover half the mountainside. "This is freakin' me out—big time. Plus, I'm on the downhill side."

Howard approached the edge with caution. Tires crunched as he crawled at a heel-to-toe pace across the broken rock. He kept a steady foot on the gas pedal so as to keep the vehicle's forward motion as smooth as possible. The Jeep held its footing. Howard smiled; his strategy was working. He drove in the lowest gear and hugged the top edge of the debris where the slope was minimal. They were half-way across when trouble began.

The Jeep crabbed sideways, defying the control Howard was struggling desperately to maintain. He stopped to take stock of his predicament. Miriam looked at him, unaware at first of what was happening. But after sitting still for the better part of a minute and with his foot firmly pressed on the brake pedal, Howard knew the mountain was winning; he felt the

Jeep shudder and shift on the loose rock. There was no hiding it from her now. She heard the grinding and felt the sideways slipping of the vehicle. She turned again toward Howard, this time, her eyes wide with terror. Instinctively, she lifted one hand off the dusty dashboard, and clutched at her stomach. On the verge of panic now, her heart raced and her mouth went dry. Howard let out the clutch slowly. They were moving again, but differently now. For every foot of forward motion, they crabbed several inches sideways. He stopped again. The Jeep held. They had barely caught their breath when there was a loud bang.

"Fuck!" screamed Miriam.

"I've blown a tire."

There was a hissing sound, and the Jeep quickly listed like a sinking ship. Miriam's side of the vehicle tilted more sharply toward the downhill side of the mountain.

"W-what're we gonna do now?" she said, her voice trembling with fear.

"I need you to climb into the backseat. Get directly behind me."

"Are you friggin' crazy? Any movement and this thing's gonna flip."

"No it won't," replied Howard.

"Why do you want me to do this?"

"I want our combined weight on the uphill side."

"What're you gonna do then?"

"Turn us so we're not sideways to the mountain. That way, there's less chance of us rolling over."

"Then what?"

"Then I'm going to climb up toward the road. See if I can get us to the top of the scree field."

Reluctantly, Miriam edged out of her seat beside Howard. She gingerly climbed into the back. As her weight shifted, there was movement and the grinding sound of rock. Then it stopped. Miriam was crosswise in the rear with her feet braced on the downhill side of the cab.

"That's not good enough," said Howard. "I need you to draw up your legs so all your weight is behind me."

She clung tightly to Howard's seatback and drew herself into the fetal position.

"Hang on tight," he said and let out the clutch.

The moment they began to move, rock shifted underneath the vehicle. He turned the steering wheel slightly to avoid making too sharp a turn and with care managed to move in a wide arc until the vehicle was pointing up the mountain. But now their position on the slope was such that Howard's view through the windshield was nothing but vehicle hood and sky. His only reference points were those he could see through the side windows—and they were not comforting. The Jeep was adrift on a sea of razor-edged rock fragments like chipped flint. When he released the clutch and attempted to climb the slope, all hell broke loose: a deafening roar of clattering rock resonated under the floor pan of the Jeep, followed by a chilling view through the rear-view mirror. Thousands of rock fragments were hurtling down the mountainside, bouncing erratically like ricocheting bullets. Like a collapsing pile of sand, the mountain was disintegrating behind them. Great sections of hillside were on the move: sliding, roaring, and tumbling spastically into the valley far below.

Quickly, Howard let out the clutch and tried to climb higher on the slope and away from the rock slide. There was another loud bang and the hiss of escaping air. A second tire had blown.

"Shit!" she screamed, clutching at her belly. "W-we're gonna die!"

With his foot jammed hard against the brake pedal, and one hand on the steering wheel, Howard reached out and held her arm, "It's OK, Mimi. We're not going to die. I need you to be calm."

"Calm," she shouted. "How the frig can I stay c-calm? We're never gonna get out o' this alive."

"Yes we are," said Howard in a composed tone.

"How?"

"I've got another job for you," he said quietly.

"What kind o' job?"

"You're going to have to get outside the Jeep."

"Are you nuts?"

"Listen to me," said Howard, his voice controlled. "Look on the back floor. There's a pair of work gloves, a long piece of angle iron with a ring on it, and a steel mallet."

"Yeah, I see 'em."

"Work with me on this."

"All right," she replied, her lower lip trembling.

"I want you to anchor us to the hill."

"How?"

"First, put on the work gloves."

"OK," she said, slipping her hands inside the cool leather. "W-what next?"

"Go to the front of the Jeep, and I'll tell you what to do."

Carefully, she opened her door and stepped onto the slope of loose rock. Her feet slipped as she made her way to the front bumper. Howard leaned out his window and issued instructions. She stuck the handle of the mallet into the belt of her jeans, released the winch drum, and slowly dragged the steel cable up the slope. With each step, she dislodged scree. It shifted, then tumbled downhill and clanged against the grill and hood of the Jeep. When she had pulled the cable out to its limit, she stopped high on the hillside, and then turned to face the vehicle below her.

"Now what?" she shouted.

"Come toward me a couple of feet. You don't want to get the bar in and find the hook won't reach."

She eased herself down the hill until Howard motioned for her to stop.

He leaned out the window and yelled, "Clear away loose rock, then pound the bar as deep into the mountain as you can."

Her hands shook as she followed his instructions, but she found it difficult to wield enough force to bury the bar. He called encouragement to her over the metallic ping of steel on steel. Finally, she had the bar in to the hilt. She snapped the cable's hook to the metal ring. He engaged the winch and the steel cable went taught. Slowly, the Jeep inched upward as the drum pulled in the cable.

By the time they had reached the road, the sun was below the peaks and the first stars were appearing. The air temperature had plunged sharply. Both donned extra layers of clothing. Miriam buried her face in her hands and broke down.

"It's OK," said Howard, wrapping his arms around her. "You did a great job."

"I've n-never been so friggin' scared," she sobbed. "I thought all of us w-were gonna die."

"All of us?"

"Yeah, *all* of us!" she repeated.

Howard stared at her.

"I'm k-keepin' the baby, Chip. I've made up my mind on it."

# CHAPTER 29

## *Stranded*

THEY WERE SAFELY OFF the scree, but now, their predicament was worse than it had been at the summit of Monarch Pass. Instead of an insulated RV with plenty of clothes and bedding, they had to ward off hypothermia in an un-insulated Jeep with only the clothes on their backs and a single wool blanket each, something Howard had put on board at the advice of Harry Kimball. Outside, it had begun to snow.

He was angry at himself. Twice he had got them into trouble in the mountains: first by ignoring a mechanic's advice on vehicle servicing, and then by ignoring a local woman's advice on the dangers of driving on scree, something that could have killed them both. Why had he been so careless? Was he so intent on showing Miriam a good time on this vacation that he had thrown caution to the wind?

As Howard assessed their situation, he realized he had made yet another mistake; he had broken the cardinal rule of the off-road traveler and failed to tell anyone where they were going and when they planned to return. He estimated their location on the mountain, and then placed a call to the campground's office on his cell phone. The line dissolved into static. He disconnected and tried again. This time, the 'low battery' warning light appeared. They were now incommunicado.

"Is the line busy?" asked Miriam

"No," he replied, breaking the grim news to her.

"What now?" she asked, already shivering in the frigid mountain air.

"First, I want you inside," he said, helping her into the back seat of the Jeep. He slid onto the driver's seat and started the engine, then turned the cab's heater control to maximum. "I'm going to do this on and off throughout the night."

"Won't we run out o' gas?"

"Not if I limit it to ten minutes an hour."

"But, aren't we likely to get carbon monoxide in here?"

"Not unless snow blocks the exhaust pipe," he said. "If it looks like it will, I'll get out and clear it."

"You gonna be in the front seat all night?" asked Miriam.

"No. We'll have to huddle under the blankets. Use each other's body heat. How are your feet right now?"

"A little cool."

"What about your hands?" he asked.

"They're gettin' cold."

"Then put these on," he said, pulling an extra pair of work socks from his backpack.

He dug deeper into his pack and retrieved a container of waterproof matches and some tea light candles. He lit one and placed it on the front floor pan of the Jeep, then climbed into the back seat with Miriam and wrapped them both in the blankets.

Given the anxiety of their situation, the cramped quarters, and the thin, high-altitude air, they slept fitfully, barely managing to ward off the cold. The worst times were toward the end of each period of running the Jeep's heater; Miriam's feet were coldest then; she worried about getting frostbite and losing her toes. High on the mountain and beyond the nearest town, there was no urban light in the sky, no antidote to the sepulchral blackness that enveloped them and magnified their seclusion. Other than their breathing, the only sound was the intermittent moan of the wind around the door and window openings.

At three o'clock in the morning, Howard wiped the condensation from the Jeep's windows and peered outside; except for the visible traces of white on the ground, it was the kind of disorienting blackness that made hair prickle on the neck.

Once before with Suzanne, he had been in this kind of darkness. Before sunset, they had found a rushing creek in a deep ravine off the side of an old logging road. It was open-range country where cattle roamed at will among the thickly forested slopes and on the roads. After climbing down the steep incline and harvesting squaw wood from the pines, they had built a crackling fire on the bank beside the tumbling water. When darkness fell, Suzanne became chilled and needed a blanket. He left her beside the creek, and then scaled the ravine on his way back to the Jeep. He had picked his way cautiously up through the trees, groping blindly and sweeping a hand ahead of him to protect his eyes from tree branches he could not see. He had almost reached the road, when he touched something that sent a chill of fear through him. Warm slime covered his fingers and he could hear the chuffing sound of heavy breathing. Instinctively he drew back his hand. When he groped forward again, he felt the bony forehead of a large steer.

He laid his cheek against Miriam's, then pulled the blanket around them and dozed off. An hour later the cold woke him. He reached into the front and turned the ignition key. The engine leapt to life and the heater fan raced, at first pumping cold air, then gradually warming the cab. Ten minutes later, he turned off the engine, but could not get comfortable; his fifty-year-old bladder was full.

He stepped into the frigid mountain air. The ground was covered with several inches of freshly fallen snow. Absently, he aimed the stream and wrote his initials, something that used to annoy Suzanne who always envied the ease with which men could pee in the outdoors. He recalled her playful revenge, giggling and chasing him while he ran from her, penis in hand, trying not to wet his trousers. Odd that he should think of her now, stranded here on a Colorado mountain. He zipped up and was about to re-enter the Jeep when something registered in his peripheral vision.

He stared down the mountainside for several minutes, but saw nothing. He cupped both hands to his ears and listened intently. All he heard was the amplified sound of the wind. He was about to turn back toward the Jeep when he saw it again—a speck of light, then two specks. They were moving. He recognized them now—vehicle headlights. Someone was slowly crawling up the winding road. Could they be hunters he wondered? No, he thought, hunting season did not start until fall, and this was early summer. Who could possibly be coming up here at this hour?

He jerked open the door, turned on the engine and switched the headlights to high beam. Then he pressed the panic button on his key fob and the horn went into a rhythmic, loud beep.

Miriam stirred, "What the fu—"

"Someone's coming."

"You're kiddin'," she shouted, jolted fully awake by the news.

"Stay inside and keep warm," he said over the sound of the heater fan.

Howard grabbed a flashlight from under his seat. He aimed it at the vehicle and waved the beam in circles. Far below, the driver flashed his headlights in acknowledgment.

"They've seen us," he shouted.

Ten minutes later, twin beams of light speared the darkness as the vehicle topped a rise in the road. It drew close and stopped. There were two people inside, a man and a woman in their forties. At the rear of their Jeep, two jerry cans and a plastic cooler were lashed to a metal platform. The driver stepped out first and came over to talk to Howard. His passenger climbed inside to be with Miriam.

"Are we glad to see *you*," said Howard, exhaling warm air on his chilled fingers.

"Mechanical troubles?" asked the man.

"No. I've blown two tires. If it'd only been one, we could've changed it and driven down."

"You were wise to stay put," said the man, looking at the flattened tires. "How long have you been up here?"

"All night."

"Damned cold place to be stranded."

"We never expected to see anyone up here," said Howard. "Especially this early."

"My wife and I are photographers. Came up to take sunrise photos. We do calendars, motivational posters, that kind of thing."

"Oh," said Howard, and then added, "Would you happen to have a cell phone? The batteries in mine are dead."

"I do. Why?"

"Could you call someone? Get them to bring us up some tires?"

The man went to reply but was interrupted by his wife who called from the Jeep.

"Chad, honey, this gal—Mimi—she's pregnant!"

The man noticed Miriam crying inside the Jeep, then turned to Howard, "No need to make that cell call. We'll help you off the mountain."

"But what about your photography?"

"There'll be other chances. We live locally."

While the woman took Miriam into their Jeep and fed her hot coffee and buns, the two men set about changing the flat tires, using the spares from both vehicles. It was well after dawn by the time they were ready to start down the mountain. Miriam found the ride down more stressful than the ride up. Only when they had backtracked along the wet highway and reached town, did she relax.

Once off the mountain, Howard got both tires, damaged beyond repair, replaced at a local garage. That evening, he and Miriam took the couple out for supper at a restaurant in Ouray. From their table at the window, they enjoyed views of the mountains and listened to the couple talk about life in the San Juans and about the mining history of the area. It was late when they returned to the RV.

"Sorry I was such a wuss up there on the mountain," said Miriam, kicking off her shoes and flopping onto the lounge sofa.

"It's me who should apologize," said Howard. "I shouldn't have taken us across the scree."

"It's a ride I'm never gonna forget."

"What made you change your mind?" he said.

"About what?"

"Keeping the baby."

"Fear o' dyin' I suppose. Knowin' that if I died, the kid would too . . . die without ever havin' had a crack at life yet. That's where the whole abortion thing hit me. Where I saw that it was wrong o' me to even consider it in the first place. And other stuff went through my mind too."

"What stuff?"

"The people we've met on this trip. Realizin' they'd been through worse troubles than me."

"Like Frank Watson?"

"Yeah. And that Mexican woman. Seein' her terror at the thought of losin' her only kid. It made me realize just how precious life is."

"How about Alice?"

"Yeah. Her for sure," said Miriam, her face lighting up at the mention of the woman's name. "She had a lot to do with my decision. But so did someone else."

"Who was that?" asked Howard.

"You."

"Really?" he said, looking surprised. "I didn't think I was having any effect on you."

"Well, you did. More than you know."

"How?"

"Until I met you, it's like I'd lived my whole life inside a box that I couldn't see out of. You lifted the lid off. Showed me I'm part o' somethin' bigger. You made me feel good about myself—that I was a decent enough person to *be* a mom. Am I makin' any sense here, Chip? I mean, I'm not as good with words as you are."

"You're doing fine, Mimi, just fine."

For the first time in a long time, Howard felt relieved. Up on the mountain, he had wondered whether her comment had been blurted out in the fear of the moment. Now, he seemed more convinced of her commitment to keep the baby. But what would the future hold for her? Did she fully realize the long struggle she was about to embark on? Years of hardship, trying to hold down a low-paying job while raising a child entirely on her own? To outward appearances, she was a grown woman to be sure. But beneath the surface, she was still a young girl in many ways. Would she be up to the challenges ahead?

And then, an idea slowly formed in Howard's mind. Perhaps, once he was settled in San Diego . . .

# CHAPTER 30

## *Desert Odyssey*

THEY STAYED THREE MORE days in the San Juans, exploring abandoned mine buildings and picnicking in the shimmering aspen forests along the Last Dollar Road on their way across Dallas Divide to the town of Telluride. South of Red Mountain Pass, they visited the historic town of Silverton, a place that except for automobiles and other modern trappings looked pretty much as it would have during Frontier days.

Beyond the east end of town, they followed a long, dusty road that paralleled the rushing waters of the Animas River to the ghost town of Animas Forks, a collection of weathered, skeletal mine buildings nestled in a spruce-studded valley near the lower edge of tree line. Towering above them were mountain slopes of rocky outcroppings and sparse grasses that lifted their eyes to alpine summits, resplendent in their glistening, white robes of snow.

On their return drive to Silverton, a sea of bleating sheep blocked the road. Howard turned off the engine. Shepherds on horseback and border collies worked constantly to keep stray animals within the flock. Hundreds of creatures spooked by their vehicle refused to budge, but when pressed by the shepherds and dogs, moved obediently and surrounded the Jeep in an ocean of fleece. As they passed, Miriam reached out and touched their shaggy backs, oily with lanolin.

THE DRIVE out of the mountains in the motor home was more stressful for Miriam than it had been traveling in the smaller Jeep. The massive vehicle seemed to fill every inch of the southbound lane of the Million Dollar Highway and made the drop-offs and curving switchbacks even more terrifying. At the narrower places and sharp bends she closed her eyes, opening them only occasionally for the views. They drove the triple passes: Red Mountain, Molas, and Coal Bank. Then at Durango, they swung west into transitional high-desert country, a vast plateau that connected the mountains to the immense expanse of red-rock desert yet to come.

Howard had not visited the American Southwest since before Suzanne died, and was eager to share his love of the desert with Miriam. He stopped just outside the town of Cortez, Colorado, at Mesa Verde National Park.

"I never dreamed I'd get to see this place," she said, barely able to contain her excitement. "I remember seein' pictures of it when I was a kid."

After getting a book from the visitor's center, they bought tickets and joined a ranger-guided tour of the cliff dwellings, a tiny enclave of masonry buildings tucked protectively under a rock overhang below the mesa top. Miriam stayed close to the ranger, intently following his presentation on the Anasazi Indians, their daily life, and their mysterious disappearance in the thirteenth century. A New York couple's precocious, pre-teen son befriended Miriam as they walked through two of the ruins: Long House and Cliff Palace. At Balcony House, the boy stuck his head through an opening in the masonry and grinned impishly.

"Can I take your order, ma'am?"

"Yes," replied Miriam, without missing a beat. "I'll have a double cheeseburger to go, with hot peppers and a large order o' fries."

"Would you like bacon on your cheeseburger?"

"Please."

"Anything to drink with that?"

"A strawberry milkshake," she giggled.

"Coming right up," he said. "That's regularly a five dollar combo, ma'am, but for you, four bucks. I'm in a generous mood today!"

The boy went off to explore on his own, leaving Miriam alone with his parents.

"Your son's not exactly a shrinkin' violet," she said, laughing.

"Tell me about it," said his attractive mother, rolling her eyes. "That boy of mine's got the gift of the gab. He sees humor in everything. I swear he's going to be doing standup comedy someday."

After the tour, they stopped at scenic overlooks, and then took a long hike to enjoy views of the surrounding mesa country. By suppertime, they had packed a lot of activity into their day—too much activity. Miriam was exhausted, her face pale and drawn.

"You don't look well," said Howard.

"I don't feel so good," she replied, cradling her head in her hands.

"In what way?"

"Headachy . . . weak."

"When did this start?" asked Howard.

"Back in the mountains."

"Why didn't you tell me?"

"Because I know how much you want to show me places."

"Not so much that I want to make you sick."

"I'll be fine. I just need to sit down. I'm a bit dizzy."

Miriam was quiet for the rest of the evening and went to bed early. Although she was not spotting as she had done before, Howard thought she seemed unusually lethargic and checked on her several times during the night.

THE FOLLOWING day Miriam was well enough to travel. They crossed into the Ute Mountain Reservation and headed for the four corners area, the common point at which four states meet: Colorado, New Mexico, Utah, and Arizona. There was no question they were in the desert now. The heat was skin-searing, like standing before the open door of a blast furnace. The dry air wicked moisture from their mouths and noses, and they blinked more often to lubricate their eyes. On the scalding asphalt, watery mirages shimmered; as Howard drove toward them they disappeared, only to be replaced by others that formed farther ahead. Surrounding them was a scorched, treeless plain of bleak, stony ground with crumbled mesas, a vista that except for sprinklings of sagebrush and other stunted vegetation could have been a NASA image captured by an unmanned rover on some distant planet. Howard paid the entrance fee at the Navajo-run attraction, and parked the motor home.

There were a dozen, dusty cars in the parking lot near the elaborate marker, a massive square patio of leveled stone that bore the inscription: "Four states here meet in freedom under God." The state lines were deeply etched from corner to corner and in the center, an embedded metal medallion marked the point of intersection. Tourists stood around talking and photographing each other, awkwardly bent over the marker with a foot and hand planted in each of the four states.

When it was Miriam's turn to have her photograph taken, she stepped to the center, planted her two feet, and then leaned forward to position her hands. Without warning, she suddenly fainted, face down. At first, Howard thought she was kibitzing for the group, but when she did not move, he rushed forward. Instantly he was joined by another tourist, a black man in his fifties. Concerned tourists gathered in a circle and looked on.

"I'm a doctor," he said, kneeling to check Miriam's pulse.

"She hasn't been feeling well for a few days," said Howard.

"Does she have any medical conditions?"

"She's pregnant."

"How far along?"

"Second month. Do you think she's got heat stroke?"

"Possibly," offered the doctor. "Has she been drinking water?"

"Some, but I'm not sure how much."

The doctor glanced toward a patch of shade, "Let's move her over there." Then he turned to his wife. "Honey, can you get my medical bag from the car?"

Howard picked Miriam up in his arms and carried her out of the sun. While the doctor checked her blood pressure and heart, she opened her eyes.

"Mimi, this gentleman's a doctor."

"Whuh?" she said, trying to focus.

"Your friend says you haven't been feeling well."

"I haven't," she replied. Dry-mouthed, she turned to Howard, "Can you . . . get me a drink o' water?"

When he returned minutes later, the doctor had finished examining her.

"The young lady tells me you're driving to California."

"That's right."

"She's dehydrated," said the doctor.

"But we've been drinking water," said Howard defensively.

"Not enough evidently," said the doctor, turning to Miriam who had now emptied her water bottle. "Being in your first trimester, it's especially important you drink large quantities of water to maintain enough amniotic fluid."

"How much water?" she asked.

"Eight glasses a day. More if you can do it. At least till you've crossed the desert."

"Do you think I'm seriously dehydrated?"

"No," he said and smiled reassuringly. "But if I were you, I'd take it easy with outdoor exertion, especially in peak sun." He put the stethoscope and blood pressure monitor in his medical bag and closed it. "You lose body fluids quickly out here in the desert. Remember, by the time you feel thirsty, you've already begun to dehydrate."

Howard was concerned at Miriam's condition. "How are you feeling right now?" he asked.

"Weak," she replied, then added, "and tired."

"Then I think we ought to call it quits for the day," he said. "No more traveling for you. I need you rested and re-hydrated before we move on."

"That would be wise," said the doctor. "She'll feel a lot better once her fluid levels are back to normal."

"But we *have* to move on, Chip," she insisted.

"Why's that?"

"Because there's no campin' around here."

"How do you know that?" he asked.

"I saw a signboard that said so," she replied. "They don't allow it."

"Then somehow, we've got to find a way of staying in the area, if only for one night," said Howard.

"Look after the young lady, sir," said the doctor, handing his medical bag back to his wife. "I'll go and ask someone."

"While we're waitin', Chip, can you get me some more water?"

When Howard returned with water, the doctor had arrived with a Navajo man about sixty-years-old. He was dressed in a straw Stetson, western shirt, frayed jeans, and heavily scuffed cowboy boots.

"I've explained your situation to this man," said the doctor. "He lives just a few miles from here, near a place called Teec Nos Pos. He says you can park your RV there overnight while the young lady is recovering."

"That's very good of you," Howard said to the man who adamantly refused to take money for his kindness.

The man climbed into a dented, turquoise-colored pickup, and led Howard for the short drive to his home, situated on a dirt road near the small hamlet whose name had been spelled out in large letters on a nearby rocky peak.

"God only knows how these folks make enough money to survive," said Howard, struck by the abject poverty as they pulled onto the man's plot of land and saw his living quarters.

His meager trailer home had a shabby, wooden porch out front made from re-cycled shipping pallets. Rusted machinery parts peppered the rocky ground. Nearby, a wire-fenced corral equipped with a livestock feeder and water trough, held two horses. The surrounding vista was stark—low mountains with jagged outcroppings of rock, and dotted with thousands of stunted bushes of varying sizes. Sparsely treed, it was arid in the extreme, with tufts of course grass, sagebrush, and clusters of prickly pear cactus all competing for sustenance from the stony soil.

At the sound of the motor home's approach, the man's wife came outside, along with two young boys, probably the man's grandchildren. The woman was unsmiling and confused by the arrival of strangers, until her husband explained the situation to her.

"I have to go back now," said the man after he had helped Howard situate the RV on a patch of level ground some distance from his dwelling. "If you need water, there's a tap beside the house."

They watched the man's vehicle as it headed back down the dirt road toward the Four Corners, raising a rooster tail of choking dust that drifted across open desert in the hot wind.

Without an electrical hookup, they could not run the RV's air conditioner in the prickly heat. Howard rolled the awning out to shield them from a blistering sun. They spent the afternoon in the shade, in remarkable comfort considering the temperature.

Hours later, the man returned home. Shortly afterward, they saw him leave his porch and walk between the sagebrush toward the motor home. Cradled in his hands was a plastic bowl.

"My wife sent this for you," he said, handing the steaming bowl of homemade bean soup to Miriam. "It will help you regain your strength."

"Tell her thank you," she said.

The man stayed for a short while, trading small talk and asking them about their journey to California. Miriam was full of questions for the man, wanting to know local history, including the English translation for Teec Nos Pos which he was happy to provide—Cottonwoods in a Circle.

"What's that medallion on your belt buckle?" she asked.

"It was awarded to my father for his military service. He served in the Pacific in World War II. He gave it to me before he died."

291

"Really!" she exclaimed. "He must have been one of the code talkers then."

"Yes," replied the old man, taken by surprise. "How do you know of this?"

"I like history," she replied.

"Then you must know also of the German's Enigma Code?"

"Uh-huh," she replied, nodding affirmatively.

"Theirs was the code that was broken, not ours," he said, proudly. "The Japanese never figured it out. Our people were there at all the great battles: Iwo Jima, Kwajalein, Bougainville, Guadalcanal, and the bloodiest of them all, Okinawa."

"Wow," said Miriam.

"But my father was not just a code talker. He was one of the 'twenty nine."

"The twenty-nine?" she said, frowning.

"He was recruited in 1942 with twenty-eight others. They were the ones who developed the first codes."

Spurred on by her keen interest and questions, the man told Miriam as much as he had learned from his father.

"Do you know any of the codes?" she asked, when he had finished.

"Yes. My father taught me many of them, after they were de-classified in '68."

"Would you tell me one?"

The man thought for a moment. "Chay-da-gahi. In our language, this means *turtle*. In the war it meant *tank*."

When the man's wife called to him from the porch, he said his goodbyes, and then re-traced his steps back through the sagebrush.

After supper, Miriam and Howard sat outside. At dusk they watched the desert landscape come alive, as nocturnal animals emerged from their burrows.

"It's so quiet here," said Miriam. "So peaceful. No wonder you and Suzanne loved the desert. I can see why now."

"Yes," he replied, then changed the subject. "How are you feeling?"

"Much better. Been drinkin' a lot o' water."

"I couldn't help but notice," said Howard, winking. "Think you'll be well enough to travel in the morning?"

"Oh, yeah, especially if I get a good night's sleep . . . and I'm sure to get one out here."

Howard did not speak for a time as he watched rabbits hopping among the sagebrush and listened to a pack of coyotes yipping somewhere in the distance; they stopped as abruptly as they had begun.

"Somethin' on your mind, Chip?" she asked.

"Yes."

"What is it?"

"I don't know how I'm going to repay this man for letting us stay here. I'd like to leave some money for him, but somehow, I think he'd be insulted if I did. How do you think I should handle this?"

"Excuse me?" she said, turning to face him. "You are asking for *my opinion*?"

"Well . . . yes," he said. "Is that a problem?"

"Guess I'm just not used to gettin' asked. Most people figure I'm not bright enough to have one."

"Mimi, you ought to know me better by now. If I didn't think your opinion counted for something, I wouldn't have asked you for it."

"You're right. I'm sorry."

"Well, what *do* you think?" he asked again.

She paused for a moment. "Get me a pencil and some paper."

She wrote out a short note, and then folded it in thirds. "Be back in a minute," she said, getting up from her chair.

"Where are you going to put it?" asked Howard.

"Under the windshield wiper of his truck," she replied.

"Do you mind if I read it?"

"Course not," she said and handed it to him.

> Thank you for giving me the most wonderful lesson from the history of your people. I will tell everyone I know about the Code Talkers now. I don't know if you ever speak to your father in your prayers, but if you do, thank him for my freedom!
>
> Mimi Kovacs

"Perfect," said Howard, handing the note back to her. "I couldn't have said it better myself."

In the dim light, he watched as she slowly made her way across the property toward the man's pickup truck and placed the note. It was, he thought, a reflection of the Miriam he had come to know: a guileless soul with a well-hidden sensitivity beneath her offhanded exterior manner. He found her comment about prayer refreshing, especially coming from a non-believer. He had seen a gradual change in her since Toledo, a mellowing of the spirit, a developing maturity, and he liked what he saw.

"You know," said Miriam, popping a wad of gum in her mouth. "It's a small world when you think about it. I mean, here we are in the middle o' hairy ass nowhere, and who do we meet? A guy whose father helped invent the Navajo codes. How friggin' cool is that!"

"Small world for sure," said Howard. "Like that encounter we had with one of my ex-students."

"Yeah, the arrogant turd," she said with contempt. "Daryl Douchebag or whatever his name was."

Howard laughed, amused by her earthiness, something that he especially loved about her.

THEY LEFT Teec Nos Pos before dawn the following morning and headed southwest into an area of magnificent desert beauty. As the sun came up behind them, it cast long shadows across the landscape with its red rock monoliths and stone-filled arroyos. Under a lapis lazuli sky, the colors of the sedimentary rock formed an earthy palette: terra cotta, burnt sienna, orange, chocolate and caramel, with paler hues of ochre, buff, and delicate yellow-beige.

"Look," said Miriam, pointing to a glittering carpet that paralleled the road. "There must be crystals in the ground. "See how beautifully they sparkle in the sun."

Miles later, Howard noticed a decrepit car coming up fast in his rear view mirror. The vehicle pulled out and went to pass, but slowed so that it remained beside the RV in the oncoming lane. Four scruffily dressed men in their twenties were singing to heavy-metal music that blared from the open windows. The man in the front passenger seat made eye contact with Howard.

"Hey, honky," he shouted menacingly. "No one else out here but you and us."

Howard glanced briefly at the man, and then re-focused on the road ahead. In the distance, an eighteen-wheeler was fast approaching.

"We gonna kill you first, honky, then fuck your woman," said the man, who joined in a communal whoop with his rowdy friends."

The oncoming truck was getting closer by the second, but the car remained beside Howard, the driver resolute in his game of chicken with the approaching behemoth.

"White pussy, white pussy, aaeeee" whooped the four men.

The truck was only a hundred yards away now. The car accelerated, and then swerved sharply in front of Howard at the last moment. The truck's air horn blasted as it hurtled past. Moments later an arm suddenly protruded from the passenger window. A wine bottle arced toward the roadside ditch and exploded in a burst of glass shards.

"So much for your crystals," said Howard, shaking his head in disgust as the car sped ahead of them. "Nothing but broken wine and liquor bottles."

"Must be thousands of 'em," said Miriam. "Can't imagine the amount o' drinkin' that must go on out here."

As they traveled west, the views varied from featureless plains to worn-down mesas and vast expanses of knee-high sage. They found a place to pull over for lunch. The moment they stepped into the blazing heat, a cone of silence enveloped them. There were no other cars on the road. The sudden arrival of a hummingbird startled them. Its iridescent chest shimmered in the sun and its wings whirred furiously as it probed the RV's red taillights with its needle beak. When it found no sustenance, it raced off across the sagebrush.

Miriam pointed out a lizard hiding under the shade of a bush. Wordlessly, they spent a few minutes watching it before it scuttled away.

When they noticed a colony of ants, they knelt in the red soil to watch them. Howard pulled a pea-sized morsel of crust from his sandwich and placed it on the ground in the shade. An ant approached to investigate. Within moments, others arrived. They walked around it, probing and pushing. When enough had gathered, they organized into a work party and carried it away.

"Now there's a lesson in cooperation," said Howard.

"Yeah," said Miriam smiling. "The United Ant Workers of America—Local 219."

They had been back on the road only ten minutes when they came to an abrupt stop. Blocking the road were free-range cattle, stupor-like in the blazing heat, swishing flies with their tails and gazing vacantly at the motor home. Then one of them dumped a cow pie; a squadron of flies suddenly appeared from nowhere and dived on their hot meal. Howard pulled forward, but the animals were determined to stake their claim on the patch of blistering pavement.

"Why don't they keep 'em fenced in?" asked Miriam.

"Ranchers don't have to," said Howard, honking the horn.

"How come?"

"The laws allow it."

Finally, a couple of steers shuffled off; Howard cautiously eased through the gap in the small herd. The stench of fecal-matted hides hung in the dry air.

Hours later they left the baked, desert floor and began the climb toward the south rim of the Grand Canyon. The vegetation had changed now; smaller pinions and junipers appeared first, and then slowly gave way to taller pines.

FOR TWO days they relaxed in the cooler temperatures. Miriam had fully recovered her strength by now. Still, they avoided the heat of mid-day and ventured to the edge of the canyon only in late evening and early morning. To avoid the hordes of tourists, they took folding chairs to quieter spots along the canyon rim where they could quietly commune with nature.

On their final morning before dawn, they bundled in warm sweaters and waited for sunrise, only mere feet away from the edge of the abyss. Cool air moved up the canyon walls like exhaled breath, carrying with it the territorial cries of birds and the raucous rasping of ravens. Slowly the sky glow lightened the canyon. Rocky features appeared one by one like specters emerging from a fog. Random patches of sunlight appeared unexpectedly throughout the canyon: here on a spire of rock, there on a patch of wall a half-mile away. The dance of light on rock continued until much of the canyon was lit.

Miriam flung herself into the moment with abandon, swaying from side to side, arms held over her head, like a born-again convert at a Pentecostal revival.

"Tell me I'm not dreamin', Chip."

"You're not dreaming, Mimi," he said, laughing.

"Isn't it wonderful," she squealed. "It's bigger than life. Almost too much for your head to take in. So many layers o' rock. That's history, Chip. The history o' the world written in rock. Millions and millions o' years. Fossils and bones and—"

She was euphoric, emotionally swept up in the grandeur of it all. With her arms outstretched and hair tossed by the wind, she ran with child-like abandon, back and forth along the rim of the canyon, imitating the ravens. "And look at those birds down there. Imagine bein' able to spread your wings and fly over somethin' as gorgeous as this. To soar and dive and spin your way down to that river just 'cause you can."

Howard grinned, "Glad we came here?"

"Oh yeah. Oh for *sure*. And you know what, Chip?"

"What, Mimi?"

"Someday I'm gonna bring my kid back here, right to this very spot. I'm gonna buy us a Greyhound bus ticket each, and we're gonna—"

Howard grabbed her arm and pulled her back, "You won't be coming back at all if you fall over the edge."

"Hey, you know what's so funny about this?"

"No."

"Remember that friend o' mine I told you about?"

"What friend?"

"Sherri. The waitress at Hooters who introduced me to Aaron."

"Yes, I remember. What about her?"

"You know what she said about this place?"

Howard shrugged.

"'Who'd want to see the Grand Canyon? It's just a big hole in the ground.' I mean, how friggin' dumb is that? Just goes to show you, she'd never been here. Never seen what I'm lookin' at right now."

They got into the Jeep and drove back to the RV. After breakfast, they disconnected the shore lines, packed up, then pulled away from the south rim. Miriam strained for her last look at the canyon, then, when trees finally cut off her view, she picked up Howard's road atlas and flipped the pages.

"Where're we goin' now?" she asked.

"Where do you want to go?"

"I know this might sound weird and all, 'specially after seein' a place as gorgeous as this, but—"

"But what?"

"I was thinkin', wouldn't it be cool to see Las Vegas?"

"Vegas?" said Howard, looking surprised.

"Not for the gamblin' o' course. Just to check it out . . . you know . . . to see the lights and all."

"Hey," said Howard, "why not."

AFTER A brief stop at Hoover Dam to take photographs, they drove into the tacky glitz and got a full hookup site in a campground on the strip.

They grabbed a quick supper, and then as dusk settled over the desert community, they joined the procession to the enclosed pedestrian mall to see a computer-animated sound and light show. Banks of speakers pounded out a heart-stopping beat. Two million lights ran phantasmagoric patterns up and down the quarter-mile-long arched ceiling. They stayed until the show was over, and then decided to visit a casino on the way back to the RV.

The moment they entered the gaming floor, they were immersed in an ocean of synthesized, electronic sounds from the gambling machines: beeps, whistles, bells, harpsichord arpeggios, and the undulating musical scales of xylophones. Somebody had just won at a one-armed bandit: sirens sounded and an avalanche of coins tumbled noisily into the machine's metal collection tray.

They strolled the carpeted floors in the huge, windowless room, a timeless hinterland without clocks or seasons, its air, filtered and re-cycled, purged of cigarette smoke and elder flatus, a fantasy palace softly illuminated by indirect lighting and the mesmeric glow of slot machines. On the ceiling, strategically placed cameras and one-way glass provided security people with an eye on the gaming floor.

Gamblers of every description filled the casino: old and young, fat and thin, beautiful and ugly, affluent and marginalized, haggard after too many years of bourbon and cigarettes. Some stood, others sat, popping in coins, pulling handles, and gazing catatonically at the rolling wheels, hoping for a three-of-a-kind match. A morbidly obese man—each cheek of his elephantine buttocks overhanging a padded stool—played the machine in front of him as well as those to his left and right. Beside him were a bride and groom, recently wedded at a nearby chapel, he, still in his rented tuxedo, sans tie, she with her train scrunched under one arm. In contrast to the youthful newlyweds, an emaciated and darkly tanned elderly couple fed the last of their coins into a poker machine. With his cloak of papery, wrinkled skin, the man appeared more mummified than human. His wife, equally skeletal with sunken cheeks and sun-bleached hair looked on with an expression of despondency; she worked her toothless gums obsessively, like a cow chewing its cud.

Back on the busy sidewalk, they were once again bathed in the neon glow of the strip.

"You don't need to gamble a cent here," said Miriam. "People watchin's entertainment enough."

"I know what you mean," replied Howard, detouring around a drunken man. "It's like another planet."

When they reached the RV, Howard turned on the TV and slumped into one of the captain's chairs. It was something that helped him get ready for sleep most nights. Usually, he handed the remote to Miriam and she picked a program for them to watch. But tonight he was tired. Within minutes he had dozed off.

She turned to look at him: at the way his cheeks puffed as he exhaled, at the little involuntary movements his mouth made during sleep, and at the assorted food stains on the front of his shirt. She smiled at these quirky things, so familiar to her after spending over a month on the road with him—a time period that had seemed so much longer and brought her closer to him than she could have imagined. Under his rumpled exterior, he was, she thought, a lovely man. The sort of man she could bare her soul to with the surety that he would treat her deepest feelings as a sacred trust. Had he always been like this, she wondered? Or was it a product of his maturity, gained through many years of marriage to a woman he had adored, and from the fathering of two girls? For a long moment, she looked down at his sleeping face. Then, she tucked a blanket around his body and under his chin. She turned off the TV, brushed her teeth, and climbed into bed.

WHEN DAWN came, they took turns in the shower, and then struck out to find the nearest restaurant. Bleary-eyed gamblers passed them on the sidewalk, their facial expressions a mirror of their luck—or lack of it—at the casinos. While waiting for traffic lights to change, they watched a family of four, panhandling for breakfast money and bus fare to get them back home. Eliciting more sympathy from passersby, the kids were having better luck than their parents.

Howard shook his head, "I wonder how many others are in their shoes this morning?"

"Lots, probably," replied Miriam. "Folks who can't afford to be gamblin'." She paused for a moment, and then continued, "There's a sort o' sadness about this place, don't you think?"

"In what way?" he said.

"I dunno. It's just a feelin' I get. People desperate to win money, maybe to pay off a debt, or to make up for bein' out o' work. It's like their lives are out o' control in some way."

"Not necessarily," said Howard. "Remember Alice?"

"What about her?"

"Gambling is fun for her. Entertainment. She didn't strike me as the out-of-control type."

"Nor me, to be honest and truthful," said Miriam. "She's got her shit together, that's for sure."

When the lights changed, they joined the throng that surged between the painted crosswalk lines. After spotting a food ad on a sidewalk display board, they stepped inside and took a window booth that overlooked the street. An indifferent waitress placed two menu folders in front of them. Minutes later, she returned to take their orders and pour coffee.

"How long to Malibu from here?" asked Miriam, stirring in cream and sugar.

Howard pulled a crumpled AAA map from his pocket, flipped it over to the distance chart, and ran his finger along the route. "Four-and-a-half hours to L.A . . . another for traffic slowdowns, plus the run up the coast. Why?"

"Oh nothin'," replied Miriam sighing wistfully. "Just sorry the trip's over."

"Me too," said Howard, then added, "and I'm glad you changed your mind."

"You mean about keepin' the baby?"

"Yes," replied Howard, spilling coffee on his shirtsleeve. "You're going to make a good mom."

She handed him a napkin from the table dispenser. "You really think so? You're not just sayin' it?"

"You're young at heart, Mimi. It's good for a kid to have that in a parent."

The waitress arrived with their orders: ham, eggs, toast, and home fries for Howard, pancakes with syrup and bacon for Miriam. They tucked into their food and for a while hardly looked up from their plates except to check the action beyond the window. In spite of the early hour, the street was already busy: pedestrians ambled along the sidewalks, and tour buses disgorged a fresh load of gamblers or picked up sightseers for the ride to nearby Hoover Dam.

As they ate, Howard thought back over the trip that had brought them together. Since Suzanne's death, his loneliness had been excruciating: no one to greet him at the end of his workday or share the evening meal with. His evenings had seemed eternal, staring at the four walls. Worst of all, had been the unspoken exile from his and Suzanne's former social network of married friends. As a widower he was considered too risky to mix with established couples. But in these last weeks, he had cherished Miriam's company and the little things they had done together: tidying the motor home, shopping at grocery stores for foods they both liked, and sitting around a campfire at dusk and watching the stars come out. He snapped out of his reverie when she tapped on the table.

"A penny for your thoughts?"

"Oh, nothing important," replied Howard, spreading jam on his last slice of toast. "I was miles away."

"Chip?" she said, now looking at him intently.

"Yes."

"Think you could you do me a small favor?"

"Sure."

"When you drop me off at my mom's, would you come inside? I'd like her to meet you."

"Why would she want to meet me? I'm sure her social circle doesn't include English teachers."

"Just humor me—OK?"

"All right then."

After breakfast they walked back to the RV, hooked the Jeep to the motor home, and then headed out of town on I-15 and into the Mohave. They quickly put Las Vegas behind them and by the time they crossed the California state line, the heat of the sun had become withering. Dust devils pirouetted randomly across the arid landscape, growing and shrinking, breaking apart, then re-assembling to resume their erratic dance. For a while, a large one ran neck-and-neck with the motor home alongside the highway, scattering sand and pebbles onto the pavement.

At Barstow, he stopped for fuel while Miriam called her mother from a pay phone, and went off to get a bucket of KFC so they could eat on the move. On the opposite side of the gas pump, a young man was filling the tank of a low-slung pickup with California plates. The banana-yellow vehicle sported chrome wheels, low profile tires, and deeply tinted windows. The cardiac beat of a sound system thumped a rap tune from inside the truck; Howard felt the vibrations in his feet.

"Y'all are from out o' state," he said, glancing at the motor home's license plates.

"Yes," replied Howard, smiling at the man.

"Headin' into L.A.?"

Howard nodded.

"Driven there b'fo'?" asked the man, dipping and swaying his shoulders to the beat of the truck's sound system.

"Never," replied Howard.

"Lemme give y'all a heads up, m' man."

"Sure."

"You watch yo' ass ever' single minute—y' hear? L.A. drivers be the craziest dudes on the planet. They's either blind, stupid, or both."

"I've heard the drivers are crazy here," said Howard, suddenly feeling ancient and straight-laced.

"Crazy don't come close to describin' 'em, man. I mean, they got shit for brains—know wha' I'm sayin' to y'all? Tailgaitin'. Speedin'. Doin' the California Cut."

"The what?" asked Howard, trying to follow the man's jerky, hip-hop speech.

"Dudes in the outside lane, too lazy to check the overhead signboards. See they exit ramp at the last second and make a three-lane jump in front of y'all. Cut yo' front bumper off, just like that," he said, snapping his fingers.

"Thanks for the tip," replied Howard. "What about driving in the city?"

"Red lights and stop signs don't mean shit. Folks run 'em all the time. A slowdown's the bes' you gon' get. Ev'body in this town is impatient—know wha' I'm sayin'? Cain't wait to get goin' again. It's like they got fleas bitin' on they ass or somethin'!"

The nozzle clicked, but he kept topping up the tank until it overflowed. A rivulet of raw gas ran down the truck's body, and dripped onto the already deeply pitted asphalt. He returned the handle to the pump, secured the gas cap, and then tore off the paper receipt sticking out like a thin, white tongue.

"Now don' forget," he cautioned again. "You watch yo' ass—else you gon' be FUBAR."

With that final bit of advice, the man reentered his rap world, throbbing frenetically behind the tinted glass.

# CHAPTER 31

## *Malibu*

THE YOUNG MAN AT the gas station had been right about L.A. traffic. The San Bernardino and Santa Monica freeways were vehicular insanity: speeding, tailgating, lane hopping, and text messaging. On the road ahead, a beat up Hyundai with mismatched fenders veered off the pavement and grazed the barrier before the driver regained control. Car stereos pounded so loudly, the motor home's windows rattled in the frames as they passed. An EMS ambulance—siren and strobe lights pleading for right of way—was blocked by vehicles that straddled all lanes. When a gap opened, it sped through and raced south on the Harbor Freeway toward Inglewood.

Miriam was pumped at her first glimpse of the Pacific Ocean. She popped a wad of bubble gum in her mouth and chomped noisily.

"Isn't it wonderful, Chip?" she shouted, bouncing excitedly in her seat. "So big and blue and oceany."

"Yes," he replied, laughing, "it certainly is oceany."

"How far across do you figure it is?"

"Ten thousand miles," replied Howard, "or thereabouts."

"Wow," she shrieked and clapped her hands. "Wouldn't you like to trade your RV for a sailboat right this minute? I mean, how friggin' cool would that be? We could sail all the way to the other side."

"I think we had better visit your mother first."

When the interstate ended at Santa Monica, Howard swung north towards Malibu on the Pacific Coast Highway. Miriam pointed to tiny figures surfing offshore, some prone on their boards, others riding the curl of an incoming wave. She unfolded the hand-drawn map with directions to her mother's house and traced the route with her finger while Howard drove.

"Turn here," she said eventually.

Howard was no stranger to large homes in wealthy neighborhoods; he had been raised in one. But the affluence here was in a league of its own. Palm trees dominated the massive properties and towered above palatial mansions. Bushes festooned with brightly colored blossoms added a fresh elegance to the streets. A lawn and pool maintenance van was parked in front of a large estate. Two Hispanic workers in white coveralls were busy grooming an expansive lawn with a riding mower and power trimmer. As he drove deeper into the heart of the community, he noticed the cars in driveways: Porsches, BMWs, Hummers, Ferraris, and outside the lavish entrance to one mansion, a flaming red Lamborghini Countach, crouched low to the brick driveway like a tiger about to pounce.

"I think that's the one," said Miriam, pointing to a gated entrance with an intercom mounted on the masonry pillar.

Howard eased the unit to the curb and waited as she paged the house. A woman's voice, tinny sounding in the small speaker, welcomed her daughter. An electric motor whined as the wrought-iron security gate slid open. He swung the coach in a wide arc, then up the long driveway in which evenly spaced in-ground lights had been buried in the pavement. The drive made a wide loop in front of the Spanish-style house, an elegant single-story building with buff-colored adobe walls and a terra cotta tiled roof. Hanging baskets overflowing with flowers hung from wrought iron brackets fastened to the building.

Miriam's mother was waiting under the arched entrance to an enclosed patio that led to the front door. When the motor home came to a stop, she rushed forward with outstretched arms to greet her daughter.

Howard held back as both women embraced. While he waited, he appraised Miriam's mother; she was tanned and slim with large breasts, and about five-and-a-half feet tall with short, blond hair. With few lines on her face, she looked to be in her mid-forties, too young to have a thirty-five-year-old daughter.

"Mom," she said, "I'd like you to meet my friend, Chip, the man who's driven me all the way from Ohio." Then she turned to Howard. "And this is my mother, Robin."

The two shook hands, and then everyone stepped into the front foyer of the luxurious home. The Santa Fe style was evident, but in a minimalist kind of way with bleached log furniture and Navajo rugs on terra cotta tile floors. The effect was attractive and orderly: colors, from wall paint to fabric throw cushions were tastefully coordinated; Georgia O'Keefe prints were hung to the perfect height and the furnishings were arranged with geometric precision. The dominant feature in the room was a three foot by five foot oil painting, a waist-up portrait of Miriam's mother, looking the epitome of elegance with coiffed hair and wearing a peach, chiffon dress. The overall ambience was one of sophistication and wealth. He noticed that there were a few books. They were neatly arranged in small groups with pottery or slabs of onyx serving as book ends. Had they actually been read, he wondered? Or had they been purchased and displayed solely to compliment the décor?

He thought about the home he had shared with Suzanne, a casually cluttered environment with a wrap-around, lived-in coziness, enhanced by an ocean of books, some scattered, some shelved. Their eclectic collection, put together over many years included novels, biographies, and memoirs; non-fiction tomes on history, geography, and politics; and more esoteric works like poetry, philosophy, and art. Books had been an integral part of their relationship from the very beginning. Just seeing the titles on the shelves was enough to evoke fond memories of something either learned, or simply enjoyed for its own sake in a comfortable chair on a rainy day, or by a crackling fire on a winter's night.

"What can I get you to drink, Chip?" Robin asked as they descended two steps into the sunken living room.

"Red wine if you have it."

"How 'bout you, honey?"

Miriam looked at Howard before she answered, "Just a ginger ale for me."

"White wine's usually your favorite, isn't it, honey?" said her mother, glancing briefly at her daughter's midriff.

"I'm not in the mood for wine, Mom," she replied defensively.

The woman smiled awkwardly, and then quickly left to get refreshments.

"There's no puttin' anythin' past her," whispered Miriam, "I swear to God."

"You think she knows?"

"I know she knows."

Minutes later, her mother returned and set a tray on the coffee table. She sat opposite Howard on the sectional sofa. The ritual of small talk began, interrupted only by forays for salsa and blue tortilla chips.

"I love your décor," said Howard, looking around the huge room. "Have you been to the Southwest?"

"Many times. I got the rugs at Hubbell's trading post . . . the cochinas and the art from galleries in Taos and Santa Fe."

"Those were Suzanne's favorite places."

"Suzanne?"

"My late wife. We traveled a lot."

"When did she die?"

"A little over a year ago."

"I'm sorry. I've been widowed twice. It takes a long time to get over losing a spouse."

Miriam interjected now, anxious to tell her mother about her RV trip across America with Howard, but the woman seemed preoccupied.

"Why do I get the feelin' you're not listenin' to me, Mom?"

"You're right, honey. I was miles away. Sorry."

Miriam picked up where she had left off; highlighting some of the places they had visited. As she spun her narrative, Howard studied the mother. She was a physically attractive woman, but more than appearance, it was her mannerisms that captivated him most: her nuances of facial expression, her body language, the way she angled her head when she talked, the gestures she made with her hands, and the dimple in her cheek that gave an asymmetrical lilt to her face.

"Excuse me," he said, interrupting their conversation.

"Yes," said Robin.

"Where's your washroom?"

"Down the hall. First door on the left."

He put a hand on the coffee table to steady himself. As he rolled forward out of the overstuffed sofa, his hand slipped. Red wine splashed onto the cuff of his long-sleeved shirt; the rest pooled on the table. "What a klutz I am," he blurted. "Sorry about that."

"Don't worry," she said, heading for her kitchen, "I've got just the thing for red wine stains."

When she returned, Howard, still apologetic for his clumsiness, had unbuttoned his sleeve and positioned the cuff on his forearm. She gripped the fabric and went to spray the stain, then reeled suddenly, as if jolted by an electric shock. The bottle slipped from her hand and thudded to the floor.

"Oh my *God!*" she screamed, eyes wide, both hands held to her face.

Miriam rushed to her mother's side, "What is it?"

"Oh . . . oh, no . . . oh surely not," she cried, gasping and clutching at her chest.

"What's wrong, Mom? Are you havin' a heart attack?"

She followed her mother's eyes, dazed with shock; they were riveted on Howard's tattoo—an inked image faded with the passage of time, but still legible.

"It's . . . not possible," Robin cried, shaking her head in denial. "No . . . it can't be true. He . . . he told me you were dead."

"Who told you I was dead?" said Howard, confused.

"Your father. He said you'd been killed . . . killed in a car accident. How could he have told such a lie? Been so cruel?"

Howard's expression changed as recognition suddenly dawned. "Your name's not, Robin," he said.

"No . . . it's not," she replied. "It's my nickname . . . and you're not, Chip either . . ."

They embraced and clung fiercely to each other, cheeks pressed tightly together as they swayed in each other's arms. After a long interval, Lisa stepped back. She ran her fingers over the contours of his middle-aged face, as if trying to turn back the years, trying to imagine the younger Howard, the boy with the full head of hair and no beard—the first boy who had loved her.

Then, gradually the full significance of it hit Miriam. She thought back to conversations she had had with Howard. One by one she connected the dots and a picture emerged. But the scope of it, and the disturbing questions it raised, seemed to knock the wind from her. She slumped onto the sofa.

"She's the one, isn't she, Chip?" said Miriam.

Howard turned at her comment.

"The one you were sweet on?"

He nodded, then, with a shocked expression, looked back at Lisa, "Good, *God*," he exclaimed. "She's *our* daughter!"

"Yes, Howard, she is."

"But . . . how could she be? Your letter from Dubai said that you were . . ."

"I know what it said," she replied, then added, "I think you'd better sit down for this. There's a lot that neither of you know."

"She already knows some of it," said Howard, sitting beside Miriam.

"How's that?" asked Lisa.

Because I've talked to her. Told her about you and me and the pregnancy."

Miriam suddenly burst into tears. "Why, Mom?" she cried. "Why were you going to abort me?"

"Give me a chance to explain," she said, feeling cornered.

She glared at her mother and continued. "And if Chip is my real father, then that makes Ray Kovacs—"

"Calm down, Mimi."

"Calm down? Dammit, Mother, I'm thirty-five years old, and I'm just findin' out *now* that I was adopted! Why'd you leave it all these years?"

"But, honey—"

"You're not standin' in my shoes, Mom," she said. "Can't you understand how angry I am? Don't you think I deserved to be told before this?"

"Yes, but I kept putting it off," said Lisa in her own defense.

"You don't put off somethin' as important as tellin' your daughter the truth. I had a right to know."

"Your mom's right, Mimi," said Howard. "We all need to calm down so we can get to the bottom of this."

Lisa took a deep breath. "Having the abortion wasn't my idea."

"Oh, sure. Like someone held a gun to your head . . . told you to dump me in a friggin' toilet bowl or else."

"Yes, Mimi. That's exactly how it was, except without the gun." She poured herself another drink of wine from the decanter and continued. "It was your grandfather's idea. My pregnancy threatened his standing in the church."

"Why? Was he the minister or somethin'?"

Lisa turned to Howard, "This must be confusing for you, but Mimi knows nothing about her grandparents—she never met them."

"Go on," he said, now understanding Miriam's attachment to the Watsons and Alice Kimball.

"They were both active in the church," said Lisa. "Mom taught Sunday school. Dad was the treasurer, plus he did youth counseling."

"That's a laugh," said Miriam, sarcastically. "He counseled other people's teens but couldn't deal with his own daughter gettin' pregnant?"

"There were two sides to your grandfather: the pious man at church, and the tyrant at home."

"Why are you tellin' me all this, Mom?"

"I'm telling you, Mimi," she said, impatiently, "so you'll have an idea of why things happened the way they did. Soon as your grandparents found out I was pregnant—"

"How'd they find out? Did you tell 'em?"

"I didn't need to. My mother had a sixth sense about things. She knew I was pregnant. Same way I know you're pregnant right now."

"See," said Miriam, turning to Howard, "Told you she'd have it figured out without me havin' to tell her."

"Who's the father?" asked Lisa.

"Never you mind," shouted Miriam. "This isn't about *my* pregnancy."

"You're right. I'm sorry," replied her mother, holding up her hand to quell her daughter's anger.

"What I don't understand," said Howard, "is how fast your family disappeared from Toledo."

"It was a case of timing," said Lisa. "The company Dad worked for had just won a large contract in the Emirates. Management was in the process of trying to find someone who'd be willing to go."

"What do you mean, the Emirates?" asked Miriam.

"The United Arab Emirates, honey. The project was in Dubai. Problem was, none of the engineer's wives wanted to go to the Middle East, but Dad jumped at it. It was a chance to kill two birds: make a lot of money as well as escape the scandal my pregnancy would've caused."

"A chance to hide you half a world away," said Miriam, shaking her head.

"Yes, and it got worse."

"How could anythin' be worse than that?"

"You grandfather made me wear a burqa soon as we got overseas."

"One o' those sacks with an eye slit?"

"Yes," said Lisa.

"Why?"

"He wanted to keep me hidden till I'd had the abortion."

"That's friggin' weird."

"That was your grandfather. Control freak and prude."

"I had no idea he forced you to wear a burqa," said Howard. "You never mentioned that in your letter."

"I did put it in the letter originally," said Lisa, "but my father censored it, made me re-write it. The main thing is, he wanted you to know about the abortion."

"But, I don't understand, Mom, if he was religious, how could he go along with something like that?"

"Because he wanted two things: to keep his image clean, and to end all contact between me and Howard."

"What stopped you from goin' through with it?"

"I flat out refused," said Lisa. "Told him I'd find a way of getting back together with Howard in the States."

"What did he say to that?" asked Howard.

"At first, he went ballistic. He'd already bought airline tickets and made arrangements to fly me out of the country to have the abortion. Eventually, my mother calmed him down."

"Why out of the country?" asked Miriam.

"Because abortions are illegal in the Emirates."

"Then what?" asked Howard.

"He made a deal, more an arrangement, really. His sister, Lois, in Philadelphia was divorced and living on her own. He told her that if she would take us in, he'd send her a generous monthly allowance to cover all expenses. But there were strings attached."

"What strings?" asked Howard.

"He said that if I left my Aunt Lois and tried to get back together with you, he'd cut off the money. Anyway, as soon as she agreed to the arrangement, he put me on a plane to the States."

"Did he stay in touch with you after that?" Howard asked.

"Uh-uh," said Lisa. "Both my parents cut us out of their lives."

"Permanently?"

"Yes," she replied, the pain of the estrangement still visible after decades.

"So," said Miriam, "that's why you told me my grandparents were dead."

"They might as well have been, honey. If I'd told you otherwise, you'd have wondered why they didn't have anything to do with us."

"Did you try to contact me after you got Stateside?" asked Howard.

"I called your home as soon as I was back," replied Lisa. "That's when your father told me you'd been killed. He was so convincing on the phone, I believed him."

"That doesn't surprise me," said Howard, shaking his head, in disgust.

"Why's that?"

"Because my father wanted me to get my degree in the worst way. He knew if I had a wife and baby to support, I'd never get it. I'm sure that's why he lied to you. And of course, he never told me you'd called the house. Not a word."

"I could kick myself now," said Lisa.

"What for?" said Howard.

"For not checking with your friends to see if it was true. It just never occurred to me."

"Hindsight's twenty twenty," replied Howard, then he changed the subject. "How long did you and Mimi live with your aunt?"

"Three years, then I met Ray at a dance."

"Why'd you marry him, Mom?"

"A bunch of reasons, honey," she said, draining her wine glass, "I wanted to break my financial dependency on your grandfather *and* get out of Aunt Lois' house."

"And?"

"Ray was willing to marry into a ready-made family. Not many men are prepared to do that. To raise another man's kid."

"Did you love him?" asked Miriam.

Lisa hesitated before answering. "I grew to love him."

"So, it was a marriage o' convenience then?"

"Well, yes, I suppose it was, but I did like him. Anyway, honey, that's all water under the bridge now. The thing is, he tried his best to be a good husband and father, in spite of his being on the road so much. He did care for you, honey. You know he did. He adopted you. Wanted you to have his name."

"And you went along with that?" said Miriam.

"Yes," said her mother.

"But why?"

"Why are you cross examining me like this, Mimi?" asked her mother.

"Because I wanna know the truth. You owe me that."

Lisa suddenly went quiet. She looked at Howard, then at her daughter.

"What is it, Mom?"

There was a long pause before she spoke.

"I guess if I have to tell the truth here . . . then two people are going to be mad as hell at me."

"Just spit it out," said Howard, wondering what she was holding back.

"When I registered the birth at the hospital, the baby's name was Holly Crandall."

"Then how the hell did I wind up as Miriam?"

"I'll get to that in a minute," said Lisa, holding up her hand, "but first I owe Howard an apology."

"What for?" he asked.

"Because when you and I picked names, we'd agreed on Holly if the baby was a girl, right?"

"That's right," he said, trying not to let his hurt show.

"Well," she continued, "when Ray wanted to adopt her, he wanted to change her first name as well."

"Why, Mom?"

"Because his mother's name was Miriam."

Miriam turned to Howard, "Now I know how shitty Frank Watson felt about losin' his real name."

"Who's he?" asked Lisa.

Neither of them answered.

"I'm sorry, Howard. Very sorry. I've felt guilty for years because I didn't put my foot down and say no."

"Did he push you on it?" Howard asked.

"No, that's the thing. I just let him talk me into it. I was eighteen-years-old. Grateful someone was prepared to marry me when I had a child. It didn't occur to me that I should've honored your choice, no matter what, especially since at the time, I thought you'd been killed. All the more reason to honor you. Please forgive me, Howard."

He changed the subject, "Mimi said your husband died on the road."

"Yes. He'd driven non-stop from Albuquerque and hadn't slept. Hit a bridge abutment. I became a single mom overnight. Mimi was thirteen."

"I think I will have another red wine after all," said Howard.

313

Lisa filled his glass from the decanter, "It must be difficult for you hearing all this."

"It is," he said, taking a long sip of wine. "I'm hearing about a life I could've had with the woman I loved." He turned to Miriam. "I missed your first steps. All your birthdays. Reading you bedtime stories. The vacations we could've had together."

"I'm sorry, Chip," said Miriam, touching his arm, "I've been thinkin' more about *my* pain than yours in all o' this."

Lisa dabbed her eyes with a tissue. "Do you remember 'our song' Howard? Remember how we used to sing the words to each other as we danced?"

"Of course I do," he replied. "'*You Are the Sunshine of My Life.*'"

"I've heard that song so many times since I last saw you," she said. "I still have that picture of us taken on a park bench back in Toledo."

"You do?" said Howard, surprised.

"Yes, I've kept it all these years. I cried so many tears on it our faces were starting to disappear."

Howard zoned out and gazed at his motor home parked outside. But for the intervention of two sets of parents, he would have shared over three decades of married life with Lisa and had a relationship with Miriam. Then he felt guilty, as if his thoughts despoiled the memory of Suzanne. She had, after all, been a good wife to him and a good mother to their girls.

"You talked about Suzanne earlier," said Lisa, breaking his reverie, "and that you'd traveled a lot. Where did you two meet?"

"On the campus of St. Martin's College. We were students at the time."

"So . . . you'd both be young, then," said Lisa, gently probing for details.

"Yes," said Howard, feeling awkward talking about his deceased wife in front of a former lover. "We were the same age . . . nineteen . . . but it worked out for us."

"Any kids?"

"Two," said Howard, pulling creased photos from his wallet. "Tina was born when I was twenty-three, Lynn two years later."

"Lovely girls," she replied, dwelling at length over the images. "This one looks athletic."

"That's Lynn. She's won plenty of swimming awards including Olympic gold."

"Any grandkids?" she asked, handing back the photos.

"No," he said quietly. "Neither of them wanted children."

"Well," said Lisa, turning to their daughter, "isn't *this* an odd twist of fate?"

"What do you mean?" asked Miriam.

"You're pregnant."

"Yes, Mom," snapped Miriam. "What of it?"

"Don't you realize something?" said Lisa.

"Realize what?"

"You're carrying our grandchild."

She looked from Howard to her mother as she processed the revelation, then blurted, "Anyway, if it weren't for, Chip, there'd be no grandkid at all."

"What do you mean?" asked her mother.

"I . . . was considerin'—"

"Oh, puh-*lease*," exclaimed Lisa, her face suddenly flushed. "Don't tell me you were planning to abort the child? Is that why you were coming out here? Thinking I'd arrange for some Beverly Hills quack to do the deed?"

"Can I help it if my boyfriend dumped me? Left me to fend for myself?"

"Good, God, Mimi, that's no reason to throw a human being in the garbage. I brought you up with better values than that. I had a gut feeling you were pregnant. Turns out I was right."

"What else is new?" shouted Miriam. "You've always been right. Do this, Mimi. Don't do that, Mimi. Go out with this boy, Mimi, not that boy. I felt like a friggin' puppet when I was a kid. You were always pullin' my strings. Always tryin' to control everythin' I did in my life. Sometimes I wish you *had* aborted me."

"How dare you say such a thing," Lisa exploded, apoplectic with rage.

"My life's been a shit heap up to now, Mom."

"And whose fault is that? You can't blame me for the choices you made. I tried to do right by you. Tried to convince you to stay in school and get an education. It was you who chose to drop out. You who chose men with no future."

"Talkin' about men with no future, why didn't you put *your* foot down and make Dad—I mean Ray—take another kind o' job instead o' truckin'? The kind where men come home to their families at the end o' the day. Maybe if I'd seen him more often, I might've picked better men . . . the kind who wouldn't have jerked me around."

"Jerked you around?" shouted her mother. "What Jason did to you was assault and battery. He got what he deserved in the end. And as for the others—"

"Don't do this to me, Mom," she cried. "I don't need remindin' what a screw up I've made o' my life. The main thing is, I'm havin' the baby. What I'm gonna *do* to support us after that, I haven't the foggiest."

"Look," said Lisa, trying to defuse the tension in the room, "let's not fight anymore, honey. I've got the guest bedroom set out nice and pretty for you. We can talk more about this later."

Miriam dried her eyes with a tissue, and then got up from the sofa. "It's gonna feel weird for me now . . . callin' you, Dad instead o', Chip."

Howard smiled, "Why change? I like my nickname."

The room went uncomfortably quiet after Miriam left. Howard and Lisa were alone for the first time in thirty-five years. There was a long, awkward pause before conversation resumed.

"I'm sorry about the upset," said Lisa. "When all the dust has settled, I *will* support her. You do know that . . . don't you?"

"Of course I do," said Howard, "but you won't be doing it on your own."

"What exactly do you mean?"

"I have no problem helping her out," he said, then added, "for as long as it takes and in any way I can . . . emotionally, financially, whatever. I'd even offer to tutor her so she could increase her education . . . perhaps get herself a better paying job."

"You would *do* that?" asked Lisa.

"In a heartbeat," replied Howard. "In fact, I had already considered it before we arrived out here. I just hadn't told her yet. She's damned good with math—I'm sure you already know that."

Lisa nodded.

"Well, with some more education under her belt she could turn that skill into money . . . get a real estate license perhaps."

"Funny isn't it," she said, changing the subject. "Even when they've left the nest, you never stop worrying about them? I take it you talked her out of having the abortion."

"I tried to, after I picked her up the first time."

"What do you mean, the first time?"

While Howard filled her in on the details of their cross-country trip, Miriam shuttled her belongings from the RV into the house. She was unusually subdued now, and avoided eye contact with her parents, who now sat beside each other on the sofa.

"Just imagine," exclaimed Lisa, "picking up our daughter on the side of the road like that. What a small world."

"Yes," he replied. "It *is* a small world, all right. In a million years I could not have guessed who she was when I took her in—in from the rain."

"I offered to give her the money to fly out here. Did she tell you that?"

"No."

"Well," said Lisa, throwing up her hands in exasperation, "that's, Mimi for you. She gets a chance to fly, and instead, she thumbs a ride. She drives me crazy with the bad choices she makes. It's like she's stuck somewhere in her teens and never grew up—thirty-five going on sixteen. Course, I take some of the blame for that. I was overprotective. But I did it out of love. Do you understand?"

"Yes, I do. Especially after all you went through just to give birth to her."

"She's had a hell of a life, Howard, and I feel guilty about that, although logically, I shouldn't. She's a grown woman and made her own choices."

"I know," he replied. "She told me some of the things that went wrong, the relationships that went sour."

"Jason was the scariest," said Lisa.

"The drug dealer?"

"Yes. I used to fear getting a phone call in the middle of the night. Finding out she was dead, either from his fists or the drugs. Did she tell you how he died?"

"She said he was beaten to death."

"Ever heard of the Sinaloa drug cartel?"

"Uh-uh," said Howard.

"The police think it was somebody from the cartel who ordered him killed. The border authorities knew he'd crossed many times into Juarez from El Paso. They figured he was trying to make contact with a man they call El Chapo—the most wanted drug lord in Mexico. DEA agents hid a GPS locator on Jason's rental car and began tracking his movements in Mexico. They believe the cartel found out about the locator device and decided to have him killed in the States before he could lead the authorities to the drug boss."

"Good thing he was killed in an alley and not in their house," said Howard. "She could have died as well."

"You don't know how many times that thought went through my mind," said Lisa. "There but for the Grace of God!"

"Too scary to think about, isn't it?" said Howard.

Lisa nodded and sighed, "I don't know where her life is going from here, Howard. It's early days yet. I worry about her, though. She's so vulnerable. I'd rather see her raise this baby on her own, even if I . . . we . . . have to help her, than hook up with another Jason, or that religious nut she lived with."

"I couldn't agree more," added Howard.

Conversation stopped as a vehicle pulled up to the front of the house. It was the landscape company's van Howard had seen earlier in the neighborhood. A man in white coveralls rang the bell.

She opened the door and spoke warmly to him, "Por favor, puede usted volver manana?"

"Si, senora," said the man. "Buenos tardes!"

"Pool maintenance," she said as she closed the door. "I've asked them to come back tomorrow."

"Come on," said Lisa. "Let's go out to the garden for a while. We've got a lot to catch up on."

They left the building through a long shaded portico, framed by hewn beams, pillars, and corbels that opened invitingly onto a lawn ringed by palms and tropical bushes. Walkways of interlocking brick encircled the kidney-shaped swimming pool and led to a quiet, private corner graced by a small waterfall and a pool with Japanese goldfish.

"It's beautiful here," said Howard, as he sat beside her on a garden bench. "A far cry from the neighborhood we grew up in."

"David provided well for me."

"How did you meet?"

"After Ray died, a girlfriend of mine in L.A. invited me to come out for a vacation. Sandra took me to a party, which is where I met David. He was a successful writer and quite the self-promoter. We hit it off and dated till I went back to Ohio. Afterwards we stayed in touch—a long distance romance. When he proposed, I followed my heart."

"He must have been successful," said Howard, looking around the property.

"David had charm, money, and connections—the three things that can take you far in this town. But hey, that's enough about my life."

Howard recounted how he had met Suzanne on the campus of St. Martin's College. He talked at greater length and with greater comfort about their relationship, his two girls, and his career on the faculty.

"Where did all those years go, Howard? It didn't seem that long ago and we were in our teens, so in love we didn't think two people had ever loved as much in the history of the world."

"Yes," he replied. "But even if we had got married, odds are we'd probably have split up. Most teen marriages don't last."

"I hate to be clichéd about it," she said, "but better late than never. At least we're sitting here now after thirty-five years. If nothing else, it's a relief to know you're not dead."

"I was bitter for a long time about the way I lost you," said Howard. "When I read your letter and looked at the postmark, I thought you had already had the abortion . . . that our baby was dead. I had no way of knowing otherwise."

"Of course you didn't. I was bitter too. I never would've believed that my parents would cut me off the way they did. That was the cruelest thing of all. Their estrangement from me hurt for a long time—tore the soul out of me. But, like you, I had to get on with my life."

"Well," said Howard, "you did the right thing by having Miriam."

"Yes, I've always felt that, in spite of the heartaches I had raising her. She was worth the pain and struggle."

Time passed quickly as they reminisced. When the sun's lower limb neared the horizon, Lisa persuaded Miriam to join them and watch the sunset. They hurried along a path between the plantings toward a clearing that afforded a view of the ocean. At a rocky outcropping, Howard noticed a tiny bird flitting among the boulders. It landed on the lower branch of a tree, and then burst into song—a bubbling cascade of liquid notes.

"Canyon wren," declared Lisa, noting Howard's interest.

"Yes."

"Lovely isn't it?"

He nodded and smiled, "You two go on ahead. I'll be there in a minute."

He leaned against a rock—an audience of one—to enjoy the wren's serenade. Its pointed beak and white throat quivered as it bestowed its melodic benediction. He recalled the many times he and Suzanne had heard its distinctive song pierce the stillness of the desert.

"Hurry, Howard," called Lisa. "You're going to miss the sunset."

The bird kept pace with him as he continued along the path., hopping from rock to tree to bush. He thought of how Suzanne had appeared in his dream and her words to him: "I just want you to know that it's OK now."

He joined Lisa and Miriam in the clearing. Three figures stood watching the sun's final descent: two former lovers, reunited after half a lifetime apart—and between them, their love child—with her own history yet to write.

# EPILOGUE

ADJUSTING TO LIFE IN Southern California was difficult for Howard, especially the climate. He missed the separate seasons of his native Ohio: the crisp, fall days when forests were ablaze with color and woodland trails glowed under golden-leafed canopies; the winter artistry of frost on windowpanes, and the wafer-thin ice that framed the banks of streams; the earthy fragrance of reawakening spring growth; and in summer, the neon dance of fireflies in the damp, night air of marshlands.

Unable to find a home close enough to commute to Rancho La Jolla High School, he was reduced to living in his RV on a private campground, while he house hunted. Although he knew it would be a temporary arrangement, it left him feeling like a displaced refugee. Even visiting local attractions like the San Diego Zoo or taking in a play at the Old Globe Theater did little to give him a sense of connection to his new community.

He knew that his greatest challenge would be building a rapport with his new students, something that had not been difficult for him at St. Martin's College, a place where his unconventional teaching style was accepted. In San Diego he was an unknown quantity, no longer a man with tenure, but a newbie starting on the bottom rung and working with unfamiliar curriculum. But he was grateful. At least he had a job, and when the opportunity presented itself, as he was sure it would, he could find a teaching position in another college.

In August, Tina, flew to L.A. to visit him and meet Lisa and Miriam. The foursome spent a leisurely week driving up the Pacific Coast Highway, stopping at the scenic overlooks and photographing the rugged coastal vistas. They spent two days in San Francisco, enjoying the antics of the sea lions at Fisherman's Wharf, touring Alcatraz, dining in Chinatown, and taking cable car rides up the steep inclines of the city. Delighted with the city, Miriam wore a permanent grin as she thrilled to the clang of trolley bells, and the views of San Francisco Bay.

After a visit to the Monterey Bay Aquarium on their return trip, they stopped for supper at a restaurant near Big Sur. They dined off slab-like wooden tables, tiered on a hillside that overlooked the Pacific, hundreds of feet below. The scenery was surreally beautiful. Behind them, the trees and peaks of the Santa Lucia range were bathed in the bronze light of late afternoon, their valleys extending sharply down toward the sea. In the distance, mountain peaks in variegated shades of hazy blue, were layered one behind the other like three-dimensional paper sculptures, their bases blurred with cotton-white tendrils of sea fog. After supper, they donned sweaters against the cool ocean breezes and gathered around the outdoor fireplace.

"How's your sister taking all of this?" asked Howard.

"Oh, she'll come around, Dad," said Tina, smiling at Lisa and Miriam. "You know Lynn, she doesn't deal easily with change. Anyway, I think it's wonderful you three have found each other after all these years."

"I'm so glad I talked to you from that campground," said Miriam.

"So am I," said Tina. "Although at the time I had no idea who you were, of course. But, here I am with a new sister and a niece or nephew on the way."

"Sorry," said Miriam, "but I can't help you on the gender thing. I haven't had an ultrasound done."

"Would you consider one?" asked Tina.

"Uh-uh."

"Want it to be a surprise?"

"Yeah. Besides, if it hadn't been for, Chip—I mean, Dad—there'd *be* no surprise to have."

"Why's that?"

"When we first met, I was considerin' an abortion."

"You never told me that."

"I know," said Miriam, casting a guilty glance in her mother's direction.

"What made you change your mind?" asked Tina.

"Oh . . . a lot o' things," said Miriam. "I'll tell you about it sometime." Then she began to laugh.

"What's so funny?" asked Tina.

"It'll be a snap lookin' after a baby after all the practice I've had," said Miriam, glancing at Howard. "I've wiped more spilled food off his clothes than I care to think about."

"Dad's been doing that forever," said Tina. "Whenever we came home from camping trips, he was dirtier than anyone else."

"Funny," said Lisa. "I don't remember you being such a slob when we were in our teens."

"We were too preoccupied with other things," said Howard with a grin. "Slaves to our raging hormones you might say."

"Yech," said Miriam, poking a finger down her throat. "Spare us the gooey details."

He threw his head back and laughed. "Why is it adult kids get so squeamish over the thought of their parents having sex?"

"Quick," said Miriam, grabbing hold of Tina's hand. "Let's go to the gift shop. If I have to listen to any more o' this, I'm gonna hurl."

With his daughters gone, Howard stared pensively into the fire, watching the random dance of the flames, and the shimmering glow of the coals.

"I'm curious," said Lisa.

"What about?" replied Howard, tossing a twig into the fire, that immediately flared brightly.

"That St. Christopher's medal around your neck. You were never religious when I knew you. Has anything changed?"

"No," he said, running a finger along the gold chain.

"Was it Suzanne's?"

"No. A Greek fellow gave it to me before I left Toledo. Said if I wore it, God would heal my heart."

"And?" asked Lisa.

"That's still a work in progress. It's taking me a long time to get over Suzanne. I have days when I imagine I hear her voice, or her footsteps, or I sense that she's standing in a room beside me. Then I'll have a day when she's not on my mind at all—and I'll feel guilty for *not* thinking about her—as if I'm somehow being disloyal to her memory. I know that doesn't make sense, because logically she *is* gone and I am free to move on with my life. But being free to move on, and actually moving on, are two different things. When you say those words 'till death do us part' you never realize that you can go on loving someone far beyond that point. I'm finding that out."

"You had a lot of history with her, Howard, not to mention having two children together. It takes a long time to heal from that. When you've been with someone that long, you carry a lot of shared memories, and the special occasions hit you hard. I know what that's like. I've been through all those things . . . twice. But if it's any comfort to you, in time the pain diminishes and joy returns to your life."

"It's odd, you know," said Howard, "but my feelings are all jumbled and confused seeing you again—meeting under these circumstances, so many years later."

"I know. I have those same feelings. There's some familiarity, because let's face it, we weren't just lovers, we conceived a child together. But that was a long time ago. Since then, our lives have taken different directions. A lot of water goes under the bridge in thirty-five years."

"Yes it does," he said, stirring the embers with an iron poker and adding fresh logs, "but still, I'm glad we met again, especially with Mimi being here, and the possibility of a grandchild."

"I am too," said Lisa, who suddenly burst out laughing.

"What's so funny?" said Howard.

"Don't ask me why," she said, "but I suddenly thought of that naughty thing you used to do in the theater when we went to the movies?"

"You mean when I cut a hole in the bottom of the popcorn bucket and stuck my—"

"Yes, yes," she said, still laughing. "I don't think we fooled anyone. I'm sure people knew what we were up to."

"We ought to tell the girls about that when they get back," he said. "That'd freak them out for sure."

In the morning, they continued their journey down the Pacific Coast, inhaling views of the steep cliffs and watching the offshore kelp beds roll in the long swells. They stopped at Moro Bay to walk the beach at low tide, and then again at Santa Barbara to visit the Spanish mission.

When they arrived back at Malibu, Lisa used her Hollywood connections to arrange a personalized tour of movie back lots, and the behind-the-scene places not normally accessible to the general public, including a unanticipated photo op with actors, Tom Hanks and Sean Penn.

Afterwards, she had a professional photographer come to her Malibu home and take enough stills of the four of them to fill a small album.

THROUGHOUT THE fall, Howard drove to Malibu every weekend. On Christmas school break, he flew east to be with Tina and Lynn, and then returned to Malibu on the day after Christmas.

He grew increasingly anxious as Miriam approached the end of her last trimester. She had had some difficulties during her pregnancy and there was still a chance that she might not carry to full term. After the New Year, he called regularly to check on her condition.

Then, on 26 February, he got the call he had been waiting for: Miriam had gone into labor. He rushed north to join Lisa at the hospital. Both were allowed into the delivery room to be with their daughter. Later that evening, Miriam delivered a seven pound, six ounce baby girl—Holly. Her grandparents were delighted and Howard spent as much time as he could in Malibu, helping Lisa to outfit the nursery, and cooing over the baby.

Yet, despite his frequent visits, Howard's relationship with Lisa never developed into a late-in-life romance. She still retained some of the warmth he had remembered in their youth, but they were like two tectonic plates that had shifted; there could be no realignment back to where they had once been. Time as well as life experience had altered them both. But such was often the case with places, friends, or lovers—none remained the same after a long absence. Life moved inexorably forward, and no amount of nostalgia could recreate the past, except in the castles of the imagination.

They shared the common love of a daughter and granddaughter of course, and that was certainly adequate to maintain a connection, but not enough to cement a loving union—a merging of souls. Lisa's Malibu lifestyle and her associations were in a league so far removed from Howard's, it was as if she inhabited an exclusive place within the cosmos, where the stars were of greater magnitude, and where the movement of planets contradicted the conventional rules of physics. Yet for all the glamour and the tinsel in Lisa's life, he did not envy her. The world she inhabited was not his kind of world.

Nevertheless, Howard continued to wear the St. Christopher's medal that Spiros Xenakis had given him back in Toledo. In a curious way, he found comfort wearing it even though he was not a religious man. The medal was a tangible reminder of his good fortune at having reunited with the daughter he thought had been lost to him forever. Most people, during the course of their life have a "small world" experience, a serendipitous crossing of paths with someone from their past. On this trip alone he had had two, the first being with Dave Morell, his former student from St. Martin's. Still, he could not help but think how easily he could have missed connecting with Miriam had he decided not to stop on a rain-soaked highway.

LISA WAS on the phone and Miriam was breast feeding Holly when the doorbell rang.

"Can you get that, Mom?" she shouted.

"I'll call you right back, Jennifer," said Lisa, quickly ending the call and rushing for the front door.

"Morning ma'am," said the uniformed UPS driver looking at the label on the box. "I've got a parcel here for . . . let's see . . . a Ms. Mimi Kovacs."

"She's busy at the moment," said Lisa. "Can I sign for it?"

"Of course," he said, giving her an electronic device and a plastic pen.

Lisa lingered for a moment in the front foyer, silently eyeing the parcel as the driver returned to his vehicle.

"Who's it from?" asked Miriam, moving the baby to her other breast.

"Packing label says, 'Mr. J. Woods,'" said Lisa.

"Lemme see it."

"Isn't that the guy who calls you on the phone?"

"Yes, Mom. That's Josh."

"You never mention him much," said her mother, setting the package on the coffee table.

Miriam offered nothing.

"Want me to get a knife so you can open it?"

"Please," replied Miriam.

Her heart pounded as she shook the box and tried to guess the contents; this was the first time he had sent her anything through the mail. Almost a year had passed since their dinner date, and he had called her often. On each occasion they had spent hours on the phone, laughing and talking about so many things—everything except their affections for each other. She had strong feelings for him, yet after three failed live-in relationships, she was scared to take another chance on love, especially with an infant daughter in the picture. She was certain Josh cared deeply for her, but for some reason, he too held back. Perhaps Howard had been right after all; long distance relationships were simply too difficult to keep up, and Josh lived over a thousand miles away. She looked again at the parcel, the size of a small microwave—probably a crib toy for the baby. It was then she noticed an envelope in a plastic pouch, stuck to the side of the box; it had been encircled with black marker and was highlighted with a printed message: "OPEN FIRST." She tore it from the box and was reading it when her mother returned with the steak knife.

"What's it say?"

Miriam held up her hand.

Her mother quietly retreated to a soft chair.

15 May
Gunnison, Colorado

Dear Mimi:

I got your letter last month with pictures of Holly. What a sweetheart! She's as beautiful a child as I've ever seen. You must be so proud of her and looking forward to spending your first summer together.

There's still plenty of winter snow pack in the high country and in the shady places below tree line. But down here in the valley, this year's crop of wildflowers has arrived in greater numbers and earlier than other years. The best surprise was seeing the first columbine. I've enclosed a photo of it for you.

I took your advice and upped the price of my carvings—more than doubled them. That seems to have gotten rid of some of the buyers who were probably flipping the pieces for higher profit. The increase hasn't put a damper on business. If anything, I seem to be getting more work than I can handle, a good thing, considering what I have planned.

I'm moving out of the barn here at Harry's. It's time I had a place of my own rather than relying on family. I got the chance to buy a parcel of land down the road from him and Gladys. You might remember passing it when we drove into town—the one with the run-down cabin on it. I went out there with a local man to check the existing well and do some water-quality tests. We found plenty of water to supply a house and a small barn for Becky, Orion, and Juniper. No more boarding for them! An extra bonus—there's enough acreage for riding and a trail that leads up into the mountains. I've already demolished the cabin. The foundation and sub-floor for the new place should be finished by next week. I'll have a full basement now and plenty of room to do my carving without having to leave the house. It's a two-story home made of squared timbers with a stone fireplace on the main level. I'll be doing the inside trim work myself to save on construction costs.

Now I've come to the most difficult part of this letter—the part I've dreaded, yet wanted to write for so long. I must have torn it up and re-written it ten times. Trying to get my feelings on paper has been hell. Where do I start? The best place would be last summer when I met you at the summit of Monarch Pass. Do you remember tripping and falling into my arms when you stepped out of the RV that morning? Not a day has passed since you left here that I haven't thought about you, especially that wonderful night we spent together. I know I've only kept in touch by phone since then, and I'm sure you must be confused as to why I haven't expressed my true feelings for you before this. A lot of that had to do with my less than ideal living arrangements, but as I say, that's about to change. Anyway, just open the box and read the brochure.

All my love:
Josh
xxx ooo

PS: By the way, I got rid of my old truck and bought something newer and safer. One accident in my life is enough!

After reading it, Miriam stared at the letter.

"Something wrong?"

"No, Mom. Would you take her for me?"

"Come to grandma, sweet pea," said Lisa, pulling the child into her arms.

Miriam slit open the parcel with the steak knife, unfolded the flaps of the cardboard box, and removed the paper packing. They both gasped when she lifted out a wood carving. It was the baby in the shell—*Gift from the Sea*—the exquisite piece that had so captured her heart in Josh's showroom.

Then she removed the glossy brochure. It showed an artist's conception of a two-story log home with a covered porch that ran the full width of the house. The first page was an introductory letter from the builder; the next was a detailed floor plan of a three-bedroom home.

"Oh my *God*," cried Miriam, bringing a hand across her mouth.

"What is it, honey?"

"I don't believe this."

"Don't believe what?"

"Look," she said, showing the layout to her mother.

"It's just a floor plan."

"No, Mom," she said, her eyes tearing up. "Look again."

She took it from her daughter and examined it closely. Penned in small script inside each room were: Master bedroom—Mimi & Josh, Second bedroom—Holly, Third bedroom—☺.

"Well?" said Lisa, smiling at her daughter.

"Would you look after the baby for a while?" said Miriam, wiping her eyes as she got up from the sofa.

"Where are you going?"

"To make a phone call."